THE ACLLA'S LEGACY
-A NOVEL-

BY

BONNIE ADAMS-LITTLE

© Copyrighted, 2016, all rights reserved by Bonnie Adams-Little
The Aclla's Legacy

Published by Farris Press (an imprint of Yawn's Publishing)
198 North Street
Canton, GA 30114
www.yawnspublishing.com

All rights reserved. No part of this book may be reproduced or transmitted in any form, electronic or mechanical, including photocopying, recording, or data storage systems without the express written permission of the publisher, except for brief quotations in reviews and articles.

Library of Congress Control Number: 2016935989

ISBN: 978-1-943529-36-0   paperback
        978-1-943529-37-7   ebook

Cover photo and image by Bonnie Adams-Little.
Cover design by Farris Yawn in consultation with Anna McBath Shelton.

Printed in the United States

This book is dedicated to
Daisy Nickels Adams, artist, humorist, mother
Tilton Hall Little, raconteur, inventor, father,
and to the
Star People,
Indigenous Peoples of the Americas,
whose blood I share,
and to
Cuzco
"…May there always be a Cuzco and may it be forever young…"
(Inca Prayer to Con Ticci)

Chapter 1

Cherry blossoms arced over the tidal basin, swirling in a copper sulfate sky, covering a marble bench near the Jefferson Memorial. Joanna Nickels-Stewart paused, hitched her purse strap higher, and calculated the distance to the bench. One last sprint should do it.

Racing in high-heeled shoes at Olympic speed, on a colder than usual morning in March, wasn't her usual form of exercise. She skidded to a halt in front of the bench, swiped it with a tissue, doffed her purse, and plopped down, gulping for air.

Petals fell from auburn hair as she bent forward, pressing a stitch in her side. How embarrassing if the senator had seen her dashing through the park, but she'd needed time to compose herself. It was her first time being alone with him.

She sat up, moved to the center of the bench, took a small bag of popcorn from her purse, placed it on the bench, and checked her wristwatch. 9:15 a.m. Fifteen minutes before the meeting.

Searching in the bottom of the purse, she located the gold compact Michael had given her, combed tangled hair, powdered shiny spots on her nose, rearranged the silk scarf, touched each ear to be sure she'd worn both earrings. Fourteen minutes.

She tossed the compact into the purse and removed a pencil-thin hand-held computer. A quick tap on the apps-icon for the Cassini Space Probe data feed, accessed NASA's secure site for scientists. She'd been observing a sector on Saturn's second largest moon for signs of eruptions for days now. No new data since 8:30 a.m.

Stashing the computer in a side pocket of the purse, she picked up the popcorn bag, tore it open and tossed kernels in a broad circle. A platoon of pigeons appeared. The more aggressive birds gobbled every morsel.

Joanna tossed with both hands, aiming the popcorn beyond the immediate circle, attempting to assure the whole bevy had equal shares. Strategic distribution might be the best solution—timed tossing, intermittent schedules of tossing, changed geometric patterns of tossing.

It was exasperating. She couldn't even engage in the simple act of feeding birds without designing a scientific experiment.

Wings flapped, the birds soared and scattered. The senator and his two bodyguards strolled toward her. 9:25 a.m. She should've guessed he'd be early.

Stuffing the popcorn bag back into her purse, she stood to greet him. Feeding pigeons was probably wasteful and frivolous to his way of thinking, an unwelcome addition to the mess the park wardens cleaned daily. She started forward and hesitated. He'd stopped a short distance away, speaking with the bodyguards.

How *did* he manage to look so impeccably groomed—a Brooks Brothers' mannequin. The molded black hair, with silver streaks at the temples, glistened in the sunlight, defying wind. If he'd been summoned to appear before news cameras this very instant, no make-up people would've been needed.

Joanna reached up to smooth her own disorderly locks. It was hopeless. Adjusting her suit jacket, she swept the toe of each shoe against the back of the opposite leg to remove dust.

Michael had laughed at her reaction when he'd informed her that his father wanted to meet with her this morning.

"No need to worry," he'd said, "the old man's as much in love with you as I am. He probably just wants to persuade us to change our honeymoon destination to please his constituency."

The senator and his bodyguards turned toward her, moved closer. She reached back to retrieve her purse. It teetered on the edge of the bench and fell, dumping the contents on the ground. 9:30 a.m. Pigeons reappeared on cue.

Threatening clouds gathered in the south as Joanna, heat flushing her face, bent to collect her things. One of the bodyguards rushed to assist. He scooped up the computer and compact, handed them to her.

"Should I gather up the popcorn?" he asked, with a mischievous grin.

Avoiding his eyes, she shook her head, smiled, and mouthed, "No thanks."

He tossed the bag in a trash bin and shifted aside. Senator Mike Vander Hurst stepped up, offering her a bright public smile, a quick hug, and a slight peck on the cheek.

"Please walk with me," he said, moving to her right side.

Like his son, he towered above her, standing at least six feet. She stifled a nervous giggle, imagining having to skip to keep pace.

"I appreciate you meeting me here. Was it difficult getting away from the observatory?"

"No sir, I have evening watch hours."

Was he going to talk about private matters in front of the bodyguards? Michael had said they were family friends and part of the senator's "Southern Mafia." She imagined they were privy to most family secrets.

"Too bad we couldn't do breakfast or lunch, but the Senate's voting on some important bills today ..." He turned to one of the guards. "Zack, bring the car to this side of the basin, and phone General Moore. Tell him the meeting's been cancelled, we'll get back to him as soon as the officials in Ulaanbaatar contact us."

Clouds roiling in the southeast reminded Joanna of vultures circling the pastures of her family farm in Virginia, their enormous wings casting huge shadows.

"As I said, we're expecting a roll call this morning, so I guess I'd better get right to the point. I've received a disturbing communication about you." He halted, facing her, "... from Peru."

She turned toward him and stumbled off the sidewalk. The remaining bodyguard grabbed her elbow to steady her.

"I don't understand," she said.

"Sam, please give me that envelope." He motioned the bodyguard away. "The contents of these documents are rather surprising, Joanna—

to put it mildly."

Stinging raindrops struck her face. Waves in the tidal basin lapped the shore, keeping time with her heartbeat.

"Our family wasn't aware of your Peruvian connections," he went on. "I'm guessing Michael doesn't know, either. I haven't mentioned anything to him. In fact, I'm requesting you keep my involvement in this matter confidential. Do you understand?"

The sun disappeared. Joanna placed her hands inside the wide sleeves of her suit coat, seeking warmth that eluded her. Laughter sounded in the distance. Two uniformed nannies, toddlers in tow, strolled in their direction.

The senator took her arm, steered her onto a meandering path ending in a willow grove, and handed her the manila envelope. She opened the flap and removed an official document with a letter attached. Scanning it twice, she felt cold perspiration trickle down her spine.

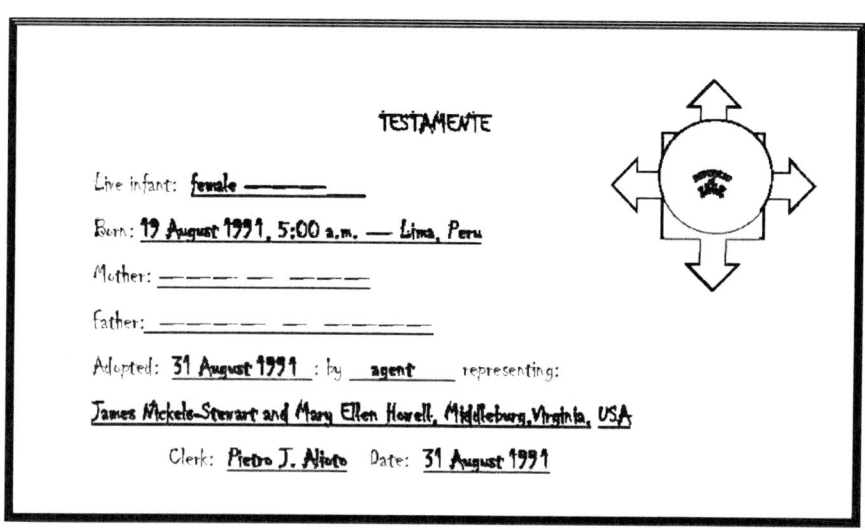

The attached letter was written on heavy linen stationery, addressed to the senator. It stated that Joanna Nickels-Stewart had been adopted in Lima, Peru in 1991. She had been named Huarana, and the records relating to her birth parents were sealed. There was no signature.

Joanna was slipping off a ledge, falling into the abyss—a recurring childhood nightmare. She turned in a half circle, in search of safe moorings.

The senator located a bench and made her sit down. Her hands fluttered in slow motion onto her lap, the envelope and documents fell toward the ground.

Bending automatically, she caught them and placed them in her purse. She drew a quick breath and settled wearily against the back of the bench.

Senator Vander Hurst patted her hand. She edged away. He leaned forward, looking at her sidewise, examining her face. "You really didn't know... ."

"You can't possibly think I'd conceal such a thing. Have you investigated this letter, to authenticate it, I mean?"

"It originated in Lima, mailed by a courier service," he said.

"It can't be true!" She shook her head. "My parents would've told me. I've never even been to Peru—"

"I can see you're shocked, Joanna." He paused. "But please try to understand the dilemma Cecile and I have."

He slid off the seat, moved a few feet away, facing her. "Michael's our only child. It's imperative that my wife and I know the ancestry of our future grandchildren."

"The ancestry—," she said, coughing, nearly losing her breath.

"Now, Joanna, more than anyone, you're certainly aware of how important family is in our Southern culture. Why the Nickels-Stewarts are among the first families of Virginia, and of course, we thought you were—" He caught himself and rubbed his hands vigorously, dry washing them. "I'm just saying this adoption business needs to be resolved. Michael would marry you, of course, and we certainly do want you to join our family, but—"

"What exactly do you want from *me*?"

"You need to clear the air. Sort this adoption business out before the wedding."

Clear the air—before the wedding... . She brushed cherry blossoms from her skirt and realized it was rain, not tears, falling in drenching sheets.

Senator Vander Hurst motioned for Sam to join them and turned to go, addressing her over his shoulder. He said he was sorry to leave, had to get back to the Senate floor, knew she'd understand.

Thinking about *Humpty-Dumpty,* recalling how it had been one of her favorite nursery rhymes, she sat staring straight ahead.

When she was five, James Nickels-Stewart had made her exercise her imagination trying to devise different ways of putting the character back together again.

As she grew a little older, he'd insisted she learn about entropy, which—he'd said—meant that poor Humpty Dumpty could never be the same again. Humpty couldn't be returned to lower disorder once he'd shattered into higher disorder.

Higher entropy, higher disorder... her new reality.

Sam lingered nearby, holding an umbrella over her. Joanna glanced up at him.

"Dr. Nickels-Stewart, may I drive you somewhere? Zack will pick me up."

She stood and took his arm, matched her stride to his as they walked in silence around the basin to the parking lot. Near her car, she pulled the keys from her purse.

Sam used the remote and opened the door for her. He fumbled with his collar, a worried look on his face, while she seated herself behind the steering wheel.

"Thank you, Sam," she said, smiling up at him. "I'll be okay."

He tipped his hat, hurried across the street, and headed toward the Capitol building. She watched him go, feeling like Robinson Crusoe losing Friday.

What to do? Where to go? Whom to call?

Michael had left for Fort Benning this morning—wouldn't be back until noon tomorrow. This certainly wasn't something she could tell him over the phone. She wanted to see his reaction, up close and personal. Ditto her parents, who were scheduled to return late tonight from a trade mission to China. She definitely wanted to see *their* reaction.

Call Sister Mary Jane, Auntie Jane. The number rang several times. She pressed the button to cut-off the call, remembering Sister was teaching college classes. Office hours weren't until 2:00 p.m.

Marva—she was with her fifth grade class. Sandra? She'd be home tending the baby, best not to disturb her. Rosa, of course. Phone Rosa.

Good God, Rosa's not going to believe this—wait a minute, maybe it isn't true.

It needed investigating before she told Rosa—best to have real facts to tell. She couldn't to go off "half-cocked" as Nana Nickels-Stewart called giving in to such unbridled emotion. She admired her grandmother and was proud of learning good self-discipline from her.

What did the senator think he was doing, anyway, interfering with their marriage plans?

Michael had joked a number of times about an arranged marriage his family had contracted with a prominent southern family—a gentlemen's agreement, he'd called it. He'd said for several years both families had been grooming the young girl in question, a Charleston debutante, to be Mrs. Michael Vander Hurst, the fifth.

That kind of long-term manipulation of a person's life was the most abhorrent thing Joanna could imagine. It absolutely froze her blood, but the Vander Hursts hadn't seemed like they'd do that sort of thing... *well, until now.*

Cherry blossoms settled on the floor of the car as she leaned against the cold leather seat. Did Senator Vander Hurst already know everything about her birth? He certainly had enough resources at his disposal.

No matter, she'd find the answers. A good detective agency could be hired to investigate in Lima, and she'd question her parents. They'd tell her.

Then again, why hadn't they?

Best not conjure up troubles. She'd go to the farm tomorrow, confront them, and hear what they had to say. Then she'd talk with Michael—and she *would* tell him everything.

What would his reaction be? Difficult to say—considering the position he'd taken during their recent argument about her career. She'd always believed he was so broadminded and modern. She'd never thought he would... oh well... here she was, borrowing more trouble.

The car engine whirred to life with the press of a button, and her heart lurched as she entered D.C. traffic. Nana always said deal with things in their own good time.

Nana Nickels-Stewart—the "eye" in the middle of the hurricane—all hell could break loose, and still she would—Joanna slammed on brakes as traffic stalled.

She may not be my grandmother.

Chapter 2

If only the day could be rewound to the point at breakfast when she and Michael were laughing together, drinking coffee, sharing plans. Sadly, that kind of thing happened only in advanced theoretical physics, and most people hadn't caught up with that paradigm yet.

She dreaded going back to the condominium, spending idle hours wrestling with the unknown, waiting to take action. What she needed was a firm place from which to make a stand against the ensuing chaos…a place with structure, some measure of anonymity, some kind of mindless activity so she could lose herself until watch hours.

McElrod Observatory—she'd go to work, locate a detective agency, fax them the documents, get them searching. She could handle this.

The windshield wipers swished hypnotically. All at once, she was poised on the tip of the wiper blade, swinging between some old and new existence. Stomping the gas pedal, she hurtled forward. Damned if she'd be tossed about by chance. She was a good scientist and knew very well how to control for contingencies.

Lincoln Memorial receded in the rearview mirror as she crossed Arlington Bridge and headed east. The drive out to the observatory was always relaxing after the hectic pace of D.C.'s traffic. McElrod Observatory was located twelve miles from Washington on the Virginia side of the Potomac.

Unfortunately, it wouldn't be long until D.C.'s creeping expanse claimed all the empty acreage. Then the observatory would have to be relocated where city lights wouldn't obscure the night skies.

Working at the observatory satisfied her great need to stay connected with her profession. She hated to think she'd soon have to leave her volunteer position there. Her wedding was set for September, and, as her mother reminded her constantly, prep time was needed for that.

Mary Ellen Nickels-Stewart and Cecile Townsend Vander Hurst were making a major production of the wedding. They'd selected Charleston, South Carolina as the site, and consequently, extra travel time was needed to make the arrangements.

The wedding plans had seemed to be progressing well except for one recent serious argument she and Michael had over her career. She'd been stunned at his insistence that while he pursued promotion in his job, her work might have to be put on hold. She'd always thought he understood a career like hers couldn't bear a lengthy hiatus. They'd had quite a stalemate, but finally agreed she'd continue working after they were married.

She was an astrophysicist, had worked hard to attain her doctorate. She'd already turned down offers from major universities in California and Arizona to stay with Michael.

"A temporary arrangement," he'd said. "My job's portable, don't worry, we'll relocate when you're ready."

Then he'd accepted a job at the DOD. The chances of their being posted elsewhere had suddenly become more than remote. His position was in a new area of expertise—drafting international law regarding interplanetary travel. It was an area apparently considered top secret.

He'd been reluctant to give specific details. One thing he had made very clear, though, he couldn't—wouldn't turn down the opportunity.

Another point of contention between them was that Michael failed to mention her work at McElrod when he introduced her to his colleagues. She'd pointed it out to him the last time it happened, and he'd apologized, offering as an excuse that he was preoccupied with important events at the DOD. She suspected he didn't tell them because he believed volunteering at McElrod wasn't exactly real work.

Her work at the observatory *was* gratifying. Recently she'd garnered a bit of attention for significant contributions to the way observations were conducted at McElrod, and those methods had paid off in increased discoveries. Dr. Benzer, director of the observatory, had expressed appreciation for her work and regret that a current freeze prevented him from hiring her permanently.

That was okay, for now, because she loved her profession and would do anything to be involved. The universe was her natural domain. She'd studied it since she was six years old, when her father had introduced her to its magnificence in his backyard observatory.

James Nickels-Stewart was an amateur astronomer, a well-respected species in professional astronomy circles. In fact, his name was listed among the discoverers of the Maradella Radiation Belt—he'd been twelve at the time. He was proud his daughter had become an astrophysicist and told everyone she'd inherited his love of astronomy.

He'd chosen global finance over astronomy. Joanna believed he'd compensated for the defection by bequeathing all his knowledge to her.

That was why she knew more about the field at seventeen, when she'd entered university, than most doctoral level astronomy majors. In addition, she'd already published papers in *Astronomy Edge*, the most respected research journal in the profession.

The bond she shared with James Nickels-Stewart was special, which made it doubly disturbing that he might not be her real father—it didn't bear thinking about just now, ditto, her marriage and career plans.

There was *one* thing she'd have to decide soon. The senator had made it clear, if she and Michael married, he'd prefer she renounce her Catholic faith and become a member of the Protestant Episcopal Church. Although her parents were devout Catholic and had made her attend a Catholic boarding school, she was probably best defined as a lapsed Catholic. Still, having to renounce the faith she'd grown up in ... that did beg sorting out. It was another issue Michael and she had dodged lately.

The parking lot at McElrod Observatory was nearly full. Joanna circled it twice, found a space and ran through the rain to the entry door.

She tried to skirt the reception area, but Delmarie Rose, who was speaking with a graduate student, looked up in surprise. Joanna waved at her and hurried on down the hall.

Unlocking the office door, she launched into menial tasks, writing reports, tidying the office. Having accomplished that, she proceeded to the lounge where she dusted everything and rearranged the furniture.

At noon, she was in the middle of moving the sofa when the receptionist entered the lounge and opened the fridge door.

"Hey girl, what're you doing here so early?" Delmarie said, as she turned around and sat down. "My God, what's happened to the furniture?"

"I've wanted to do this since I first came to McElrod. Don't you think there's a better view with the sofa facing the windows?"

"I declare, Joanna, you're looking right *pea... ked!* You sure you're okay?" Delmarie placed her lunch tote on the coffee table and took out her sandwich and drink.

"It's the weather." Joanna shifted the chair she was moving to another position. "Your brother's on the Alexandria Police Force, right?"

"Okay, Joanna, now you're asking me about the police, something's going on. I just know it."

"A friend of mine received an anonymous letter and needs to find the identity of the person who sent it. Do you mind asking your brother if he knows of a good detective agency, particularly one with operatives in foreign countries?"

"I'll call him now." Delmarie patted her sweater pocket and pulled out her cell phone.

Joanna skipped lunch and returned to the office. Using her cell phone, she tapped in the number Delmarie had given her. She cleaned desk drawers as she waited for a response.

The Quick Pro Quo Detective Agency had connections in Peru and would get on the job, right away. They directed her to fax copies of the birth certificate and letter to them.

She sat at her desk and searched the computer for websites related to Lima. Time passed quickly as she viewed images of what could be the city of her birth and read about its history. She clicked through a number of sites having information on hospitals in the city, but the search was futile. She needed more information.

Numbers flashed on the bottom of the computer screen alerting her to the time. Logging off, she cleaned the desktop, put on her lab coat, and took the elevator to the top floor of the observatory.

At 6:00 p.m., Daylight Savings Time, the night skies, at this latitude in early spring, were gradually phasing into darkness. This was Joanna's personal witching hour. No matter how many times she approached a telescope, her body still reacted with the same tingling excitement.

She climbed the spiral staircase to the high dome and, using the remote control, adjusted the McElrod 60″ reflector telescope, which was augmented by the space-based relay system of transmissions from the Hubble and Kepler Space Telescopes. It had been built in 1994 and had a single mirror, with an aperture diameter of 1.524 m., and a focal length of 138″.

The telescope wasn't the most technically advanced, but, with a system of adaptive optics and data feeds from Pasadena and Houston, it was on a par with those in many well-respected lower-tier observatories. Joanna sat in the swivel chair and looked into the eyepiece, adjusting it again.

The telescopic extension of her eyes catapulted a million miles into space, and she focused on Rhea, noticing what appeared to be greater density in streaks of bright ice deposits accruing along a deep escarpment. She'd been observing that area for several weeks.

Of course, eruptions had occurred in the past on the surface of Saturn's second largest moon. NASA's Cassini Space Probe had photographed the debris fields, and earlier analysis had determined the eruptions were mostly ice.

Both Voyager 2 and Cassini had picked up indications that Rhea had a wispy hemispheric atmosphere, consisting of oxygen and carbon dioxide, which might have come from cryo-volcanic eruptions or some surface organic source—*organic source*—now that was a significant phrase. It suggested life might be sustainable.

Long hours at the telescope could lessen observational precision. Joanna stared into space and shook her head occasionally, redirecting attention. It was important to stay alert.

Refocusing the lens, she gazed more intently. Was she hallucinating? She'd been sleep-deprived for some time now, but... there it was again. M*ovement...* She recalibrated the lens, checked the coordinates, looked again, swept her eyes across the array of blinking screens to the right and left of the telescope, and placed a hand over her heart to force a calmer beat.

She repeated the checklist, logged the coordinates in a neat, precise hand, and yelled to the graduate student in the room below. "Jared, come up here. *Quick*."

She saw him look up through the iron mesh, his mouth open. The clipboard he'd been holding hit the floor, and he raced up the steps, two at a time.

"Dr. Nickels-Stewart, what's wrong—what is it?"

She motioned for him to come closer. "Look." She stepped aside.

He inspected the lens for a long moment, adjusted them, looked again, and turned toward her, eyes wide in astonishment.

"Damn, I don't believe it." He went to the data screens. "You check the coordinates? What about the feed from Cassini?"

The questions irked her—even the greenest neophyte would have done those things. He glanced toward her again, waiting for a response. She nodded, indicating she'd performed the procedures.

"Okay, record all the observations and repeat all the protocols. I'm calling Dr. Benzer —hope to God he's near a telescope. We've hit it big this time."

Joanna studied the pulsing screens and heard the words of her doctoral advisor during his first lecture to new students. "What privileged blokes you are, you've got a *ringside seat* on the universe."

She trembled, thinking about the eruptions. Of course, consideration had to be given to the distance and the delay related to that, but the age of the other eruptions had never been determined. *This was a real-time event. The eruption* was *occurring now.*

Some scientists thought water might have been present on Rhea in the distant past, but, if there was evidence of water in these eruptions, the possibility of life on Rhea was more likely. Even more importantly, the possibility of future human habitation might prove viable.

Jared rushed back up the stairs. "I left a message at the conference desk. They said they'd get it to him immediately. Boy, we've hit it big! Did you capture the audio and visuals from NASA? Let me see your recordings."

Rewinding the tapes, she checked the latest data transmissions relayed by NASA, scanned the images to the computer and superimposed grids. She brought the printed copies to the table and displayed them for Jared to see.

"This is really great," he said. "We need to stake a claim—before anyone else announces it. Professionals and amateur astronomers in the worldwide Deep Space Network may have seen it—let's hope not. Why were you looking in that particular sector?"

We—there it was, he'd said it again, and it was more than annoying the way he was questioning her on protocol. She knew he thought she was doing nothing more than marking time at McElrod until her society wedding. She'd overheard him say as much to Delmarie.

She'd been on her way out of the office when she heard him proclaiming to the receptionist that he thought it was awful for someone like Joanna to dabble—to play at doing astronomy. It was way beyond waste for her to throw away a terribly expensive education, because everyone knew after marriage to that rich senator's son, she'd never work again.

The receptionist had caught Joanna's eye and shook her head with a look of disgust. Later she'd remarked, "Poor boy, I do declare he's experiencing failure to thrive, stuck as he is in that unnaturally extended prepubescent stage."

Joanna pointed to the printout. "Rhea's the only one of Saturn's moons to have recent eruptions. It's difficult to say *how* recent, but, of course—"

"Well, this is certainly happening now. We need to measure the light intensity, calculate distances, figure time lapse, analyze the spectrum. I guess you've verified the dates on the Cassini recordings with Pasadena?"

She wouldn't focus on his put-down, his implications that she hadn't followed standard protocol—protocols not established until she'd instituted them, only weeks ago.

"The eruptions are coming from the interior, near Tirawa impact basin. They're not spewing ice like the other eruptions have done in the past," she said.

The observatory phone rang. Jared darted down the steps to answer it. Joanna picked up the data printout and followed him.

"Yes, sir... no, I hated to disturb you... we thought you should know about our latest discovery…yes! Our latest discovery! We've seen eruptions on Rhea!"

The gall started deep in her gut, threatening to exceed the velocity of the eruptions she'd just observed on Rhea. She choked it back. She wasn't about to let him see how his stupidity roweled her.

"Yes sir... . Yes! Joanna got pictures... . We've recorded the observations and got the feed from Hubble and Cassini... . How do you want this handled? No, you're right, others may have observed it... . You'll handle the press... Okay, I'll fax you the info —"

"Jared, let me speak with Dr. Benzer—*now*!" His mouth opened, he handed her the phone.

"This is Dr. Nickels-Stewart. I need a meeting with you before this goes public... There's important information Jared doesn't have." She glanced over at him.

"You may give him credit for verifying my data, but he didn't participate in the prior research, observations, or discovery of this event... Eight o'clock tomorrow morning will be fine. Thank you."

She put the phone in its cradle and faced Jared.

"You're on your own now," she said, handing him the telescope's remote control. "Good luck with that."

Chapter 3

Strange to think her interlude at McElrod had ended. True, it had been a subscript to her life, but she hated to admit that. It should have loomed larger. The groundwork and protocols she'd put into place for future discoveries were substantial contributions.

This morning's meeting with Dr. Benzer had gone well. She'd pointed out a number of specific points missing from faxes Jared had sent and approved the final press release.

Wedding prep, she'd said, was her reason for leaving. She expressed her gratitude to the director for the opportunity to volunteer, and he'd stated, once again, his appreciation for her work at the observatory.

Now it was a relief to have the way cleared so she could devote full time to her immediate problems. She'd get the facts about her adoption if that certificate proved to be valid, and she'd go to Peru to meet her birth family. After that, she'd get busy and apply for a long-term paying position with a reputable university.

Custis Memorial Parkway had less traffic by 9:30 a.m. in lanes going west toward Middleburg, Virginia. Driving out to the family farm was usually one of her favorite things to do.

The passing scene was spectacular. Flowering redbud and dogwood trees were woven into an exquisite natural Aubusson carpet that stretched across the landscape and rose gradually to the distant Blue Ridge Mountains.

Last evening, she'd rehearsed incessantly the upcoming conversation with her parents and now her thoughts whiplashed between devising questions to pose to them and dissecting Michael's phone call.

He'd sensed her turmoil but she'd lied, saying it had been a long tiring day. He'd queried her about the meeting with his father. She'd said the venue for the honeymoon was settled—it was Tagalo Island, South Carolina—she'd sort that out later. She was determined to conceal her adoption until he returned home.

The turn-off onto the dirt road leading home churned up her anxiety all over again. She was glad she'd called to say she was coming to lunch, at least she was expected.

The make-up mirror on the visor reflected a pale worn face she hardly recognized, the display on the dashboard flashed 11:00 a.m. She opened the car door and stood for a moment gazing at the greening, dew-diamonded pastures she loved.

It was time. She had to do this.

Taking the gravel path to the rear of the house, she opened the back screen door, hung her coat in the mudroom, and walked down the wide central hallway. No sound came from the dining room or the library. She turned toward the kitchen and nearly upended the housekeeper, who was hastening in the opposite direction.

Vivian lifted her chin, smiled up at Joanna, and threw her arms wide for a hug. Joanna clung to her. Vivian was her "second mother," and had been with the family as long as she could remember.

"Mrs. Nickels-Stewart is exercising Ginger, took the dogs with her—shouldn't be long. Tell you what, why don't you go on down to the barn, we're not quite ready here—she'll be happy to see you. Go on."

Leaning on the fence, Joanna watched her mother trotting Ginger around the paddock. Mrs. Nickels-Stewart saw her, waved, and pointed toward the barn.

Joanna rounded the fence and followed her into the barn. She patted the horse's neck while her mother dismounted.

Mary Ellen Nickels-Stewart kissed her forehead and handed her a currycomb. Grooming the horses alongside her mother was one of her fondest childhood memories.

They worked in companionable silence, and, when they'd finished, Joanna brought fresh oats for the feed bucket and opened the spigot to fill Ginger's water trough. Her mother handed the horse a carrot and reached to examine a hoof. She spread lanolin on it and checked the other hooves in turn.

"Your visit's unexpected. What's the occasion?" Mary Ellen Nickels-Stewart stood, stroking the horse's muzzle, her back to Joanna. "It's always a delight to see you, of course!"

"Let's talk after lunch, okay? Is Dad home?"

"My goodness, this sounds rather ominous." Mary Ellen turned to stare at her. "I'd hoped you were here to talk dish and silver patterns. We haven't done that, you know. Of course, you'll want to duplicate my Raynaud Scheherazade—that way you'll have extra place settings, when I retire from the hostess business."

Joanna hurried ahead to open the door for her mother and the dogs. The dogs romped into the hall but lunged back toward the porch when they heard her father's car turn into the gravel drive. Joanna opened the screen door just in time to prevent a disaster.

James Nickels-Stewart exited his car, pushed back a dark wavy forelock that fell across his deeply tanned brow, and cleared the porch steps in easy strides. He engulfed Joanna in a one-armed embrace and extended the other arm to field the dogs' licks and jumps.

"This whole place explodes in excitement when the laird of the manor appears." Joanna laughed, returning his hug.

Several times since the senator had given her the birth certificate, she'd studied her image in the mirror and had to admit she looked Hispanic. That didn't prove anything, because her father had told her the earliest Scotts were believed by anthropologists to have migrated from the Iberian Peninsula sometime after the last Ice Age, so they really did have Spanish DNA in their blood!

The Nickels-Stewarts actually had Hispanic coloring. Both were descended from the Black Scots, so-called because of jet-black curly hair and a light olive complexion. In fact, people said her father resembled Sean Connery.

Mary Ellen called from the end of the hallway, "Why don't you two have an aperitif while I go change?"

"Great idea," James Nickels-Stewart said. "Just a second and I'll settle E.T. and Misty in the study—Bloody Mary's all around? Good!"

He entered the room, smiling at her, and placed the drinks on the table. "Let's have lunch in here. Run tell Vivian we're relocating the festivities."

From her place at the breakfast room table Joanna could see through to the main hall. Mrs. Nickels-Stewart was descending the grand staircase, dressed in a suit that set her tiny frame off to perfection.

Her mother could have worn a patched bath towel and that regal carriage would have lent it elegance. It irked her that her own posture and grace was a matter of constant studied effort.

Given that small stature, Joanna had often wondered how her mother managed to have such a commanding presence. Like a general, she advanced to the foot of the table opposite her husband and nodded toward Vivian, who directed the staff to serve lunch. Vivian, having executed Mrs. Nickels-Stewart's orders, seated herself across the table from Joanna.

Polite chatter, accompanied by rhythmic rounds of food consumption, progressed inexorably toward the conclusion Joanna dreaded. Meals at the farm were always a delight with fruits and vegetables fresh from the garden, but all that was lost on her today as she chewed automatically.

She watched her mother closely—waiting for her to sit up straight, square her shoulders, and stare pointedly at James Nickels-Stewart. It was the signal that conversation was about to turn deadly serious.

"Did Joanna tell you there's something she wishes to discuss with us? She's been very secretive about it since her arrival."

Her father turned toward her, an expectant look on his face.

"Mama, Daddy, there's been a letter—from Peru—with a birth certificate."

Forks clattered against dessert plates. Vivian rose in a flutter, excused herself, and hurried from the room. Mrs. Nickels-Stewart dropped her napkin and pushed back from the table.

"Oh, God, Joanna—"

"Please tell me the truth." Joanna brushed tears away.

Mary Ellen rounded the table and stopped abruptly.

"James, *do something... .*"

"Joanna, darling, we never had any reason to tell you," he said, reaching her side and bending to embrace her.

"Then it's true?" She wrenched herself from his embrace and looked up, pleading.

"But, darling girl, you couldn't be more—"

"What do you know about my birth parents?"

"We reared you from an infant," her mother said, kneeling by her side and clasping Joanna's hands. "You were available for adoption, considered abandoned by the Peruvian courts. We couldn't have children, and it was so thrilling when you came into our lives."

"Who was your agent—the certificate mentioned an agent?"

"Aunt Jane was stationed in Cuzco back then." James Nickels-Stewart stood to face her. "She took care of the adoption and brought you home to us."

"But my parents—surely you know who they are?" She leaned back in the chair and caught a glimpse of her mother moving her head in a quick "no" directed at her father.

He glared back, anger etching lines on either side of his mouth.

"There are... only a few details." He stumbled over his words, unlike anything she'd ever heard him do. "You were born in a hospital...

in Lima to—to a woman of Hispanic lineage and a man who was a Quechua Indian."

"We assumed your family was too poor to keep you," her mother said, not missing a beat as though the lines were rehearsed. "Many Quechua families put their children up for adoption back then, and Catholic families in the states were eager to adopt those children."

They were hiding something, not trusting her to deal with whatever it was.

She didn't want a fight, especially with her mother. It could be disastrous. "I want you both to pay close attention." She struggled to keep her voice even. "I do love you very much, always will, but I need to know about my birth family, and, since you don't seem to want to tell me, I'll have to go to Peru and find the truth for myself."

"Oh please, Joanna, don't do that, I'm begging you." Mary Ellen Nickels-Stewart wrung her hands. "I'm just sick to think you'd go down there. There's instability down there. Foreigners are put in jail at the drop of a hat. I know—don't say it—it's usually because of drugs, but—"

"Mama, I—"

"James, you tell her. You know what they do down there!"

"I've quit my job," Joanna said, "today, in fact. That'll make it easier to—"

Mary Ellen pulled her lace handkerchief from her suit pocket. "Darling, that's *not* a problem, you don't have to work."

"Why in God's name doesn't she understand?" Joanna looked helplessly toward her father.

Mary Ellen rose from her kneeling position, waved her hand, as though dismissing the whole affair, and straightened her suit coat.

"Darling, we'll work this all out—I've got to run—got a Providence Hospital board meeting. Please call Michael, tell him to come on out. Stay for dinner—stay the weekend. We'll have lots of time to discuss all this."

"We can't, we have—" Her words were smothered in a cloud of

Chanel N°5.

Joanna dropped her arms in defeat. Her mother made a cheerful exit, waving and blowing a kiss to her husband, obviously pleased everything was conveniently on hold.

"I guess I'm always going to be in a one-way conversation with her," she said, glancing over at her father.

He shook his head with a look of disgust and settled into a corner chair. Hurrying to his side, she pulled him to his feet, and hugged him.

"Daddy, please walk me to the door. I'm so sorry I can't stay, Michael and I have plans this evening."

"Does Michael know about this?" He draped his arm around her shoulder as they entered the hall.

"No, I wanted to discuss it with you all first."

"Listen to me, darling, call Sister Jane as soon as you can." He paused and removed her coat from the closet. "When you're ready, I'll go with you to Peru. Will you let me come with you?"

"You're the dearest person," she said, slipping into the coat he held for her. "I haven't actually decided to go. I've engaged a detective agency. They'll probably get all the information I need. Maybe I won't even have to go, not until there's an opportunity to meet my birth family."

Hugging him at the door, she felt him watching her as she descended the stairs to the driveway. At the bottom, she turned.

"Daddy, this doesn't change anything."

He bounded down the steps and hugged her again.

"Of course it doesn't. It'll *never* change anything. It can only reveal richer and deeper aspects of you. All the rest is accidental."

Chapter 4

The drive home to D.C., with spurts of speed and the slow crawl of traffic heading into the Capitol, punctuated her frustration. James and Mary Ellen were dear, well-meaning people, but they *were* concealing something. Mainly it was her mother, because her father wanted to tell—but what could possibly be so terrifying, so devastating, that they couldn't—*stop it, Joanna.*

There was the dinner party to orchestrate. She'd wait until after the party to tell Michael about the adoption. He would have returned from Georgia at noon and gone straight to the Pentagon.

Parking the car in the condominium garage, she hurried through the lobby door and halted at the row of mailboxes. A letter with a colorful foreign postmark fell to the floor. She grabbed it up, put her briefcase on a Louis Quinze settee, and perched on the edge.

7 April 2016
Joanna Nickels-Stewart, Ph.D.
2320 M Street, NW - Claiborne Place, 1402
Washington, D.C. 20057-3847

Dear Dr. Nickels-Stewart:
The Executive Council of the National Astronomical Observatory in Cuzco, Peru extends an invitation to you to do post-doctoral work at the Observatory. In addition, you would have an appointment as assistant professor at Franciscan University.

Our senior projects manager, Dr. Pedro Lopez, recommended you for the position. He witnessed the presentation of your research on frequencies of matter at the Astronomy Conference in Denver. He is convinced you will contribute greatly to our work here. We sincerely hope your response will be in the affirmative.

Very truly yours,
Juan Alderez
Juan Alderez, Ph.D., Chairman of the Executive Council

Holding it up like some rare specimen, she examined the letter, front and back. She'd hardly ever given a thought to Peru—actually, it only came to mind when she imagined Rosa at home. Now, in just two days, she'd learned she was born in Lima, and here she was, being invited to work in Cuzco. What were the odds?

Could the one incident have anything to do with the other? Did the person who sent the letter to Senator Vander Hurst have anything to do with this? Never—it was impossible, but it sure was one hell of a coincidence!

She closed her eyes and imagined the ancient observatory. She'd read that Cuzco Observatory was among the oldest in the world. It was very prestigious, and still preserved the ancient astronomical towers used by the Incas. How thrilling to think about working there, but she and Michael would *never* have any reason to re-locate to Peru—well Michael wouldn't.

Placing the letter back in its envelope, she reached for her briefcase, hurried to the elevator, pushed the button. She had a party to get underway. General Moore, Michael's boss, was coming.

Michael had said something was brewing at the office. He'd said the general was being evasive, but had intimated there was a new development in Asia that would shake up their branch of the covert service.

Joanna took the elevator to the fourteenth floor, unlocked the condo door and paused, mesmerized by the view of the Potomac through plate glass windows. It was heart stopping. The river stretched in a wide arc from dining room to living room and, at night, the lights were like a diamond necklace surrounding their aerie in the sky. No pair of eagles had a more beautiful nest.

She entered the study, threw her things on a chair, and dropped the letter from Peru into the middle desk drawer. Hurrying to the master suite, she went through to the dressing room and selected clothes for the evening.

There was just enough time to shower and do her hair before the caterers arrived. From the top drawer of the dresser she took out the gift her family had given her when she'd received her doctoral hood.

It was a magnificent emerald necklace with matching earrings from Bogotá. Michael had said to impress his boss and colleagues tonight. *Well, that should do the trick.*

At the bottom of the drawer lay a newspaper article she'd clipped from the Denver Post. The article announced that Dr. Joanna Nickels-Stewart, a bright young astrophysicist, had stunned conference attendees with her research findings. It seemed so long ago—only a year—but so much had happened.

She slammed the drawer shut, went through to the bathroom, got into the shower, and turned on the water. Memories of Denver flooded her thoughts.

Her presentation had ended, and she'd thanked the audience for their attention, inviting their questions. Unexpectedly, she'd received a standing ovation. Afterwards, people streamed forward to query her about the research.

Her eager inquisitors ignored the passage of time, and Joanna began to plot an excuse to leave. Apologizing, she grasped the handle of the computer projection cart and attempted to roll it toward the exit. Her audience accompanied her, remaining oblivious to her intentions.

Nearly despairing, she looked up to see a young man approaching. She recognized him—he'd winked at her from a front row seat in the auditorium and had signed "good luck" just prior to the beginning of the lecture.

Turning away from her latest questioner, she aimed a couple of surreptitious glances in his direction. She was determined not to look again, when she felt his eyes compelling her.

Now she stared openly. He was very tall. *Damn!* He fit every cliché—Greek god was one of them—the handsomely sculpted face, the black curly hair, the eyes of lapis lazuli blue, all topped off by the nonchalant grace of an athlete.

How embarrassing—he'd caught her gawping—Rosa's favorite word for gawking.

Suddenly, to her surprise, his voice sounded several decibels above the general noise. "Joanna, you've got to come with me this minute! We're late for our luncheon with Sir John Notherby."

It had been quite a "disconnect" as she watched him elbow his way toward her, grab the handle of the computer cart, take her arm, and steer her toward the back exit. She'd attempted to retain a vestige of dignity, apologizing to her captive audience, but he'd dragged her willy-nilly into the back hall, near the kitchen, where they were alone.

"What the hell do you think you're doing?" She'd jerked her arm away, straightening her scarf.

He stepped back, laughing, pretending to dodge a right hook. "Go ahead! Admit you needed rescuing. You'd have been stuck there all day with those people."

"But—"

"By the way, if we can't do lunch, at least allow me to escort you to the banquet tonight. Wait! Don't say anything—you owe me! What'll it be, lunch or the banquet?"

"Well, if a ransom has to be paid, I guess lunch."

"Okay—lunch it is—by the way, in case it's important, I'm Michael Vander Hurst. No, no, don't introduce yourself, I know who—"

"I wasn't about to introduce myself."

Turning off the hair dryer, she heard loud clattering noises coming from the kitchen. Michael had obviously arrived, admitting the caterers who were now invading the premises.

She finished dressing and listened as he greeted his basset hound Skylex and entered the hall lavatory. Slipping into her shoes, she hurried to the antique sideboard in the dining room. It was an heirloom piece that Michael had inherited from his grandmother in Charleston.

The ornate eighteenth-century silver serving pieces were in the center drawer. She took them out and placed them on the marble top, arranging them in the European pattern she'd learned at boarding school. She didn't trust the caterers to know how to do that, nor was she pleased they'd insisted on using rented china and silverware.

Worse still was the realization that the source of her irritation had to do with her mother's prejudices. Mary Ellen Nickels-Stewart commanded a full serving staff and never used caterers, but, if she'd been reduced to using them, she'd never have permitted rented service pieces.

Michael entered the room. In the sideboard mirror, she saw him halt and stand very still, letting his gaze sweep over her, head-to-foot.

"Hot damn, young lady—I'll have to lock you in the closet. I can't hire enough guards to keep the fellows off you tonight. Is that a new dress?"

"You've seen it before—last week when you called saying, 'Get dressed, we're going to dinner.' You arrived home, took one look, and the dress wound up on the floor."

He shook his head and ambled toward the master bedroom with Skylex shadowing him. Joanna turned around and stepped directly in front of one of the pier mirrors that flanked the sideboard.

She rearranged the high mandarin collar of the filmy jade-green silk overcoat. Reaching underneath, she placed hands on her hips and smoothed down the matching slender satin strapless sheath. The emerald necklace, glowing through thin veils of silk, nestled its large pendant in her cleavage. Luxuriant dark hair, pulled back from forehead and ears, was held in place by tiny emerald encrusted combs, revealing a widow's peak that emphasized her heart-shaped face.

Several months ago, while on a shopping spree, she and Kristy Lynn had covered D.C.'s own Rodeo Drive. They'd found an exclusive dress shop.

Joanna had tried on several dresses and finally emerged wearing the dress.

"My God, Joanna, that's stunning," Kristy Lynn had gasped. "You look just like Kwan Yin, or maybe an Inca princess."

Seeing her reflection in the mirror, she had to agree with Kristy Lynn.

The spacious living/dining room pulsated with jazz and excited talk—everyone seemed lighthearted, enjoying the party.

Lively celebrations with witty, intelligent conversation—ranging from recent discoveries in astronomy, to gourmet cooking, to the latest trends in literature—were high on Joanna's list of favorite things. Added to that, the charismatic presence of her beloved Michael should have made the occasion perfect, but the events of the day shadowed her mood. Now she moved like an actor on a stage, reciting lines of inconsequence, waiting for her real life outside the stage door to begin.

She squared her shoulders with determined cheerfulness and made her way toward a cluster of people who were looking out the plate glass windows. They were exclaiming in fascination at the light patterns made by landing aircraft at Dulles International Airport ten miles to the southeast.

"Joanna, where *did* you get that recipe for cornbread salad?" General Dan Moore's wife Linda called from a spot near the grand piano. "I know D.C. caterers didn't come up with that concoction all by themselves!"

"*The Tomato Shed*, Johns Island, South Carolina, the cornmeal is milled at *The Geechie Boy* on Edisto Island." She turned, calling over her shoulder. "Ask Michael, he'll give you the recipe. He loves making it."

Listening to snippets of conversation, she circulated, greeting people, smiling through a mask that hid inner turmoil. There'd been other times she'd questioned who she was—everyone did—but this was different. It was no longer a philosophical exercise.

She glanced across the room, noticing General Moore leaning on the bar that fronted on the windows overlooking the Potomac. He was impressive in evening dress uniform but appeared nervous as he scanned the room. He looked in her direction, straightened, rapped on the bar, and called for attention.

"Hey, everybody, I've an important announcement to make. Michael, my boy, come on over here this minute. I don't believe I've delivered such good news in ages."

Michael exchanged a quizzical look with her and crossed the room. The general shook his hand and slapped him on the back. "You lucky brute, you're being promoted to chief executive officer at a very important field unit of ours in Mongolia—Ulaanbaatar—the Khurel Togoot. And your team will relocate with you."

The general looked over the crowd once more. She felt his eyes on her. "Joanna, now don't you fret, darling—we've got a job over there for you, too." He raised his glass, "To the happy couple! Congratulations, Michael, my boy!"

Glasses clinked and shouts sounded as friends and colleagues crowded around Michael. He shook hands, laughing and bantering with them. She knew she should go to his side—show her happiness for him—but Lot's wife couldn't have been more riveted to the spot.

A job for her—and they hadn't even felt the need to consult her? What if she hadn't left that position at McElrod—did they really expect her to drop everything, pick up, and move halfway around the world? Did General Moore even know she held a doctorate in astrophysics?

One of the waiters was making a swift pass-by through the crowd with a large tray of champagne-filled flutes. Joanna intercepted him, swiped a glass, and fantasized about taking the whole tray—maybe even snagging the refill tank, attaching a long hose, and sitting in the corner, sucking the damn thing dry.

She knocked the glass back in two swallows. At least the general hadn't told her not to worry her 'pretty li'l ole head.'

The last guests departed at 2:00 a.m. She and Michael escorted them to the elevator. General Moore and Linda lingered, commenting on the party.

Finally, the general entered the elevator, pushing Linda ahead of him. He pressed *hold* and stepped out of the elevator to shake Michael's hand again. He kissed Joanna on the cheek, and, as the door closed, he blocked it.

"Don't you worry your pretty little head, Joanna, sweetheart," he called out, "We'll take good care of you over there!"

She stared at the closing elevator door, mouth agape. Michael grasped her arm and steered her toward the living room. She drew back, still grappling with her anger at General Moore's insensitivity.

"Come here," he said, pulling her into his arms, holding her tightly. His chest was heaving. Was he crying?

"This promotion means more than I thought," she whispered.

"It means I'm finally free. My father, the goddamned king of control freaks, has planned every other moment of my life. At least this time, he had nothing to do with it. It's all my own doing."

She feigned interest in the Potomac, not wanting to meet his eyes. What would he do if he knew the senator had staked another claim on his life—if he knew his future wife had been told to check her heritage before their marriage?

Chapter 5

Saturday, 10:00 a.m., Joanna sat up in bed. Michael was still sleeping. She watched him breathing softly. *Their sons would look like that... .*

There were times she'd questioned the traits he shared with most men who comprised the dating-pool from which everyone said she was privileged to draw. Those men were ambitious, driven, and narrow-focused. Women in their universes were the bright moons, satellites to their Earth, never planets on an equal footing.

Lately, Michael's job had taken top priority. She knew that was to be expected now and then—no relationship could be equal all the time—but things would be different in the future. *Of course, they would.*

She pulled on her robe and quietly closed the bedroom door. In the kitchen, she thanked the gods of automatically timed cappuccino machines for their bounty, and savored the cup warming her hands as she headed toward the study.

She sat at the desk, letting the view of the Potomac hold her gaze. Small pleasure craft flashed silver waves in the sunlight. Puffy clouds drifted eastward. She felt rested—glad she hadn't indulged in more champagne last night.

The thought of the letter in the middle-desk drawer was intriguing. What would it be like to work in Cuzco? She needed to call Rosa, get the scoop on that observatory.

Nope, couldn't do that. Not Rosa, not yet.

If she told Rosa now, half of Peru would know by lunchtime. Michael would be up soon. In the meantime, she'd call Aunt Jane in Cleveland.

Sister Jane's Dominican Order had stationed her in Cuzco at the Franciscan College, earlier in her career. Joanna's mother had always held her sister up to Joanna as a role model to emulate. Auntie Jane would be delighted about the invitation to work at the observatory. She'd been instrumental in getting her favorite niece placed in the best astronomy program in the east and always rejoiced in Joanna's career triumphs.

Was it too early to call her on Saturday? Did nuns sleep in on weekends? *Doubtful that!* Anyway, by this hour the morning rituals and breakfast at the convent should be over.

Joanna placed the letter on the desk and picked up her cell phone, tapping in the numbers. She swung her chair toward the large landscape painting of Machu Picchu that hung in the hall, in an alcove near the dining room. It had been a gift for her tenth birthday from Auntie Jane and was the only object of décor in the condo that belonged to her.

The phone rang repeatedly. It would take the convent portress a while to answer. Usually the oldest retired nuns were assigned that duty—that had been the case in Joanna's boarding school days. Parents, eager to call daughters, were always complaining about the inefficiency of the arrangement.

"Joanna, what's this?"

Startled, she turned toward the desk and saw Michael holding the letter. She pushed the button to stop the ringing phone.

"My goodness—an invitation to work at the National Observatory in Cuzco," he said. "What a feather in your cap."

She'd been slouching in the chair. She straightened and felt her shoulders tense.

"I didn't want to wake you—I thought you needed sleep," she said. "The letter came yesterday and there wasn't time to tell you."

The clock ticked loudly. *Michael, please get this right.*

He gave one brief cursory look and dropped the letter back on the desk.

"Ulaanbaatar trumps Cuzco, right?"

She tried to stand, her legs buckled, she braced herself against the desk. He was already retreating toward the kitchen.

"Michael, wait." She hurried after him. "There's something you ought to know."

He turned, giving her a curious look.

"I don't think I have to tell you my career's going nowhere. I've quit that job at McElrod—yesterday."

"But that's great! It'll give you more time to pack for Mongolia—I really need your help to get this relocation under way. Hey, let's get dressed and go to *Celsius* to celebrate."

Turning his back again, he rummaged in the refrigerator, found a peanut butter jar and a bag of English muffins. He placed them on the kitchen island and opened the flatware drawer, taking out a butter knife, holding it up in triumph.

"There's something else." She cleared her throat, aiming for more volume. "Your father received an anonymous letter about me. It seems I'm adopted from Peru."

Michael's hand froze, suspended in mid-air. The knife dripped peanut butter above the English muffin. "What the hell're you saying…?"

"Adopted—that's right—you heard it. I went to see my parents yesterday, and they admit it's true."

He searched her face, his stare penetrating. The peanut butter settled in a blob on the counter. He looked down, busied himself scraping it up, put the knife on the plate, and aligned the muffin beside it.

She drew the letter containing the birth certificate from her briefcase and handed it to him. "I've hired a detective agency to investigate," she said.

He perused the documents multiple times, dropped them on the island, and studied the design in the granite counter top. Finally, he pushed the papers toward her.

She felt him scrutinizing her again. It reminded her of someone seeing a moon rock for the first time, searching memory for points of comparison to Earth rocks.

"I see you're wondering about my identity, too," she said.

"How dare you—presuming to know what I'm thinking." He stood, grabbed the plate from the island, and dumped the contents into the disposal.

"You know what—you're so right. I've no idea what you're

thinking. But, silly me, there was hope your thoughts might reflect a little human compassion."

"What the hell do you want me to say? Of course, I'm as shocked as you are."

She scooped the papers from the island, stuffed everything back into the briefcase, and hurried into the bedroom. Dressing quickly, she left the condo for a run in the park.

Having detoured for coffee, and cooled off sufficiently, she took the elevator to the top floor, and opened the door to find Michael standing in the hall, reaching for his coat.

"I know this adoption thing knocked you for a loop," he said. "Sorry I wasn't more sympathetic. It's just, there are so many things on my mind, it's hard to deal with one more."

"No sweat, not your problem—"

"Don't lay that goddamned injured victim act on me!"

"Hey, not to worry—I won't be doing any more laying or being laid, for that matter."

She jammed her jacket on a hook inside the closet door. Michael ignored her as he emptied his coat pockets of gloves and slips of paper, obviously searching for something. She struggled with emotions that were heading for a roller coaster ride.

"Joanna, we've got to put all our efforts into getting ready for this Khurel Togoot assignment." He wrapped his wool scarf around his neck. "It's the maker or breaker of our lives together. Not only will my career success be cemented, but our financial future will be, too."

She stared at him in silence, watching him pick up his briefcase and reach for the doorknob.

"Can't you see this is my opportunity to contribute to the family coffers, not just subsist on the old inheritance dole? Besides, you'll have a job, too."

"You're expecting me to throw away my career on some

meaningless make-work job?"

"That's what you've been doing—volunteering at McElrod! For God's sake, you don't even have to work—you'd have leisure to do research, to write, whatever you choose."

Her blood exceeded boiling point, neurons firing red into optic nerves. "Tell me, just why did you scoop me up in Denver?"

"Hey, it was your choice to volunteer at that goddamned observatory—I had nothing to do with it. Jesus, Joanna, don't be like that. Of course your career's important, but this job in Mongolia is my ticket to the top—"

"What if Cuzco's my ticket to the top? I've a brilliant idea, why don't you come with me to Peru. I'm betting somebody down there can find work to occupy you."

"That's so adolescent! You know I respect the contributions you've made to science, but this job in Mongolia is vital—I'm doing important research and I'm damned lucky to be heading that team."

"So my career bites the dust, but, hey, that's not your problem. There's room for only one bright star in the future Senator Vander Hurst's galaxy."

His fist clenched, his face reddened, he looked somewhere above her head. He was his father's exact replica as he hurtled down the hallway. Skylex rose to follow. The bedroom door slammed, cutting the dog off before he could navigate the distance.

Joanna addressed the dog, patting its head. "Oops! Scored a direct hit, didn't I Skylex, smack dab to the old phallic id, right where good ole boys fear emasculation by their women folk."

From the study, she heard Michael stalk out of the bedroom and bang the entrance door. The house was silent. Skylex wiggled his long ears at her. Joanna ignored him and nestled into the sofa, staring out the window, drifting with the Potomac, viewing life's strange twists and turns.

What the hell am I doing!

She hated being idle. May as well take Skylex for another walk, clean the house, sort papers, shred outdated documents, organize things she'd long put off doing. Maybe she'd even pack for Mongolia, but she'd be damned if she'd pack for Michael.

At dinnertime, she searched the cupboard and decided against pasta. Left over potato salad and a piece of ham were the only things in the refrigerator. She put them on a plate, went to the sofa, and set the plate on the coffee table. Skylex eyed the food, licking his jowls. She'd fed him breakfast and given him two walks. Had she fed him the evening meal? She put the plate on the floor, turned on the news, and fell asleep.

The mantel clock chimed twelve times. Michael unlocked the door and went straight to the master bedroom. Slowly, deliberately, Joanna got up from the sofa and headed toward the dressing room.

It was difficult enough to think she didn't know who she was, but now Michael had become a mystery. They'd lived together for nearly a year. How long did it take to know a person, really know?

She was tired—bone tired—may as well dress for bed and shower in the morning. Opening the dresser drawer, she pushed aside her mother's latest contribution to her wedding trousseau, an antique lace trimmed batiste nightgown and matching negligée.

Underneath the negligée lay another gift from her mother. It was a delicately monogrammed silk camisole, embroidered by a congregation of cloistered French nuns.

The money spent on those three items alone would have fed a poor highland Peruvian village of a hundred souls for a month. In her mother's mind, those items were utterly necessary for a bride's trousseau.

Holding the camisole, Joanna sat on the bench for a moment,

examining the exquisite stitches. She would never have chosen such a garment. The very notion of its purpose seemed so ironic, so contrary to her way of thinking.

She'd been mulling over one question all day. What had Michael seen in her—why had he pursued her and proposed? Surely, it wasn't her family connections, which she *now* knew was the source of her desirability to Senator Vander Hurst and his wife Cecile.

Her fantasy had been that Michael was attracted to her brilliant mind, the fact that she was a rising star in the field of astrophysics. Certainly, she was attractive enough, but she'd hoped that wasn't the only draw.

Standing, she rummaged under her mother's gifts for a cotton nightgown, found it and closed the drawer. She thought about parading around in that negligée and laughed out loud. What she usually paraded around in was a lab coat.

Glancing up, she saw her image in the mirror above the dresser. She stepped back, reaching for the bench.

My God! I am Cecile Townsend Vander Hurst.

Recalling Michael's mother following behind the senator with mincing steps, an adoring look plastered on her countenance, valiantly avoiding public scrutiny, Joanna knew the truth had to be faced. Her career as an astrophysicist wasn't part of the Vander Hursts' master plan. She pressed her hand to her heart to slow its pounding.

She was having a panic attack. It had to be. She'd never experienced one before, but had heard others describe them—pounding heart, weak legs, breathing in short gasps. Her whole life was spinning out of control.

She had to get a grip—breathe deeply, pause, breathe, relax, force the air out... she could handle this.

When the senator had given her that birth certificate, her self-concept had been ripped apart like an exploding machine, scattering the bolts and screws that held her life together. Her identity had taken a major blow, but now it tottered on the edge of complete oblivion.

I'll be damned if I'll be a Vander Hurst geisha!

By all that was holy, she did have control over one thing. She'd go to Peru. First thing tomorrow morning she'd inform Michael she was going.

If she stayed three months, she'd have time to search for her birth parents *and* sort out how she really felt about marriage to this family. And, who knew, maybe with time in Mongolia, away from his parents, Michael might just learn to appreciate her for herself, rather than the "image" he and his family were trying to superimpose.

It was possible…

Her super-sized suitcase was in the hall closet. She got it, returned to the dressing room, placed it on the table, and closed the interior door to the master bedroom.

She tossed jeans and t-shirts into it, intending to pack only essentials. *Maybe, it was a good idea to pack all her belongings, just in case.* Later, she'd phone the part-time housekeeper and ask her to pack Michael's things.

Forcing the suitcase closed, she rolled it to the front door where it sat upright, engorged, looking like some exclamation point to their lives together. Best to put it in the closet—that wasn't a view she wanted to inflict on Michael first thing in the morning.

Moving to the hall entrance to the master bedroom, she reached to open the door. It was locked. *Michael had locked the door.* She turned away, tiptoed to the guest room, and lay across the bed, feeling more exhausted than she could remember.

She counted each passing hour and then tried counting sheep. Still, she was wide-awake, staring at the ceiling, thinking of recent happenings. Something had been bothering her since that meeting with the senator. It was his instructions to the bodyguard.

"Call General Moore, cancel that meeting. Tell him we'll get back to him as soon as we hear from the officials in Ulaanbaatar."

Chapter 6

Sunday morning, 7:00 a.m., the Potomac was lost in a viscous gray fog that wouldn't lift until noon. Joanna paused by the breakfast bar and noticed Michael at his desk stuffing papers into his briefcase. She walked into the room and stood near the desk.

"Michael …."

"Come here," he said, holding his arms wide. "Are we okay? I'm sorry. Really, I am."

Every cell in her body registered his embrace. She remained silent, wanting to capture the moment, store it.

"I've got to leave town for a few days," he said. "General Moore called and said he wants a meeting with the team early Monday morning at Fort Benning. Why don't we fly down to Tagalo Island next weekend, walk in the sunshine, it'll be great, and we can personally make the reservations for our honeymoon—"

"Michael, I'm going to Peru."

He stepped back, ending the embrace, giving her a look he reserved for children and persons whom he considered feeble minded.

"Isn't that a waste of time and money? You've hired a detective agency." He assumed an air of extreme patience, emphasizing each word. "When they get the information, you can get in touch with your birth family. We can fly them to Mongolia—hell, we'll fly them to the wedding."

"It's important to me to go down there. I need to find myself—find my birth parents."

"Okay, so I'll go with you. We can spend a few days visiting with Rosa. You'd like that, wouldn't you? Then we'll fly to Mongolia, I don't have to report to work until the end of the month."

"I want to spend at least two months down there, maybe three. I'll join you in Mongolia afterwards."

He resumed the deliberate selection of documents, then directed an angry gaze at her.

"You don't even know if they want to be found—they may not—you know. Furthermore, have you thought about what your decision will do to us?"

"I'm going to the farm for a few days before I fly to Lima," she said.

"You packed last night, didn't you?"

"Michael—"

"Don't do this to us. Wait until I get back from this meeting with General Moore. We can settle it then. I've got to run—I'll phone you when I get to Georgia."

He kissed her and hurried out the door.

She removed the Machu Picchu painting from the wall. May as well take it back to the farm and put it in its old place in the bedroom.

Tucking the painting under her arm, she slung her laptop carrying case over her shoulder and rolled the luggage to the open the door. Pausing, she took in the panoramic view of the Potomac. One thing she knew for sure, her life would be very different the next time she saw that view.

The elevator stopped at the lobby. She dropped the condo key in Michael's mailbox and rolled the suitcase to the parking garage.

The painting would travel best on the back seat of the car. Everything else could go in the trunk. She took one last look around, threw her suitcase in the trunk, and slammed the lid.

Traffic was heavy on Francis Scot Key Bridge but less so on the parkway on weekends. Vivian wasn't expecting her, but, when Michael was out of town, she often drove over for Sunday brunch. She'd leave her things in the car and explain afterwards—no sense upsetting household routines.

Michael would be angry, of course, but it couldn't be helped. She wasn't going to let him go with her to Peru.

She punched the phone keypad on the car console, entering the number for Rosa's home in Cuzco. Western South America's time zone was the same as Virginia's.

It was too early on a weekend for Rosa to be awake. *Just as well, catch her off guard, prevent her from asking too many questions—save the big news for face time.*

"Hola, Casa de la Reyna."

"Hola. Señorita Rosa, por favor. Me llamo Joanna, la amiga de Estados Unidos."

She'd last seen Rosa a little less than a year ago. Their shared birthdate was the reason as twelve-year-olds they'd become instant friends back at boarding school. Last year they'd planned a celebration in New York City for their 24th birthday. Rosa had brought Juan Diego Garcia, her fiancé, to meet Joanna. He'd wined and dined them extravagantly.

"Joanna! Is it you? I can't believe it—tell me you're pregnant—go ahead, tell me, hurry!"

"Almost as momentous, I'm coming to Peru—"

"Hello, hola—there *is* a bad connection—¿cómo?"

"Coming to Peru."

"¡Madre de Dios!"

Joanna heard a thump, silence, footsteps. She guessed the maid was rushing to Rosa's assistance.

"Doñita Rosa, ¿está bien usted?" There were sipping sounds, more silence.

"Rosa, are you okay? Listen to me, please. Michael's on his way to Mongolia, and I'm coming for a visit. Can you arrange to meet me in Lima next weekend? I've something important to tell you. I'm booking the flight for next Friday overnight —"

"¡Un momento! You must permit me to adjust my mind to this. Of course, I'll make the arrangements for you, but what is this occasion? I've only begged for years that you should come to Peru—for years!

You haven't broken up with Michael—"

"No, no, tell you when I get there. Do you think your family would mind if I stayed with them in Cuzco for a few days?"

"Mind—are you loca, Joanna? It you didn't, they would be mucho offended."

"I'll email my arrival time—got to go—I'm on the road to Middleburg. Love you, bye."

It was good to have a few days with her parents, but she wasn't going to let her mother talk her out of going to Peru. Although she was a bit apprehensive, still, it was thrilling to think she might have a whole other family.

Were they urban dwellers or highland villagers? Why had they given her up? Maybe they were unwed, not exactly the acceptable thing in Catholic Hispanic culture. Maybe the young woman—assuming she was young—had been forced by her parents to conceal the birth. Maybe she had a new husband and children now. Maybe she didn't want her past revealed.

What had the person who mailed the letter to the senator hoped to accomplish? Why hadn't they sent it directly to her? Was the 'sender' some member of her birth family? Maybe it was really Senator Vander Hurst. Maybe he'd run a background check on her and discovered the adoption and had someone mail the letter and birth certificate from Lima. She wouldn't put it past him, knowing what she did now.

In a few days, she'd know one way or another. She couldn't wait to get to Lima—it'd be wonderful seeing Rosa and her family, but more importantly, the detective agency would probably have info by then. They might have already found something. She'd check first thing tomorrow morning.

Birdsong awakened her to springtime outside the open window. The bedside clock flashed 8:00 a.m.—Monday morning. She brushed fingers through tangled hair, plumped the tear-stained pillow, and propped herself against the padded headboard. Michael hadn't called yet.

There was a knock at her door and Vivian cracked it open a small space. "Joanna, are you awake? Good morning, darling, you've a call on the house phone."

"Thanks, Viv."

Was it Michael? Why hadn't he used her cell phone? She punched # 7 on the console, pushed the speaker button, and settled back against the headboard.

"This is Joanna."

"Good morning, sleepy head,"

"Auntie Jane! I tried calling you Saturday morning. How are you?"

"I've just spoken to Mary Ellen. More importantly, how are *you*, my sweet girl?"

"Auntie Jane." Tears ambushed her. "I'm adopted and mama and daddy won't tell me anything about it. They said you were the agent."

"I can't deny that, now can I?"

"Please, tell me about my birth parents, you must know everything."

"I signed the papers as a proxy for Mary Ellen and James, but the person who brought you to our attention handled the other arrangements. The main condition of your adoption was that the rest of that information should remain a secret."

"Who was the person making the arrangements?"

"My dear, I promised never to divulge that. I love you, but I can't break that promise."

"I'll find out anyway. I'm going to Peru."

Silence on the other end. Joanna waited, watching a robin fly to the ground, scurry about, gather twigs, return to drop them into the rain gutter near her window, a precarious place for a nest.

"Since you're determined to go down there, I'd like to ask a favor.

A cloistered nun, whom I met while teaching at Franciscan University, lives in Cuzco. She's elderly and resides in Santa Maria Monastery. Her name is Sister Elena de la Cruz. Rosa's Grandmother de la Reyna knows her well. Anyway, after you're settled in, please go introduce yourself, will you?"

"Auntie Jane, you know I hate cloistered convents—I'd do anything in the world for you, but please, don't' ask that."

She had a touch of claustrophobia, loathed the very thought of being inside such a place, cloistered meant "locked-up." Auntie Jane's convent was different, modern, almost like a hotel, where members of the religious order lived but went outside to engage in various professions, like education and medicine.

"Sister Elena's very knowledgeable about Incan mythology, and I know you've always had an interest. She's brilliant. I think you'll not regret spending a little time with her. Please do this for me, and give her my best wishes along with a package I'll send to you later."

"Did mama tell you that Dr. Juan Alderez from Cuzco Observatory invited me to work and teach there? It's amazing—the letter arrived last week, soon after the senator gave me the letter about my adoption. It would be tremendous to work in that historic place!"

There was no answer.

"Auntie Jane—Sister Jane, did you hear me?"

"Yes... did the senator have any idea who sent that letter? Surely, of all people, he should've been able to track that information down."

"I think he considers it my problem. Michael says his father is 'cleverly efficient' at delegating tasks. Anyway, I've hired a detective agency."

"Your mother said you'll be going to Mongolia at the end of the summer…"

"General Moore's finding work for me."

She hoped that statement had yielded some small inflection of joy and excitement. She couldn't hide much from her aunt.

"How's Rosa? Will you be staying with her family while you're in

Peru?"

"Rosa's meeting me in Lima to sight-see. She's become her country's equivalent of a starlet, can you believe it! She's featured in the gossip columns of *La Vida Nocturna* magazine now that she's engaged to Juan Diego Garcia—he's a big name in Peruvian politics. I met him last year when he came to New York with her. It's awful to be judgmental, but he acted like a spoiled jerk. I can't think what she sees in him."

"What's Carlos doing now?"

"Finished a graduate degree at London School of Economics last year and Rosa said he was recently elected to represent the Department of Cuzco. She says everyone believes he ought to run for the presidency someday."

"Joanna, this is certainly a huge adventure for you—almost like a pilgrimage, isn't it? I remember how delighted you were with that little book about Peru I gave you for your twelfth birthday."

"*The Secret of the Andes*, by Ann Nolan Clark— you actually gave it to me for Christmas when I was eleven. Llamas were the secret treasure, not gold.

"In college, I learned that the Incas named two dark cloud constellations for a mother llama and her baby—those constellations represent major tribal lineage symbols."

"If I were you, I'd go ahead and meet with Dr. Alderez— see the work they're doing at that historic observatory. You'll find Cuzco's an extraordinary place. And, Joanna... please visit Sister Elena for me. You're going to do just fine down there. *Vaya con Dios.*"

Chapter 7

Michael hadn't called, but that wasn't unusual. The meetings were typically two day affairs and participants were kept busy every minute.

A real physical ache for his presence had started, and she'd begun to dread the thought of spending the next few months without him. It worried her that she hadn't told him the senator might have arranged his promotion. Would he come to her defense if she told him there were also clear indicators his father intended to script her life, as well?

She was glad to be at the farm. Each morning she was up early and exercised the horses with her mother. Afterwards, they sat on the back porch drinking coffee and talking, waiting for the rest of the household to begin morning routines.

"Joanna, have you considered that you and Michael may grow apart if you spend this whole summer in Peru? I'd sure hate to see you throw away this opportunity for happiness—my goodness, most girls would die for such an exciting future."

"Dying may be what's required ..."

Mrs. Nickels-Stewart's hand shook, the coffee splashed on her linen napkin. She set the cup carefully on the side table.

"What's wrong with you, Joanna? I'm beginning to be concerned."

"Believe me, so am I, when I see how the Vander Hurst family sacrifices its members to an era frozen in time, and I'm about to be their latest victim."

"God almighty, what *are* you talking about?"

"Don't you see, Mama? Tagalo Island's an exquisite metaphor for a past that may never have existed, except in the minds of people like the Vander Hursts. People who must constantly be vigilant, giving all their being to feed that image, constantly living careers that don't bring satisfaction in order to support that lifestyle, arranging and contracting sham marriages to assure blood lines, forcing their children into the same mold to preserve tradition. They doggedly hold that line—repainting, re-upholstering, restoring, re-plating, refurbishing, and relinquishing self on the altar of a nonexistent dream."

"You're condemning your father and me, too…"

"That's not true—you're nothing like the Vander Hursts. You grow, change, adapt, and open yourselves to new possibilities. That's why I love and admire you both so much."

"I love you, too, darling." Mary Ellen sighed, wiping tears with her napkin. "I just want you to be happy and secure."

"Mama, are you worried this trip to Peru will change my relationship with you? It won't, you know. I won't let it."

"How can it not? What you find down there may swallow your whole existence, no matter how much you might wish it wouldn't."

"You're my mother, period—always will be—you represent all the things that word means to me, every resonance it has, and there's no changing that."

Mrs. Nickels-Stewart reached over and pulled her close. Joanna stared out at the hills, wishing she could tie the moment up neatly and store it in her little pouch of treasures.

In the evenings, her father joined her at his backyard observatory where they discussed astronomy for hours. She sensed he felt a strong need to give her tips about foreign travel. He was quite the expert based on his many trips abroad for the U.S. Government.

"Whatever you do, don't wear good jewelry out in public," he told her. "Lima is a city of a little more than eight million people packed into a narrow strip of land along the coast. There are recent signs of an economic up-turn, but actually, the country has only two strata of people, the very rich and the very poor. Sadly, many desperate people live in primitive shantytowns. El Salvador is an exception, an exemplar of good 'bootstrap determination' on the part of the inhabitants. You might want to visit that little community, if you have the opportunity."

"I recall a few years back, after a trip down there, you said the new

U. S. Embassy was built like a fortress. You said it was a real 'over-the-top reaction' to the Tupac Amaru guerrillas' hostage-taking incident in the 90's at the Japanese embassy."

Joanna adjusted the telescope lens and sensed her father watching her. She turned her head, seeing the worried look.

"Those terrorist groups are still active in remote places, Joanna. Please be careful."

Vivian insisted Joanna weigh carefully the decisions about what clothes to take in order to pack more efficiently. It was Wednesday morning, and they were in the midst of yet another bout of organized chaos when Joanna's cell phone alerted her to a call from Michael.

She hurried from the bedroom into the hall, out through the screen door onto the upstairs porch, and sat in a wicker rocker. "Michael! Where are you? I thought you'd call yesterday."

"I've just returned from Georgia. So you couldn't wait."

"I had to—"

"Good luck with your little Peruvian adventure. By the way, I'm leaving for Ulaanbaatar earlier than anticipated. The military shuttle departs Anacostia-Bolling this evening. Thanks for asking Gert to pack my things—I'll call you when I land."

"Michael, please be safe. I love you." Crackling static announced the call had ended.

The shadow of a cloud passed across the peaceful hills, changing them from serene and beautiful to desolate and lonely. Joanna left the porch and called after the housekeeper who was descending the stairs, "Viv, have you seen that small carry-on case I used back in college?"

"Check the attic."

It'd been a good while since she'd been to the third-floor attic. The huge fan-shaped windows in each gable had made a perfect place for a child to play on rainy days. She'd imagined herself as Jo in *Little Women* and had spent endless hours reading and dreaming about the future.

Her father called it the plunder room, a room ubiquitous in southern homes where all cast-off treasures were stored. Leaning against one wall was a lavishly carved Tudor bedstead. She'd been told Great-Great-Grandpa Stewart had died in it. It had occupied that exact spot for at least a hundred and fifty years, leaving its ghost undisturbed. Eight rare walnut chairs, cane backs and seats shredded, lurked under the eaves nearby, concealing mysterious stories of their dismantling.

Huge trunks containing clothes from two previous centuries stood in soldierly rows on either side of an aisle that formed a sort of reviewing corridor leading to the gables at either end. During Joanna's tenure at boarding school, the drama department had greatly benefited from the costumes she'd liberated from those trunks.

The corridor had a crosswalk at its center that formed two alcoves. Joanna turned left into one of them. It would be the likely location of the carry-on case. Searching the shelves for the suitcase, she spotted, pushed far back on the top shelf, an old tan portmanteau with rattan sides on which were pasted glorious multi-colored stickers, bearing witness to passages through many worldwide ports-of-call.

Around her fifth birthday, she'd climbed on a rickety chair and pulled the portmanteau off the shelf to examine it more closely. It had been locked. A rattling sound caught her attention, and she sat down on the spot, attempting to pry it open with an old rusted fireplace poker.

Vivian, who'd been searching for her, discovered her "damaging" the suitcase and threatened to punish her bodily for the first and last time in her young life.

"Don't touch that," she'd screamed. "It belongs to Sister Jane. Whatever possessed you, Joanna?"

She'd cried hysterically while Vivian, still scolding, dragged her down the stairs. As far as she knew, the portmanteau had sat gathering dust since then.

Standing on tiptoe and reaching far back on the top shelf, she grasped it firmly, swinging it over her head and down to the floor. Why would Sister Jane have stored it here?

Forgetting her original purpose, Joanna clutched the portmanteau to her chest, returned to her bedroom, and locked the door. She placed it on the bed and got the poker from the fireplace.

The first well-positioned pry popped the lid. A scrap of paper stapled to the top of several other documents lay on the bottom of the case.

She picked it up and saw that it was part of a letter ripped from the middle of a page. It had no greeting and no signature. The stationery reminded her of the box of Crane's in her mother's writing desk.

> *History will exact a price and that price must be paid. Nothing must be allowed to preclude the obligation to preserve the legacy.*
>
> *Neither you, nor J, will know the year, but we will most certainly know the event that precipitates it. I regret the upheaval in our lives when that time comes.*
>
> *The paperwork has been completed. If you and all parties are agreed and the conditions are met, tomorrow at noon you may sign the documents that transfer the baby to your care.*

The portmanteau must have been given to Aunt Jane when the adoption occurred. Maybe it had been filled with baby clothes ...

Aunt Jane said the person's name had to be kept secret. Would revealing that person's name cause disturbance in everybody's lives? What was *"the price history would exact"* and what was the *legacy*?

The message was certainly enigmatic. No use asking either Aunt Jane or her parents to explain it. Was the author of this note the person who'd sent the anonymous letter to the senator? Could that person possibly be her real mother or father?

She worked the staple loose from the scrap of paper and found a duplicate of the birth certificate the senator had given her. Attached to it was an envelope with several faded snapshots. Placing the scrap of paper on the bed, she sat down to study the pictures.

One was a photo of a young woman who looked Hispanic. She wore a white dress—not a wedding dress, maybe a debutante gown. She was holding a bouquet and was posed in front of a familiar building. Joanna had seen that building somewhere before... Madrid, the El Escorial. She'd toured there a few years back.

Another photo was of a young man who resembled a Sephardic Jew from Spain, but he was dressed in what appeared to be a native Incan costume. His headdress was a crown-like affair with a fringe that stretched across the forehead, covering the top portion of his eyes.

Were these pictures of her parents? Chilblains covered her arms.

She examined the third snapshot. It was of Machu Picchu and resembled the landscape painting Aunt Jane had given her. At the very bottom of the suitcase was a photograph of a much younger Aunt Jane, in her religious habit and veil, standing in front of an ancient church. The name Monasterio de Santa Maria was worked into the wrought iron sign above the gate. That was the name of the monastery where Aunt Jane said her friend Sister Elena lived.

Joanna placed the scrap of paper and birth certificate, along with the photos, in the zippered side pocket of her large suitcase. She grabbed the portmanteau, peeped around the bedroom door to be sure Vivian was nowhere in sight, and hurried back up the stairs to the attic.

Sliding the portmanteau back into its place on the top shelf, she sat for a moment on a discarded hassock thinking about what she'd found. Her gaze wandered to the row of shelves opposite, and she saw a plastic wrapped bundle stuffed far back on the second shelf from the top.

Inside the plastic was the suitcase she'd originally hoped to find. She felt a sense of urgency to finish the packing and get on with the trip to Peru. The mystery surrounding her birth had just become an exploding super nova.

Chapter 8

The remainder of the week was taken up by visits to the family physician for the last round of preventive inoculations, and a gala dinner at Stancey's Tavern in Alexandria to say goodbye to all her best friends, minus Rosa.

The girls had attended boarding school with Rosa and her. The bonds they'd forged were greater than any sorority, more like blood kin.

"What do you mean you're going to Peru, when did this happen?" Wilma demanded, following her to the reserved table near the fireplace. "I didn't know that particular continent was on the way to Mongolia!"

"I want to spend some time at the historic observatory in Cuzco—it's on every astronomer's list of things to do."

She wasn't fibbing. It was true she would've wanted that, if she'd thought about it before the letter of invitation had arrived from Dr. Alderez.

"You can't be serious," Marva said. "Surely, you can come up with a better excuse for visiting Rosa. By the by, I've been fantasizing about our photos appearing in *People Magazine* because our famous South American friend Doña Rosa de la Reyna is your maid of honor."

"It's not Rosa's photos that'll attract media attention," Mary said. "Isn't it more about Senator Mike Vander Hurst's only son getting married?"

"God, this place is to die for, Joanna, I'm so glad you invited us to Stancey's," Linda said. "I can just see Thomas Jefferson and George Washington walking in, wigs askew. Did you all know James Madison brought Dollie here?"

"Are you coming down with something, Joanna?" Sandra scrutinized her. "I've never seen you this quiet."

"What can I say? You've all been out to the farm. You know how mama can render anybody speechless, and I've been there for a whole week."

"Wow, you're staying in Mongolia two whole years," Marsha said.

"I hope you remember you're the main attraction in that Charleston wedding in September."

"For sure…" Barbara said. "Those one-occasion electric-blue-waltz-length dresses with gold dahlia bosom accents take up a whole lot of room in our closets."

"Just for the record, I'm putting you on notice now," Wilma said. "I'm ditching that damned giant gold dahlia. It looks too much like the bull's eye on a dartboard, and my décolletage already attracts too much attention."

"I'm gonna pin that gold dahlia on my ass, it'll make a better bull's eye there," Marsha said. "That way those cupids hanging from the pillars in Summerall Chapel can aim their arrows at me."

"Good heavens! Those are Rococo cherubs," Gail said. "It's more likely those Citadel Cadets will sink their swords into your derriere."

"It's so romantic, being married in Summerall Chapel! Terry sighed, reaching for one of the hors d'oeuvres.

"I just love that ceremony on the steps outside, after the wedding, where the cadets form an arch with their swords for the couple to walk through," Kimberly said. "When the bride passes by, each cadet taps her lightly on the tush with his sword. It's *so* sweet."

"I can't imagine loving *any man* enough to choose his favorite race car driver's colors for my brides' maids' gowns!" Shannon said.

"How can you possibly leave Michael alone for the whole summer?" Dollie asked. "He's so handsome, I wouldn't trust—"

"Break it down, he's going to Outer Mongolia," Sandra said, turning toward Dollie. "All those girls wear multi-layered down-filled snowsuits with mukluks. They're not exactly competition for Joanna. Besides, he's Southern—he'll be frozen most of the time, especially his—"

"Okay, enough already!" Joanna said. "I can't believe I'm admitting this, but I'll miss you all terribly. I won't have anybody to harass me—well, except for Rosa."

Terry had been leaning her chin on her hand. "Did you all know *harass* comes from the medieval French word *harer* which means *to set the dogs on*?"

Everyone turned to look at Terry, eyes wide with amazement. Joanna laughed.

"What the hell does that have to do with the price of oats?" Marsha said. "I'm ordering another drink." She signaled the waiter. "Joanna, I don't know if I can sustain this friendship much longer, it's just plain 'nageratin,' as great Aunt Elsa would say."

"Well, too bad. Y'all've been with me for my whole entire life, and now you're in it for the long haul, get over it!"

"I know you're not telling the whole story," Mary said. "You think your BFFs wouldn't know you're holding something back?"

They knew each other too well, could read the changes in one another's moods like emotional barometers. They always knew a storm was brewing, long before it erupted on the surface. Still, she couldn't tell them. If she even hinted at the latest upheaval in her life, they'd all be pulled into a raging torrent of emotion.

Despite a few last minute glitches, with all preparations completed for a vacation in Peru and a longer stint in Mongolia, Joanna was on her way. She'd said goodbye to her father earlier in the day on Friday when he'd left on a business trip to Europe. They'd discussed her plans several times.

"Joanna, you know your mother and I'll welcome any new family members you may acquire. Maybe, we can even get down to Peru while you're there. I've never visited Machu Picchu. God keep you safe, baby girl."

She'd hugged him. "Daddy, I love you."

After dinner, her mother said good-bye on the front doorstep, declaring she hated public displays of emotion, saying she would break down if she went to the airport. She thanked Vivian for offering to see Joanna off.

At 10:00 p.m., on the dot, Vivian maneuvered the car into the departure lane at Dulles International and jumped out to alert a porter. She embraced Joanna, sweeping tears away with manicured fingertips.

"What a fantastic journey you're on, dear girl! Just don't forget your family and friends back in Virginia—we love you."

Joanna lingered on the curb, as the farm utility vehicle merged into traffic. Watching the red taillights streak like laser beams in the darkness, she felt the abandonment of a five-year-old on the first day of school.

The airline attendant helped her scan her printed ticket and check her luggage. She rolled the carry-on case forward and caught the escalator to the departure concourse for the over-night flight to Lima. The lengthy security checkpoints had to be endured and then she scurried to find her gate.

A glassed-in observation deck, permitting family members to watch international departures, loomed above where she sat waiting to board her flight. She'd chosen a seat with its back to the observation deck and was staring out the windows, following the activity on the airfield.

Sensing someone watching her, she turned and nearly choked on the bottle of water she'd been sipping. A dark haired man with a striking resemblance to Michael towered above the people on the observation deck. When she glanced in his direction again, he dropped back into the crowd. It wasn't Michael, it couldn't be—he was on his way to Mongolia.

During the first hours of flight, Joanna peered out the plane's small window into a sea of thick cloud, its blankness mirroring her loneliness. She was annoyed to be "wallowing in such misery" as Nana would say.

She had to lighten up. It wasn't fair to Rosa, arriving in Peru like this.

At 30,000 feet above Florida, a full moon shone down on a cloudless Caribbean and Joanna's attention was drawn for a while to lights etching the shapes of the Florida Keys. Later she spotted Jamaica, an oval sapphire brooch pinned to a moonlit sea.

Several hours into the flight, she noticed tiny boats queuing up in an orderly fashion. She was curious to know why they were waiting in line when she saw that one-by-one they were entering what appeared, from the altitude of the plane, to be a long narrow channel.

"It's the Canal—good Lord, that's the Panama Canal!" She blushed and looked around to see if her fellow passengers had heard her.

The lights in the cabin were dim, the other passengers appeared to be asleep, their window shades pulled down. She checked her watch. It was 4:15 a.m. No wonder no one shared her excitement.

The plane flew on, out over the Pacific, into a violent storm. Lightning flicked across the sky like horse whips in some cosmic rodeo, snapping and cracking electrically charged air currents against the plane.

"Please fasten your seat belts, we've encountered turbulence. Keep them fastened until further notice." The flight attendants hastened to their seats as the plane hit an air pocket.

Joanna dropped twenty stories in an express elevator, heart lurching into her throat. She gripped the seat and barely had enough time to rearrange internal organs before the plane became a toy boat jerked about in a whirlpool. She did a quick "life review" and closed her eyes.

Suddenly the attendants announced a reprieve, unbuckled seatbelts, and continued their ceaseless drink-serving rounds. Passengers settled once again into restless stupors. Although the turbulence seemed endless, it had only lasted minutes, and now she saw that the surface of the Pacific was appropriately reflecting its name.

Sleep seemed impossible. She was spellbound by moonbeams shining into the depths of the ocean, illuminating streaks of phosphorescent flying fish.

The plane droned on, flying southward, skirting the coasts of Columbia, Ecuador, and northern Peru. Once she saw a lone ship making its way westward and fantasized about her soul on some eternal journey on that ghost freighter.

Einstein's theory of relativity and parallel universes came to mind. How many journeys had she made across that starry realm, and with whom? Was the journey with Michael, would it be this time?

Lately they seemed like two elements in a highly unstable molecule, with atoms held briefly together by apparent electron deficits in outer shells, yet the union appeared doomed because those extra electrons weren't essential.

The plane's engines droned hypnotically. Joanna continued staring into the depths of the Pacific, and it became a serendipitous crystal ball.

She posed another question. "What would life have been like had I not chosen a career in astronomy?"

That's unimaginable! Why haven't I realized that before?

Astronomy was in every fiber of her being. It gave purpose to her life. Everything else could disappear—that would remain.

The dam of long-held restraint broke, and a flood of emotion poured through. Muscles released and mind eased for the first time in months, maybe years. How long had she held that pose, living someone else's dreams, attempting to shape a life not her own?

She leaned against the headrest and closed her eyes.

Chapter 9

Bright light streaming through the plane's windows awakened Joanna to a stunning view. The sun was rising over the Andes through air so clear the outlines of the endless snow-covered peaks were sharply etched, looming ever higher, row-after-row, stretching toward the curvature of the far distant horizon.

The view lasted only minutes before the aircraft plunged into thick clouds in a quick descent into Lima. It skidded to a landing and taxied to a spot near the terminal. In stark contrast to the shining world above, smog smothered the landscape. Off to the left, two rusted fuselages lay randomly scattered, littering a grass-pocked runway.

It was disconcerting to step directly from the plane into the opposite season of autumn in the Southern Hemisphere, even though the nearly equatorial climate made the difference barely discernable.

A pungent stench from the nearby tanning facilities on the Rimac River assaulted her, raising a tickle in her throat. She held a tissue to her nose as she walked the short distance across the tarmac to Aero Puerto Internacional Jorge Chávez.

Hurrying into the building, she found a scene of barely controlled chaos. Long lines of anxious passengers waited at baggage claim and customs. She was glad she could avoid the currency exchange—her father had supplied her with Peruvian sols from his bank.

Armed police in brown uniforms milled about. Before leaving home, she'd checked the state department website for warnings about foreign travel.

The site reported that terrorist activity still raged in the remote countryside. In the cities, express kidnappings, in which foreign tourists were made to use their credit cards to obtain money from ATMs, were on the rise. Joanna had concealed that information from her mother but had to admit, now that she was facing it, the reality was a bit intimidating.

She lifted her luggage onto a wheeled cart and maneuvered it toward a corridor with windows on either side. Rosa had said to meet her near the entrance, in the area adjacent to the duty-free shops.

The windows displayed jewelry replicating Inca artifacts. The precious metal content alone was probably worth thousands, to say nothing of the cost of the emerald gemstones set in many of them. In one window, a mannequin wore a superb full-length rare vicuna coat, a modern day rendition of Inca royalty's coat-of-choice. Joanna stopped to gawk.

Someone was staring at her. She turned, relieved to see Rosa rushing toward her. She was caught in an exuberant embrace. Rosa circled with her in an excited dance.

Suddenly they came to a halt and Rosa pushed her away. "Let me look at you, I can't believe you're here! Sorry to be late, traffic's at a standstill out there."

"It's okay, I barely had time to ask a policeman for directions," she said, as Rosa grasped the handle of the luggage cart with one hand and guided her to the front entrance with the other.

A taxi was waiting at the curb, engine running. Several paparazzi had gathered at a respectful distance. Joanna ducked into the back seat. Rosa smiled, waved, and posed briefly while the taxi driver collected the luggage.

"Mother and dad so are excited," Rosa said, settling into the taxi. "By-the-by, while we're in Lima, we'll be staying in Miraflores. It has wonderful beaches, the shopping's divine, and the dining choices are on par with NYC. I thought you'd like that."

As the taxi dodged through crowded central city streets and turned onto the Paseo de la República, heading toward the southern suburbs, Joanna noticed how the smog gradually became a yellow-tinted lens, turning the vivid colors of flowers into scenes straight out of a Monet painting. She was thrilled to think this was the city of her birth, La Ciudad de los Reyes, founded by Pizarro in 1535.

She relaxed against the car seat and brought Rosa up to speed on recent happenings: Michael's mission to Mongolia, her discovery of tectonic activity on Rhea, her surprise at being invited to work at Cuzco Observatory.

"How I wish there was some way you could accept that job at the observatory," Rosa said. "The place is so historic and they're working on some very exciting stuff related to your research, did you know that?"

"How do you know so much about my research? Has the Princess of Peru finally remembered her degree from MIT?"

Rosa reached out to pinch her. Joanna slapped her hand and giggled.

Miraflores seemed a fashionable suburb, Lima's "country cousin come to town," as Nana would have said. Their hotel was a converted colonial home with a guarded gatehouse and walled enclosure that encircled luxurious gardens.

The architecture and grounds reminded Joanna of Michael's family plantation home, but the view from the high cliffs overlooking the Pacific rivaled any of South Carolina's coastal views.

 The taxi driver opened the door, assisted them out, extracted the luggage, and wheeled it to the desk. Rosa thanked him and let her friend pay the fare and tip. Joanna smiled. The same old Rosa, refusing, like royalty, to carry any form of cash or credit cards on her person. Not a bad policy since everybody always stepped forward to foot the bill for la Doña Rosa de la Reyna.

Reservations were in order and an attendant led them up the grand staircase to their connecting rooms. Joanna placed her luggage in the closet and went through the door into the opposite room where Rosa was hanging up dresses.

She glanced with dismay at Rosa's two bulging suitcases. "How long did you say we're staying in Miraflores?"

Rosa made a face and continued unpacking. Joanna went to stand in front of the French doors that opened onto a balcony. "Rosa, do that later. Please order some tea. Let's sit on the balcony. There's something

I want to tell you."

Rosa studied her while dialing room service. Joanna turned and walked through the open doors onto the balcony.

She leaned over the railing and sucked in her breath. A dizzying cliff descended in a sheer drop to the beach below. She stepped back and glanced up at the blue painted ceiling where ceiling fans created a gentle breeze that stirred bougainvillea entwined around white columns.

The color of the porch ceiling made her think of her home in Virginia. Southerners painted their porch ceilings that color to repel insects—mosquitoes found the color repugnant. Apparently, so did ghosts, because that particular shade was known as *haint blue*.

Two chaise lounges invited leisurely sea gazing. Joanna selected one and lay against the cool webbing, soaking up the languid, exotic atmosphere.

Room service knocked at the door. Rosa brought the tray out on the balcony and placed it on the wicker coffee table. On the tray was a silver bowl of icy cold water with two antique hand-cut crystal flutes submerged in it and next to that was a bottle of Dom Pérignon 1976, elegantly presented in a silver ice bucket.

"That doesn't resemble any tea I ever had—"

"Your voice suggested we needed something stronger," Rosa said, wrapping a linen towel around the bottle. "Besides, we need to properly toast your finally coming to Peru."

Decanting the cork with an expert twist of the bottle, Rosa filled the frosted flutes and handed one to Joanna. "You can lose that worried look," she said, raising her glass for the toast. "This hotel is under contract to Father's business. His accounting department will pay *all* our bills."

The crystal glasses struck in bell tones and the effervescence flowed into Joanna's nostrils as she tilted the flute and let the bubbles swirl in her mouth. She held the rare liquid a moment, allowing it to excite the back of her tongue before it slipped into her throat.

Rosa held up her glass, watching the bubbles rise to the top. "Ah, incomparable—the rich distilled fruit of Verzenay ..."

Joanna regarded her warmly and turned her attention to the boats plying their nets out beyond the ocean tides. *Time to tell Rosa, she had to do it now.*

"Rosa, I'm adopted."

The crystal glass splashed expensive wine and shattered as it hit the tiled floor. Rosa swabbed the front of her dress with a napkin, dropped it, jumped up, and grabbed Joanna's wrist.

"Say again! *Slowly*, please."

"I'm adopted ..." Joanna paused, allowing the words to hit their mark. "... and this part you're not going to believe—from Peru. Right here in Lima, in fact."

Rosa slapped one hand over her mouth and one over her heart, doing a dramatic pretend "faint" onto the chaise longue. Minutes passed. Still, she sat staring. Suddenly whacking her forehead, she jumped to her feet, hugged Joanna, released her, and reached for the cell phone.

"Got to call the family—Carlos will be astounded—nobody's going to believe this. No wonder we've always been friends—"

"Please wait, Rosa. I haven't told anybody else. Except for Michael, you're the first outside the family to know."

The phone was stowed away, and Rosa sat expectantly on the edge of the chaise lounge, giving Joanna her undivided attention.

"First I want to gather all the information," Joanna said. "I know absolutely nothing except that an anonymous letter and a birth certificate were sent to Senator Vander Hurst."

"Why to him?"

"I don't know. The letter says my name is Huarana. Please don't say anything to anyone until I'm ready. While we're in Lima, I want to go to the Office of Records—"

"We'll go together. This is so exciting! We'll pretend we're Nancy Drew and Bess. No, I can't be Bess—she was pleasingly plump. Who was the athletic one? George, I'll be George. We'll call it *The Secret of Joanna's Birth!*"

"Is 'Huarana' a common name in Peru?"

"It's Quechua." Rosa's mouth formed a broad circle. "¡Madre de Dios! Joanna, what if you're Quechua Indian?"

"Well, the only thing my parents told me was that my dad is Quechua and my mother is Hispanic, but they're hiding something."

"You said anonymous letter. Who sent it? Was it someone in D.C.?" Her eyes opened even wider. "You don't know!"

"I've hired a detective agency. I hope they'll find something soon." She pulled the torn letter and photographs she'd found in the portmanteau from her purse and handed the paper to Rosa. "Take a look at this, I found it in Auntie Jane's old discarded suitcase."

Rosa read the lines, turned the scrap over, looking for more information, and read the front again. "History exacting a price—events precipitating upheaval in lives—a legacy to preserve.... My God, Joanna, this *is* a mystery!"

"I found these snapshots along with the letter and birth certificate in that suitcase. Who knows, they could be my parents."

She handed Rosa the photographs and stood, leaning far out over the balcony. "I'm absolutely driven to find them. I've lived almost twenty-five years thinking I was Joanna Nickels-Stewart and my life's unravelling."

Rosa studied the images. "I've got it! You're royalty, directly related to the last Russian Tsar. Your parents were hiding out, pretending to be Limenos. Oh, it's so exciting! Soon after you were born, they were killed by secret agents, then, like in the Greek Tragedy *Oresteia*, a faithful servant spirited you away, entrusting you, like the infant Oedipus, to impoverished peasant farm people who would rear you until you were old enough to inherit and—"

"Lord, have mercy! Didn't you hear the one important fact I do know? My birth parents were Hispanic and Quechua. Furthermore, James and Mary Ellen Nickels-Stewart hardly fit your 'peasant farm family' characterization—"

"Oh, Joanna, don't be so literal! Wait—I have it! You're the love child of a former U.S. president and his Hispanic mistress. She was banished to Lima when she became pregnant and secretly married to a Quechua man who was paid to—"

"Get a grip, for heaven's sake!" Joanna took a deep sip of the champagne. "There's mystery enough here without embellishing it beyond recognition."

"Seriously, Joanna, there has to be a reason for all the drama surrounding your birth, legacies and debts owed to history!"

"I've thought that, too. If that young girl is my mother, who could she be that she was presented at the royal court in Spain. I mean look at what she's wearing…doesn't that look like a debutante gown? She had to be from a prominent family, right?"

"I simply can't contain it—I'm bursting to share this with everybody—don't worry, I won't. We'll go to the Hall of Records Monday morning, but Sunday we're going to church, to the shrine of my patron saint, Rose of Lima—we'll pray for success in finding your birth family."

She reached for Joanna's champagne glass, filled it to the brim, chugged it down, and wiped her mouth with the back of her hand.

"Did you know that Rose of Lima was the first canonized saint of the new world?"

"No, but there's one thing I do know for sure, her namesake's neither a first, nor a last *saint of anything*!"

The Hall of Records was an imposing seventeenth-century building with visible damage from some recent destructive event. Joanna introduced herself to the information clerk and asked about procedures for a birth records search.

"Señorita Nickels-Stewart, unfortunately, we had an earthquake in 2007, and the oldest part of our building collapsed. Sadly, many of our archives were subjected to fires. An archeological team from the Universidad Del Lima is trying to piece together the burnt remains of such records, but it takes time."

"Is there anything we can do now?"

"Our researchers will work on your request and will forward the document to Doña de la Reyna's home in Cuzco as soon as possible. Will that be acceptable, Senorita?"

"I'll only be in Peru a short while—how can we speed up the process?"

"Señorita, it is not possible. Now please, you must fill out these forms and sign them."

"Joanna, don't despair," Rosa said. "We've simply got to tell Carlos about this. We need his help. He's acquainted with important people among the Quechuas. They have 'memory keepers' who may know about your birth."

"I don't know—I'd like to wait a little longer—do some digging on my own. The agency I hired has contacts here in Lima. Surely I'll get the full story soon."

"Well, you tell me when, and I'll put Carlos on it—he's like a bloodhound about solving mysteries and he has a large staff who'll help, both at his law practice in Cuzco, and the offices here in Lima."

"The clerk knew your name! Does everybody in Peru know who you are?"

"Unfortunately, the paparazzi have made sure I need no introductions."

Chapter 10

Rosa, determined to make up for the disappointing outcome of the records search, scheduled several days of sightseeing that stretched far into the night. Finally, on Thursday, Joanna saw the historic district with its Palacio de Gobierno. Their tour of the governmental palace ended at 11:30 a.m., as the Marshal Nieto Dragoons performed their ceremonial spectacle of the changing of the guard.

"So where are we going to lunch?" Joanna said. "Let's go someplace special and expensive—the tab's on me."

Rosa turned and walked back inside the palacio, heading toward the bank of elevators. Joanna caught up with her just as she pressed number two, marked "private" on the brass panel.

The door opened, and an attendant admitted them. "Buenos días, Doña Rosa de la Reyna, Señorita Nickels-Stewart, ¿cómo está?" He touched his uniform cap, saluting and smiling.

"What's going on?" Joanna whispered. Rosa ignored her. The elevator stopped on the second floor. The attendant opened the door and bowed once more.

Rosa thanked him and darted forward, pulling Joanna after her as she made her way toward an impressive door about midway down the hall, where an elaborately costumed soldier guarded the door. He greeted them and placed a gloved hand on the doorknob to open it.

Joanna, mouth agape, followed Rosa into the room where a middle-aged man approached. He looked familiar. Rosa advanced on him with arms outstretched.

Of course, he looked familiar—his picture had been in yesterday's newspaper. In person, he looked even more like a duke in an 'El Greco' painting—physique ascetic to the point of emaciation, his torso elongated. He had silver white hair, randomly dusted with streaks of ebony.

The President of Peru ended the embrace with Rosa and bowed over Joanna's hand.

"I am delighted to meet you, Dr. Nickels-Stewart. You are so kind to accept our invitation to lunch. We are honored you are visiting Peru. Don de la Reyna has told us of your brilliant work in astronomy. He is so proud of you. One might conclude you are his second daughter."

"Sir, thank you for inviting us to lunch," Rosa said.

The president showed them to their places at table, and Rosa signed 'CEDAR' to Joanna. **CEDAR**—their old game of one-upmanship dreamed up during their freshman year of high school at boarding school—**C**-count your blessings; **E**-enjoy; **D**-don't ask; **A**-accept; **R**-relax. Their only rule was that the surprise had to be something wonderful and impossibly rare.

This certainly fit that description.

Bragging rights for being the first to spring a "CEDAR Surprise" belonged to Joanna. Her grandfather James Stewart had grown up with a famous actor who just happened to be Rosa's idol. She'd swooned over him, renting all his movies, hanging posters of him on the wall above her desk, and she'd talked about him incessantly.

Joanna's family had invited Rosa to the farm for a weekend visit. The two girls arrived shortly after the family was seated at the dining table and the butler had shown Rosa to a seat next to the actor. She'd nearly collapsed.

"Count your blessings, enjoy, don't ask, accept, relax," Joanna had signed across the table to Rosa that evening. They'd both learned sign language for a service project at school. It came in handy when they needed to convey private messages.

The President of Peru assisted them as they were seated on either side of his place at the head of the table. He sat down and rang the bell for service while smiling fondly at Rosa. "My dear, why haven't Catarina and I seen you lately? Surely, you're not that busy."

Joanna eyed the table décor. Near the place settings were menus, written in gold embellished calligraphy, announcing each course in words guaranteed to fire off every salivary gland.

The first course was a spiced potato soup, and the second was a fish course of seafood delicacies. Following that was a lime sorbet and then a salad of parched rainbow-hued corn kernels on a bed of quinoa, sprinkled with tiny bits of herbed alpaca cheese and a vinaigrette dressing.

The main course was pollo al horno with tropical fruit salsa and yeast rolls. The dessert was a rich dark chocolate mousse. Joanna had seen a documentary about how the cocoa plant had originated in Peru. She couldn't wait to taste the mousse. Each course was accompanied by appropriate wines from the western slopes of the Andes.

There was a fourth place setting near Rosa. Joanna wondered who else would be joining them.

She thought about signing the question to Rosa when His Excellency, El Presidente Emilio Duarte, excused himself and turned aside to engage in a brief conversation with an aide who had just entered the room.

Joanna took advantage of the moment and spoke to Rosa. "Let me compliment you on your excellent choice of a dining establishment!"

"Only the best for my best friend," Rosa said.

"By the way, who's going to sit over there?"

The aide went to open the door, El Presidente stood, grinning from ear-to-ear, and hurried across the room, hand extended.

"What a pleasure! I'm so glad you could join us, Carlos."

"Thank you, Emilio." Carlos de la Reyna shook El Presidente's hand and moved toward Joanna with the grace of a dancer

She and Rosa stood at his approach. He blew a kiss to Rosa and bowed over Joanna's hand, tenderly brushing it with a kiss. Still caressing her hand lightly, he rose to his full height, looked into her eyes, and held the glance.

"It's been far too long," he said.

She blushed. "Goodness gracious, Carlos! If you had been Cinderella's Prince Charming those stepsisters would have fought to the death for that glass slipper."

His laughter reverberated throughout the room. He clicked his heels and bowed to her again.

"Since his return from England, every female in Peru old enough to hold her own spoon has made a play for my dear brother," Rosa said. "We suspect Prince William was his charm school tutor."

El Presidente returned to the head of the table and picked up his napkin. "Please everyone, be seated," he said.

Rosa and Joanna seated themselves on El Presidente's left and right, while Carlos chose the chair next to Joanna. The butler removed the extra setting from Rosa's side of the table and placed it in front of Carlos.

"We're so proud to serve you our national produce, Dr. Nickels-Stewart," El Presidente said. "You know, contrary to what everyone thinks, the Irish did not invent the potato. It originated in Peru, and we've thousands of varieties in every color and flavor to prove it. Did you know genetic engineering actually originated with the Incas? They had special plots all over the empire for developing seedlings for the differing soils and climates. I hope you'll enjoy all our great foods while you're here."

"And you must taste our many varieties of corn," Carlos added. "Peru is the original source of that grain, as well. It'll be my pleasure to take you on a sampling tour of all the gourmet restaurants, but I refuse to be blamed for any excess weight gain."

"I saw Juan Diego at the bullfights on Monday," El Presidente said to Rosa. "He exuded the same fierce energy as the bulls. He certainly seems a very popular candidate in the upcoming campaign for my position."

"Your Excellency, my preference would be to settle quietly on his family's estancia in the Sacred Valley and raise llamas."

"I can see the magazine covers now," Carlos said, laughing. "Rosa posed in high-heeled, open-toed Pradas™ standing in barn muck, wielding an enormous pair of scissors, pretending to shear llamas."

Joanna laughed at the apt description of her friend.

"My allegiances are divided," Rosa said. "I guess if I were really truthful, I'd prefer to have Carlos be our next president."

"As would I, my dear." El Presidente paused, gazing out the window for a long moment. "I hope you don't mind, Dr. Nickels-Stewart, if I'm informal here—please, may I call you by your christening name? I believe we shall become good friends."

"Sir, I'd be honored."

"How long will you be in Peru?" El Presidente asked.

"Your Excellency…"

"Oh, my dear, please call me *Emilio*. You will see me frequently at Casa de la Reyna. My wife and I stay there when we're in Cuzco. Rosa and Carlos have known me since they were babies. Rosa seems unable to drop the formalities, but I insist you do so."

"I'm staying the summer, Emilio. Oops! I mean winter. It's such a rare privilege for me to visit Cuzco. While I'm here, I'm hoping to learn more about Incan astronomy."

"Joanna's quite the scholar in world mythology and astronomy. Also, the origins of astronomy in astrology," Rosa said.

"While I was studying in England, a scholar unearthed some of Newton's original writings revealing his preoccupation with how astrology and alchemy influenced civilizations. There was quite a bit of buzz about it at the time," Carlos said.

"I thought those writings had disappeared—or should I say, *were disappeared*," Rosa said. "I'm thinking the Royal Society can hardly have wanted them in wide distribution."

"Certainly the Incas ruled their empire according to astrology's dictates," Emilio said, "but I can't imagine the father of modern science giving much credence to such matters."

Joanna put her steepled fingers to her mouth. Like Newton, her research had left her with some radical ideas about the fundamental building blocks of the universe.

"Joanna, doesn't your work relate to that?" Carlos said. "When I was in D.C. last fall and dropped by the farm to see your family, your father told me you were researching the frequencies of matter."

So much for self-restraint when your friends were determined to "out" you.

"Quite obviously, astronomy has its roots in astrology," she said. "As you can imagine, the night skies would have been the big-screen televisions of our cave-dwelling ancestors. It wouldn't have taken them long to identify patterns and start tracking them."

"I can well picture the Incas on remote mountain tops observing the skies," El Presidente said.

"As the stars in the zodiac seemed to change positions coincidentally with events on earth, our early ancestors learned to devise mathematics, calendars, music, philosophy, and religion related to the changes they observed.

"They were convinced all things were interdependent—which probably gave rise to that famous line from antiquity, '... As above, so below... .'"

"I get it," Rosa said. "They built temples and offered sacrifices, hoping to influence the flow of events in outer space to avert disasters like drought or whatever, on Earth." She looked toward Joanna, seeking confirmation.

"The fact is, people *are* directly affected by everything in the universe," Joanna said. "It's all held together by strong and weak nuclear forces, electromagnetic forces, and gravitational forces that are in constant greater or lesser interaction with everything, including us."

"I never thought much about those forces influencing us," Carlos said.

"We're certainly aware of how sun flares affect the earth—our power grids can be interrupted, even wiped out. Our bodies have their own electrical systems, so why wouldn't they be disturbed, also? I think we're only just beginning to understand how closely interconnected, whether organic or inorganic, *everything* is in the universe."

"Electromagnetism and cosmic rays accounting for human health and behavior," Carlos said, shaking his head. "Old Newton may have been on to something!"

"So my astrological sign could really tell a great deal about my character!" Rosa said. "That sure gives me a whole new repertoire of excuses for 'sinful' acts!"

"Joanna, you make me glad I have nothing more to worry about than governing Peru." El Presidente chuckled. "Should I be consulting an astrologist just to hedge my bets, do you think? I believe I read somewhere that one of your presidents did so."

On their last day in Lima, Joanna and Rosa walked the short distance from the hotel to San Isidro to see the Enrico Poli private collection of Escuela Cusqueña paintings and pre-Columbian gold artifacts. Afterwards, Rosa insisted on going to Jockey Plaza Shopping Mall in Miraflores where photographers clustered around her, snapping "exclusive" photos.

Joanna hid behind a mannequin to avoid them. "How do you put up with that constant attention? I'd be mortified."

"Oh, you get used to it. I figure they need the money, and what does it cost me?"

"Rosa, is that man over by the perfume counter a reporter? He's obviously not a photographer."

"Handsome devil, isn't he? Why do you ask?"

"I think he's following us—I thought I saw him yesterday. It's probably my imagination. He doesn't have a camera. There, he changed his position. Did you see that?" She grabbed Rosa's arm. "Know what, I think I saw him at Dulles airport, too."

Rosa had been examining a dress. Her happy demeanor changed. She threw the dress across a rack, dug into her purse for the cell phone, and punched a number.

"Carlos, we're in Miraflores—the Mall—Davila's. Joanna believes someone's been following her, she thinks she saw him at the airport in

D. C.... No, he's definitely not paparazzi... About six feet, black hair—forelock keeps falling in his eyes. Definitely not Hispanic, maybe Irish... Okay, right away."

She tapped the cell phone again as she spoke to Joanna. "He'll put somebody on it—and I'm calling a taxi—don't argue with me."

The taxi dropped them at the hotel. They were on their way to the elevator when the desk clerk called to Joanna and handed her a message.

"Michael phoned," she said.

"Probably not a good idea to tell him about the stalker," Rosa said.

They rode the elevator to the second floor in silence and paused outside their rooms.

"I'd better call him back. We can go to dinner afterwards, okay?"

"Why don't we order room service—the hotel menu's excellent," Rosa said. "We can dine on our private balcony and watch the sun set over the Pacific! What more could you ask?"

Joanna opened the door to her room, set the shopping bags on the chair, and perched on the bed next to the nightstand. She dialed the desk and asked the clerk to put the international call through for her. She pressed the speaker button and put her purchases away while she waited.

She missed Michael terribly, saving interesting bits of conversation to share with him, or funny incidents she knew he'd relish. She dreamed of his caresses, sleeping and waking. No matter how absorbing her time in Peru was—fascinating, exotic, beyond her wildest imagination—none of it compared with Michael's remembered presence. She'd played back a dozen times in her mind the angry words they'd exchanged on their last day together and grieved over them.

"This is Michael Vander Hurst." Joanna raced across the room, sat on the bed, and leaned close to the phone.

"It's me. I've missed you so much!"

"Joanna, please tell me you've found your family and you're getting on the next plane to Mongolia. I can't stand another minute without you."

"Rosa's helping me, but it's taking time. We've been sightseeing all over Lima! Would you believe, we had lunch with the president of Peru at the Palacio de Gobierno? I wish you'd been there. El Presidente and the de la Reynas are best friends and he seems to think that makes me a friend, too!"

"Joanna, what are your plans?"

"Rosa and I went to the Hall of Records and I had to fill out all kinds of forms. They promised to do a thorough search and send the results to Cuzco. We're flying there in the morning."

"What happens when you don't find something in the next two weeks?"

"It's probably going to take a little longer than that. Then I'll need a little time to visit with my family when I find them. I can't just locate them and disappear." She hesitated, dreading to tell him her latest decision. "While I'm looking, I figured I may as well volunteer briefly at the Cuzco Observatory."

The moments ticked by. He cleared his throat. "When are you coming to Mongolia?"

"I'm thinking near the beginning of August—"

"I'll be in the field, out of cell phone range all next week. I'll call you when I get back."

"Michael, I love you," she said.

The line clicked.

She sat a while looking at the phone, then got up, and stretched across the bed face downward, giving in to helpless sobs.

A loud knock sounded at the connecting door. Rosa pushed it open and entered.

"You look awful," she said. "What's happened? Don't shake your head like that. You must tell me *now*."

"Okay, sit down—it's a long story."

Chapter 11

Cuzco's National Astronomical Observatory was outlined against an azure sky with puffy cumulonimbus clouds stretching thousands of feet into the stratosphere. Joanna studied the four towers surrounded by modern buildings.

The towers were obviously pre-Columbian—Inca built. The stonework was exquisite. The sight of them gave her the same tingling excitement she'd felt when she was nine-years-old, and her parents had taken her to New York City to see the gigantic Christmas tree in Rockefeller Center.

She crossed the wide landscaped area that formed a rectangle in front of the building and entered the revolving door. Earlier she'd gotten directions to Dr. Alderez's office in the main building, on the seventh floor. Moving quickly toward the reception desk, she took in her surroundings.

The central reception lobby rose up ten stories, in open tiers, to a skylight covering the whole of the interior. People were standing near the railings on each tier. They cheered, whistled, applauded. Joanna stopped to look over her shoulder, attempting to catch a glimpse of the person inspiring the enthusiastic greeting.

A receptionist stepped forward and handed her a beautiful bouquet of wild flowers in vibrant colors.

"Welcome to Cuzco, Dr. Nickels-Stewart! Go ahead, wave to everybody. They're excited about your arrival."

Joanna looked up and waved, turning in every direction to acknowledge the welcome. Like her mother, she tried to hide displays of public emotion but could feel the heat rising in her face. The applause increased as she waved. She glanced up again and saw a large billowing banner suspended from an upper story balcony. A star filled night sky formed the backdrop and, spread across it, foot-high block letters proclaimed:

WELCOME TO CUZCO, DR. NICKELS-STEWART!

"Dr. Alderez told us you were going to work here," the receptionist said. "He announced this morning that you were on your way to see him. He's in a meeting now, but he'll be free very soon. I'm Anita Sanchez. May I give you a little tour?"

Dr. Alderez stood up and came from behind his desk. "Dr. Nickels-Stewart, please tell me you've come to accept our offer."

Joanna went immediately to shake his hand. "Thanks to you and your staff for the lovely bouquet of flowers. I must have someone identify them for me."

"We're honored by your presence. Of course, you've seen that for yourself! I was delighted you'd called for an appointment."

"I had business in Lima so I decided to come see you personally instead of replying in writing. Your job offer is very flattering. I'm so sorry to have to turn it down. I'll be married soon and will be in Mongolia for two years, where my future husband has been posted. If you'd permit, I'd like to volunteer for the next two months while I'm here in Cuzco."

"We'll be glad to have you here, in whatever capacity, for however long you can stay. Please, let me show you the lab we'd hoped you'd supervise."

The lab encompassed the whole of the top floor. Offices were located off halls that encircled the huge glass-enclosed space. The roof of the lab operated hydraulically, by remote control, to permit the huge telescope to sweep in an arc in the rectangular opening.

"I've never seen a lab as up-to-date as this, even in D.C.," Joanna said. "You must have a phenomenal funding source."

"There are some very wealthy donors who're eager for us to advance the research for which they'd hoped you'd be responsible."

That was a stunning bit of information. She'd never imagined anyone in South America was aware of her work, except for a very few astrophysicists.

Dr. Alderez went on, responding quickly to her questioning look. "Members of our Board of Trustees and their families are well-informed about your research. Would you like to see one of our ancient Incan Observatory towers? There's an even bigger telescope in one of them."

From the east tower, Joanna could see all of Cuzco and the surrounding mountains, some with permanent peaks of snow.

"Cuzco was designed by the Incas in the shape of a puma," Dr. Alderez said. "On that high promontory to our right is Sacsayhuamán, presumably the Puma's mouth. The zigzagged walls of the fortress form its teeth."

He indicated a point south of the fortress. "Down there, toward the middle, is the Plaza des Armas, which would be the puma's heart, while further on is Coricancha in the puma's lower body. Coricancha actually means 'circle of gold,' which may refer to the earth's path of revolution around the sun. It seems our Inca priest-amautas were brilliant astronomers."

Joanna turned slowly in every direction, impressed by the sights. "I read that Francisco Pizarro's secretary, Pero Sancho, wrote home in 1533 that the city rivaled any he'd seen in Europe," she said.

Office and lab routines absorbed Joanna for the next few days. By Friday, she'd started to worry that no mail had arrived at Casa de la Reyna from the Hall of Records.

The Quick Pro Quo agency had finally contacted her. They'd determined that her mother's name was Sarafina Alma, though they couldn't say whether Alma was a surname or her married name.

Maybe now that she had a little more information, she could encourage the Hall of Records to work more diligently on her case. She'd take a quick trip back to Lima.

Joanna had worked all morning in the lab. At noon, she grabbed her sweater from the coat tree, took her purse from a concealed drawer in the desk, and hurried down the corridor toward the stairway. The massive spread of atrium windows overlooking the city and surrounding mountains provided an arresting view.

Mount Anahuarque loomed in the distance. Dr. Alderez had told her the mountain was where the god of war was honored, the place where young Inca males had begun their initiation into manhood. From bedtime reading, she'd discovered the Incas had associated their god of war with the planet Mars, a planet referred to as the "troublesome one" in worldwide myths. She tore herself away from the view, hurried down the stairs and stopped in the reception area to chat with Ms. Sanchez.

"Hola, Señora Sanchez, I wonder if you could help me. I've a friend from the states who's coming to visit while I'm in Cuzco. She was adopted from Peru. She hopes to search for her birth parents while she visits here. Can you tell me some agencies that might have information?"

"Sí, you've come to the right person! My husband is adopted. He located his mother and siblings. I know what must be done."

"May I buy you lunch?"

"I'd be honored to go to lunch with you. You don't have to pay."

Chapter 12

Joanna booked the flight back to Lima. She was on her way to MIMDES, the Ministerio de la Mujer y Desarrollo Social. Ms. Sanchez had told her that agency would have information about adoptions.

It was important to check the statistics on children adopted in early 90's, all the records of those labeled "abandoned" by the courts, names of babies adopted to the states in years surrounding her birthdate, the locations of hospitals where the babies had been born.

Surely, her mother's name would appear somewhere in those sets of data clusters. She entered MIMDES and the attendant hurried forward, eager to help. Joanna was shown to a small reference room where she spent the morning searching record books and computer databases.

She'd systematically checked hospitals for babies born on her birthdate and made a list. She'd visit them later—sometimes more information could be obtained from sympathetic employees.

"Were you successful in your search, Señorita?"

"Somewhat, I guess. I found several places where I might get some answers."

"In the years before our ministry was formed, adoptions were frequently arranged privately by families who did not want the family name dishonored when a child was born to an unwed daughter. The family went to court, paid fees, and handed the child over to an adopting family. Lines of succession, titles, and property were at stake. So the families would pay to have the records concealed or destroyed."

Was that why the anonymous letter had been sent to the senator? Was it possible someone was benefiting in some way from revealing the information about her birth? She leaned on the counter, worry knotting her shoulders.

"You're saying if this adoption was handled privately, there might not be a trace of it in the public records?"

"Well, you mentioned there was an agent in your case. You might search for the name of the person handing over the child to that agent. Look for the application for a visa to carry a baby across international borders during the years surrounding your birth, and you'll want to check with the Hall of Records."

Joanna exited MIMDES and decided to lunch at the Café Conquistador. It was located near the Post Office, opposite the Chapel of Vera Cruz.

She'd stop in and purchase postcards for Aunt Jane. Maybe even light a candle at Rosa of Lima's altar—she needed all the help she could get.

The Hall of Records was on her way. Surely, they should've found information by now, but why hadn't they mailed it to Rosa as promised? She'd tried to contact them by email but all their systems were down, and the last time she'd checked the situation was the same.

Entering the baroque building, she headed straight for the clerk who had assisted her when she and Rosa filled out the papers.

"¡Hola, Señorita, my name is Joanna Nickels-Stewart, I was here nearly two weeks ago looking for information on my birth parents."

"Si, I remember you. I mailed the documents as soon as we had the information. They must have arrived in Cuzco by now."

Joanna looked down at the counter to hide her amazement.

"Do you have copies of what you sent?"

"Certainly, but it will take a few minutes." The clerk returned almost immediately and placed a file on the counter, opened it, and took out a copy of the original questionnaire plus a sheet of narrative. She handed the copies to Joanna.

Two names in bold type jumped out from the page: **Sarafina Alma**, mother, deceased in childbirth; **Manuel Curisimay**, father, address unknown.

The word "deceased" made the page blur. Frustration and disappointment were responsible for the tears—not grief. How did you grieve a mother you'd never known? She'd deal with her "might-have-been" fantasies later.

"Señorita, these things are never easy," the clerk said. "I could run an identity check on those names. Perhaps we might find more information."

Joanna accepted the tissue the clerk offered and watched as she tapped the computer keyboard. After a moment, she frowned.

"I'm so sorry, Señorita, there is nothing. It's possible if the couple was unwed the families gave false names."

Joanna thanked her, put the copy of the paper in her purse, and exited the building. She walked in a daze down the street to the Café Conquistador.

There was still hope. At least her father was alive, and obviously, someone from among one or the other of her birth parents' families wanted to protect their good name. Had one of them had a momentary prick of conscience and sent the letter to the senator? What about the scrap of letter she'd found in Aunt Jane's portmanteau?

At the lunch counter, she selected a light salad along with an Inka Cola™, and made her way to a small outdoor table near the sidewalk. She wasn't far from the Palacio de Gobierno.

Maybe after lunch, she'd drop in and ask El Presidente for help in her search. She laughed aloud, imagining him commandeering the whole of the Peruvian government in an effort to locate Manuel Curisimay.

"Joanna, is that you! What *are* you doing in Lima?"

She looked up, swallowed a grape, and took a sip of warm Inka Cola.

"¡Hola, Carlos!"

He placed his lunch tray with a sandwich and bottle of water on the bistro table, pulled out the chair opposite her, and sat down.

"I demand to know what you're doing here. I know you too well, so don't prevaricate. That's a guilty look if ever I saw one."

She laughed and shifted her plate aside to give him room on the small table. His face had a sincere look of concern. She fought another onslaught of tears.

"I didn't want to bother anyone about all this. Not until I was sure."

"I'm offended, don't you know we're family, you can tell us anything. If you've murdered somebody, I'll represent you and get you off."

He picked up his water bottle and took several sips. "I'll just cover as many palms as it takes with cold hard cash and make sure the police immediately jail all persons refusing to keep their mouths shut. See, we can handle this. Now, go on and tell Carlos! After all, I'm your honorary—make that 'ornery'—older brother."

Tears started again. She swiped at them. "I've been searching for my birth parents."

He slowly put the bottle down, his eyes urging her to continue.

"Michael's father got an anonymous letter from here in Lima saying I was adopted. He told me to find out about my origins, because he needed to know the heritage of his grandchildren, needed to know whether I was good breeding stock. Well, he didn't exactly say that last part, but that's what he meant ..." She took a deep breath. "Now I have no idea who I really am."

Carlos pushed the sandwich away, placed his arms on the table, and leaned forward.

"I'm sorry you found out that way. Listen, you may think you don't know who you are, but Rosa and I sure do! You're still the same wonderful person we've always known."

"That's what Daddy said, but I need to know. It seems like I've been living on the surface of things for a very long time."

"That's a universal condition," he said. "I've grown increasingly sick of myself and a number of others in my social circle who live superficially."

He put his sandwich down and stared off into the distance. "Most of us are cookie-cutter people, living our lives in the shape we think society demands."

"I guess I would've been happy with my shape," Joanna said, "if I hadn't been forced to examine it."

"It concerns me you felt you couldn't tell me—us—about the adoption."

"I told Rosa, begged her to *not* tell you and the family. I wanted to get the facts, before I revealed anything. James and Mary Ellen adopted me through Sister Jane, who was teaching over here at the time. She's listed as the agent on my birth certificate."

"So none of them were willing to help you with the information?"

"Neither she nor my parents. They're hiding something." Joanna held the warm Inka Cola. She was thirsty but hated drinking it without ice. "I'm angry they didn't tell me earlier. It might have made things easier. I wouldn't feel so alone now."

Carlos scooted his chair around to her side, put his arm around her, and hugged her to him. Sobs from pent up grief escaped her attempts to suppress them, and she pulled away in embarrassment.

He reached for her again, folding her into his chest. She relaxed into his arms and let her tears flow freely, tears she'd needed to release when the senator gave her the letter. Tears unshed because she'd stuffed them back when her adoptive parents had been untruthful with her, tears denied expression when Michael failed to understand how much the search for her identity meant to her, and tears she needed to shed for a dead birth mother.

With his left hand, Carlos extracted a large white handkerchief from the breast pocket of his suit coat and gently wiped her eyes. Joanna registered the thoughtful, tender, loving gesture.

He hadn't even tried to stop her crying. Nor had he discounted her feelings with some inane remark about how everything was going to be all right. Every other man she knew would've been squirming by now.

The handkerchief was still in his hand. She took it from him and blew her nose robustly.

He pretended dismay. "Don't you dare give that thing back to me before you've laundered it."

"Then I've got to buy you a new one, 'cause I don't have a washing machine and the laundry service will lose it just like they do my sports socks."

"So…Rosa knows?"

"I told her when I arrived. She went with me to the Hall of Records and the clerk said she'd mail the information to the estate address in Cuzco. Rosa checked every day but the info never arrived. Today when I went there, the clerk said she'd mailed it. I asked her for a copy."

"That's the longest Rosa's ever kept anything from me—and you were planning to tell me when?"

"Carlos, I didn't know how difficult it would be to track down my birth parents. I did find out this morning that my mother's deceased. Other than that, there's no information! So, I guess you could say I still don't know anything."

"Okay, *now* I'm definitely offended! What better person to help, I ask, than an attorney! Surely, you remember how clever I—"

"When you walked up just now I was amusing myself with fantasies about going to the Palacio de Gobierno and asking El Presidente to help find my father."

"Hey, now that's *not* a bad idea!"

"Don't you even think about it, Carlos de la Reyna, I'll sue you for breach of confidence!"

"You can't, I'm not under contract."

"The detective agency I hired found out my mother's name was Sarafina Alma. The Hall of Records people helped me find the hospital where I was born, and it showed she'd died in childbirth. My father's name is Manuel Curisimay, but he was listed with "address unknown."

Joanna wiped her eyes with the handkerchief and stuffed it in her pocket. "The clerk ran a computer check of those names and found no birth records, no marriage records, or work records, not even a driver's license—nothing—it's like they never even existed! She did remark that sometimes families wanted secrecy, especially if the daughter wasn't married. Do you think that could be the case?"

"I'll do some digging and we'll see what turns up. We should be able to verify your information. The adoption wouldn't have been completed here, anyway. Who did you say the agent was?"

"You've met her. Auntie Jane, Sister Jane."

"The Nickels-Stewarts would've been listed as your 'parents of record' on a new certificate they would've been required to obtain in the state of Virginia. Although your 'birth parents' names were concealed, the courts, by law, still had to record them."

"I found a copy of the birth certificate in an old portmanteau in the attic at Middleburg, but it's exactly like the one Senator Mike received with the names eliminated." Joanna pulled the certificate from her purse and handed it to Carlos.

"When I asked Auntie Jane, she said secrecy had been imposed as a condition of the adoption and she wouldn't break her word. It's the most frustrating thing!"

"I know some people in Virginia who could get a copy," Carlos said. "It's difficult, mind you, to get the records unsealed—but there are ways around that."

Joanna glanced toward him as he bent to place the certificate in his brief case. Her heart skipped a beat.

"Carlos, don't turn around. There's a man near Santo Domingo, opposite us, at the corner. He looks a little bit like Michael. I believe he's been following me. He was at Dulles when I left D.C., and I saw someone who looked exactly like him at the mall in Miraflores."

"Rosa phoned me and I alerted the police about that," Carlos said. "They said they'd put out a *Bolo*."

"Why would anyone stalk me? What could he possibly want?"

"Okay, tell you what—I'm going to get up and walk away. Just act natural, pretend we're saying goodbye. I'll handle this." He left a tip on the table and bent to kiss her cheek. "Get a taxi to the airport, I'll call you later. I'll see you at dinner with the family on Friday."

Joanna gathered the paper plates and discarded them in the trash bin. She watched Carlos walk briskly down the street, using his cell phone. Several minutes passed, and a police cruiser came trolling down the street.

The stalker seemed to sense something was awry. He crossed the street and headed into the alley next to the post office. The squad car pulled to the curb in front of Santo Domingo and two police officers jumped out, scanning the crowd. They milled about, questioning bystanders near the church.

Joanna was nearest to the alley. If she stopped to alert the police, the stalker would escape. She sped toward the post office, shoved the doors open, and raced toward the back entrance–she'd cut the stalker off as he came out of the alley.

Great idea, so what do I do when I catch him?

People in the post office gasped as she ran headlong through the center of the building. She scanned the plate glass windows in the rear, and saw the stalker emerge from the alley. He glanced about, apparently trying to decide where to go next.

Joanna grabbed a small wooden stool from a nearby customer station, raised it in front of her like a shield, and dashed through the back door.

She exited into a parking lot, and out of the corner of her eye, saw an armed guard rushing after her, brandishing his gun. "¡El ladrón, Thief! Thief!" he roared.

The stalker, hearing the commotion, stopped to look over his shoulder. Joanna, holding the stool with legs extended, ran directly into him.

He stumbled. She lost balance. They both hit the ground. The stool broke, scattering slats all over the pavement.

"What the hell!" The stalker bellowed and rolled away from her.

"¡Socorro, ¡socorro, policía," Joanna yelled, as the postal guard arrived.

He stood above them, pistol trained on Joanna, demanding, "¡Levantese, ¡levantese!"

Two other guards came running up as the city police barreled down the alley. One of the guards grabbed Joanna's arm and hauled her to her feet. "You have destroyed government property," he shouted.

"I was trying to stop this—"

"¡Cállese! ¡cállese! You have attacked this poor man," the first guard said, grasping the stalker's jacket in an attempt to help him stand.

The stalker ducked, slipped out of the jacket, fell to his knees, and crawled between two enormous pots that separated the building from the parking lot. When he'd made it to the other side, he stood up and ran pell-mell down the street. The guards and police stood immobile, staring in astonishment.

"He's getting away," Joanna shrieked.

The two police officers, finally surmising the situation, tore after the stalker. The second postal guard pulled on Joanna's arm, jerking her back toward the building.

She tried to reason with him. "I didn't steal that stool. I was only trying to—"

"But, Señorita, the evidence, it is here."

"Why in the world would I steal an old stool like that?"

"You have destroyed this item by hitting a poor man. You must go to jail where you will be charged with assaulting a citizen."

"He's no citizen, he's a stalker. Here, use my phone—call Congressman Carlos de la Reyna—he'll vouch for me."

Shouting came from across the street. Joanna looked out from under the guard's arm in time to see the stalker make a mad dash, scale Santo Domingo's fence, and disappear into the bushes at the back of the church. One of the cops headed back toward her and the guards. "Give me that jacket," he ordered.

"That poor man is innocent," the guard said.

"No, ¡non ¡Me está siguiendo," Joanna said.

"Here is your thief," the guard said. "She has stolen government

Chapter 13

Against the protests of the whole de la Reyna clan, Joanna signed a contract for a one-room-long-term rental apartment in Hotel San Pablo. She pleaded that she needed to avoid traffic and be nearer to the observatory.

It was difficult to believe another week had gone by, with only two months left. Her search had yielded nothing but the names of her birth parents. Nor had Carlos received word from his contact in Virginia about the birth certificate.

She'd eagerly anticipated a reunion with some member of her family by this time. It was her hope that she'd have time to explore Cuzco, perhaps in the company of her birth father, or at least some other close relative.

In the meantime, she'd made an effort to get to know her colleagues at the observatory and introduce herself to her neighbors. One of the neighbors, Maribel Valladres, had previously been a police officer and was now working in Carlos' Cuzco office. Her latest assignment was to shadow Joanna until the stalker was captured.

The stalker had eluded both the local constabulary and the National Police Force in Lima. Joanna didn't like the idea of a bodyguard, but relented when Carlos assured her the woman would be discreet and stay out-of-sight.

Another matter nagged at her. Aunt Jane had phoned several times to inquire about her request that Joanna visit Santa Maria Monastery.

She was chagrined to admit she'd been too busy to carry out her aunt's wishes. The truth was she dreaded the visit to the monastery, but promised to do so before another week had passed.

Dialing Rosa's number, she pushed the speaker button, and began dusting the small apartment. The dial tone sounded repeatedly. She picked up clothes she'd left strewn over the table, chair, and single bed that constituted the items of furniture provided by the hotel.

"Hola."

property and destroyed it by hitting that poor innocent man, and now he has lost his jacket."

"Please don't cuff me. I'll pay you for that stool. Here, I'll give you all enough money to buy two stools, see, here take this." She extracted several bills from her wallet. "I was just trying to stop that man before he got away. He was after *me*! Please call Don Carlos de la Reyna."

"Joanna, put that away—*now*!" Carlos shouted, dashing from the alley.

Joanna smiled up at the postal guard and eased the bills back into her purse. Carlos grabbed the guard's hand and shook it vigorously.

"Gracias, Señor Officer, you've saved Dr. Nickels-Stewart. El Presidente will want to commend you personally. She's a friend of his and a very important personage. Here's my card, send the bill to my office. Now let me record your names so I may give them to El Presidente."

"Hey Rosa, what does one have to do to visit a nun in Santa Maria Monastery?"

"¡Madre de Dios! That's the last place on earth I'd expect you to visit. What can you possibly have to say to cloistered nuns?"

She could imagine Rosa pacing up and down. It's what she did when confronted with unreasonable demands.

"Actually, I need to visit the monastery because of Auntie Jane."

"Well, why didn't you say so? Probably, the best time to contact someone in authority for permission would be to attend Mass on Saturday morning. No use to call, if the extern nun doesn't recognize your phone number she won't answer. Go figure—*Caller-ID* is their one concession to modern conveniences."

"I have to get permission?"

"Saturday morning mass, 5:00 a.m., and after that, you should be able to talk to the extern nun who tends the altar. Then it'd be a matter of waiting, sometimes weeks, until the abbess gives permission and sends a message to summon you to the locutorio."

"What's a locutorio? Why does it take that long?"

Rosa giggled. "There's real time and then there's cloistered convent time. I guess when you believe you're already living in eternity a few extra weeks don't matter. The locutorio's where conversations take place between the nuns and their visitors—wait till you encounter that medieval relic!"

At 4:00 a.m. on Saturday morning, Joanna flagged down a taxi to take her across town to the Plaza de San Francisco. After detouring to collect Rosa, who'd insisted on accompanying her, the driver dropped them on the street near the padlocked front gates of Santa Maria Monastery.

The cabbie, eyes narrowed and mouth turned downward, registered his disapproval while accepting the fare from Joanna.

"He's probably worked out for himself what sort of profession we're practicing, at this hour, in this section of town," Rosa said in

English, winking at the man and giving a coquettish little laugh as she unbuttoned the top two buttons of her bodice.

"Good God, Rosa!"

"Delicious, isn't it? I've always wondered how it felt to be regarded so."

Joanna cornered her eyes in exasperation. "Good thing no paparazzi are around to record this for posterity."

Rosa ignored her and indicated the plaza. "This place is a busy impromptu market during the week. I love shopping here. The central market's only a block away," she continued, "and we're near the train station. It's a direct conduit to town from the Quechua villages located in the mountains and along the Urubamba River."

Joanna stared at the monastery's ten-foot-high wrought iron fence, with makeshift sunshades attached to the top of it, covering the stalls. The colorful spectacle encompassed a huge variety of vegetables and ceramics. Museum quality textiles woven with Incan symbols were displayed on the fence. The owners slept on pallets on the ground near their stalls.

Rosa maneuvered past the stalls and positioned herself near the monastery's grand entrance. Joanna followed and experienced several moments of fright as they stood in front of the padlocked gates. It was 4:30 a.m.—similar areas in D.C. had become drug-dealing venues.

On either side of Santa Maria's gate, people, under newspapers or thin blankets, were stretched out on the sidewalk. Clearly, they weren't waiting for church services to commence. It looked more like a scene outside a major chain store in D.C. on Thanksgiving night before Black Friday.

It occurred to Joanna that the jewel-toned cotton batiste dresses, white lace mantillas, and high-heeled sandals, which Rosa had insisted they wear, didn't constitute the best attire for a street fight. An image of herself and Rosa, scarred from battle, flitted across her mind.

She turned, surveying the scene once again. "Are you sure the church is open on—"

A blur caught her eye as Rosa rounded the corner of the fence, scurrying onto the side street, motioning frantically for her to follow. She didn't question the need to run.

High-heels wobbling, lace veil straining to take flight, Joanna cursed loudly and experienced a moment of embarrassment remembering her close proximity to the monastery.

Halfway down the block, a vender was off-loading bins of vegetables from a pick-up truck parked near the curb. Rosa sped in his direction. An extern nun had just emerged from massive double wooden doors and was holding them open while another nun took the containers from the vendor. Joanna increased her speed to catch up with Rosa.

The vendor returned to his vehicle, slammed the tailgate shut, and drove away. Rusty iron hinges creaked loudly and the nuns disappeared inside the door.

Rosa, waving and yelling as she ran, arrived just as the door settled into place. She grabbed the wrought iron knocker, wielding it in a desperate attack on the door—no response. Joanna halted nearby.

"Don't you think we'd better check the front gate? It's ten minutes past five."

Rosa ceased the onslaught and trailed along behind Joanna. They rounded the curve of the high monastery walls, back to the plaza, where the scene remained exactly as they'd left it.

"Rosa, let's give up. I'm calling a cab."

Rosa was hurrying down the side street, heading back toward the wooden doors. When Joanna caught up with her, she was knocking on the door, singing loudly in heavily accented Spanish, "I hear you knocking, but you can't come in, I hear you knocking, go back where you've been... ."

"You're going to get us arrested," she stage whispered, grabbing Rosa's arm and pulling her toward the front gates.

An aged male caretaker was unlocking a small inset-gate in the lower half of one of the tall iron gates. Joanna shoved Rosa ahead of her and hurried through the narrow opening. She ventured a glance over her shoulder, expecting to be jostled by large crowds of enthusiastic churchgoers. No need to worry—no other worshipers were storming the gates at this hour.

The caretaker directed them to a small door at the side of the church. It was concealed within a six-foot high panel, cleverly set into the silver encrusted, beautifully carved, fifteen-foot high wooden doors of Santa Maria Monastery Church.

Only the dim glow of vigil lights at side altars lit the way as Joanna made a sharp turn to the right and followed Rosa up the center aisle. The thick adobe walls made the space silent as a tomb. A lingering fragrance of beeswax, starch, and incense brought back memories of the chapel at boarding school.

Joanna paused, rubbing her arms, shivering from the penetrating cold. Swishing cloth and wooden beads, clicking like muted castanets, sounded near the rear of the church.

She turned toward the sound. It seemed to be emanating from behind a nearly opaque gauze curtain, which served as a backdrop for the delicate tracery of wooden bars extending the height and width of the wall at the back of the church. Ghostly shapes of black draped nuns were settling into choir stalls behind the curtained screen.

At the front of the church, near the high altar, a nun was busy lighting tall candles for the Mass. She was probably the extern.

Rosa had told her the externs were lay sisters whose job it was to act as intermediaries between the cloistered nuns and the external world. They wore the same habit as the cloistered nuns but their veils were white instead of black.

Midway up the aisle, Rosa stood next to a pew, motioning for her. She hurried forward, slipped into the space between the two pews and stumbled into a padded cushion kneeler attached to a step that folded down from the back of the pew.

Dropping onto the kneeler, she took in the baroque decor of the church. The cedar pews were richly carved. The altar cloths and furnishings were of linen, silks, and brocade, while the candlesticks and sacred vessels sparkled in silver and gold—pure, no doubt. The entire interior was covered in tiny mosaic mirrors, thousands of tiny mosaic mirrors—the effect was stunning.

Over the centuries, the mirrors had obviously become crazed—and appeared to have flecks of gold in them. *Given the history of the Inca Empire and their Conquerors, those mirrors probably were embedded with gold particles.*

The flickering light of multiple candles bouncing off the mirrors caused rays to dance about the vast open spaces in the church's high-vaulted ceiling. Joanna recalled reading somewhere that alternate states of consciousness could be triggered by less intensely hypnotic displays of light.

When she was a child, she'd walked in the woods on the farm, wading in a shallow stream with willow branches entwined overhead. She'd become transfixed by the light patterns and in some strange way, had felt as though God needed her eyes to see His creation, to praise it.

She'd knelt in that natural sanctuary, appreciating His creation for Him. The Mass always made her think of that experience. Her father had said the telescopic history of the Christian religion was enacted daily in the Mass. The pageantry and ritual made the sacred seem close and real to her.

She watched the altar boy hold the silver basin for the priest to wash his hands in preparation for the sacrifice of the Mass and, by chance, glanced up toward a huge cross in the form of an "**X**" that was suspended above the altar. Unlike most crucifixes, this one had no corpus, no figure of Christ.

The boarding school nuns had informed their students that such a cross was known as a Saint Andrew's cross. They'd said the Apostle Andrew chose to be crucified that way since he believed he was unworthy to be crucified like Christ on an upright cross.

Dr. Alderez had told her the city of Cuzco and, indeed, each Incan village was laid out to represent an interstitial cross, an "**X**" that marked the yearly solstice and equinoctial paths of the sun. He said villagers believed it was a way of maintaining contact with Viracocha, the god who ordered the universe.

Apparently, the interstitial cross also represented the two "branches" of the Milky Way. She supposed the sixteenth-century Santa Maria nuns had deliberately selected that symbol for their church, knowing it would resonate with the Quechua people.

She had responded automatically to the words and motions of the Mass, and had received Holy Communion reverently, yet failed to notice the celebration had ended.

"Ite missa est," the priest intoned. Her father had told her the ending meant, "You are sent'—return to the world to tell them what you now know."

Sister Jane had explained to her that the Mass recapitulated the stages of the Hero's Journey. She'd said, "How tragic that most people don't understand that deeper symbolic meaning."

Joanna glanced at Rosa, who was lost in her own private world, head bowed, hands folded in intense supplication. Wonder what she was thinking, how was she experiencing these moments? Rosa had always been open about everything but her spiritual life—saying it was off limits because sacred things were best left unexpressed.

The sun exploded into the twilight of the vast church, quickening the stained-glass windows, diffusing their colors like a million prisms that joined the play of candlelight bouncing off the mosaic mirrors.

It was like being inside a kaleidoscope. Joanna was beginning to think the heavenly light show was the most sublime thing a soul could experience when a clarion wave of musical notes swept over her.

Rosa leaned near and whispered, "The nuns are chanting *Prime*, the prayers of the Divine Office for the first hour of daylight."

Gregorian chant, of course.

The Chant had originated, in earliest Christian times, with monks who had devised the musical scale. There was no denying it was heavenly music.

Plainsong was the sound of the human voice in its purest form, the rhythm attuned to the heartbeat, expressed in the timbre of disciplined voices, singing together many times a day, over many years. No musical instruments accompanied the chant—nothing was allowed to distract from the clarity of the voices that poured forth praise and love for the creator. It was sublime and almost poignantly unbearable.

The sound seemed to lift Joanna's spirit up among the dancing rays, making her one with both light and sound. She let her body absorb the beauty, becoming oblivious to the world around her.

She felt a touch on her arm and saw Rosa gesticulate toward the altar where the extern nun had returned from the sacristy to extinguish the candles. She barely had time to grab her purse before Rosa dragged her from the pew and pulled her up the aisle.

Rosa opened the gate in the middle of the communion rail and hastened up the steps to the high altar. She did a quick bow of the head toward the tabernacle that held the reserved transubstantiated communion bread. Joanna followed her and genuflected in front of the tabernacle. She saw Rosa ascend the last altar step and tug at the drooping sleeve of the extern nun.

The nun's back was to them, her arms raised high, holding the long wooden handle of the silver candlesnuffer to extinguish the tall altar candles. Joanna watched in horror as the nun registered the tug on her sleeve and swung around with a look of amazement.

The heavy metal candlesnuffer swung with her, dipping and whizzing past Rosa's head, missing it by a mere quarter of an inch.

"Damn it!" Rosa ducked and moved to the bottom step of the altar.

Joanna gasped and murmured a prayer of thanks, with a sigh of relief that the frightened nun hadn't taken Rosa out with one well-aimed blow.

"Sóror, perdón, me llamo Rosa de la Reyna. Por favor, quisiera para usted hablar," Rosa called loudly.

The "de la Reyna" name seemed to be familiar to the nun. She composed herself, smiled at them, descended the steps, and came forward.

"Sóror, le presenta mi amiga, Doctor Joanna Nickels-Stewart, de los Estados Unidos." Rosa gave a rambling explanation of how Joanna had made a promise to her aunt—a nun of the Order of Saint Dominic in the states—to visit Sister Elena de la Cruz.

"I will place your request before Abbess Antonia," the extern nun said. "Where should I have the messenger deliver the response?"

Rosa looked toward Joanna, a deep shade of red infusing her face, and supplied her own address. The nun inquired about Rosa's family and Joanna suppressed a groan. When Rosa was asked about family, she usually started with *Genesis*.

At the back of the church, the small inset door creaked loudly. The elderly caretaker jingled his key ring and inserted a huge iron skeleton key into the lock plate.

Pointing toward the exit, Joanna signed to Rosa, "He's locking the door, let's go."

Rosa ignored her, blithely continuing with the recitation of family exploits.

Giving a last nod to the nun, Joanna smiled, mouthed "thank you," and bolted to freedom.

Chapter 14

Joanna longed for more time to discover all the interesting people, places, and things in Peru. It was like a parallel universe compared to the one in which she'd been reared. The essentials were the same, but their varied expressions were exotic and wonder-filled for her.

She especially enjoyed the opportunity to visit with Rosa and get to know the de la Reynas better in their own environment, but she worried time was running out. For that reason, she wasn't looking forward to the next phone call from Michael.

What occupied many days, made them most stimulating, were the projects Dr. Alderez had assigned. Today she was meeting with her new lab partners, Marisol and Vinny. The purpose was to review areas on which they could focus in the short time she had to work with them. In addition, they'd asked her to discuss her research.

She described work she'd done on the vibrational frequencies of chemical elements, directing the lab technicians' attention to facts such as their precise numerical positions along the electro-magnetic, infrared, and sonar spectrums.

"The molecules of various elements, which make up every kind of matter in the universe, also have their own individual frequencies, like 'theme songs' for each one. Not only rocks and planets, but even humans have such a frequency," Joanna said.

"Scientists have captured some of those sequences of musical notes on sensitive recording instruments. There's an article about it in a recent issue of *Astronomy Edge*," Vinny said.

"NASA has recorded some of them. I found a website they set up where the 'music of the spheres' can be heard. It's really cool to hear Earth's theme song," Marisol said.

"The main question to consider is what conclusions might be drawn by comparing and contrasting current data related to various known frequencies given off by objects in deep space," Joanna said, delighted at the excitement the dialogue had generated.

The intercom buzzed and Ms. Sanchez announced a personal call for Joanna. Reluctantly, she excused herself and left the lab. She sat at her desk and pushed the receiver button.

"Joanna, it's me. Are you there? Joanna—"

"Rosa, what's going on?"

"You've received a letter from Abbess Antonia. I'm sure it's the first instantaneous response in the history of that monastery. You should see the envelope, the stationery is straight out of a Victorian parlor—they actually make it themselves and sell it, so it doesn't cost them anything. It's embossed with a lovely script imprinted with all of Mother Abbess's formal titles. Shall I read it to you?"

"Yes, please."

"Dr. Joanna Nickels-Stewart is kindly requested to meet Thursday at 2:00 p.m., with Sister Elena de la Cruz in the convent locutorio at Santa Maria Monastery. Sister Petrina de la Encarnación will chaperone."

"Wait a minute, what's up with this chaperone business?"

"Presumably to assure that nothing untoward, either unacceptable verbal exchanges or physical signs of affection, occur between the nun and the visitor."

"Sounds like a prison."

"What shall we wear? Actually, I think nice dresses, you know, like the ones we wore to Mass, with the mantillas, and possibly high-heeled sandals with silk stockings would be appropriate," Rosa said.

"Good God! It sounds like *Visitors Day* at boarding school—I always felt like wearing dirty underwear in protest."

"Joanna, clothes are important—lab coats aren't socially acceptable everywhere, you know."

"Listen, why don't we meet in front of the monastery on Thursday? You think it'd be kosher to take along recent pictures of Aunt Jane?"

Joanna was surprised to find she was actually looking forward to meeting the nun, since the experiences she'd had visiting Santa Maria Church. Her eagerness increased as she and Rosa walked alongside the monastery's stucco wall that extended a full block.

Midway down the block, set into the wall, a hand-carved eight-by-six-foot wooden frame held an antique door firmly in place. Heavy cross-braces decorated the door. No handle was visible, but a richly embossed tarnished silver button was affixed to the center of the middle cross-brace.

Rosa hurried ahead and pushed the button. The sound reverberated somewhere inside the 450-year-old building.

"What's that for?" Joanna pointed to a 3-by-2-foot rectangular opening cut into the wall next to the door.

"It's a turnstile. Patrons of the convent can put things in there for the nuns."

"Should I place Aunt Jane's gift to Sister Elena in there?"

"Probably... I have a friend who's a cloistered Carmelite, and she can't have gifts presented directly to her. She told me any presents or letters go directly to the prioress, and she decides whether the nuns will get their stuff—you know, if it's acceptable, under the rules of the monastery."

Joanna put the gift in the turnstile and pressed the button. She'd recently bought a book at the tourist shop in her hotel to learn more about Santa Maria Monastery. The author said people left all sorts of things in monastery turnstiles, even newborn infants. Previously, she'd thought the term referred to the convent door. *Imagine finding a baby in that cylinder!*

There was something else she'd read about Santa Maria Monastery that was most unusual. Contrary to the way monasteries were traditionally founded, Santa Maria had been established by the Conquistadors shortly after they'd conquered Cuzco. Why had they done that, when they probably had greater need for any number of other types of institutions?

The massive door groaned and swung open. Rosa pinched her arm in excitement and pushed her forward.

Just inside the door, she halted. Rosa stumbled into her back and gave her a shove.

"Damn it, Joanna, keep moving."

"Why didn't you tell me about *this*?"

About six feet into the interior was a massive barrier of wrought-iron bars extending from floor-to-ceiling and wall-to-wall, splitting the room in half. The bars were crisscrossed by intricately shaped metal curlicues on which were mounted silver circles with repoussé gold flowers. An opaque black curtain, suspended from the ceiling, stretched the full length, concealing the part of the room behind the bars.

"Get the hell out of my way." Rosa gave her another push. "This nail-studded door's cutting into my ass."

Behind the curtain a chair scraped the floor. "For God's sake, Rosa, hush! Somebody's back there."

Willing herself forward, she sat on one of the two antique carved mahogany chairs that occupied a space in front of the bars. Rosa brushed past her to claim the other.

"Those bars are called a grille," Rosa commented, her voice bouncing loudly off the stone walls. "Sister Elena will be behind that curtain."

Seconds ticked by. Finally, the exterior door settled firmly into place, sealing the windowless room.

"Espéreme, por favor, traigo Sóror Elena." A voice sounded from behind the bars.

Joanna glanced furtively at Rosa. Receding footsteps echoed loudly on the stone floor and a key turned in the interior door's lock plate.

"Like we have a choice about whether to wait here when we're locked up real tight in this room with no windows," Rosa said.

Joanna felt blood drain from her face. A rising envelope of terror gripped her. She tried replacing horrifying thoughts with an image of open fields, but breathing intensified in harsh successive gulps.

"I can't imagine why they feel they have to lock us up—"

"Rosa, for God's sake, shut up. I'm about to jump up and start clawing at that door."

Rosa pantomimed zipping her mouth and reached over to pat Joanna's hand.

"It'll be okay, just breathe deeply, that's it ..."

Joanna jerked away and jabbed sharp fingernails into her right palm. Pain replaced panic. Time stood still, she closed her eyes, forcing herself to remain calm, silently reciting lines from Richard Lovelace, *"Stone walls do not a prison make, nor iron bars a cage... ."*

The monastery bells clanged twice, counting the hour. The door on the other side of the bars creaked open. There was a sound like the whirr of birds' wings and then a brief period of silence.

"Benedícite," a well-modulated voice said from behind the curtain.

"Dóminus," Joanna and Rosa chorused.

Joanna hadn't used that greeting since boarding school. "Blessed be" one person said in greeting, and the other completed the phrase with "... the Lord!" The students had been told it was one of the earliest greetings used by Christians in the first centuries A.D. in Rome.

A delighted giggle sounded from behind the grille, and the voice said in lyrical, barely-accented English, "Dr. Nickels-Stewart, how much I've looked forward to meeting you."

"My aunt—that is Sister Mary Jane Howell requested I visit you. She sent you a gift. It's in the uh—the turnstile. Oh, and I would like to introduce my friend, Rosa de la Reyna, who is here with me—"

"Rosa, this *is* delightful! Your grandmother and I were BFFs in grammar school... ... isn't that what you young people say nowadays—BFFs?"

Joanna remembered Grandmother de la Reyna visiting Rosa at boarding school and entertaining all the little girls with stories about the unholy scrapes she and her childhood friend Clara de Almagro had managed to get into together.

"Is she really Clara de Almagro?" Eyes wide in disbelief, Joanna signed the question to Rosa.

"I hope you'll give your grandmother my affectionate greeting," Sister Elena said. "How is she?"

"Boy, do I know some juicy stories!" Rosa signed back and leaned forward, staring intently at the curtain as though she might see beyond it.

Joanna pointed toward the curtain and pantomimed slapping Rosa up the side of the head, reminding her Sister Elena was waiting for a response.

Rosa smirked at her and spoke directly into the grille. "Sister Elena, perhaps you would like to see some pictures of my grandmother and our family. May I pass them through the curtain?"

Rosa removed the photos from her wallet and held them between the bars where the curtains came together at the center. A delicate hand, with unwrinkled skin like eggshell-thin porcelain, reached through the curtain to take the pictures.

"Rosa, the last time I saw your brother, he was about five-years-old. He has an uncanny resemblance to your grandfather."

Joanna took the opportunity to examine the black curtain more closely while Rosa and Sister Elena chatted about the pictures. Shapes could easily be detected.

The two nuns on the other side were dressed in the regulation black habits of Santa Maria Monastery with black veils covering their heads, signifying vowed religious profession, but, astonishingly, there were veils covering their faces as well, like Iranian Muslim chadors with niqābs.

The room had grown silent, a silence intensified by the walls. *Was Sister Elena addressing her? Was it about her work?*

Rosa looked at her expectantly. She hastened to fill the conversation gap, words jumbling out, as she launched into a meandering narrative about her invitation to do research at the Cuzco Observatory—how she couldn't take the job and was just volunteering because she had soon to join her fiancé in Mongolia.

"Joanna, does your work include looking at the frequencies of matter expressed as sonar waves? I've read that a process related to that may have accounted for earlier civilizations being able to carve and position enormous boulders."

Wait a minute! How did a cloistered nun know about the frequencies of matter?

"That's certainly an area of interest. Sound waves may well have been utilized by ancient peoples in that way," she said, responding as she would to a colleague. "Many scientists, including myself, are looking into the properties of matter when their frequencies are artificially altered." She paused. "Please forgive me, but I'm amazed that you know about this."

"We offer editorial services here at Santa Maria, a job able to be performed in the isolation of our cloistered lives. I've recently edited Dr. Juan Alderez's book on astronomy."

"That's a technically advanced treatise on electromagnetism—what a monumental task you've had!"

"One learns a great deal in the process of editing. Some of the content is extraordinarily engaging—such as the work of Dr. Alderez—and some *not* so much. I recently edited a manuscript on how to construct and tie fishing lures, written by one of our Santa Maria cloistered nuns in Italy. The subject matter was so mind numbing it nearly drove me to knuckle gnawing." Sister Elena's tinkling laugh sounded through the curtain. "But I understand the book has become an international best seller. Who knew there were so many fly-fishermen all over the world! Of course, its success may be due to the original trout recipes."

"And you expected her to be boring!" Rosa signed, hand held high, fingers moving quickly.

"Joanna, in the last letter I had from your aunt, she said you had learned you were adopted and that the reason you're in Peru is to find your birth parents. Have you been successful?"

Rosa spoke up. "She's made all the rounds of the governmental offices in Lima and managed to find the names of her parents—we aren't sure if they're accurate, seems her mother is dead and her father has vamoosed. Now we're searching for her father or at least some living relative."

"How frustrating to come all this way and not find what you seek," Sister Elena said.

"Rosa and Carlos are helping me. I'm sure it won't take much longer."

"Sister Jane wrote that you're interested in mythology. Does that interest extend to Incan mythology?" Sister Elena said.

"Greek and Roman mythology are required in grad school because, historically, the names of planets and other objects in space are named for those gods and other minor deities, but I haven't had the opportunity to study South American myths. I'd hoped to do that while I'm here."

"And I thought she came to Cuzco just to see me, well, besides looking for her family, of course!" Rosa said.

Sister Elena chuckled. There was a soft purring sound, like a snore. Joanna wondered if the companion nun had been put to sleep by their talk about astronomy. She dared not look at Rosa. In the past, far less provocation had caused them to dissolve into laughing fits.

"There's an Incan myth I've been studying for some time, trying to understand its meaning," Sister Elena said. "Dr. Alderez cited a book in his manuscript that claims myths may have coded references to astronomy." The nun's voice stopped for a few seconds. "Goodness—I'm carrying coals to Newcastle, prattling on, when you're the expert, Joanna!"

"Sister, what myth are you trying to decode?" Rosa asked. "I've studied a little bit about pre-Columbian mythologies. I may be familiar with it."

"It isn't part of the collected literature."

"You've discovered a previously unknown myth?" Joanna said.

"Well... something like that." Sister Elena said. "I know it may be presumptuous, but it just occurred to me. With your great knowledge of astronomy, Joanna, you'd be the perfect person to examine the myth. Perhaps, you'd be willing to take a look at it—see if really does contain astronomical references?"

"I don't know if I have the knowledge to do what you're asking, but, yes, I'd be eager to try. It'll certainly motivate me to investigate Incan myths."

"Our extern, Sister Ana, will place a sealed envelope in the turnstile for you to take as you leave. May I request that this matter be kept confidential between us? I believe the myth shouldn't become public knowledge just yet."

The monastery bells clanged three times, announcing the hour. Chairs scraped the floor and the black curtain rippled slightly. "That's our call to prayer. How enjoyable this visit has been, I hope you'll both visit again soon. Goodbye, God bless you."

Chapter 15

The raucous sound of the buzzer shattered the silence and the door to the street popped open. A cold wet breeze enveloped Joanna.

She checked her watch, astounded that an hour had passed and her claustrophobia had been forgotten. She shielded her eyes from the afternoon sunrays, diffused to hyper-brightness by raindrops, and saw Rosa point toward the distant street corner.

"I'll get a taxi, you get that envelope."

Joanna pressed the silver button and waited while the turnstile opened. She took the envelope from the half-cylinder and glanced at its contents. The myth was entitled *The Llama Road*. Glancing at the first lines, she felt the raindrops start, and reluctantly dropped the envelope into her purse. She hastened up the block to the street corner.

The taxi maneuvered out of traffic and stopped at the curb just as she arrived. Rosa pulled her into the back seat and instructed the driver to go to the Plaza des Armas.

"I need a drink," Rosa announced. "We're going to the Via Làctea, I'm buying."

Joanna leaned forward, turning her whole body to look directly at Rosa. "I wasn't aware you carried anything even remotely resembling cash. Did something happen back there to make you dig deep into that exorbitantly expensive purse?"

"For your information, I've got a running tab at the Via Làctea. Carlos has Jamie his chauffeur pay my bills once a week."

The taxi advanced a few feet. Rosa drummed her nails on the armrest. Joanna gazed out the window, trying to ignore the sound. Traffic at 3:15 p.m. in Cuzco assured that a trip to the Plaza des Armas was going to be anything but quick.

Suddenly, the cab door was flung open, and Rosa hit the sidewalk running. Joanna reached into her purse for sols and handed them to the driver. "I doubt Jamie will track *you* down to pay this fare," she said.

The man regarded her blankly. She smiled at him and dashed after

Rosa, who was shouting over her shoulder, "It's only four blocks to the Pub."

A cold drumming rain had set in and Joanna was soaked, chilled to the bone, with hair shedding streams of water all over her new silk dress. The cobbled streets made the going rough but she stumbled doggedly after Rosa, who'd disappeared around a corner, apparently intent on winning some personal marathon.

She was seriously considering ditching the high-heeled sandals. *How, in the name of all that's holy, can Rosa run like that in those high-heels? Solemn pledge to myself—I'll never again take her advice about appropriate apparel. We could've worn biker boots and nail-studded leather miniskirts for all those nuns could see from behind those veils.*

Feet aching, clothes clinging like saran wrap, she trudged through the rain and sighed with relief when she spied the cathedral. The Via Làctea Pub was at a right angle to it, across the Plaza des Armas from La Compañía de Jesús Church.

Although she'd only been in Cuzco a short time, the pub had become one of her favorite haunts. She enjoyed sitting on the second-story balcony, sipping a glass of wine, and watching the ever-changing cloud display over the valley of Cuzco. The pub had an excellent cellar, but what people really came to Via Làctea for was the chocolate cake.

Cocoa in Peru was the real thing and death by chocolate was a less than remote possibility. Via Làctea chocolate cake had no icing—didn't need any. It was moist but not gooey, and the chocolate so rich it almost hurt the palate. Coffee had to be drunk with it—coffee with no sugar, no cream, just weak black coffee—the caffeine in the cake more than made up for its scarcity in the coffee.

Joanna had read that when the Conquistadors exported cocoa from Peru to Spain, Pope Clement VII had been given samples of the exports. He'd immediately decreed it sinful for the laity to use cocoa because he deemed it too great a sensual pleasure.

However, the pope didn't apply the ban to himself and his friends. They didn't have to abstain from the indulgence that had become the rage of Europe, presumably, because they were well along the road to sainthood. Joanna felt great empathy for the sixteenth-century pope's need to sin shamelessly in the matter.

She crossed the plaza and climbed the stairs to the pub. Rosa was on the balcony, a drink in hand, shoes kicked under the table.

A huge piece of chocolate cake had already been ordered and placed at Joanna's side of the table. A waiter appeared immediately and put a steaming cup of coffee next to the cake.

Rosa smiled, thanked him, and gestured toward Joanna's feet. "Lose those shoes. Eat cake."

Joanna slipped out of the high heels and took a quick bite of the chocolate cake, followed by a restorative sip of coffee.

"Okay, Rosa, let's talk. You signed something in that locutorio about scandal—"

"Sister Elena... she's descended from Diego de Almagro and an Inca princess. Almagro didn't marry the princess—most of the conquistadors didn't marry their mistresses."

Joanna eyed the last half of her chocolate cake, deciding she might take it home for a snack.

"What's so scandalous about that? I thought maybe you knew really personal stuff—like why she entered that cloister or something."

"My mom probably knows. She keeps up with everybody's gossip. Actually, I do know one thing. Sister Elena was engaged to some dude distantly related to my grandfather. It was after she'd débuted at the Spanish royal court at eighteen. Imagine having to submit to that anachronistic ceremony!"

"You'd do it—you'd be in your glory," Joanna said.

"Anyway, her fiancé died in some tragic accident, the family sent her to France to be educated. She earned a doctorate in fine arts at the

Sorbonne and entered the monastery soon after returning home. That's all I know."

Joanna savored the warmth of the coffee. She touched the cup to her cheek and pondered Rosa's description of the nun's life. "What a waste... ."

"Wait—*now* I remember what I really wanted to tell you," Rosa said. "There's an old man who walks in disguise down Calle Santa Maria every Sunday morning before Mass and deposits a bouquet of roses in the turnstile for Sister Elena. He even leaves donations of money in her name. No one knows who he is, and he's done that since she first entered the monastery." Rosa sipped her wine slowly, looking around at the other patrons in the restaurant.

"You're telling me no one has identified that man in all this time," Joanna said.

"There's another thing—the florist delivers fresh flowers every morning for the altars in Santa Maria with a card announcing they are given in Sister Elena's honor."

"That's beyond belief —," Joanna said.

"The florist was interviewed by a T.V. reporter—brought him tons of publicity—but he wouldn't reveal the name." Rosa tore off a piece of Joanna's cake. "Listen to this! A few months back my mother and I were visiting Grandmother de la Reyna at the nursing home. She babbled something about *Sister Elena's child*. Mother became very flustered, said, 'That's ridiculous! Pay no attention to that, Rosa.' Later she commented that Grandmother de la Reyna was just having one of her 'crazy' spells."

"It's a tragic story." Joanna forked down the last piece of chocolate cake, assuaging sadness at Sister Elena's plight. She leaned back, a faraway look in her eyes. "So Clara falls in love, becomes pregnant, her parents send her away to have the child. She gives it up for adoption, and enters a convent. When we go see her again, let's ask—"

"You're kidding, right?" Rosa regarded her, wide-eyed. "Don't you dare even go there, they're not allowed to talk about personal—

Good God! I didn't say she was *pregnant*!"

"How do you know so much about cloistered nuns?"

"Joanna, I've told you a million times Katrina has a cousin who took the veil at the Discalced Carmelite Monastery in Lima and she said ..."

Rosa's voice was a low humming counterpoint as Joanna used her fork to gather up the last cake crumbs and made a decision to request a visit with Sister Elena for next Thursday. She wouldn't take Rosa along. She had some residual compunction about that, but maybe, with no one else present, the nun would reveal more about the myth... and her personal life.

Chapter 16

The taxi wove its way through rain-sparkled streets toward Casa de la Reyna. Rosa and Carlos had insisted Joanna come to dinner at least once a week, and Friday had become party night. Don Remondo and Doña Isabella always left early on Fridays to spend the weekend at their country home in the Sacred Valley, which left the huge "in town" estate house deserted except for a skeleton staff.

Joanna had considered cancelling this evening's invitation. She'd wanted to spend more time examining the myth Sister Elena had given her. She'd already consulted the works of several sixteenth-century chroniclers who'd arrived with the Conquistadors, as well as some modern reference works by archeoastronomers. Dr. Alderez had suggested she read three books: *Hamlet's Mill* by Georgio de Santillana and Hertha von Dechend (Boston: David R. Godine, 2005); *The Secret of the Incas: Myth, Astronomy, and the War Against Time* by William Sullivan (New York: Three Rivers Press, 1997); and *The Sacred Valley of the Incas: Myth and Symbols* by Fernando E. Elorrieta Salazar and Edgar Elorrieta Salazar (Cuzco, Peru: Aedo Productions, Inc., 2004). He said the books were essential to understanding Incan mythology.

She'd compared Incan names and descriptions for planets and constellations with those found in other myths. The experts were unsure about the number of planets the Incas could have observed. William Sullivan found that the Anonymous Chronicler mentioned five planets the Incas knew.

The cab slowed to a crawl—stalled in traffic. She pulled her portable computer from her purse and located Sister Elena's myth, which she'd scanned into her files. Last evening she'd highlighted passages and made notes related to her research.

The title was puzzling. The "paved" road system of the Incas wound for thousands of miles across the Andes, along the Pacific coast, and down into the jungle, but in modern times the part referred to as "The *Inca Trail*" followed a route roughly parallel to the Urubamba River.

THE LLAMA ROAD*

(The Inca Trail???)
<u>Possible Amarya Words</u>
<u>Viracocha</u> (supreme god of the Inca...perhaps representing the planet Saturn); <u>Con</u> (god, thunder); <u>Ticci</u> (source)

<u>Con Ticci Viracocha</u> once walked among the people, teaching his ways before the <u>death of the first sun</u>, before he journeyed across the <u>great endless sea.</u> In those days, he instructed <u>Manco Capàc</u> and Mama Ocllo to build places of remembrance, so the people would know his teachings.

<u>endless sea</u> = celestial sea, the sky ocean?
<u>death of first sun</u> = often coded reference for the passage of time, of one World Age [like Pisces] about to change to the next world age [example: changing from Pisces to Aquarius] when it would be necessary for king/priest/astronomers to establish the new "star markers" that showed Earth's "place" in the heavens
<u>Manco Capàc</u> (possibly Pirua—mythical first "king" who gave Peru its name)

In his time, <u>Pachakuti Inca</u>[a] chose as his <u>mita</u>[b] to make visible on the face of <u>Pacha Mama</u>[c] all the teachings of Viracocha. He did this according to Viracocha's instructions to Manco Capac.

[a] Pachakuti = Earth turner-over
[b] Mita = the Reciprocal obligations people owe to Con Ticci

and vice versa

◦ *Pacha Mama = mother earth*

Pachakuti built the Llama Road on Pacha Mama to mirror the road above. The Great Mother Llama and her suckling walk down the middle toward the land of the gods. Long ago, Viracocha first commanded the puma, in his own image, to guard the land of the living, at the navel above the abyss where the fresh waters whirl. He set the partridge to mark the entrance to the land of the dead. Paco, the Great Male Llama, he commanded to stand with the plumed war lance at the entrance to the land of the gods. Paco stands on the tallest mountain, sounding the conch shell, to remind the people of Viracocha's teachings.

Viracocha is depicted as a Puma (mountain lion) and guards Cuzco. Does overall shape of the Puma in Cuzco also represent the Milky Way on the ground?

Pachakuti Inca made beautiful, above all others, the home of Viracocha and all things are revealed there. In his abode, Viracocha bids the condor to bear the souls of men to the Life Tree, near the entrance to his home in the sky, where they rest until once again they enter the land of the living. The great warrior stands watch over Pacaritampu where the Sapa Inca is born anew into the house of the sun. *(Life Tree—located near Orion, the warrior in the Milky Way)*

Mama Quilla, the moon goddess, lights the way along the Llama Road, and her servants know the secrets of its path. *(Who were the servants of Mama Quilla?)*

The teachings of Viracocha are written in the sky and on the land. When Viracocha's brother, the Angry One *(same as planet*

Mars in world mythology???), stirs the waters and the Life Tree shakes and Inti the Sun God dies, the people have no fear for the Llama Road forever tells of Con Ticci's promise:

"I am Con Ticci Viracocha, I <u>weave the pattern endlessly</u>. I am born, I live, I grow old, I die, and I am reborn again. I look on the place of dawning at the <u>confluence of the Twin Rivers</u>, where I give to Pirua the means to measure all things and to the people the cluster of <u>seeds</u>, that is their treasure, seeds growing near the place of the First Time, of life's beginning."

Weave the pattern endlessly = Saturn giving the "measures" to Jupiter....conjunctions of Saturn and Jupiter?

Confluence of the Twin Rivers in the sky = Milky Way's two branches that appear to rise at different times of the year—because Earth is between two "arms" of the galaxy

Seeds = Pleiades constellation?

The mythology of the Incas appeared to have concepts related to the technical language of worldwide myth, as the scholarly work of William Sullivan, in his book *The Secret of the Incas: Myth, Astronomy, and the War Against Time*, seemed to prove. Given that, it would seem that the *places* in Sister Elena's myth: "land of the living"— "land of the dead"— "land of the gods"—should be able to be found on the ground.

"¿Señorita? Señorita, ¡llegamos!"

Joanna stared blankly at the driver. He pointed toward Casa de la Reyna's high walls as the cab turned the corner and pulled into the driveway. The wrought iron gates swung open. The guard at the gatehouse saluted Joanna and waved the driver forward. The cabbie maneuvered along the concealed driveway and finally turned onto the circle in front of the main house.

Joanna eased the computer into her purse, paid the fare and exited the taxi in a daze. Bartles greeted her at the door and showed her into the study where Carlos was seated, warming himself in front of a roaring fire. He stood to greet her.

"Joanna, you look lovely, glad you could join us. Come sit by the fire. Bartles, please bring martinis."

"Did Rosa tell you about our adventures at Santa Maria Monastery on Thursday?" Joanna asked.

"She said you were both entranced by Sister Elena and that the nun had asked you to decipher some kind of Incan myth."

Joanna stretched her feet toward the fire, remembering the painful journey in high heels to the Plaza des Armas. "I would never have believed such places existed in the modern world, if I hadn't seen that locutorio for myself," she said. "And the myth Sister Elena gave me has become an obsession. It's an extraordinary document."

"I'm eager to hear all about it, but I won't ask. Rosa said Sister Elena wanted it kept mum for the meanwhile." He stood and took the martinis from Bartles, handing her one. "May I switch the subject? We've another mystery."

"Another mystery?"

"My attorney friend Tim, in Virginia, phoned to ask if I'd received the notarized copy of your original birth certificate, he'd mailed it early last week. It seems someone has definitely been intercepting our mail."

Joanna slumped in the chair. "So we still have no way of knowing if the names I've found are the real ones? Intercepting the mail, you said—"

"Tim read the names over the phone," he said. "Plus, El Presidente asked the U.S. Embassy to courier this in for us!" He grinned and waved a sheet of paper.

"Carlos, you didn't, you shouldn't have involved Emilio." She was on her feet and went to stand next to him, as he handed her the document. "Are the names the same?"

Next to 'mother of infant' was the name Sarafina Almagro, not *Alma* as on the documents she'd gotten from the Hall of Records. Her father's name was listed as Alejandro Huaman Ayaviri not "Manuel Curisimay."

"I think I know why the names were changed." Carlos sat down in the wing-backed chair near the fire and regarded her with interest. "Any chance you've ever heard the name Alejandro Ayaviri?"

"No, I don't think so." She sat in the chair next to him.

"That name's a hot item here in Peru. Alejandro Huaman Ayaviri, a Quechua Indian, is reputed to be the last direct descendent of Incan royalty. Various terrorist groups have claimed him and committed acts in his name."

Her father, a Quechua Indian, like in the picture. She waited for Carlos to continue.

"Their actions landed Ayaviri in prison about twenty years ago. I'd heard he'd escaped recently, or was let out, or something, but the news media have been rather quiet about him lately."

The words stuck in her throat. She tried vocalizing them. They came out in a whisper.

"My father's *a terrorist*?"

"The government portrays him that way, but I'm not sure I agree. He was implicated in an attempt to bring about an Incan restoration. He sued the government for tribal lands and tried to stake a claim for a separatist Quechua nation near the site of Vilcabamba."

"Vilcabamba…"

"The so-called 'lost city of the Incas,' their last stronghold after they'd revolted against the Spanish in 1536. I'd be willing to bet that's why there's so much secrecy surrounding your birth, Joanna. It's very possible someone was taking extreme measures to protect you when you were adopted."

Of all the scenarios that she and Rosa had imagined for her birth parents, the notion of a "terrorist" father hadn't been one of them.

"Do you think Senator Vander Hurst knows about this?"

"It's certainly a possibility. I have another piece of information for you, Joanna. When I was in Lima today, the head of the National Police dropped by my office and told me they'd found a piece of paper in your stalker's jacket with two names on it."

"Don't make me wait, tell me, please."

"One of the names was Professor Geraldo Jiménez and this you're not going to believe— the other was Alejandro Huamán Ayaviri. I'm terribly worried about this stalking business."

"Why would anybody want to stalk me? What possible benefit could they…?"

"Joanna, you saw the man once in D.C., twice in Lima, and now he's been discovered with a piece of paper having a name associated with you."

She took her cell phone from her pocket, did a quick Internet search. "I'm not wasting another minute." *Geraldo Jiménez* was listed with the Department of History, Universidad Nacional de Huamanga in Ayacucho. She handed the phone across to Carlos.

"Look at this. I'm getting an appointment tomorrow. I can rent a car and drive over. It's only about 170 miles from Cuzco—"

Carlos roared with laughter. Joanna's face flushed. "What's so funny?"

"As the crow flies, you're right, but translate that *one hundred seventy miles* into gouged-out gravel shelves that snake around mile high mountains with no guardrails." He shook his head. "Even if you manage to drive successfully over those high passes, the bandits will make sure the rest of your trip is far more eventful."

Rosa floated into the room like a sunlit butterfly, planting kisses on her brother's cheek and Joanna's forehead. She sat on the sofa, drawing her legs up beneath her. Joanna noticed how the light beige velveteen dress draped her like a second skin, the broad hem rippling over the edge of the sofa like molten gold.

"You two are so solemn!" Rosa said. "To think I've just come from coaxing J.D. out of the mulligrubs, and now I've got to do the same for you. What have I missed?"

"My father's a terrorist!"

Carlos set his drink down hard. "Joanna, stop that—"

Rosa jumped up and came to perch on the arm of Joanna's chair. "See, I told you, this *is* a Nancy Drew Mystery. Remember the *Clue in the Old Diary* where Nancy, Bess and George—"

"God help me, please spare us the details," Carlos said.

"Okay, so tell me, who's your father?"

"Alejandro Huaman Ayaviri."

Rosa's mouth formed a silent 'o' as she stood and faced Joanna.

"Don't look at me that way," Joanna said. "Who knows? It could be interesting to have a terrorist in the family."

Rosa found her voice. "I'm betting Michael's family wouldn't use the word *interesting*."

Carlos stared into the blazing fire. "Senator Vander Hurst probably started a thorough investigation the minute he got that letter about your adoption, Joanna. If anybody could force the Virginia courts to unseal birth records, it would surely be a U.S. Senator."

"Have you heard anything from that detective agency lately?" Rosa said. "I still think we need to know the identity of the person who sent that letter."

"It's really strange somebody in this country wanted the senator to know about my adoption. Do you think that person could be a relative of mine?"

"We're not going to solve this any time soon." Carlos rang for Bartles. "I'm starved. Let's have dinner in here where we'll be more comfortable."

Bartles carried a large tray into the room and arranged place settings on the coffee table. "I thought you might prefer an informal supper of pizza and chicha," he said.

"Thank you, Bartles. Listen, Joanna wants to go to Ayacucho by car," Carlos said. "Please tell her about your experiences traveling there a few weeks back."

"Oh no, Miss Joanna, you mustn't do that—not by car. I was chased by marauders who intended to take my vehicle, a most unfortunate incident. Had I not *accidentally* hit the gear release that popped open my Highland Utility Vehicle's boot and fired off the concealed weapon mounted inside it, I might never have managed to escape."

Joanna pictured the poor unsuspecting bandits encountering Bartles. Rosa had confided years ago that her family had engaged the retired British Special Forces operative to train their estate guards when the terrorist activity was at its worst in Peru.

"Okay, everybody, not to worry, I'll buy a plane ticket, I promise."

Bartles handed her a plate with a wedge of pizza. She chomped down on a mouthful of fresh vegetables, homegrown beef and chicken. She washed it down with a swig of chicha.

"This is—" She took another bite. "This is, by far, the most scrumptious food I've ever tasted. Now, please, everyone, tell me everything you've ever heard about Ayaviri."

"Miss Joanna!' Bartles set the tray down and faced Rosa and Carlos with a stern look of disapproval. "Don Carlos, Doñita Rosa, I am *most* surprised—most surprised. You must protect your friend better than this." His demeanor suggested he'd issued them orders to "cease and desist." He bowed his head slightly, and left the room.

Absently, Rosa watched Bartles close the door and turned toward Carlos.

"Wasn't Ayaviri from Ayacucho?"

"Attended university there," Carlos said. "A few years ago, he wrote an op-ed column, published in the Lima papers, calling for better treatment of the Quechua people. He seemed to have some brilliant ideas about governmental benefits associated with better treatment of oppressed peoples, and he was right on target with many of his demands."

"I'm curious, why did you think Joanna's birth certificate in

Virginia would reveal her birth parents' names?" Rosa said.

"Joanna told me the clerk at the Hall of Records suggested there was a possibility the names had been concealed here in Peru, but I knew the adoption wouldn't have been completed in this country." Carlos stood and used the poker to break up the logs Bartles had added to the fire. "During the years Joanna was adopted, the adopting agent had to get an IR-4 Visa before taking her out of the country. R*e-adoption* would have occurred in Virginia, and an American birth certificate would have been issued showing James and Mary Ellen as the 'real' parents."

Carlos came back to his chair, took a sip of chicha, and set the glass down. "Typically, the original foreign birth certificate would've been sealed at that time. Fortunately, Virginia has recently changed stipulations related to all that, and I was—"

"What's your mother's real name?" Rosa asked, reaching for her second slice of pizza.

"Sarafina Alma—no, that's the name the clerk gave me in Lima. The Virginia certificate shows *Sarafina Almagro*."

Rosa choked on the pizza. "¡Madre de Dios! That's Sister Elena's family name!"

"Easy now, don't go jumping to conclusions," Carlos said. "Thousands of the old Conquistador's descendants dot the landscape in Peru, even in Panama. Hell, Rosa, you and I are probably Joanna's 'n^{th}' cousins, thrice removed!"

Laughing, Joanna placed her chicha on the table and regarded Rosa.

"Well, anyway, it might need to be checked." Rosa frowned at Carlos.

"Joanna, you did say your Aunt Jane is well-acquainted with those nuns at Santa Maria," he said. "Is there any possibility Sister Elena did have something to do with your adoption?"

"A *cloistered* nun," Joanna and Rosa howled in chorus.

Carlos placed his hands over his ears. "Damned screeching harpies... surely I've earned my peace and quiet this evening." He got up, pulled his chair to the opposite side of the hearth. "I'm just saying... Sister Elena may have put your aunt in touch with Ayaviri. Picture it... his wife was dead, he was about to be imprisoned, he may have appealed to the monastery to find someone to care for his child."

"Wait, *now* I have it." Rosa stood, assuming a Vaudevillian pose. "Your father left you in the turnstile, and Sister Elena contacted Sister Jane to find someone to adopt you." She placed the back of her hand across her forehead and continued. "It's like your all-time favorite old-timey Hallmark drama, called *Cradle Song*! Just think you might have grown up in the cloisters, like the girl in that story. The nuns would've mothered you and grieved when you left to marry, but they would've made your wedding dress, and given you away, and you would've marched down the aisle of Santa Maria Monastery, just like in the story... that is, if you hadn't been adopted." Rosa draped herself across the sofa and leaned back with a satisfied smile.

Carlos applauded. "Fine performance, Rosa, only it's a most unlikely plot, especially in Joanna's case. Still, Ayaviri might have gotten help from Sister Elena."

Joanna slowly drained her glass of chicha and reached for the jug to replenish it. She scrutinized Carlos and suddenly swiveled toward Rosa. "Do you remember I told you Auntie Jane insisted—absolutely insisted—I visit Sister Elena? She kept calling to remind me."

"So you're thinking Sister Jane was tossing you a clue, despite her promise to conceal the identity of the person who arranged your adoption," Carlos said.

"Joanna, you may be onto something," Rosa said. "Let's go confront Sister Elena on Monday morning."

Chapter 17

Monday morning Joanna contacted Santa Maria Monastery seeking permission to visit Sister Elena. The extern nun informed her that the professed nuns were on retreat for the entire week, preparing for a major feast day celebration of the monastery's patron saint. However, an appointment *could be* scheduled for early the following week.

Exasperated, Joanna made the appointment for the following Monday. She decided to proceed with her original plans to travel to Ayacucho. Meanwhile, she'd get some work done at the observatory.

She'd been assigned two graduate assistants and they were waiting to see her first thing this morning to work on the special project Dr. Alderez had given her. Hurriedly, she sent off an email to Ms. Sanchez requesting that she arrange an appointment with Dr. Geraldo Jiménez for tomorrow afternoon.

Finishing her morning rituals, Joanna left early for the lab and stopped at the observatory restaurant to get coffee. Carrying the coffee outside, she stepped onto the open wrought-iron viewing area surrounding the tower. The nearly 360° view from the top of the tower was a source of wonder for her.

She looked northeast toward a hill above the city where the Inca fortress was located. All the guidebooks said Sacsayhuamán had been constructed of massive boulders, weighing tons, which formed defensive zigzag walls meant to outline the teeth of the puma.

She pulled her tablet from her briefcase and tapped the Apps icon for historic landmarks in Cuzco. Mainly, she was interested in the Inca shrines situated within the old city boundaries.

The website noted that two river courses, the Tullumayo on the eastern boundary, and the Huatanay on the western boundary, had been diverted to form the shape of the puma. The two rivers came together at the lower end of the city, beyond Coricancha—one of the major shrines—to form the tail of the puma. Old maps showed the rivers but, in modern times, one of the courses was no longer clearly discernible on the landscape.

Huaycaypata Plaza, now the Plaza des Armas, in the puma's heart and the lowest part of Cuzco, had been filled with two feet of beach sand brought up over the Andes from the Pacific Ocean. In addition, dirt from regions conquered by the Incas was mixed with the ocean sand in that plaza, along with particles of gold. That particular area was apparently very symbolic and represented the center of the empire. The name "Cuzco'" meant *navel of the world.*

Sister Elena's myth referred to that in much the same way. Joanna knew sacred centers all over the world were called the "navel," or the "center of the world." The *abyss*—the maelstrom—in mythology was located below that sacred center and was where the vertical "world tree" connected, like an axis, the world above with the world below. Even the temple in Jerusalem was designated *center of the world* by the Hebrew people.

Joanna sipped her coffee and shivered in the morning chill. The website said the Incas flooded Cuzco once a year, opening the dam of a reservoir located high up on Sacsayhuamán—the mouth of the puma—to permit the water to flow across the city, through the rivers—the outline of the body of the puma—and on out near or through Coricancha, the Sun Temple.

That temple was located near what was probably the birth canal of the puma. In the geoglyph, it would be located where the sun intersected the Milky Way's branches. That is, if Cuzco's puma shape represented the Milky Way. The signs were there that it did.

Gifts and the remains of yearly sacrifices were thrown into the Inca "manmade'" flood, which carried them down north eastward to the Urubamba River. From there, the river flowed northwest, toward Ollantaytambo, and on out, ultimately to the Amazon, and thus to the Atlantic Ocean. Did the Incas believe they were sending the gifts to the "celestial sea" out in the universe, out to Viracocha who had left Earth via the celestial sea?

Joanna ordered another coffee. Where had the time gone! She

grabbed her computer, put it in her backpack, and dashed across the quadrangle to meet with her assistants. She was excited about her Cuzco Puma as Milky Way theory—it had elegance and symmetry!

Cuzco lay above the Sacred Valley. Maybe it symbolized the "other" branch of the Milky Way. All over the world, ancient peoples shaped features along their rivers—for example, the Nile and the Tigris and Euphrates—to conform to the Milky Way.

In the minds of people in past civilizations, the Milky Way began as one river, flowing from the *land of the gods*—the headwaters—and then separated into two branches flowing around the sacred center, the navel, the *land of the living*. Eventually, it came together again at the other end, the *land of the dead*, where it flowed, once again, back to the gateway of the *land of the gods,* in an eternal cycle. It looked as though the Incas had depicted that same symbolic image in the way they'd shaped Cuzco, as well as the way they'd engineered the Sacred Valley.

Actually, it appeared that the image was ubiquitous throughout the empire, spread across the landscape of the Andes from the north, in Quito, all the way to the southern tip of Chile.

What was stunning about the concept was how well it matched the images of the Milky Way Galaxy as viewed from the Hubble Space Telescope. The galaxy was spiral, but viewed from Earth it appeared to have a long single "arm" that separated into two branches surrounding a central open area, and then it came back together to form another single "arm."

Recently astronomers had found a monstrous black hole in that central area, from which the material for life forms may have emanated, possibly carried by Fermi Bubbles throughout the galaxy. Maybe Cuzco, the Center of the World, high above the Sacred Valley, represented that place where the living could remain in constant communication with the Land of the Dead and the Land of the Gods.

Dr. Alderez had asked if she'd be willing to work on the creation of a star map of the Sacred Valley, as it would have looked in the early years of the Inca Empire. It might help in determining if recently discovered geoglyphs on mountainsides actually mirrored the constellations during that time span.

The wall chart she'd hung at her apartment, on which she hoped to plot major Inca shrines that figured in Sister Elena's myth, would come in handy to sort out the material she and the students would generate. In fact, the map Dr. Alderez had asked her to construct should intermesh with the work she was doing for Sister Elena.

Joanna and her assistants spent the morning generating a list of symbols and elements: numbers, colors, animals, gods, directions, sequences, and patterns found in the Incan myths. They compared their list to material in scholarly works outlining certain common features in myths from around the world—features which might well be recurring because of their common astronomical valences.

Around 11:00 o'clock, she made plans to meet with the graduate assistants later in the week and thanked them as they headed off to classes. She stopped by Ms. Sanchez's desk to inform her that she intended to spend the afternoon at her apartment working on the items she and her assistants had selected to test the myths and symbols under scrutiny.

Ms. Sanchez handed her the info for her appointment with Dr. Geraldo Jiménez. It was scheduled for tomorrow at 1:00 p.m., and the round-trip ticket would be waiting at the departure gate for her.

"Gosh, how much do I owe you—I didn't expect you to book the flight," Joanna said.

"Está bien, it was less than 335 soles. You may pay me when I get the credit card bill."

Joanna hugged her. "Expect a special gift from Ayacucho."

She had finished organizing everything for her afternoon's work at the apartment when her cell phone rang. She saw Michael's number, touched the "speaker" button and laid the phone near her computer.

"Michael! How wonderful to hear your voice! I tried calling you Sunday. They said you were out."

"We had a mission in the Gobi Desert."

She waited for him to continue. The phone was silent.

"You must be exhausted. Geeze, I've missed you so much."

"You wouldn't be missing me if you were in Mongolia."

"It's just I can't leave now, not when I'm close to finding something. Carlos located my parents' real names. My birth mother is dead and my father is missing, but a professor in Ayacucho may know about him, I'm going there tomorrow." She wouldn't mention her father's terrorist activities, not yet.

"Mother's getting anxious about the wedding. What should I tell her?"

"Tell her I'm not leaving Peru until I find some trace of my family."

"Joanna, for God's sake, your mother's dead, and it doesn't sound to me like your father wants to be found—"

"But somebody sure wanted *me* to be found or they wouldn't have sent that letter."

"Joanna, I don't have time to talk, I've got to run—I'll call you soon."

Ms. Sanchez had scheduled Joanna's flight so she could arrive two hours earlier than the appointment. It gave her an opportunity to stroll around the campus of the University of Huamanga and acquaint herself with the area.

It was good to have time to walk the same streets her father had probably walked. She imagined him discussing ideas with fellow students.

She'd Googled the op-ed columns he'd written. He had definitely been a student at this university. It was clear why Ayaviri had attracted radical followers.

He'd argued the case of the Quechuas within the historical context of other conquered minorities and had laid out the logic of the premise that the social condition of the majority is always enhanced when a minority has lawful rights and privileges. Obviously, his position had not been popular with the establishment.

The library attracted her attention and she went in to peer at the display cases of priceless documents from the 16th Century. Afterwards, on her way back to the History Department, she stopped frequently to admire the many historical and architecturally important buildings.

The university bell tower announced the hour as she approached the receptionist's desk.

Señorita Inés informed her that Professor Jiménez was still meeting with a student, but would see her in about half an hour. She offered Joanna a cup of tea and showed her to a conference room where she could wait.

Joanna decided to spend the time working on Sister Elena's myth. Pulling out a map of Cuzco from her purse, she placed it on the table next to the copy of the myth. She sketched an outline of the puma with a red marker and circled the sacred sites in blue. So the puma was meant to mirror the Milky Way... but why a puma, specifically?

She trolled her brain, remembering and recording on the notepad what she'd read about the puma as a symbolic creature in the Andes. Sister Elena's myth also seemed to be about the symbolism of some place called the Llama Road.

The china cup warmed Joanna's hands as she breathed in the tea's orange spice aroma. She looked up and saw, through the conference room windows, a blur of movement. A man approached, opened the door, and entered.

"Dr. Nickels-Stewart, to what do I owe the honor of this visit from such a famous personage?"

"I'm not—that is, thank you, sir. I appreciate that you could give me a few minutes of your time. It's a long story and I'll try to make it brief."

"Please, let's go to my office where we can be more comfortable."

He fit the stereotype of the aging professor, beard neatly trimmed, hair white and just touching his shirt collar, no tie, and a tweed suit. He had a kindly face, a distracted manner, and eyes that resembled computer screens processing data at warp speed.

"I've read in the papers about the work you're doing in astrophysics at the Cuzco Observatory. It's an area of interest of mine too, because of the astronomy in ancient myths, which, of course, form part of my own scholarly endeavors."

"I've only recently had the opportunity to study Andean myths. I'm looking forward to examining your research into their history," she said. It would have been helpful to have him examine Sister Elena's myth but the nun had imposed secrecy. Maybe in the future she could get permission to discuss it with him.

Joanna enjoyed seeing another person's office. The artifacts displayed revealed much about personalities and passions. Dr. Jiménez's interest was obviously ancient history.

He sat at the desk, laid his eyeglasses to one side of the green blotter, leaned forward, and indicated that she should sit in the chair opposite. "Now, tell me, my dear, what may I do for you?"

"I guess the best way to explain my reason for being here is to mention the name Alejandro Huaman Ayaviri."

Dr. Jiménez reached for his glasses, put them back on, and studied her intently, waiting for her to continue.

"I was adopted from Peru as an infant. Recently, information was given to me indicating Ayaviri is my father. I'd hoped you might know something about him."

The professor leaned further back in his chair and looked at Joanna with greater interest.

"Well, that's certainly a name from my past," he said. "Ayaviri was a student in several of my classes. A professor hopes for at least one student like that in a long career. He grasped subtle nuances, was very inquisitive, wanting to probe ideas, trying to understand the complex influences that shaped them."

"Do you know if he had other children?"

"He married shortly before being arrested and imprisoned. I don't recall any children."

"Was he originally from Ayacucho? Were his parents here?"

"The old files are housed—I should say buried—in our central administration building. My secretary will make a request for exhumation—leave your particulars with her and she'll mail you any pertinent information. His last known address, as well as parent names and addresses should be listed in those records." He hesitated. "You know, I do seem to recall that it was reported he died in prison recently, although I've heard rumors...."

Ever since Carlos had revealed her father's identity, she'd constructed elaborate scenes in which they'd met and she'd talk with him about his ideas for the betterment of the Quechua people. It was hard to accept that he might— "I'm sorry, sir, I missed your last statement."

"I said I'd heard recently of a new group, ¡Dése Prisa. Their leader sounds very much like Ayaviri. I'm not the only one to have noticed that—there are rumors all over the highlands that he may still be alive, that he escaped from prison, and the authorities hushed the whole thing up out of embarrassment. It certainly wouldn't be the first time they've concealed such matters."

"Do you know anyone who might know the truth of those rumors?"

The professor shook his head. "I'm so sorry. I wish I could be of more help."

The search had become relentless like the endless sweeps she'd made across Rhea's barren landscape, but at least Saturn's moon had ultimately offered up a few of its secrets.

"Wait a minute!" Dr. Jiménez said. "There *is* something—something you must see."

Joanna watched him rummage in a file cabinet, feeling like an eight-year-old with her birthday present next to her place at the dining table, having to wait until she'd eaten her dinner to open it.

"He wrote a paper," Professor Jiménez said, "on his ancestors—a most interesting paper—used original sources, said they'd been handed down in his family. He was descended from Sapa Inca Huáscar the last *legitimate* Emperor of Peru. Atahualpa, who is usually portrayed as the last emperor, was a younger son by a Quito concubine of Huayna Capàc's. On his deathbed, Huayna Capac appointed him to govern *only* the Northern provinces, leaving Huáscar to be the sole Sapa Inca in Cuzco. But, forgive me, I digress…I have that paper somewhere…."

He buzzed his secretary, "Señorita Inés, please locate my Primary Documents File and make a copy of a paper you'll find in it, last name Ayaviri. Be sure to copy the two documents clipped to it. Thank you."

"Dr. Jiménez, has anyone else been here to question you about Ayaviri?"

"Not that I recall, I would've remembered such a person."

"There is someone who may come inquiring about my father. He's about six feet, Caucasian, has jet-black hair with a silver streak cutting through it on the left side. If he should come here, please inform the special services police in Lima. A note was found in his pocket having your name and my father's name on it. We believe he's been stalking me."

Dr. Jiménez returned to his desk and placed his glasses once more to the side of the blotter. He looked pensively at Joanna and then stared at some point slightly above her head.

She pulled her wallet from her purse and took out the photo of the young Quechua man she'd found in Aunt Jane's portmanteau. "Do you recognize this?"

The professor held the picture, smiling, studying it. "Ayaviri was Inca royalty, you know. He's wearing the *borla*—that red fringe you see across his forehead. It signifies the kingship of the Sapa Inca. What a magnificent ruler he would've made."

Joanna reached for the photo. "I wish I could have met him."

There was a knock at the door. The secretary entered. "Thank you Inés, please give those to Dr. Nickels-Stewart."

"Gracias," Joanna said, glancing at the copies of the papers her father had written. "Where would Ayaviri have gotten original sixteenth-century documents?"

"The Inca aristocracy learned Spanish very quickly. We know of many instances in which they wrote documents, even whole books, to chronicle the exploits of their people in an attempt to record events before the memory was forgotten. Three very famous examples of such authors were Garsilasco de la Vega, Guaman Poma de Ayala, and Juan de Santacruz Pachakuti Yamqui Salcamaygua."

The intercom buzzed. "Sir, your next class is in fifteen minutes."

Joanna stood, extended her hand, but the professor turned away and moved to the credenza behind his desk. He took down a painting of El Misti Volcano that was hanging on the wall above it. There was an opening behind the painting. In it was a carved wooden box approximately eight by eleven by two inches deep. He lifted the box from the recessed area and walked toward Joanna.

"Your father said a very strange thing when he gave me this box. 'Someday, someone may come searching for me,' he said. 'Please keep this and give it to that person.'"

The professor lowered his gaze and looked directly at Joanna as he handed her the box. "This contains the very precious records written by Ayaviri's ancestors in 1545. I believe it was meant for you, Nusta."

Joanna hugged the box to her breast. "It has been a privilege to meet you," she said.

He stepped back and bowed to her. "My dear, it's I who am honored, beyond measure, to have met Ayaviri's daughter."

Chapter 18

The plane ride back to Cuzco was short, but long enough to allow Joanna to read the papers her father had written.

She let her hands rest on the first page for a moment, seeing her father in the faded photograph she'd shown Professor Jiménez. His words streamed effortlessly across the page, speaking directly to the reader, to her. Moments passed, and she became lost in the world he'd created from his ancestors' writings.

After a while, she put down her father's manuscript and picked up the source document titled *Mita*. She recalled that the word signified the concept of reciprocal obligations the Sapa Inca and his people owed to one another and to Viracocha.

MITA

High on a cliff, opposite Old Mountain, a wondrous bird turned eastward, his golden face and azure head mirroring the sun's own image in the sky. He flapped lustrous green wings and shook himself, settling each feather into place, and sang an exuberant greeting song to the rising light.

He was perched on a platform, built by the kuraka and people of the ayllu, on a promontory overlooking the Urubamba River. It served as a lookout post and was the place where gifts of sacrifice were offered to Inti, the sun god.

Each morning, on that platform, Huarana, the kuraka's eight-year-old daughter, sang the required greeting song to Inti. She was proud of her mita that made her a valued member of her ayllu. Because of her piercing sweet bird-voice, she had been chosen to sing the greeting and awaken the village to daily work.

This morning she had paused on her way to the platform. She was entranced with the scene around her. Hummingbirds sipped nectar from pendulous fuchsia cups entwined in the rocks above. Orchids, in rainbow colors, clung to fern-like tree branches interlacing high overhead, and the green first light of dawn filtered down through the fronds, illuminating huge yellow butterflies floating lazily through perfume-scented air.

The secluded spot was a favorite refuge for Huarana and her parrot Coco. They often lingered for hours absorbing the beauty.

She sat for a moment on the outcropping of moss-covered rock, closed her eyes, and imagined herself soaring with the butterflies, tasting nectar. The insects droned hypnotically, lulling her to sleep.

The greeting song awakened her. She shook her small tan body, rubbed sleep from huge emerald green eyes, and scrambled along the narrow rock ledge, stepping cautiously to avoid the abyss at the edge. The sun god rose ever higher in the sky.

"Oh, Inti, please forgive me, I didn't mean to fall asleep. Mama will be furious. I've failed my mita. What will I do? Inti, please help me!"

The sun god, choosing not to answer, traveled upward toward mist-enshrouded Old Mountain. Huarana's heartbeat joined the rushing river torrent, sounding like the glacier-fed waters pouring over boulders thousands of feet below.

Placing one foot in front of the other, she circled the chiseled ledge leading to the platform. She rounded the cliff and made her way onto the level space with its low wall of stacked stones.

Coco was perched on the wall's edge where it jutted out over the river valley. His soprano voice, sounding exactly like her's, echoed across the mountains and through the cannon walls.

Huarana hated going near the edge of that platform. Sacrificial llamas tossed from those heights, fell spiraling in ever-smaller circles, crying out with the same terror she felt.

She gasped at the danger, but the beauty awed her. Far below, the dark foliage breathed wispy clouds that rose with mist from the river, while across the gorge Old Mountain appeared in ghostly outline against the brightening sky.

Tearing herself from the view, she turned toward the parrot and noticed his eyes flashing yellow in excitement. Keeping her eyes on the bird, walking toward him, she willed him not to fly out over the gorge.

He knew the greeting song well and skillfully improvised high notes only he could reach. She blended her voice with his, singing the haunting, slow nostalgic notes, telling of the human heart's love and longing for life. The melody suddenly increased in tempo and burst forth with high-pitched trilling sounds, announcing that Inti stood atop Old Mountain once more, bringing light to the world. The song ended, the parrot flapped his wings and squawked, prancing joyfully on his precarious perch.

Huarana was grateful to Coco for serving her mita and amazed at how smart he was. The parrot had taken her place today so the sun god would not fail to be greeted at the very moment he rose from the underworld.

In the village below, on the banks of the Vilcanota, the River of the Sun, now called Urubamba, the ayllu took up the song, repeating it as they readied themselves to serve Inti and the Sapa

Inca. The dawning was Inti's promise that he would light their way, giving them life for another day.

Across the river gorge, higher still, up on the ridge that joined Old Mountain to Young Mountain, a carillon of voices intoned the same greeting song.

That song, sung by Inti's Brides accompanied the sun god on his journey across the world. His brides, the acllas, priestesses of the Moon, kept constant vigil on Old Mountain. Their mita was to assist the sun in his daily journey.

Huarana, ashamed of her own failure, thought about how the acllas never neglected their mita. The very life of the world depended on their devotion to their duty. That duty included tending the sacred fire that was the spirit of Viracocha, The Invisible One, and his fire must never be extinguished.

She lingered, listening to the acllas' song, while Coco fluttered his wings in anticipation. It was time for breakfast, time for them to leave the platform and make their way down the mountainside to the small stone house, their cancha, with its ichu grass roof that was home to the family.

The cancha was built low on the mountainside in a small clearing above the river. It was near enough to the riverbank so water could easily be obtained, but high enough to assure the family wasn't swept away during autumn floods. Mama Willa was standing near the door of the cancha and waved as the little girl and her parrot increased their headlong passage down the path.

Huarana hurled herself into mama's arms, and Coco swooped around several times, landing on her shoulder.

"Mama," he squawked.

"Hello, Coco," she said, laughing, offering him her hand to

stand on.

"Ha, Ha, Ha," Coco chortled, losing his breath in imitation of Huarana's spasms of laughter.

Huarana wanted to confess her failed mita, but mama wasn't showing any signs of anger. Maybe it was best to keep the secret between herself and the parrot. Surely, Coco wouldn't tell.

"Huarana, please sit on the stone bench, I need to braid your hair."

Mama Willa pulled the long shiny black hair into place and tied it with colorful bands depicting tribal symbols that had been woven on the handloom she'd brought from the jungle.

"These bands are so pretty," Huarana said. "I like to wear them every day."

The braiding finished, Huarana stood and held out her hand for Coco to perch. The two followed Mama Willa inside the cancha where Coco fluttered to Huarana's shoulder as she sat at the low table used for meals.

"You and Coco hurry and eat your corn mush. You must go to the terraces and tell your father I'll be later than usual with his breakfast."

Coco leaned toward Huarana, begging her to give him a bite of bread from her mouth. The parrot wanted to be fed as his mother had fed him when he was a nestling.

Most mornings Huarana refused, but this morning she didn't mind. Coco deserved a special treat.

The food mama was cooking would be taken by her and the other women of the ayllu to the crop terraces where the men had gone immediately after the greeting song. Huarana watched mama intently, trying to gauge her reactions about Inti's greeting song. Sensing her stare, Willa glanced over with a loving expression.

"Huarana, the greeting song was especially beautiful this morning. Have you been practicing?"

"Especially beautiful," the parrot mimicked. Huarana laughed, took a last bite of the mush, and smiled up at mama. "Coco helped me."

"But I heard only one voice!"

"We've learned to make our voices sound like one." Huarana lowered her eyes and concentrated on stroking the parrot's head. She hated being deceitful to mama. She needed to run away before she blurted out the story of her failed mita.

"May Coco and I go now, Mama? I ate as much as I could."

"Watch Coco, you know how angry your father gets when the parrot strips the corn. We really can't afford such waste. Just give the bird one of the cobs to nibble, and that'll prevent him from getting into trouble."

Huarana jumped up, blew a kiss to Willa, and bounded off with Coco swooping after her.

The parrot was Huarana's best friend. She laughed at his antics while he flew ahead as she ran. Now and then, he'd circle behind and pull her braids with his extended talons.

He'd come to live in their ayllu as a newly fledged nestling when father brought mama to the community after they were married. Coco and mama had been born in the dense jungles that lay beyond the eastern slopes of the mountains.

How wonderful it must be to live out there. Father said the jungles were very much like their home here below Old Mountain. He said the cloud forests here—with orchids, insects of every variety, condors, small parrots, cocks-of-the rock, quetzals, pumas, spectacled bears, and woolly monkeys—were just high jungles.

Huarana stopped walking and looked up toward the royal village that rested on the narrow ridge high above the river. People of her ayllu told legends about how the village was built in the shape of a condor. She wished she could see it.

Terraces stair-stepped up the mountainside, even up to the highest peaks, and they were filled with flowering plants and shrubs of every imaginable color. Father and mother had few fights, but they did argue over the flowers on Old Mountain's terraces.

"Why does the Sapa Inca use those terraces to grow flowers? Shouldn't they be used for food crops?" Mama had asked.

"Those flower-filled terraces are meant to show the love and praise we owe Con Ticci Viracocha. After all, the Sacred Village and gardens belong to him," Father had said.

Huarana dreamed about going up there, but she knew only the Sapa Inca, close members of the royal family, the temple priests, and the acllas with their servants, were permitted to visit or live up on the mountain. Unless she was chosen as a servant to the acllas, she would never have the opportunity to see the sacred village up close.

She didn't really want to leave her family. To be chosen to serve in the acllahuasi would mean that she would be shut away from her family for at least thirty years—that was a long time—too long for Huarana.

The parrot was begging for attention, picking up one of her braids and trying to fly away with it. "Coco, stop it, you're going to snatch me bald!"

The bird circled, landed on her shoulder, pulled at her earring, and flashed his eyes yellow in anger. Flapping his wings once again, he lifted off.

Soaring high above Huarana, he spied the shiny green cornstalks with golden succulent kernels draped in dark silk tassels on the terraces below. He plunged toward the tallest stalks.

Huarana screamed, "No, Coco! No!"

She saw her father glance up in alarm as she scrambled down the terrace retaining wall.

"Be careful, Huarana," he yelled as he extended his hand, inviting Coco to land. He stroked the parrot's head, plucked an ear of corn, gave it to the bird, and placed him on a nearby tree limb. "It seems Coco wants to help us pick corn today," he said.

"Father, may I help? It'll take Coco a while to strip that cob. I won't have to mind him. I can pick the corn and put it in the bags just like you. I almost forgot, mama said she'd be late with your breakfast."

"You may help for a little while. Truth be told, I do enjoy having you and Coco here, despite his naughtiness."

Huarana laughed and grabbed a bag. She moved along the row on the terrace above her father, pulling the corn from the stalks. The cobs were huge, and the kernels made Huarana think of Inti's golden disc in Cuzco. She'd seen the disc when her family traveled to Cuzco for a special holiday.

The high priest had stood on Inti's balcony at Coricancha, above the golden garden, holding the disc high to reflect Inti's dawning first light. She'd never forgotten how her heart tinkled like a bell at the sight.

The corn kernels tasted so good when mama roasted them. Huarana also liked the bread mama made from the cornmeal ground by the ayllu women. They ground the corn kernels by rocking the half-moon tuna inside the maray grindstone. She often begged mama to let her grind the corn kernels, but the mush mama cooked from the ground corn wasn't one of Huarana's favorite foods.

The bags of corn picked by the ayllu men were divided into three piles. One pile was for Inti's priests and acllas, the second was for the Sapa Inca so he could feed the warriors and needy tribes throughout the empire, and the third pile was for their own ayllu, their village. Father said this was a good practice, because everyone benefited from it.

Huarana liked thinking about helping others. She lifted her head and noticed father looking in her direction.

"Huarana, your greeting song was especially beautiful this morning," he said.

Huarana and Coco spent the morning helping father and sharing in the tasty meal that Mama Willa and the ayllu women brought to feed the men.

Now it was time for her to gather the herbs the family used to flavor foods and make medicines. Mama had taught her how to find the helpful plants, and she liked that job almost as much as singing the greeting song.

She waved to her father and climbed carefully down the steps of the terrace with Coco clinging to her shoulder. She would check along the river's bank for the cantut flowers. They were good for sweetening the corn mush, which made it taste better.

At the bottom terrace, Huarana halted. A young boy, about her age, was sitting on the retaining wall sobbing and biting a balled up piece of his sleeve.

Drawing near, she paused, willing him to see her. It wasn't polite to interrupt. She stomped her feet, hoping he'd notice.

"Has something hurt you?" she asked, unable to wait any longer. "Coco can sing for you—it always helps when I'm sad."

The boy jumped at the sound of her voice. Huarana turned to run.

"It's alright. Don't go," he said. "You're very kind. What's your name? What does your parrot sing?"

"I'm Huarana. All the songs I know, and some he learned from mama's people out in the jungle."

"Make him sing a jungle song," the boy said, sitting down again.

"I'll have to start it." Huarana began to sing, "The caiman swallowed the anaconda …"

Yellow haloes encircled the pupils of Coco's eyes. "… who swallowed the capybara, who swallowed the parrot, who screamed 'Let me out of here,' and they were all so frightened, the caiman threw up, the anaconda threw up, the capybara threw up, and the parrot flew away. Oh, the parrot flew away, he flew away home, the parrot flew away home." Coco ended the song with shrill cackling sounds like a child laughing and losing its breath.

The parrot repeated the song over-and-over again and, each time, laughed even more uproariously. The boy, wiping his eyes with his sleeve, joined Huarana in the infectious laughter.

"Why were you so sad?" Huarana asked. That wasn't polite, but she needed to know.

"My parents were buried up there." There was a catch in his voice. "My name is Joré Inca. My uncle is the Uillac Umu, the High Priest of Coricancha. He entombed my parents under the Temple of the Sun, up there." He pointed once again up toward the Sacred Village. "I wasn't allowed to cry. Afterwards, I came down here to hide my tears."

"That's terrible. What happened to them?"

"They had some disease. The Uillac Umu said he couldn't cure it. We think they got it from the seacoast, brought by the chasquis, who run the relays to bring seafood up here and to Cuzco."

Huarana had never lost anyone close to her, she felt sad for Joré. "I know you miss your parents. I would miss mine terribly."

"Aren't you the girl who sings the greeting song to Inti?"

"Coco helps me."

"We heard you just before the death ritual started this morning. Our relatives at the funeral were impressed. My uncle told them he'd chosen you to sing the greeting song because you're very talented."

Huarana and Coco had returned to the terraces each day to visit with Joré while he spent the required month of mourning for his parents at Old Mountain. Each day he laughed more frequently, relaxing and telling her with excitement about his life in Cuzco.

At the end of that month, her parents informed her that the

high priest had selected her to serve and learn in Cuzco. They were so proud of her. She would become an aclla by choice, a chosen one. She guessed it was a great honor, but she wasn't exactly happy about leaving Old Mountain.

"My uncle said you're going to Cuzco to live in the acllahuasi," Joré said.

"My heart hurts to leave my parents. Have your heart's empty places been filled?"

"... heart's empty places ...," Coco echoed, squawking loudly.

"Yes, but there's about to be a new one," Joré said, and looked away.

Joanna glanced out the small window of the plane and gasped at the nearness of the Andean peaks. They seemed to rush right up and then recede just as quickly, now a high granite triangle covered in fuzzy lush green moss, and then, a higher mountain in a wash of dazzling snow... her homeland.

She'd marveled at the story she'd just read, that had introduced her to her great—to the nth degree, as Carlos would say—grandmother, the woman for whom she'd apparently been named. The view blurred. Joanna reached up to flick away tears.

So, Huarana had lived near Old Mountain, which was Machu Picchu, and had been chosen to greet the sun god because of her beautiful voice. Then she'd become a *chosen woman*. Rosa had said Huarana meant *sacred*.

There was so much more she wanted to know about her ancestors. She had to get busy, time was running out, and she still had to find her father. The professor said there might be a chance he was still alive.

She'd already arranged to tour Machu Picchu next weekend, since she had a three-day holiday from the lab. Rosa couldn't come along because of a prior engagement in Lima.

It was probably best to go alone. She'd be able to reflect on and absorb the atmosphere of the place. It would be enormously exciting, knowing Huarana had once lived there.

The second source document lay on the tray, inviting her to open it. She was soon lost in its pages.

THE TALISMAN

Joré and his cousin Bethuär hurried out of Amarucancha, the palace belonging to their panaca. Joré was proud to belong to the family of Pachakuti Inca and to live in the palace he'd built. He'd been told the palace was the envy of succeeding Sapa Incas who'd been required to build their own palaces around Huacaypata Plaza, after they'd succeeded to the kingship.

The panaca palace, Amarucancha, was located near the acllahuasi with a direct view of Coricancha, the Sun Temple. It was not far from the Wisdom Academy, toward which the boys were hastening to avoid being late for the first gong.

"My tutor makes me memorize the sacred stories recorded on the quipus," Joré said. "It's such a waste of time. Isn't that why we have the quipus?"

"I hate to be the one to tell you this, but my father told me the amautas in the Wisdom Academy instruct in exactly the same way," Bethuär said.

"I don't know why I need to attend the academy since I have my own tutor," Joré said.

He liked being free to choose his afternoon activities. His tutor had told him when he attended the academy he'd be in school all day.

"Great-grandfather Sapa Inca Huayna Capàc, on his deathbed, commanded that I should be sent to Cuzco to attend the academy for the final year before I undergo the courage ordeals," Bethuär said.

"I'm glad you're here, otherwise I wouldn't be able to bear this confinement. I hope I'm successful in my courage ordeals. I can't wait to have my ears bored. I know it's very painful, but—"

"In Quito, Great-grandfather Huayna Capàc bored my ears just before he died. It wasn't supposed to happen until after I'm tested, but he said he wanted to do it himself."

"Some of the people have been saying that young men of the Royal Family and the sons of the kurakas shouldn't have to undergo such trials," Joré said.

"Great-grandfather told me if we don't face the challenges and survive them, the peace of the empire can't be maintained. He said people who witness the ceremonies tell stories that are retold throughout the empire. Even citizens unable to attend the games hear about our heroic deeds, and all the people learn to fear and respect the might of the empire."

Bethuär had been walking beside Joré. He stopped and turned to face him. "The most important thing is that we become real men by surviving the ordeals. If we didn't do that we'd be useless to the empire."

"But still, there should be an easier way to prove our manliness."

"Quick, Joré, pluck an eyelash! Blow it to Viracocha. Ask forgiveness. You mustn't question the wisdom of the ancestors!"

"May I tell you something? Please keep it a secret, please promise."

Joré waited for Bethuär to nod agreement and cross his hands over his heart.

"I'm terrified about the courage ordeals," he said "I'm afraid of what we might have to do, and I'm very afraid that I'll fail. I've heard horrible stories from the older boys—"

"First of all, the men who have been through the ordeals never speak of them except to their favored sons. That's part of their code," Bethuär said. "Those boys are teasing you! Sapa Inca Huayna Capàc said we don't have to worry if we study and learn all we can from the amautas. He said the most important thing of all is something they can't teach us and that's to believe in ourselves. We have to learn that on our own."

"I envy you. You don't seem to be afraid of anything," Joré said.

"What's your greatest fear?" Bethuär asked. "Don't answer, just think about it!"

During the long months of preparation, Joré trembled every time the ordeals were mentioned. He'd heard that participants who hadn't prepared well were badly injured and some even died.

The question his cousin had asked last year, "What's your greatest fear?" had been on his mind every day, and now he thought he knew the answer. His greatest fear had to do with dark underground places. He'd feared them ever since his parents had been entombed on Old Mountain.

Old Mountain! Thinking of that sacred place always made him think of Huarana. He'd often wondered how she was doing in the Cuzco Acllahuasi. It was strange to think she lived only a short distance away from the Wisdom Academy and he wasn't even allowed to see her.

Joré had been fasting on bread and water for a week. For three days he'd had to endure endless knowledge drills in which the amautas questioned him about Incan creation stories. He was surprised they weren't interested in how much he knew about all the other subjects he'd studied.

Yesterday, and last night, he'd been required to keep an extreme fasting vigil, but his most difficult trial was scheduled for today. He would have to find his way through the labyrinth at Qenqo, in total darkness. After that, he and the other initiates would have to race northwest, along the Vilcanota, the Urubamba—an endurance trial that would make him a warrior.

The ear-boring ceremony followed that, and then there would be a fabulous feast. It was the special celebration of Capàc Raymi, the Summer Solstice, and Joré would break his fast by feasting with the mummies of his ancestors and the lineage huacas of all the tribes.

Conch shells were blown at sunset on the day preceding Capàc Raymi. They sounded all over the mountains, announcing the opening of the Land of the Dead. The spirits of the ancestors would return along the Llama Road to visit with the living for a brief period.

Earlier in the morning, his only sibling, Nusta Chola, had visited Cuzco Acllahuasi. She had come to see him afterwards and had given him a small pouch embroidered in gold thread by one of the acllas—a good luck talisman. "The aclla told me you should carry it with you," Princess Chola had told him. "It will protect you."

The chasquis waited by the door with a sedan chair to bear Joré to Qenqo. Climbing quickly onto the seat, he straightened his back and closed his eyes. He would use the time to rehearse survival strategies.

The runners began at a trot and gradually increased speed. Joré was traveling so fast he had to grab the arms of the chair and hang on with all his might.

After about ten minutes, he was rudely dumped in the middle of a level circular area in front of a cave. The priests had instructed the initiates to assemble in silence and wait. Joré sat on the ground, trying to calm himself. He breathed deeply and exhaled until his lungs almost collapsed.

The Uillac Umu, his uncle, the high priest at Coricancha, arrived and assisted the other priests to blindfold the boys. Afterwards, a prayer was intoned and the priests were directed to lead the initiates into various tunnels that branched out from several directions into the main labyrinth.

Each initiate, left in one of the tunnels, had to find his way into the central maze. There were different obstacles in each tunnel that had to be overcome before the maze could be entered. The obstacles were chosen randomly so no one knew exactly what each boy must face. The obstacle could be a puma, a caiman, poisonous snakes, lizards, even poisonous spiders.

Only a young boy's wits, honed by the strategies he'd been taught, would keep him alive. The ordeal had been handed down from the First Time and it was considered a hero's journey to the underworld while the person was still alive.

The initiate set out on the journey desiring greater knowledge and long life. If successful, he was given the greatest gift of all: self-knowledge.

In the impenetrable darkness of the tunnel, the blindfold was taken off. The escorts left quickly. Joré stood alone, shivering.

His chest constricted, his body trembled, breathing seemed impossible. It was as though he'd been entombed.

The remaining air seeped slowly from his lungs. His legs crumpled. He reached out to steady himself and touched cold slimy walls.

Imagining himself lying down, rolling into a ball, he began to scream and cry. He was crying the tears that hadn't been permitted, when his parents died. He was crying with a child's inconsolable abandon.

He slipped slowly toward the ground. He had to stop. He couldn't lie down. He had to keep moving. Where? Which way? What were the strategies? He knew strategies, but which strategies?

He stood tall, extending his arms wide, groping for the walls. His left hand touched cold moist stone again, and he steadied himself, leaning against it, inching his way along until the wall ended.

Cold, musty air streamed in from the left. The pungent smell of feces and wet animal fur choked him. The hairs on his arms stood up. Something was galloping, approaching at incredible speed. He backed against the wall, worried his thumping heart would reveal his location.

Snarling, scratching, pawing, snorting sounds, magnified by the high cavernous walls, assaulted his ears. The thing came closer.

It screamed like a dying woman from somewhere behind his left shoulder. Urine trickled down his legs. The nightmares of his childhood stalked him as he grasped his sides to stop the chills that were shaking him.

He waited. Death was near. It screamed again, almost in his ear, rendering him immobile. He steeled himself, waiting to die.

Suddenly the screams receded and then there was silence. Joré opened his eyes and saw tiny flashes of light snapping about twenty feet ahead. It was difficult to tell if the thing was coming toward him or moving away.

He needed to run. His legs wobbled. His loincloth rubbed wet against his legs. Shame replaced fear. He grasped the cold wall, casting about for some safe place in the darkness before sanity deserted him.

His loincloth would interfere with running. He needed to move it higher. He adjusted his belt and felt something strange dangling from it.

"The talisman," he shouted. The contours of the embroidered symbols, their outlines worked in raised gold threads, seemed alive beneath his fingertips.

What did they symbolize? Why hadn't he looked at them more carefully this morning? He traced each one again—a caiman and a capybara—but why? Those weren't the usual good luck charms.

"Huarana!" His voice came out in a high-pitched shrill of excitement. "Huarana put those symbols on this pouch!" He laughed, remembering Coco singing *The Caiman and Capybara*.

Holding the pouch tightly to his chest, like a shield, he ran forward, belting *The Caiman and Capybara* song so loudly his voice echoed eerily throughout the chambers of the tunnel.

Each time he ended a round, he laughed with Coco's hysterical laughter, and tears coursed down his cheeks. He sang louder and laughed even harder.

The growling and snarling sounded from a tunnel on his right. He belted out the song again and increased his gait. He jogged faster and felt himself propelled further through the twists and turns of the tunnel.

Was it possible? Had the sound grown fainter? He held the image of Huarana and the parrot in his mind's eye, becoming braver and more creative, adding embellishments of screams and screeches to the song as he loped along.

Halting suddenly, he listened intently. The thing had stopped growling, but the staccato sound of its feet slapping the ground meant it had increased speed.

He guessed he'd covered about a mile by now. Had he reached the *labyrinth*? If he continued following the beast, would he find his way out? It was well known that animals were skilled at escaping from mazes and traps.

The fasting had made him bone-tired, but his senses seemed sharpened. The thought that the beast might lead him out of the maze strengthened his determination to keep going.

He ran automatically now, legs working independently. He was singing at the top of his voice, screaming and laughing up and down the pentatonic scale, mimicking the snarls and screeches of the thing that lurked somewhere ahead of him. Maybe he *could* find a way through the maze.

It was difficult to judge time. He might have been in the tunnel for hours, and his laughter, added to the hunger and thirst, had weakened him. No matter—he couldn't stop, had to go on. It might prove fatal to pause or stop, nor could he slow down.

There was pain in his side, unlike anything he'd ever experienced. It forced him to halt. He bent forward, attempting to slow his breathing so he could listen, gauge where the beast might be.

A fresh breeze brushed his face. He straightened and started running again, pushing the pain away, hearing only his bare feet thudding against the stone floor. He couldn't slow down.

The thing might have found a connecting tunnel and would pounce from behind. Maybe he should stop singing, rest his voice for a moment, but he had to keep jogging.

The pain in his side gripped him again, forcing him to bend double. His breath came in short gasps, and he braced his hands against his knees, crouching forward.

He peered down at his ichu grass sandals. They were soaking

wet from the stream of water trickling along the floor of the tunnel.

"The floor of the tunnel... ," he screamed. "I can *see* the stone floor." He stood up with one last spurt of energy and dashed forward.

Blinding light stunned him as he charged out of the labyrinth into the amphitheater at Qenqo. He shot forward like a javelin, the pain gone, feet moving faster than an escaping guinea pig. He circled the amphitheater, unable to stop running.

From ringside seats, the Coricancha priests and amautas stood, cheering, applauding, shouting, "Joré, Joré, Joré!"

He lifted his head and looked further down the track. The largest puma he'd ever seen was running ahead of him. Stretched horizontally, the stalker of his ordeal was running from *him*.

But pumas didn't attack humans, unless they were extremely hungry! The maze tenders must have made sure the animals were starving. It didn't bear thinking about.

Laughter rang out across the vast amphitheater. The puma was still racing for its life, tongue lolling to the side of its mouth, body slung low to the ground. Now and then, it glanced over its shoulder, making sure it was out of reach of its mad pursuer.

Chasquis jumped into the ring, two lengths in front of the beast, in an effort to corral it, but the puma wasn't cooperating. It was in a race for survival.

Pride surged through Jore. He did two more victory laps before halting in front of the carved-stone throne where Sapa Inca Huáscar sat watching the spectacle. Joré bent low in obeisance.

He ventured a glance upward. The Emperor of all

Tahuantinsuyu stood and bowed toward him, silently saluting him. The crowd went wild, cheering even louder.

"Joré, Joré, Joré!"

Heart heaving, lungs near bursting, he fell to his knees. Tomorrow, he would complete the grueling race from Cuzco to Ollantaytambo, along the Llama Road. That race would consecrate his life as an Inca Warrior to the Invisible One Viracocha. It would prove that he was a warrior.

"But now I know I'm a man," he whispered. He could feel it to the very core of his being. Tomorrow his ear-boring ceremony would make it official—but at this moment, he lived the very meaning of it. *I am a man.*

Tomorrow a great banquet would celebrate the new warriors. All his family and friends would be present, but Huarana wouldn't be there.

She was still in training as an aclla. It was possible he might never see her again. The empty place might never be filled, but he did have her talisman. He would wear it always next to his heart, her talisman that had helped him become a man.

Joanna put the document down. She had worried with Huarana about failing her mita, shared Joré's fear and laughter as he conquered the maze, and now shed tears over Huarana's absence from the ear-boring ceremony. She'd been charmed by the parrot's song and the symbolic message Huarana had embroidered on the pouch for Joré.

How had those two finally gotten together to have children and start the line that eventually produced Ayaviri... and herself? *Nusta,* Professor Jiménez had called her... *Princess.*

Chapter 19

Joanna adjusted her skirt and checked the collar of her blouse for the third time as she stood in front of the locutorio. She'd managed to thwart Rosa's demands to accompany her. This battle she meant to fight alone.

What could possibly cause Sister Elena to be so secretive about helping arrange her adoption? Even if Carlos was right and all the subterfuge was meant to protect her... why conceal the facts now?

The massive door creaked open. She took a seat and waited for the extern nun to bring Sister Elena to the locutorio.

There was a rustle of cloth and the soft scrape of a chair behind the grille. "Benedicite, Joanna, there's no one with me today. Mother Abbess decided I should meet with you unchaperoned."

"Dominus," she gave the automatic response and plopped down, nearly missing the chair. Bracing her hands on the arms, she dragged the chair nearer the grille.

Unchaperoned! It was almost as though they'd been tipped off that she was about to broach a sensitive subject.

"There's something I'd like to ask you before we talk about the myth."

"Of course you may, my dear."

"Carlos has uncovered the fact that my birth mother's maiden name is Almagro. Rosa told me your family name is Almagro. Sister, please tell me, are you and I related in some way?"

Joanna sat very still, listening to the low hum of the flickering wall sconces, determined to let her silence force an explanation.

"Diego de Almagro was quite a virile man." Sister Elena paused. "To a certain extent, one might say everyone in Peru is related."

"No offense, Sister, but that's not what I asked you."

"I know, I know, and I'm sorry. Anything I'm permitted to say to you at this time would be a lie, and I can't lie to you."

"Then please, why can't you tell me the truth!"

"I know it's difficult, but I must ask you to be patient, to wait a little longer. We have so little time today, please let's—"

"—let's stop wasting it!" Dead silence. Joanna coughed and lowered her voice. "I'm sorry, Sister. It's just…I've traveled so far to learn about my parents. I feel like I've turned over every rock in Peru, and now it seems you may know something, and yet you —"

"I will tell you that I did know your birth mother…and believe me, I'm sadly aware that she's dead." A soft sigh came from behind the grille.

"You knew her ..." Joanna struggled with her thoughts as they tumbled into chaos at the unexpected revelation. "... and my father... did you know—"

"There are confidences I've vowed to keep, please don't press me any further."

"But—"

"Now please tell me about the myth, or we'll have to cut our visit short."

Joanna wanted to rage, but Mary Ellen Nickels-Stewart's first commandment of politeness prevented it. She'd comply with the old nun's wishes at this moment, but she wasn't giving up. Not a chance.

"I've done really extensive research," she said, clearing her throat, stuffing back the emotion in her voice. "I think I've discovered some possible clues to its meaning."

"I knew you could do it!"

"Tourist pamphlets say the Sacred Valley replicates the Milky Way. I figured that might be a good place to start. Also, I remembered Dr. Alderez said the Inca architects designed Cuzco in the shape of a Puma, so I decided to look at how both topographical features might fit together."

"We learned about Cuzco's puma shape in grammar school," Sister said.

"The puma is a symbol of Viracocha. As far as I can tell after a cursory look at the sacred sites in Cuzco, it seems that the city might also replicate the Milky Way."

"The city and valley both, you say."

The Incan priest-astronomers told the Spanish Chroniclers that Cuzco was the 'center of the world.' Many old world sites, ancient Jerusalem for instance, were called *navel of the world*—and that always refers to the Land of the Living."

"How fascinating…so Cuzco represents *the navel of the world*—the Land of the Living?"

"Yes, but this is where it gets tricky," Joanna said. "In worldwide mythology, these three lands were perceived as being both vertical *and* horizontal. Cuzco would have occupied a space in the middle of the vertical axis, with the Land of the Gods above and the Land of the Dead below. At the same time, the Land of the Living occupies the same space on the horizontal axis, as Cuzco seems to do."

She paused, grasping for the first time the cognitive expanse of the concepts. "Those images appear to have been stamped on everything in the empire. It just occurred to me that the geoglyphs symbolize everything a person living in the Inca Empire needed to know to live well in all dimensions!"

"I'm amazed, Joanna! That does make a great deal of sense."

"Cuzco, as the Puma, is meant to honor Viracocha, the 'creator god' who brought civilization to the Andes. According to William Sullivan, Viracocha has all the characteristics that would qualify him to be a personification of the planet Saturn."

"Viracocha as Saturn…that's certainly intriguing!" Sister Elena's voice had taken on a new edge of excitement.

"The Spanish Chroniclers, as did Garcilaso de la Vega in *The Royal Commentaries of the Incas* in 1609, mentioned a curious annual event." Joanna leaned forward, forgetting that the nun could barely see her. "The Incas deliberately flooded the streets of Cuzco by opening a dam on Sacsayhuamán. The water flooded down the hill to Huacaypata Plaza, from where it rushed on out through the 'tail' of the Puma toward the southeast, which would probably be toward the 'gateway to the Land of the Dead,' *ukhu pacha*."

"I was aware of that ritual flooding of Cuzco—which would have been a very sanitary practice." Sister Elena chuckled. "Too bad European capitals of that era didn't adopt the same practice!"

"Coricancha, the Sun Temple, lies not too far from the Puma's tail, in what would be the part of the Milky Way where the ecliptic path—the sun's path—crosses it."

"Dr. Alderez said in his book that for the Incas, Coricancha might represent the "womb of the puma," Sister Elena said. "Thus, it would be the place where the seed of humans was poised to come to life, quickened by the sun." There was a long silence. "Joanna, this is all so amazing."

"The image fits," Joanna said. "In world mythology, the two branches of the Milky Way, called the Twin Rivers in the Sky, arise as a single river in the northwest skies at the 'headwaters' near the Land of the Gods, where they then split and flow above and below the Land of the Living—the Center, the Navel, the place above the abyss. Finally, the Twin Rivers come together again in the southeast near the Land of the Dead."

Joanna paused, imagining the Milky Way superimposed on the Sacred Valley. "The river below is probably the "underworld river, the route back to the 'headwaters' of the Milky Way which is replicated along the Urubamba/Vilcanota. Think of a globe with the rivers circling it, with Cuzco like a line running through the center, a vertical axis connecting all three lands."

"So, Joanna—and, please correct me if I've misunderstood—you're saying the waters of the Twin Rivers in the sky, the Milky Way, represent for ancient peoples some sort of cycle of rebirth, with one river carrying the souls from their homes among the stars to a birth on earth. When they die, the second river carries them from the Land of the Dead back to the headwaters near the Land of the Gods where they set out, once again, on their journey to the Land of the Living?"

Joanna wished she could see the nun's face. She could hear the animation in her voice—she'd felt the same way when she'd begun to grasp the ancient religious and astronomical implications.

"That same idea pops up again and again in world mythology," Joanna said. "Near Cuzco, beyond the puma's tail, should be the 'gateway' to the Land of the Dead, but I'm still working on just where that might be. According to the Spanish Chroniclers, the flooding waters from Sacsayhuamán converged and spilled into the abyss."

Joanna heard a sharp intake of breath from the other side of the curtain.

"Oh my dear... have you traveled to that area yet? It's not many miles beyond the city and the views are breathtaking. From those heights, one can look down toward the northeast end of the Sacred Valley. How thrilling if that should be the abyss you're talking about!'

"Is there a burial ground—?"

"There is!" Sister Elena's voice had become even more enlivened. "That's Pisac, Joanna! Do you think the 'underworld' in Incan mythology meant a celestial underworld, not really a place *underground*? Oh, you must go to Pisac soon, my dear!" The nun's voice died away and the silence became palpable before she spoke again. "It's really amazing how you've put all this together."

Joanna prided herself on being a good researcher, skills she'd honed during the years she'd studied for the doctorate. How nice it was to have someone else acknowledge it.

"I've constructed a sort of concept map of how the Incan sacred sites might be connected," she said. "I've begun to see that the megahieroglyph of the puma was meant to recapitulate every aspect of astronomical observations that influenced the Incan solar and lunar calendars."

"Then you've tentatively concluded the myth is some sort of 'shorthand' way of saying, go figure what this puma is all about, and you'll find the key to the Andean peoples' beliefs about astronomy?" Sister Elena said.

"Oh, much more, I believe." Joanna paused, collecting her thoughts. "What's really astounding is that when it's all finally put together, we may be able to understand just how that one geoglyph of the Puma, with its sacred sites related to celestial mechanics, summarizes all of Incan philosophy, religion, and history, like a giant concept map imprinted on the landscape of the whole Inca Empire. William Sullivan, in his book *The Secret of the Incas: Myth, Astronomy, and the War Against Time,* demonstrated how Andean mythology, with its astronomical references, recapitulates the pre-Columbian history of the indigenous peoples and may account for what motivated all their endeavors."

A cacophony of church bells rang out above them. "Joanna, those bells are the voice of God for me, I must run to chapel. We chant the Divine Office at this hour. Bless you, my dear."

"Please wait, can't you tell me—?" The curtain behind the grille swished in concert with the door's soft closing.

Damn it, how did you argue with the voice of divinity!

Chapter 20

It was Saturday. Joanna silenced the alarm and sat up in semi-darkness, staring out the small window where the rising sun backlit the distant mountains.

She turned on the bedside lamp and noticed the copy of Sister Elena's myth on the nightstand. The thing occupied her mind, waking and sleeping.

Sister Elena believed Pisac had to be the Land of the Dead. There were references in the sixteenth-century Spanish Chroniclers to a myth about a partridge. Animals had gathered on a high mountain—usually meaning the world's axis— to avoid a flood. The partridge had cried "pisc!" and caused the other animals to fall down the mountainside, and the waters of the flood had hidden fox's tail.

In the minds of early people, the 'flood' probably occurred when the constellations in the celestial ocean gradually changed to what seemed like a new position in the sky caused by precession of the equinoxes. Fox's tail would have disappeared from view.

In mythology the coal sack constellation was near the same gateway mentioned in Sister Elena's myth—the gateway to the Land of the Dead. The dark cloud constellation of the partridge lay near that gateway. The bird fashioned a hole in the ground where it laid its eggs.

What a fitting imagery for a necropolis, a "resting place" for the dead!

The delayed snooze alarm sounded again. Joanna had just enough time to dress. The train to Machu Picchu was scheduled to leave in less than thirty minutes. Machu Picchu! It had been a part of her life since Aunt Jane had given her the painting of the ruins when she was a child.

She pulled on sturdy hiking boots, fastened the Velcro straps, and grabbed her rain poncho. She'd packed a light bag the night before, as she'd learned to do early in her world travels. Hurrying from the room onto the small balcony, that encircled the interior courtyard, she descended the staircase to the lobby. She'd arranged for a taxi yesterday, and it was waiting.

The train station was located near Santa Maria Monastery. There were a few tourists, but mainly the train held the local Quechuas who were returning to their homes after a week of selling wares in the market places in Cuzco. Their homes were in little hamlets tucked high in the mountains and reached only by dirt roads.

The train exited the station, and Joanna felt dizzy as it wove its way back and forth, climbing to the heights above Cuzco. Finally, an upland plateau was reached where vast rectangular fields of beans, corn, and potato plants divided the landscape like a patchwork quilt.

Joanna snapped pictures continuously, amazed that each new scene was more dazzling than the last. Slowly the train snaked its way down to the banks of the Urubamba River that flowed through the Sacred Valley.

This valley was a spectacular sight. Joanna would be gazing at quaint villages at the foot of mile high mountains, with Incan terraces rising to the very tops, when, all at once, in the "v" between two peaks, an even higher snow-crowned cordillera would appear.

I don't have eyes enough to see all this! I'm coming back someday soon to explore every inch of this valley.

The train stopped at Ollantaytambo. While more passengers boarded, Joanna looked out on treacherous cliffs rising in sharp peaks from the river to the ruins atop terraced steps. Carlos told her that the stones in those ruins, believed to be part of a temple and probably an astronomical complex, were among the oldest and most beautiful stonework in the Sacred Valley.

The place was named for Ollantay, a great warrior, who, because of success in battle, was much favored by the Sapa Inca. There was an historical drama about Ollantay enacted during Incan times.

Quipucamayocs, the quipu-keepers, had described it to the Spanish Chroniclers who had recorded it.

The plot had to do with Ollantay requesting to marry one of the Sapa Inca's daughters. His request was rejected because he was not of royal blood. To prevent the marriage, her father sent his daughter to the acllahuasi in Cuzco, where she was locked up for the rest of her life. Unfortunately, or fortunately, she was already pregnant. The play was performed frequently in Lima. Joanna planned to see it before she left for Mongolia.

Surely, an advanced civilization, such as the Incas clearly were, must have had some form of written language. There was, of course, the system for recording information on the intricately knotted colorful cords called quipus, and there were the special hieroglyphics carved into stone at numerous ruins and woven into magnificent textiles.

In addition, there had been innumerable paintings, with symbols meant to communicate their stories. Those had been deliberately destroyed by the conquerors. Good thing the Spanish Chroniclers had been excellent record keepers, describing everything they saw and heard, but it was sad to think so much of the Incan art and artifacts had been lost to history.

The train surged forward, backed up, started again, and began gaining momentum, winding its way along the Rio Urubamba through a narrow gorge with mountains rising to incredible heights on either side.

Joanna marveled at the bromeliads and mosses clinging to sheer granite faces. Her travel book said that during rainy season, the sparse soil was released in landslides that crept to the edge of the tracks and sometimes obliterated them.

She'd read in the newspapers that a massive landslide had blocked the tracks several months ago and prevented the train from making the trip to Machu Picchu. Helicopters became the only means of access unless one wanted to walk the Inca Trail, which required a very healthy constitution.

The cloud-forest environment increased as the train drew nearer to Machu Picchu Pueblo, formerly called Aguas Calientes. Her guidebook said the village was the last stop on the railroad, and, also, the place on the Rio Urubamba from which a dirt road pig-tailed up, rising in ever-more dizzying tiers, to the ruins above.

It was difficult to describe the unrestrained glee she felt at finally being exactly in the middle of the painting Sister Jane had given her. She was *Alice* and this was most certainly a *Wonderland*.

She checked in with the desk clerk and got her room key. "I want to tour the ruins immediately," she said. "What's the best way to get up there?"

"Travel through the village, cross the bridge," he said. "You can either walk up the mountainside or take a bus ride. The bus is not for the faint-hearted, because of the one-lane road with hairpin curves and no guardrails. It's rather nerve-wracking if you're not used to it. A walk up the mountainside is a far better choice, but that can be terribly exhausting."

Joanna thanked him, took the room key, and walked up the crushed stone path to one of the many detached small hut-like structures.

The interior walls were shaped like those inside a Navaho hogan. There was a small fireplace, and the room's ceiling was rounded and ribbed in natural wood beams.

The furniture—a double bed and armoire—was heavy mahogany and handsomely carved. The bathroom was small and spotlessly clean.

Paths led from each hut through a lush landscape of gigantic split-leaf philodendrons and trees with brightly colored orchids entwined in their branches. Small parrots, red-orange cocks-of-the-rock, and humming-birds flitted about. Joyous bird chatter broke the deep silence. It was paradise.

Joanna checked her wristwatch. It was a few minutes before noon. She decided to see the ruins as soon as possible. Maybe lunch would lure people away, and she'd have the place mostly to herself. She wanted pictures of the landscape without live subjects.

She grabbed a walking stick provided by the hotel and hurried down the path into the small village of Machu Picchu Pueblo. Despite being a tourist destination, the town had retained its primitive appearance. The path through the town crisscrossed the train tracks and meandered to the bridge over the Urubamba.

The river raged beneath the bridge. She crossed it, keeping her eyes on the water. The river source must be the high sierras. She wondered if it was always at flood stage.

Beyond the bridge, she commenced the walk up Machu Picchu. She was following the narrow path which paralleled the dirt road, when she heard a noise behind her and saw a young Quechua boy cross at a right angle about ten feet from where she stood.

Dropping back to check where he'd gone, she saw, in the underbrush, a path with stone steps that led straight up the steep mountainside. She rejected any desire to follow the kid, figuring her lowlander lungs couldn't adjust that quickly to the altitude.

A Japanese man and woman, standing a few feet behind her, had obviously been considering the same possibility. The man said something to the woman and they laughed.

Joanna greeted them. "I wish I had the stamina to follow him," she said.

The man laughed again. "We say same. I'm Mikeo and this wife Nikki. We walk with you?"

"Please, I'd be delighted to have company."

The approximately two hours needed to climb up the mountain was considerably lengthened as the three hikers stopped constantly to admire the views and gawk at the luxuriant plant life. Tropical plants that were tiny tabletop specimens in New York, Atlanta, and Tokyo were tree-sized here. The blossoms of the begonias were as big as saucers and acted as spectacular groundcover all over the mountainside.

Joanna couldn't remember seeing in the guidebooks any mention of the insect life except for mosquitoes. What she was wondering about was, given the size of everything else and the excellent climate—just how big were the spiders?

"Do either of you know anything about the insects in this region—particularly the spiders? I imagine they must get pretty enormous in this climate."

Nikki moved her head up and down. "You see boxes childlen sell at tlain? One-meter-by-two meter with glass cover, huge talantulas inside."

"Too bad they not ship," Mikeo said, chuckling. "I buy and put display box on coffee table. Friends would be freaked out."

Joanna, hoping to avoid being freaked out, shifted to the outer edge of the road. She glanced back at the lush jungle growth on the opposite side that grew densely, almost up to the tree line.

"Those spiders in the boxes are probably only exoskeletons," she said. "I've been told that tarantulas shed their outer 'skins' like snakes and briefly have a pink color until the oxygen changes them to black."

"I see pink spider, I not run," Nikki said, chuckling.

"I'm betting, seeing those super-sized exoskeletons in the underbrush could make a person hurt themselves just as badly though, trying to get away from them," Joanna said.

She and her companions arrived at the last bend in the road where it leveled out onto a granite shelf carved into the lee of the mountain. It was a daunting prospect—sheer drop-offs presented sharp edges where the granite shelf met the sky, and, in such an implausible place, a Government Hostel was perched precariously on its gouged-out foothold.

The approach to the hostel was from the right, where it faced outward toward the precipice. To the left were the magnificent terraces leading to the ruins that rested on a ridge stretching between Machu Picchu, the "Old Mountain," and Huayna Picchu, the "Young Mountain."

Joanna was transfixed by the stone ruins glowing green in the late afternoon sunlight, an exquisite symbiotic creation of nature and the human hand. Her two companions seemed similarly affected. No one spoke. After a while, Nikki and Mikeo shook hands with her, wished her a good tour, and headed for the entrance to the hostel.

Chapter 21

Joanna followed several other people along the path that led to the entrance to Machu Picchu ruins and paid the fee at the access gate. Backpacks weren't allowed inside, so she took out her camera, poncho, and notebook before stowing the pack in the bin provided. She'd decided to use her guidebook instead of following the guided tour. Just ahead of her, a length of steep steps descended to a terrace that wound around toward the Temple of the Sun.

Edging near the stacked-stone-wall to the left of the stairs, she let her hand slide along it as she descended. There was no guardrail and the dizzying depth of the gaping gorge in front of her seemed to pull her toward it.

She exhaled a long held breath as she reached the wide top of the terrace, in the lee of the high wall. Several yards ahead, the precision-carved stones in the base of the Temple of the Sun loomed above the mouth of a cave. Could that be the place where Joré's parents had been entombed.

In front of her and across a stairway was a level area—almost like a parade ground—stretching toward Huayna Picchu. To the right of the Temple of the Sun, as she turned to face it, was the Fountain Stair, a series of stone steps, bisected at intervals by water fountains, that led up to the Royal Sector and the main temple complex.

To the left of the Temple of the Sun, next to the burial cave, were partial remains of structures where the acllas had once lived.

Joanna climbed the stairs to the first fountain that was adjacent to the cave. She entered the cave and noticed an intricately dressed stone, carved to depict a sort of ladder with three steps. It resembled the shape of Huayna Picchu and the two smaller hills beside it. The guidebook said the carving was meant to represent the three "worlds" of Incan cosmology: hanaq pacha, world above; kay pacha, the earth; and ukhu pacha, the underworld.

Moving back outside and to the right of the cave entrance, she looked up toward the larger temple complex, near a pyramidal mound on which the *intihuatana*, referred to as the "hitching post of the sun," was located. Before going up there, she wanted to explore the acllas' quarters.

The quarters overlooked the deep river gorge and, as she walked through the rectangular foundations and half-walls of the ruins, she tried to imagine the acllas' lives. They had worked and performed their required rituals near stunning views that could be glimpsed from every window of their humble dwellings. Did they pause to contemplate that beauty?

Every vantage point offered scenes Joanna hoped to capture. She snapped pictures from various angles, even holding the camera high above her head to take a picture over the top of the wall where the view would have been straight down into the river gorge, thousands of feet below.

The terrace on which Huarana and Joré had met must be down there near the river. Joanna stepped back, and thrilled at the thought that her ancestors had actually been in this very place.

She lost track of time exploring the Temple of the Sun. Suddenly lightning, zigzagging between mountain peaks and blazing across the sky, sent her scurrying back down to the cave.

She threw her rain poncho over her head as she ran. Watching storms was usually an enjoyment, but she didn't relish being struck by lightning.

There was a rock ledge toward the back of the cave. She could watch the storm in relative safety from there and maybe write in her journal.

Looking up, now and then, collecting her thoughts as the fog increased in density, she began to view the scene as a *tabula rasa* on which she could project her images of the acllas' world.

Mist swirled through the deep gorge and enclosed the

mountaintops. Thunder echoed in reverberating waves through the cave, and a jagged streak of light struck sparks near the rock where she sat.

There was a sizzling sound and the electrically charged force lifted her and slammed her against the back of the cave. She threw her hands up, attempting to shield her head.

Sliding toward the cold stone floor, she tried to struggle. Gravity pulled her with a stronger force and she felt herself lose consciousness.

Machu Picchu glistened in semi-darkness, an emerald in a carved granite setting. The storm topped the mountains, blowing toward the southeast. It was impossible to tell if it was late evening or early morning.

She stepped out of the cave, and felt the wind lift her tunic, whipping it around her as she carefully placed one foot onto the slippery stairs near the fountain. The low light of the storm and the rivulets of water running down the stairway made ascent difficult, but her ichu grass sandals found a sure-footing on the wet stones. She pushed the pleated headdress back from her face and climbed steadily toward the top of the stair.

Reaching the top, she took the path to the first observation point, crossed the leveled plaza, and climbed the five stone steps to the top of the pyramid. The *Intihuatana,* a rectangular-shaped stele, projecting nearly five feet above the flattened top of the pyramid, loomed in front of her. It had been carved from solid rock, and she knew it was used to measure and mark the sun's progress through the ecliptic.

She reverently placed her hands on the *Intihuatana*, and looked eastward, where a rainbow stretched across the Vilcanota gorge, linking the mountains like a bridge. *It was all so familiar.*

The early morning hours before Inti appeared above the mountains were the most sacred and she knew how privileged she was to assist the high priest at the rituals performed at this hour.

The Uillac Umu, high priest of Coricancha, was already standing at the altar. The Tumi, the knife used to slash the sacrificial llama's throat, was lying in its place on the stone shelf. She lifted the handle and extended it to him.

This morning's sacrifice would be different. The high priest was about to offer the last sacred llama to be given to Viracocha on Old Mountain.

He took the tumi from her and made the prescribed incisions. Then he grasped the taper she'd brought from the eternal flame and lit the consuming fire. He bowed toward the sacrifice, honoring the released spirit of the llama as it rose skyward toward hanaq pacha.

Two cups of herbal medicine, prepared earlier, had been placed on a rock ledge near the altar. The Uillac Umu chose one of the cups and handed the other to her.

She'd expected this, knew it was the wise thing to do. They really had no choice. The chaskas had unwittingly carried disease from the seacoast, and it had already ravaged their elite community. It would soon claim his life and hers. They were the last to be left alive. The medicine would not cure. It could only ease their suffering.

The Uillac Umu held his cup, studying the liquid. He turned toward the *Intihuatana,* raised his arms, and dashed the liquid on the sacred stele, offering his life to Viracocha.

She thought briefly of the consequences of not drinking the liquid. Then she dashed it onto the altar. It was her gift to Pacha Mama. Like Uillac Umu, she had been trained to endure pain.

The high priest turned slowly and paused briefly, honoring each of the cardinal directions, until he faced finally toward Vilcanota, the birthplace of the sun. He stopped and bowed low, saluting the rising sun.

The ceremonial robes draping his shoulders whipped about him as he returned to the step in front of the Intihuatana. He stumbled slightly and grasped the edge of the altar as he knelt.

A piercing sweet song enveloped the mountains. The small villages in the surrounding valleys were greeting the rising sun. She knew the song well. As a child, she had intoned it at break of day for the nearby ayllus.

That had been a time of great joy as well as sadness, for she had learned she would be chosen to join the acllas in Cuzco. It also meant that she would leave her parents and the boy whose friendship had blossomed into love. Little did she know then that she would one day serve at his side in this sacred place.

Kneeling on the step below him, she spoke softly, without emotion, reciting the poem she'd written for him thirty years ago. It was her farewell gift to him, the tiny skein of gossamer threads that linked them together.

He inclined his head toward her and joined in the recitation. The wind whipped their voices together, rendering them faint as a hummingbird's cry and then strong as the ties that bound them to Pachamama.

The words melded together, became a leitmotiv, a golden roundelay, a song of joy and longing, the mountain's voice.

CON TICCI

Once on a moon-bridge we glanced into waters that smiled back lilies of every hue.

Hand loved canoes, sky-lanterns, spunned-glassed fish starred our world.

You recounted strange tales I heard only in your eyes, because

we knew we would taste the frozen ice, not the substance of

dreams. We drank, in celebration, the only toast we could,

you with that warmed in distillation and I, with that

chilled by early rending. You would have carried

away ticcis

too big for us,

only people might

have laughed or cried,

and ticcis weren't

for sale, anyway.

Who could have

bought them

with multi-hued lilies,

on a moon-bridge.

But, they were ours, we had paid the price long ago,

in temple chimes and memories with an infinite love, needing neither hands nor eyes.

Whispered on the winds, played on panpipes, wafted on bright morning sunrays that illuminated the peaks around Machu Picchu, the words, echoed forever from their hearts to the top of the tall mountains and on, beyond the Andean snowfields, drifting away with the smoke of the sacrificial llama, across the rainbow, along the Milky Way back to the First Time.

Joanna sat up. Beyond the mouth of the cave, a rainbow's ultraviolet rays shaded gradually to infrared and formed a moon bridge connecting the peaks rising from the banks of the Urubamba.

She shook herself, trying to clear her head. Shapes, ideas, words, emotions swirled vividly through jumbled thoughts. She looked down at her feet. Hiking boots had replaced the sandals. Her warm woolen jacket shielded her from the wind blowing through the cave.

She stood, shook herself again. It had to be a dream, just a dream. Her journal lay on the ground beside her, pages blank. She picked it up and tucked it, along with the digital camera, into the pouch pinned to the inside of her jacket. Pulling the rain poncho over her head, she searched in its pocket for her small flashlight. It wasn't there.

Shadows stalked the ruins as Joanna headed toward the exit gate. Tomorrow, she'd return to see the sunrise and explore the rest of Machu Picchu, but now she needed to leave before the gates were locked.

Only two people were in line behind her as she exited the ruins, collected her backpack, and began the walk down the mountainside. The other tourists must have left as soon as the storm broke. The last bus had obviously departed.

She decided the fastest descent would be the path she'd seen the young Quechua boy use earlier. Although she couldn't have managed the upward climb, it shouldn't be a problem going down. Veering off the road, she headed onto the steep, roughly cut stepping-stones that were barely visible in the cloud-streaked moonlight.

The trip down proved treacherous, requiring a pattern of careful visual inspection of the next step and a quick upward glance to avoid overhanging branches. The moonlight was an unreliable flashlight and Joanna marshalled all her skills of concentration to avoid a crippling fall.

Focused as she was on the stair-step routine, she hadn't been aware of the loose pebbles falling on either side of the path until one struck her ankle. Turning to see what might be causing the minor landslide, she realized the darkness was impenetrable.

It was threatening to rain again. She hated to be caught in a deluge and dreaded to think of the devastation caused by landslides she'd seen in the valleys near Cuzco. She increased her speed and imagined crossing her fingers and toes for luck.

Slipping, she grabbed a shrub to break her fall. "Damn it," she yelled at the offending thorn bush.

Thumps reverberated off the stones above her. Something was definitely back there. It sounded like footsteps. Her scalp tingled. She felt someone staring intently at her back. Panic heaved her chest. She turned sharply. For an instant, the moonlight silhouetted two men hurrying toward her.

She recognized them. They'd been near the hostel when she'd exited the ruins. She stepped to the side and indicated they should go ahead of her.

The first man darted in front and, stopping on the step below, turned to face her. The second man remained on the step behind her.

"I don't want to walk too fast on this path, it's really very slick. Please go on ahead," she urged.

The man behind grabbed her arm and twisted it into her back. She screamed, and the man below struck her across the face.

The blow seared through her body causing an eruption of involuntary tears. "What do you want with me?"

"¡Cállese! ¡Cállese!" The man hissed the words between clenched teeth. She stared at him and shook her head as though she didn't understand.

"¡Silencio! ¡Vamos!" The man behind barked into her left ear and shoved her down the stairs. She could feel the blade of a knife piercing her ribs.

Putting one foot in front of the other to avoid falling, she tried to deal with increasing fear. She reasoned they wouldn't harm her. Whatever it was they wanted, they needed her alive. She'd cooperate. It wouldn't accomplish anything to struggle.

She trudged along, growing angrier with each passing moment. Why hadn't she prepared for something like this? Rosa had warned her. Any fool would've taken precautions.

The man in back still held her arm. Every move forward brought waves of pain, but she spared no tears on it. She needed to devise a plan of escape. There had to be a way.

Lifting her right foot to set it cautiously on the next step down, she held it a long moment in mid-air, staring at it, examining it like she would a meteorite. *That's it!*

Suddenly, she leaned too far forward, bent her knee sharply, and deliberately stumbled. The weight of her falling body shoved the man in front of her down the stairs. He careened headlong for a few steps and went down with a loud groan.

As she fell, her arm wrenched free from the man behind. He lost balance and sprawled wildly into the thorn bushes at her left side, cursing and struggling to right himself.

Minutes passed, and she heard him scrambling down the steps after her. She stood and felt excruciating pain in her knees. Her hands stung, scraped raw from the harsh encounter with the stone steps. She began to hobble down the stairs, dodging to the right, skirting the body of the other man lying on the stairs below her. The fall must have knocked him out.

Looking back, she saw that the man running after her had slipped and was catapulting down the hill again, rolling toward a clump of thorn bushes opposite her. She had to get away from him.

Falling to the ground at the side of the stairs, she covered her head with her hands and began to roll, propelling herself down the mountainside, jerking sideways to avoid tree trunks. She heard thumping feet running behind her and glanced back to see both men staggering down the hill, bellowing with rage as she increased her distance from them.

Voices sounded somewhere near the bottom of the stairs. She grabbed a tree trunk to stop her momentum and pulled herself up. Still holding tightly to the trunk, gasping for breath, she recalled a visual trick to stop her head from spinning. Closing her eyes for an instant, she envisioned a peg on a wall directly in front of her. Her sense of balance returned.

She was covered with scratches from the briar patches that blanketed the sides of the stone stairs and her body ached, but she found enough energy to dart out onto the dirt road where she joined a group of tourists. Her would-be abductors had disappeared.

Stopping by the police station, she alerted the police that two men were targeting tourists in what could be an express kidnapping. She reported the stolen backpack, declaring that the few items in it were of no particular value.

She'd checked for her cell phone and found it, along with her camera and journal, in the padded pouch pinned inside her jacket. Nor had she lost credit cards, passport, or driver's license, since those things were kept in a cloth envelope suspended from a string around her neck.

The officer took her information and assured her they would investigate and be on the lookout for the men. She imagined Carlos should be told, but then she'd have to tell him she'd ditched the bodyguard he'd assigned her. She didn't like thinking about his reaction.

She'd plead difficulty getting a signal, since cell phones were notoriously useless in this remote region. Meanwhile, she needed to find the *farmacia* and get meds to alleviate the pain in her knees and the swelling in her arm. Next on the agenda was a long soaking bath and application of an antiseptic cream to all the scratches.

Chapter 22

Joanna was back in Cuzco when Carlos phoned to say he'd gotten a call from the local police at Machu Picchu Pueblo.

"They called you? ... Good God, does everybody in Peru know I'm associated with the de la Reyna family. ... No, no it wasn't too bad... I can't believe they told you that. Yeah, that's exactly what I did—deliberately stumbled.... Really, I'm fine, just some sore muscles. I thought I'd broken my arm, but it's okay... no, just a lot of scratches from rolling in the briar patches... I'm going to tell Rosa I got in a fight with a puma.... Not exactly, it was more like an episode of the Three Stooges... Don't you dare, Carlos! Ms. Valladres couldn't help it, I left before the chickens were up, she had no idea I was going... Okay, okay, I promise, she can trail me from now on.... I'm not sure... you really believe those men might be connected to the stalker? I thought they were just express kidnappers... Thanks, Carlos, see you all tomorrow."

Cuzco's Inca acllahuasi was located on Calle Loreto, one of Joanna's favorite places to walk. That was the route most convenient for reaching her apartment, so she frequently enjoyed the views along the way.

Today she had an appointment with a nun to tour the acllahuasi. It was the very same place where Huarana had lived after she'd been chosen by the high priest. The Spanish had given the building to cloistered nuns of the Order of St. Dominic in 1605—nearly fifty years after the conquest—when the second cloistered monastery was founded. Sister Elena's monastery had been the first established for nuns in Cuzco.

Joanna was glad to have a connection inside the monastery—in a recent phone conversation, Sister Jane had mentioned that a member of her own Cleveland Dominican congregation resided at Santa Catalina. The nun, Sister Mary Verona, was doing a study on the lives of the acllas in pre-Columbian Cuzco for a Ph.D. in Anthropology.

The beautifully carved massive cedar wood doors caught her attention as she rang the doorbell. A narrow inset door was opened almost immediately and Joanna found herself in a long corridor with walls covered by priceless murals depicting the life of St. Catherine of Siena.

The nun who greeted her was tall, thin, and elegantly garbed in a simple light cream woolen tunic with long sleeves and a rectangular piece of cloth, called a scapular. Sister Jane, who wore the same clothing, had said the scapular symbolized the yoke of Christ. It was worn over the shoulders, and fell, back and front, to the hem of the mid-calf length dress. A short black veil was attached to a sort of half-moon white headband that curved at the center and lifted slightly above the nun's dark hair.

"Welcome, Joanna. Your aunt told me you're here for the summer. I mean winter! It's difficult remembering I'm in the Southern Hemisphere. How interesting it must be to work near those Incan observatory towers."

"You're kind to take the time to show me the acllahuasi. If you'd like, I could arrange a tour of the observatory for you."

The liquid-brown eyes glowed. "Could you really?"

"Of course, any time you like. You've an interesting name, is it from Shakespeare?"

Sister Verona laughed. "Although our Mother General, Mother Rosalia, is a closet romantic and lover of Shakespeare, she selected the name for me for other reasons. St. Peter of Verona, an early Dominican, a convert to Catholicism, was martyred rather than renounce his faith. I'm a convert too, so Mother thought the name appropriate."

Joanna followed the nun into a spacious atrium. Carved arches of Mediterranean loggias formed the perimeter of the interior courtyard where huge pots of geraniums and ferns flourished in an enclosed microclimate. A large fountain, in the center of the courtyard, splashed a rhythmic counterpoint to the hushed atmosphere.

"The loggias were added by the Spanish," Sister Verona said. "The stone paving and fountain are original to the acllahuasi. Apparently, the acllas used this area, as do our cloistered nuns now, for outdoor exercise and meditation."

Joanna learned that the acllas were priestesses of Mama Quilla, the moon goddess, one of the most important deities in the Incan religion. Sister Verona said the acllas had many different sub-groups but the mamaconas were the highest level, related to the royal families, well-educated, and married for life to the sun. They could be buried alive for breaking the vow of celibacy.

"The Sapa Inca's wife, the royal coya, was the earthly embodiment of the moon goddess and the high priestess of all the acllahuasis in the empire—the Tahuantinsuyu," Sister said.

"I'm intrigued by the maze-like arrangement of these rooms," Joanna said. "So, you say there were different levels of the acllas?"

"The lowest consisted of daughters of chieftains from conquered tribes, who were selected for the acllahuasi because of beauty and talent."

Sister Verona put her index finger to her lips to signal silence. They were passing through a corridor adjacent to the cloistered nuns' refectory. She pointed to the massive stones in the corridor walls, which Joanna recognized as Incan. At the end of the corridor, they turned left and Sister resumed speaking.

"The Sapa Inca married the lower-level acllas to members of the aristocracy, or to heroic warriors, and also gave them as rewards to the chieftains of conquered tribes. It was a very effective method for transmitting culture."

She turned to look at Joanna. "Those who weren't chosen for marriage remained in service in the temples until they were thirty years old, at which time they could choose to return to their villages."

"Did any of the lower level acllas ever marry into the royal family?" Joanna had wondered how Huarana, who wasn't royalty, had been able to marry Joré.

"The Inca royal males practiced a kind of polygamy. They could have many concubines, but they only ever married another royal. Of course, that rule could be 'bent'—sometimes lower-level acllas of exceptional talent and beauty were raised to the aristocracy."

They were moving through the center of the oldest part of the acllahuasi. Joanna noticed the trapezoidal niches in the original outer wall that bordered on Calle Loreto. "What purpose did those have?"

"The acllas tended the mummy bundles of the coyas—the Inca queens. They were kept in those niches."

"Are there any of those mummies still remaining?" Joanna asked.

"Tragically in the sixteenth-century, Spanish Church authorities burned all the royal mummies they could find. However, there are stories that circulate among the Quechua Indians that royal mummies may be buried in tombs under diverted riverbeds. After the tombs were constructed, the rivers were allowed to return to their natural courses."

"I've seen some mummy bundles in museums," Joanna said.

"Those are typically of people of lesser rank."

Joanna followed the nun along a corridor with small rooms opening onto it. "Are these their living spaces?"

"Work spaces *and* living spaces. The acllas were trained to weave all the religious vestments for the priests and the clothing for the royal family. The textiles, made from spinning cotton fibers, were said to be like finest silk and ranged from heavy opaque to light diaphanous fabrics. In addition, the acllas brewed the sacred chicha that was used in religious ceremonies and consumed by the aristocracy. Apparently, there was a permanent production crew that chewed the corn kernels, thus starting the long fermentation process to brew the 'beer.' I know—disgusting!—but, they were considered sacred and very healthy."

"Were they allowed visitors?"

"The coya, her daughters, and granddaughters were the only persons, external to the acllahuasi, who were allowed to visit. Not even her husband, the Sapa Inca, was supposed to violate the sanctity of this acllahuasi. However, he could choose any aclla from the lower ranks as a concubine for himself."

"Does this area parallel Calle Loreto?"

"The street, in the past, was called the Avenue of the Sun. There's a narrow stretch located on the outside of this wall where the Inca youth participated in tests of discipline and courage to initiate them into manhood. They were made to line up on either side, and a highly trained warrior would run down the center of the street, twirling a lance from side-to-side. If a young man even twitched, he could be severely wounded or killed. It must have been a frightful experience."

"I'm amazed, Sister, the daily lives of the acllas sound almost like cloistered convent life," Joanna said. "I've learned something about that from visiting Sister Elena at Santa Maria Monastery."

"I know Sister Elena, she's an extraordinary person. Well, interestingly, the living spaces of the Sumerian temple servants, the Greek and Egyptian priestesses, the Vestal Virgins of Rome, Buddhist nuns, and the acllas, are all quite similar. Institutions of consecrated celibates, both men and women, seem to have been an extremely early societal need. The members were considered repositories/preservers, not only of religious beliefs, but of civilization's accumulated knowledge."

"Were the acllas involved in astronomical observations like the priests?" Joanna remembered recognizing in her "dream" the purpose of the Intihuatana on Machu Picchu.

"Archaic people believed life was attuned to the rhythms of the universe. Myths, as stories of cosmic happenings, were direct links to divinity and informed their rituals so they would be able to relive, eternally, their interactions with the gods."

Sister Verona motioned for Joanna to go ahead of her into the corridor. "It seems clear form the vestiges of local agricultural and astronomical 'lore' that inhere in the Quechua women here that the acllas did have a major part in observations, particularly of the moon."

"What happened to the acllas here in Cuzco when their acllahuasis were dissolved by the Conquistadors?"

"At first, when the Spaniards were told the virgins were dedicated to the sun and moon, they apparently felt justified in raping women they considered pagans. They systematically destroyed the acllahuasis and defiled the acllas in the various regions they passed through on their way to conquer Cuzco."

"And the acllas in Cuzco?" Joanna was shocked by such brutality and hoped Huarana had not been subjected it.

"Fortunately, Francisco Pizarro became aware that the Incas prized the Cuzcanean mamaconas as much as the Spanish honored their own religious orders of nuns back home. He seemed to have recognized that if he didn't respect the occupants of the Cuzco acllahuasi, he would have massive rebellion on his hands. Another thing he seemed to have grasped was that the institution of acllas was an efficient system for spreading culture."

"Rather astute, I'd say, for an illiterate battle-hardened conqueror," Joanna said.

"Once the conquistadors realized that this particular Inca institution was a clever way to gain hegemony among the conquered, it wasn't long before Pizarro's lieutenants founded convents of nuns in Cuzco."

"I was really surprised to learn that they'd founded women's cloisters so early."

"The nuns would be useful for transmitting Hispanic culture to the conquistadors' mestiza daughters born to their noble Incan mistresses. Those daughters, placed in the convent at an early age to be schooled by the nuns, were—exactly like the acllas—considered highly-prized marriage commodities, capable of securing the conquistadors' lines of descent, a sure way to pass on their recently acquired vast real estate holdings and other objects of stolen wealth."

"So, essentially the Conquistadors copied Incan policy." Joanna paused to take in the view of the courtyard from an upper story window. She noticed the surrounding walls were too high to permit views of

Cuzco.

"After the Spanish monasteries were fully operative, many of the occupants of the acllahuasis found themselves enclosed in the Christian convents. Certainly, after the Incas revolted, the acllas who still resided in Cuzco—who hadn't had an opportunity to escape to the remote regions of the empire—were forced to live in the Christian convents," Sister Verona said.

"Can you tell me something about Incan religion?"

"Chroniclers reported that the Christian Conquistadors were shocked that the Incas had a religion that very much paralleled their own."

Sister Verona indicated that Joanna should descend the stairs.

"Records show that the Incas had a *confession of sins* and a kind of *baptism* or *ritual cleansing with water* performed for the sake of returning to a state of innocence. There was also a *communion ceremony*, featuring sacred bread and alcoholic spirits called chicha—that 'communion' food, as I mentioned earlier, was prepared by the acllas. The Incas even had a story of a worldwide flood."

"I imagine the Conquistadors were in a stir about all that," Joanna said, thrilled to be learning so much about her newly acquired ancestors.

Sister Verona laughed. "They believed they were being, in their words, 'confounded by the work of the devil,' and that he was deliberately mimicking their religion in this 'pagan' land."

"I've been studying astronomy in Andean myths. I'm still having difficulty visualizing the acllas' daily lives as they related to astronomical events," Joanna said.

"Major duties had to do with re-enacting rituals honoring solstices and equinoxes. The acllas recapitulated Earth's—the Incas called her *Pacha Mama*, Earth Mother—cycles of birth, evolution, destruction, and re-birth in the way they structured their lives. Even the twenty to thirty year cycles of their initiation and terms of service may have been related to the conjunctions of Saturn and Jupiter."

"That's really astounding. I recall reading somewhere that

historians depicted the acllas as mindless automatons sitting for hours, gazing blankly, chewing corn kernels for the chicha, or working day and night weaving cotton cloth."

Sister Verona's laughter bordered on the boisterous. "Historians have also depicted our cloistered Christian nuns as similarly occupied. The majority of acllas never did anything mindlessly, and I can assure you, cloistered nuns know what to do with their minds while their hands are occupied with repetitive work. Can you imagine Sister Elena doing anything mindlessly? It's ludicrous!"

Joanna thanked the nun, promising to arrange a tour of the observatory for the near future. She left the storied acllahuasi that had claimed new life as a Catholic monastery and walked alongside its walls. She noted the stones paving the street, the solidity of the buildings on either side of the street and thought about the pre-Columbian grandeur of Cuzco. The Incas had indeed been master engineers and builders.

At the apex of the street, which steadily inclined, was Santo Domingo Church, built in the sixteenth-century by Dominican monks atop Coricancha, the Temple of the Sun, the "Mecca" of the Inca Empire. Incan shrines, within the Sun Temple, were dedicated to the rainbow and the Pleiades, which had been recently excavated from beneath the central quadrangle of the Dominican monastery.

The temple's beautiful convex precision-shaped wall was still intact on the outer northeastern wall of the church. Was that the "balcony" on which Huarana had seen the golden disc of the sun displayed by the high priest?

The Spanish Chroniclers reported that the garden below the "balcony" contained solid gold precious gem-encrusted statues of people, animals, insects, even butterflies, birds, and plants, representing flora and fauna from every part of the empire.

Tahuantinsuyu, the empire, had extended from Columbia to Chile and from the Pacific Coast to the Amazon Jungle. Joanna had seen a few remaining rare objects in museums in Lima. They were fashioned as delicately and skillfully as Tiffany jewelry.

The Conquistadors had been astounded by the skill of the goldsmiths. It was miraculous that they'd recorded every detail before the artifacts were melted and shipped as ingots to Spain.

The Spanish Chroniclers noted that the Sun Temple had forty sequential lines radiating out from it, laid out by Inca engineers. The lines ran straight across high mountains and through coastal deserts.

Lineage huacas, representing the "star" totems of various conquered tribes, were located along the lines. People knelt to honor the Cuzco priests who walked those lines once a year, carrying the ashes of sacrifices in clay pots to distribute in every corner of Tahuantinsuyu.

Joanna had read that some archeoastronomers believed those lines signified the forty conjunctions of Saturn and Jupiter. Keeping up with the conjunctions had been an ancient way of tracking precession, as the constellations of the celestial equator moved backward over time. The two planets "met" approximately every eighteen to twenty years as they moved around the ecliptic plane, the path of the sun as it appeared from a vantage point on Earth. The Spanish Chroniclers related that after forty of those conjunctions, the Incas believed a Pachakuti, "a turning over of space and time," had occurred.

A lecture she'd given as a Ph.D. candidate when she'd worked briefly as a graduate assistant came to mind. She'd set up the planetarium to illustrate the conjunctions and had her freshmen students predict the changes that the ancient people would have seen in the night skies.

She'd emphasized that those forty conjunctions of Saturn and Jupiter were not only among the premier ideas in world mythology, but had also occupied the thoughts and efforts of Johannes Kepler. He'd diagrammed the complete cycle of conjunctions of the two planets, which seemed to be markers pointing to the constellations at different positions on the zodiac, like the points of an equilateral triangle, as they came together every twenty years. The complete cycle, equaling 26,000 years, was called the *Trigon of Conjunctions of the Greatest Day*.

Her students had been delighted with the idea of the zodiac. She'd pointed out that the Earth's equator, projected out into space, was called its *celestial equator*, and above that "equator" was a very prominent band of constellations called the *zodiac*. That zodiac made a convenient instrument for tracking the sun and planets, as they appeared form Earth to weave in and out of the band of constellations, like the "pointers" on a clock face.

She'd gone on to explain that in 40 conjunctions—taking about 720 years—the points of the triangles, described by Saturn and Jupiter as they met, had moved through only one third of the constellations positioned at different points around the zodiac.

It took 2,160 years (720 years times 3) for all three points of the triangle to move through the whole zodiac, after which the two planets finally met *one constellation beyond* the one in which they'd first met.

She'd demonstrated to the students how at that time, at the spring equinox—the vernal equinox—the sun's path intersected the celestial equator in a *new constellation of the zodiac*. The sun was then termed to be a new "sun" by early civilizations and it was considered to bring a "new world age" with new "moorings" that needed to be established in the stars.

The early peoples believed the god Saturn "gave the measures" to Jupiter (the god represented by their priest/kings) that would indicate the new constellations rising heliacally with the sun to mark the solstices and equinoxes. It was that X marking the spot that gave them their location in the universe.

Joanna had wondered why the Incas might have been so focused on the 40 "meetings" of Saturn and Jupiter. She'd concluded that they'd noticed how the night skies changed with the movement of Earth, and how that would cause familiar stars, like those marking the "gateways" to the Land of the Dead and to the Land of the Gods, to appear or disappear for vast periods-of-time.

Such events would have been disturbing to the Incas who depended on contact with their ancestors, who were believed to return at winter solstice through the gateway from the Land of the Dead. Equally disturbing would have been loss of contact with the Land of the Gods.

*Little wonder that those 40 conjunctions were significant to the Inca*s! The awareness of precession and its consequences of change over time was a huge catalyst to development of early civilizations. Saturn appeared to control the movements of the universe and the personification of that planet was viewed as the supreme god who brought the gifts of civilization to humankind. It would seem that all those same notions were at play in the Inca Empire.

Dodging late afternoon traffic, Joanna headed across the street from Coricancha and entered Hotel San Pablo. She was glad to have the evening free. The tour of the acllahuasi and her experiences on Machu Picchu had made her even more committed to decoding Sister Elena's myth.

Chapter 23

Several days of celebration were planned for the birthday Joanna shared with Rosa. Today, Friday, a shopping spree was on the agenda with a leisurely lunch afterwards. On Saturday, the actual day of the event, Doña Isabella was giving a dinner and formal dance. Rosa had glowed with excitement all week—Juan Diego had been teasing her about a special present he was giving her.

Joanna had to admit that she was looking forward to the celebrations, despite missing Michael. In the early spring, he'd booked a suite at a private resort on Barbados to celebrate her 25th birthday, but those plans were history now.

Selecting birthday presents wasn't on Joanna's list of favorite things. She'd asked Rosa to help her select a special necklace to wear with a party dress for the formal dance, hoping she'd show enthusiasm for some bauble and voilà, gift hunting would be over. Rosa said to meet her at the artisans' shops near San Blas that were famous for handcrafted gold and silver jewelry.

Joanna, nearing the windows of Casita Mandaval, was struck by the exquisite displays. She lingered, admiring the unique designs.

"What type of jewelry are you looking for?" Rosa asked, coming to stand alongside her.

"You're the one with the fashion sense, something to complement the dress I'm wearing on Saturday."

Rosa pulled her through the door of the shop and they stopped in front of a counter with displays of silver jewelry fastened to rectangular rough planks under glass domes. The filigreed necklaces and earrings were so delicately wrought they looked as though they'd been constructed under a microscope.

Rosa asked the clerk to bring out one of the trays of earrings. Joanna wandered toward the owner's workbench. He was shaping a silver setting that had a series of cabochon cut emeralds in a circlet around a center to which he was fitting a turquoise stone. The piece, obviously meant to be a pendant, was really a work of art.

She turned away when she heard a low squeal. Rosa was trying on a pair of filigreed earrings that descended in tiers of liquid silver from her earlobes to her shoulders.

"Why don't I buy those for your birthday?" Joanna said.

Rosa's joy was infectious. She twirled about, watching herself in the mirror as the earrings swung in counterpoint to her movement. Each time she stopped, the earrings settled into ghosts of pyramids that emitted silver sparkles in the sunlight.

"They're perfect, but you shouldn't spend that much for my gift," Rosa said, removing the earrings and handing them to the clerk.

Joanna proffered a traveler's check and asked that the box be wrapped in birthday paper.

"Damn it, I would've bought them myself if I'd known I had to wait until Saturday to wear them! What about your necklace—aren't you going to... ."

Joanna laughed and waved her away. "I already own a necklace I intend to wear."

They exited the shop and Rosa stopped just outside the door. "I've got a great idea! Let's go to J.D.'s apartment for lunch. He usually meets me there on Fridays. I've wanted you two to get to know one another better. I told him we were going to lunch, but he'll still be at the apartment. We can order in from the restaurant next door. He won't mind. In fact, he'll be delighted."

Rosa unlocked the door to the first floor veranda and motioned Joanna to follow as she climbed the outdoor staircase. The apartment building was a small two-story structure of colonial vintage with a central hallway extending from the second floor veranda to a back balcony where a stairway descended into an enclosed garden.

The architecture of the building's central open hallways was referred to as a "dog-trot" back in the states. Both open "hallways," downstairs and up, had six bedrooms opening off them, three on each side—twelve bedrooms in all. Each room had a transom above the door that opened inward for air circulation.

"This building belongs to Juan Diego," Rosa said. "He had a decorator from Lima provide every bodily comfort for these 'pied-à-terre' apartments."

Rosa searched in her purse for the key. "Each one serves as a bed-sitting room with a sumptuous king-sized bed and a hot tub in the center of the bathroom. J.D.'s best friends pay him well for the luxury of having in-town abodes."

"Sounds like a fantastic money-making venture," Joanna said, moving her umbrella to her other arm.

"Since our engagement, Juan Diego and I've been meeting here three times a week, after his City Council meetings," Rosa said. "We dine on liver pâté and wine, play in the hot tub, and fall asleep until late afternoon."

"My imagination has already filled in most of the gaps in that story," Joanna said. "This place is hugely sybaritic—even the Romans couldn't have dreamed up a more sensual place—I'm betting just being in one of those rooms is like foreplay!"

They neared J.D.'s suite, and Joanna saw that the transom above the door was leaning inward.

"See, I knew he'd be here!" Rosa said.

"Maybe we should've called," Joanna said.

Rosa placed her hand on the door, inserted the key, and turned the doorknob. Groans and short-gasping breaths erupted from somewhere inside the apartment.

"He's hurt!" Rosa shrieked, rushing toward the bedroom. Joanna hurried after her. A frenzied scream froze them in their tracks.

"Please, oh God, please God, oh GOD—oh, J.D.! Oh God, yes, yes, YES!"

The sound extended into a series of ear piercing yelps, accompanied by industrial-strength thumping noises, like a piston in an overworked engine, vibrating the bedsprings.

Rosa, trance-like, backed towards the entrance, pulled Joanna into the hallway, and closed the door. Letting her hand drop from the doorknob, she leaned against the doorjamb for a moment, and went limp.

Joanna caught her, dragged her to the back balcony and made her sit on the top step of the stairway. Rosa crumpled slowly forward, wracked by dry heaves.

Quelling a temptation to return to the room and murder J.D., Joanna dialed Casa de la Reyna. "Bartles, is Don Carlos in town? ... Thank you."

She patted Rosa's shoulder and waited interminable minutes with the cell phone pressed to her ear. "Carlos, we're at J.D.'s apartment building on the back balcony... No, Rosa... Right... Please hurry. She's in a bad way."

It was the most excruciating twenty minutes she'd ever spent. Carlos finally raced up the back stairs, and knelt at his sister's side, picked her up in his arms, and stood, holding her tenderly.

"I knew this would happen sooner or later—J.D. has always been a sleazy bastard."

"It was all I could do to keep from going back in there and beating him with my umbrella," Joanna said.

"I'd gladly do it, but we need to get Rosa home as soon as possible."

Seeing Carlos cradling his sister, Joanna had a flashback to a picture on Rosa's dresser at boarding school. It was a snapshot of six-year-old Carlos, standing in front of a crib, holding his newborn sister.

Then, as now, there was a look of pure adoration on his face. What a rare human being, she thought, and the image of her father James Nickels-Stewart became superimposed upon Carlos' tall frame. She knew she'd never forget the moment.

"Give me your coat, Joanna. We need to conceal her—those

damned paparazzi are camped outside. They must've seen the two of you come into the building. I parked on a side street and walked around the block. Take the car keys and drive several blocks away, circle back to the lane back here, near the garden entrance. I'll meet you down there."

Carlos placed Rosa on the back seat of the car and sat next to her with his arm draped around her, the coat pulled over her head. He gave Joanna directions. She maneuvered the car out of the back alley and entered the stream of traffic.

Glancing in the rear-view mirror, she fought back tears at the sight of her grief-stricken friend. Rosa was leaning lifelessly against Carlos. Deep worry lines creased his brow as he looked down at her and adjusted the coat.

They'd gone only a few blocks when the streets became congested, and the car was stalled in heavy traffic. Joanna checked the rear view mirror again. Rosa sighed as she sat up and pulled away from Carlos.

Carlos repositioned himself and settled her back on his shoulder. "Rosa, you want to talk about it?"

"I can't—can't think about it... I don't know what to say ..."

"You don't have to say anything. I can guess—he's a rotten bastard—by god, I'll go shoot him. You want me to go shoot him? I'll go do it now!"

Rosa stifled sobs and laughter. "Carlos, you're the best brother a girl ever had. I can't bear to think I'd lose you in a shoot-out."

"What! I could hit that myopic bastard at thirty paces, blindfolded."

"Carlos, darling, I don't doubt your shooting prowess." Rosa laughed hysterically.

"Joanna, help me out here! You heard her!"

"Hey buddy, you're on your own—my dog's definitely not in *this* fight!"

"Well, at least I made you both laugh. Okay, Rosa, what *do* you want me to do? Tell me and I'll make it happen."

"I want to disappear, but I can't—I love you and mama and daddy and Joanna, too, so I can't do that, and I've got to help Joanna search for her relatives—I can't give up now, I owe it to her for all the years she helped me in the states."

"Now that's my girl!" Carlos said. "Do let's carry on... Mrs. Grundy—stiff upper lip and all that British rot—"

"I couldn't bear it without you and Joanna."

"We're here, sweetheart," Carlos said.

Rosa was silent for a moment and then spoke in a thin small voice. "He said he loved me—"

"That's really something he can't comprehend," Joanna said. "I worried about that the first time I met him. He's just plain shallow, totally undeserving of your love."

"But what does that say about me? Am I shallow, too? Why didn't you say anything?"

"Rosa, no one could have told you anything," Carlos said. "You had to discover that for yourself. I'm just sorry you had to find it out in this painful way."

At Casa de la Reyna, Joanna parked near the service entrance and jumped out. She opened the car door and Carlos lifted Rosa from the back seat. She ran ahead, opening doors, as he carried his sister up the back stairs to her suite of rooms on the second floor.

From the bathroom medicine cabinet Joanna got a bottle of aspirin and turned on the faucet for a glass of water. She stood by while Carlos placed Rosa on the bed and took off her shoes. He held Rosa in a sitting position so she could swallow the pills, and then gently propped pillows at her back. He kissed her forehead, nodded to Joanna, and left the room. Rosa stared at the diamond on her right hand and slowly slipped it off, letting it drop to the floor. Tears glistened at the corners of her eyes as she shut them.

Joanna closed the plantation shutters and pulled a chair to the bedside. She leaned on the coverlet and took her friend's limp cold hand, holding it to her cheek. Rosa opened her eyes, smiled at her, and drifted off to sleep.

Joanna dozed fitfully, waking frequently to check on Rosa. Startled by a noise at the bedroom door, she sat up, trying to orient herself. It took minutes for her eyes to adjust to the twilight glow of a nightlight. Carlos had opened the door and stood gazing down at her and Rosa.

"I've placed a call to Dr. Aubrey. He's on his way," he said. "He'll check her and perhaps give her a sedative, so at least she'll sleep through the night."

"Goodness, is it evening already?" Joanna said.

"Catarina will get her ready for bed. Come on downstairs and have some food, I know you probably missed lunch. Bartles is whipping up something. We'll eat in the library. The folks are in Lima overnight—just as well—Rosa won't have to put up with Father's ranting."

Carlos' calm, take-charge demeanor was reassuring. Joanna felt light-headed after all the emotional drama they'd been through, but the cold air blowing across the courtyard was refreshing.

She dashed after Carlos and caught up with him as they reached the library wing. Just inside the entrance, he stopped and went into the coatroom. Finally emerging with a silk shawl, he draped it around her shoulders. She accepted it gladly.

"Carlos, I can't bear to see Rosa suffer like this."

He placed his hands on her elbows, pulling her close in a hug.

She was startled but hugged back, savoring the comfort. He took her chin in his right hand, kissed her lips lightly, and laying his open palm against her cheek, pretended to smack her.

"That's to remind you of something you knew a very long time ago... ." He walked away, paused and looked back. "Don't worry about Rosa. She's made of the same resilient steel as you." Hurrying to the fireplace, he used the poker to stir the logs. The flames shot up renewed. Joanna felt the warmth and pushed back the thrill she'd felt at Carlo's embrace.

She parsed his words. "Something she knew... something she knew a long time ago."

Stop it—you witless twit! Stop it now!

The logs crackled, the flames glowed. Bartles had positioned two chairs with footstools on either side of the fireplace. A bottle of brandy with snifters waited on the table between the chairs.

Joanna sat down, and Carlos lifted her feet to the stool. The butler appeared immediately with a tray of canapés and offered them to her.

"Thank you, Bartles," she said.

Carlos sat down on the other footstool and pulled it near.

"There's some news." He paused, watching her. "I had intended to tell you after the birthday party tomorrow. I didn't want to spoil the festivities. After today, I'm guessing our celebration will be a bit subdued. So, it's probably best to tell you now. The police here in Cuzco tracked down your stalker."

"Did they arrest him? Who is he, do they know?"

"Our security guards caught him going through mail at the gatehouse box. He was captured and detained, but the American Embassy intervened, so he's been extradited to the states. His name is Granville Townsend."

"Granville!—but that's Michael's cousin! I've never met him. I've heard Michael joke about his being the senator's errand boy. He was stalking *me*—why?"

"He told the national police he was sent to spy on you, said the senator wanted to know immediately what you'd discovered about your adoption. Here's the part you're not going to believe. Apparently, Townsend hatched some harebrained scheme on his own when he learned you were Ayaviri's daughter. He hired men to kidnap you and hold you for ransom!"

"Hold me for ransom—good Lord!"

"He said it would be a way to expose your terrorist father to the international press and give the Vander Hursts a reason to call off the wedding."

Joanna raised her hands to her face, trying to stop her head from spinning. "What if they'd killed me?"

"I doubt he wanted that. He said he knew your family would pay the ransom and with the media exposé, the senator would have the ammunition to persuade Michael to call off the engagement. As I said, it's real harebrained stuff."

Betrayal spread through her like glue, thickening her throat, pooling in her stomach, immobilizing her. Carlos knelt beside her chair, placing an arm around her. She shuddered and a wave of sadness washed over her.

"I've been nothing but a chess piece in the senator's power game," she said.

"Joanna, I'm afraid I'm the bearer of even more bad news. El Presidente asked about you several days ago, and I told him you were searching for your father. He insisted on having the Elite National Police look into your case."

"But I didn't want to bother—"

Carlos took her hands and gripped them tightly. "They conducted a thorough search. Ayaviri is dead. There's no trace of any other relatives."

Chapter 24

The urgent message from Sister Elena requesting Joanna visit the locutorio on Wednesday morning had been a shock.

She'd arrived earlier than usual for the appointment. For the past few days, she'd been up since dawn, frustrated and unable to sleep. It had never occurred to her that her search would end with the discovery that both birth parents were dead.

The nun would be disappointed that she couldn't finish decoding the myth. She dreaded telling her that, but she needed to leave for Mongolia as soon as possible. She had no further reason for staying in Peru.

She'd hoped there was a chance Sister Elena might know of some distant relative who might still be alive. That would be compensation, at least. The bottom line was, she needed answers about her family and the nun had implied she knew something. Well, she had to have the answers today. This was probably her last opportunity to visit the monastery.

The door swung open as she pressed the buzzer.

"*Benedícite,* my dear."

Joanna's umbrella clattered to the floor.

"*Dóminus*," she replied, bumping the chair aside as she bent to retrieve the umbrella. "I didn't realize you were back there already!"

"I didn't mean to startle you. You're up quite early yourself! How's your work going at the observatory?"

"What? Oh, my work ..." She repositioned the chair and sat down. "It's been a wonderful experience working with Dr. Alderez and the assistants."

"I can see from his books that he's an exceptional person."

"Sister, do you remember I told you Carlos was helping me track down my birth parents?" She took a deep breath. "The national police told him my father died in prison."

"How very disturbing for you."

"The thing is he tracked down my father's real name. Last week I went to the University of Huamanga to meet a professor who may have known him, and he gave me a paper my father had written that included two stories recorded in the late 1600s by one of my paternal ancestors. One story was about an aclla named Huarana …"

"Please go on."

"Well, last weekend I visited Machu Picchu, and —"

Why had she said that? She hadn't intended the conversation take that course—no stopping now.

"—a strange thing happened. I fell asleep during a storm, and I dreamed —"

"… Dreamed you were an aclla?"

Joanna stared at the nun's silhouette behind the grill. "How could you possibly know that?"

"Does your excellent scientific education allow for a belief in the supernatural?"

"I'm not sure," Joanna said. "Many of my colleagues in science believe religion is a necessary fairy tale. Others feel there's a 'worthy opponent at work,' arranging the universe and leading us on unending treasure hunts for knowledge."

There was no comment from behind the curtain. Joanna realized she hadn't answered the question.

"When I view distant galaxies, in their myriad variations," Joanna said, "I feel transported, as though I'm in touch with some vast intelligence, and everything in me resonates with that. I see order in the midst of apparent cataclysmic chaos, a never-ending cycle of order out of chaos."

"Sounds like your work is your religion," Sister Elena said, lifting her voice slightly.

"I never thought of it that way, but it's probably true."

"Your aunt told me your birth certificate had the name 'Huarana' on it."

Amazing!—she'd been ready for a fight, prepared to demand

answers—now she'd been handed an opening.

"I guess I'm named for my ancestor—the aclla Huarana." She plunged forward. "Sister, please tell me what you know about my birth family. It would mean so much to me. Did they have other children? Who are my grandparents? Please—I've so little time before I leave for Mongolia."

There was a soft sigh from behind the grille, a long pause and a rustle of fabric.

"Joanna, you may not believe this, but there are reasons that I can't do as you ask—and no, I can't tell you what they are. One day soon, I'll be able to tell you what you're asking." When she spoke again, her voice was sad. "I hope you're not too terribly angry with me."

She was beyond angry, wanted to beg—a horrible breach of her mother's code of conduct—wanted to burst into tears, like a child crying for the impossible.

"I understand that you're unwilling to tell me what you know, and I've no choice but to comply with that. But, Sister, I'm not giving up— I'll find the answers whether you help me or not," she forced the words through clenched teeth, struggling to stem the flood of emotion.

"Thank you." There was a pause. "I'm eager to know what further things you've discovered about the myth."

Didn't the nun know how wrenching it was for her to talk about the myth, or anything else, after what had just been said?

"It's intriguing," she coughed to cover the crack in her voice. "It's like many of the discoveries I've made in astronomy—the more I think I know about the myth, the more complex it becomes."

"You said there really may be references to astronomy," Sister said. "It sounds like you've found something else as well."

"Well obviously the myth was important. Not only was it committed to memory, but its symbolism was carved right into the landscape—a massive undertaking." Joanna paused.

"I can't shake the feeling this goes beyond religion, beyond philosophy—that it isn't just trying to teach descendants about astronomy, although that's certainly a huge part of it.

"They took extraordinary measures to ensure that certain clues were repeated over and over, enticing us to search for a deeper meaning."

"And what do you think that meaning could be?" Sister Elena asked.

"I think the Incas, and maybe other civilizations all over the world, were trying to warn future generations about some celestial occurrence—but what that is still baffles me."

"Do you really think it was possible that the Inca priest-astronomers observed and gave a name to Saturn?"

"Somebody in the Inca Empire sure did! Whether that knowledge was passed down by a more sophisticated civilization from a remote past, or whether their 'astronomers' were just highly skilled... that's still something for which there doesn't seem to be a definitive answer."

"You said 'a sophisticated civilization from a remote past,' that's a stunning statement."

"The facts are there. The Incas described Viracocha as 'the old god' who brought the 'tools' of civilization to mankind, just as Saturn is described in other myths around the world. Pirua, from which Peru is named, was the first Incan priest-astronomer-king Manco Capac, and like Jupiter in Roman mythology, he was given knowledge of how to 'rule' by Saturn—by Viracocha."

Joanna stood and moved about the room, as she had done so often when instructing her students. "Since these themes repeat in myths world-wide, it seems reasonable to conclude that they were handed down from remote antiquity–they're not just something humans dreamed up while observing similar phenomena."

"In other words," Sister Elena said, "these myths share common symbolism because they may share a common source?"

"Exactly," Joanna said. "Saturn gives Jupiter the means to 'rule'—and that concept of 'how to rule' seems to be a coded reference to the conjunctions of Saturn and Jupiter, which early people believed were in 'control' of the mechanics of the universe. 'How to rule' meant how to establish new star markers that told them their "location" in the universe."

She paused, giving Sister Elena a chance to comment. When there was no response, she moved nearer to where the curtain showed a slight opening.

"Kepler drew a wonderful graphic, the concept which he'd clearly copied from more ancient sources, of the 'Trigon of Great Conjunctions' of the triangles that Saturn and Jupiter describe as they conjunct over time around the zodiac, which, taken all together, shows their repetitive conjunctions over, the Double Hour, 2167 years, and the Greatest Day, of 26,000 years."

"Do you know, Joanna, I recall studying about Kepler's diagram at the Sorbonne. Those conjunctions around the zodiac mark significant cycles of precession, don't they—like a gigantic "clock" face of the universe?"

"That's why I think such knowledge—like your myth—must be a memory from some very remote civilization. Such observations had to be made and recorded over incredibly long periods of time, far longer than the Inca civilization would have had."

The nun's shape behind the grille suddenly shifted. Joanna sensed the subject was about to change.

"There's another document I'd like you to read. It was dictated to our first abbess centuries ago by a former aclla who once resided in the acllahuasi here in Cuzco. I think it may shed light on the final layer of meaning you're seeking."

Another document! One actually dictated by an aclla.

Joanna felt a surge of excitement. "I imagine it's very valuable to your monastery," she said.

"Oh, it is. Only a select few in our monastery even know of its existence—to protect the innocent, you might say. As you may be aware, in Sixteenth and early Seventeenth-Century Peru, anyone aiding the Incas in perpetuating so-called *pagan* religious practices could be dragged before the Inquisition."

"I feel honored that your abbess would permit me to read it," Joanna said.

"I'll request that the extern sister place the document in the turnstile for you. Please sit in Santa Maria Church to read it and then put it back in the turnstile. I'll be anxious to meet with you again soon to discuss it."

It felt like she was being thrown a life preserver. Sister Elena had said she'd reveal something about Joanna's family *soon*, and now there was another historic source being handed her that might help decode the myth. She'd have to postpone leaving Peru—maybe stay another month. She'd deal with Michael about that later.

Chapter 25

The fragile document was encased in a linen wrap inside an envelope that also held a pair of white cotton gloves. Joanna pulled the gloves on and slid the pages from the protective covering. Her gaze took in the florid Spanish script.

Ad Majorum Dei Gloriam
Anno Domini 4 August 1551, Feast of St. Dominic, Cuzco, Peru
Nuevo Mundo Colony of His Glorious Majesty, Charles V Hapsburg, Holy Roman Emperor
Scribe: Madre Ángela Marie Ortiz de la Navidad, Abbas, Santa María Monasterio

We are in the first year of the founding of our Order in Cuzco. The story that follows was told to me by a former aclla of the noble Inca Acllahuasi in Cuzco, who was placed in our monastery by the son of Diego de Almagro. The aclla knew Spanish before coming to us and was in her thirty-fifth year. Not long after dictating this story, she left our monastery for the remote highlands.

She was the daughter of a Kuraka and had been chosen to live in the acllahuasi at about age eight. After ten years of training, she was elevated to be an Inca-by-Privilege, a member of the aristocracy, because of her special talent for music.

At twenty, she was selected by the Sapa Inca and his Coya to join the next level of acllas. To be a chosen woman in Cuzco was one of the highest honors in the empire. As events ensued, in 1536, the Incas revolted against the Spanish, and the acllahuasi in Cuzco was dissolved, thus she came to live with us. This is her story.

THE ACLLA'S LEGACY

It was not easy for me to be content in the house of the acllas. I was haunted by memories of my home, my family, and the memory of a kiss I once shared with a young prince of the empire.

The head of the Acllahuasi, Mamacona Yulli, told me that all acllas had memories that they must wipe from their minds. It was a matter of focus, she said, of turning one's mind to the sacred duties for which each of us was responsible. Still, I could not forget that kiss, and the memory remained fresh as cool water quenching thirst.

Our acllas in Cuzco, the mamaconas, were royals by birth, sacred brides of Inti and were vowed for life. But those acllas who were not royal, Incas-by-Privilege--like myself— had three paths: we could either be chosen as one of the Sapa Inca's concubines, we could be given in marriage to a member of Inca royalty or to a chieftain, or we could become a mamacona and remain a bride of Inti always. I was among those chosen to pass to the higher levels of initiation to become a mamacona.

If a Cuzco aclla lived an exemplary life and passed all her levels of initiation, she would walk the Llama Road—our last journey, the journey to the Land of the Gods.

Finally, the day came for our first initiation, the first step on the path to becoming a bride of Inti. The other acllas and I had just come from spending two days in prayer and fasting. Everyone's face was rosy with excitement as we assembled in the sacred space.

Mamacona Yulli approached the fire altar and knelt, prostrating herself on the sacrificial stone in front. She stayed there for a long while, finally stood, and turned toward us.

"You've undergone strenuous training, and I know your hearts are full of joy." She turned her head slightly and inclined it toward the altar. "But before we continue with the rites for this special occasion, there is something I must tell you."

We waited in eagerness and fear.

"The people of our empire have attempted to live in peace with the conquerors. We thought we could survive, but our attempts have failed."

The smiles faded from our faces.

"Matters have become so desperate that our Sapa Inca has revolted," she said. "It grieves me now to tell you that after losing Cuzco to the Spanish, our warriors have fled to the high jungles." Mamacona Yulli wiped her eyes before continuing.

"Now our acllahuasi is in grave danger—especially the acllas related to the Royal Family or those raised by privilege to our ranks."

The room was silent. I trembled at the horrors I imagined and feared for the safety of my young prince, whom I knew would be fighting at the side of his uncle.

"Many of our acllahuasis in other parts of the empire have been burned and the acllas defiled," Mamacona Yulli said. "It's only because of the Sapa Inca's special protection that we in Cuzco have been spared." She paused as though the next words were too painful to speak. "This morning a royal messenger arrived with orders from Sapa Inca Manco Inca Yupanqui. We must abandon our acllahuasi tonight and escape along the Llama Road to Old Mountain."

In shock, we lifted our heads as one to stare at Mamacona Yulli, but she raised her right hand to calm us.

"Now you must finish the consecration of your lives to Inti so you may become like Mama Quilla in her service to him."

One-by-one we came forward, took a golden cup filled with chicha from the altar, drank half of it, and poured the rest over the sacred fire as a symbol of our sacrifice to the Invisible One. The fire flared brightly as I poured my chicha on the altar.

When that part of the ritual was finished, we knelt together in a semi-circle and prostrated ourselves before the altar while Mamacona Yulli repeated prayers to seal our sacrifice.

"Inti and Mama Quilla, protect these acllas who have given their lives to you. Guide them so they may serve you well. Viracocha, supreme of all the gods, grant that we may dwell with you in the Land of the Gods."

After the prayer was finished, we returned to our places and awaited Mamacona Yulli's instruction.

"The lesson for today," she said, "is a very appropriate one, considering our present circumstances. The lesson is about death."

There was a sharp intake of breath from all of us.

"You will one day reach the highest position as Inti's brides, so you must learn to come to terms with death: the death of Cuzco, the death of the Empire, the death of Pacha Mama...and your own deaths as well, for all these things will surely end."

It was difficult to hear her words because we were all so young. Such thoughts had never occurred to us.

"From your studies you've learned about the changes in the land and sky. You've watched the ice the sun god melts with his breath. You've seen it flow through the rivers that are the veins of Pacha Mama, and finally you've watched it rise with Inti's warm breath to be released into the sky as clouds destined to make their way into the heavens. We are no different."

We nodded our heads for the image was familiar to us.

"I saw you tremble at the thought of leaving Cuzco this very night," she said. "Such an ending is most certainly like a death."

Her voice was silent for a moment and then she called for a chair to be placed at the foot of the altar and sat down. A strange look appeared on her face and she lifted her voice, as I'd been taught to do when I intoned the sacred songs.

"Many ages ago our priests realized that Pacha Mama, our Earth mother, was the same as the five wandering lights in the night skies. They became aware that all things around them were like themselves, and they yearned to travel throughout the universe, to explore time, and to understand all that we see, as well as many things we can only imagine.

"For generations they studied. They abstained from food, consumed sacred substances, and finally learned to free their minds from the physical bonds of the body. They learned much of other humans, animals, plants, even the stars, since all are one in the universe.

"In this way every kind of knowledge was revealed to them, and may be revealed to us."

I was surprised to find that I had the beginnings of understanding of what she said, for we had already learned to fast in order to sharpen our thoughts, and to use the sacred plants to free our minds to peer into other worlds.

"Pacha Mama is very old," Mamacona Yulli said, "and our ancestors were born a long, long time ago in the First Time. They studied many things, including the skies, and acquired deep knowledge. This is how they learned to anticipate the cycles of Pacha Mama's growth.

"As the First Time drew to a close, people knew they must prepare. They saw that in the near future Pacha Mama would undergo many terrible changes and be unable to sustain them. Their greatest grief, as they pondered the destruction to come, was that they wouldn't be able to preserve the beautiful things they had built, the knowledge they'd accumulated. Even if they survived Pacha Mama's death cycle, much would be destroyed and forgotten. They were overcome with despair.

"But, dear Acllas, our people knew the only way to preserve this knowledge was to imprint it on everything around them—upon the very earth on which we walk and, most importantly, in the minds of our children. All the stories you've learned since childhood—even the story I tell you now—has been handed down from the First Time. When the time is right, you will hand it on to others.

"The quipus you carry in the pouches fastened to your belts tell the tale of our ancestors, those who discovered the cycles as they walked the Llama Road in the First Time. Guard it well and always carry it with you."

I sat in a stupor. I could sense both wonder and fear in all those around me, yet I felt only dread.

Mamacona Yulli stood and walked to the middle of the circular room, where words of great importance were always spoken.

"Our way of life as acllas was established long-ago, during the First Time. Our mita has always been to assure that this knowledge goes on, that humanity's story goes on."

She paused and looked deeply into each of our eyes before she spoke.

"Let your minds be at peace," she said. "You will survive—not as *finite* individuals, but as *infinite* souls, forever re-emerging, born again into the new cycle.

"Always live as though you are in the First Time. Living so, you will transcend the cycles, eventually reaching the highest levels of awareness and knowledge. Set your minds so that, like the flowing river moving over boulders, you will never permit the Present Time's discords and obstacles to encumber you. In that way, your souls will be free to live always in the First Time."

A long period of silence followed, no one moved. I was entranced by the ecstatic look on her face, and I repeated her words, trying to understand, wanting to remember.

Once again, she went to the altar and prostrated herself on the stone of sacrifice. She stayed that way for several moments then gave the signal for each of us to perform the same ritual act of self-immolation to Viracocha. When we had finished, she led us in procession outside the sanctuary.

"Return to your stations," she said, "and the mamaconas will help you organize your belongings for departure at midnight."

People scurried about and heavy containers were being moved as I hurried down the long passageway. Usually at that hour, the only sounds were of fountains splashing and birds singing. I felt a tug on my sleeve. When I turned, I saw that it was

Mamacona Yulli.

"I need to speak with you alone," she whispered. "Please come with me."

I followed Mamacona Yulli through the door into the central acllahuasi. Everywhere I heard the sounds of acllas bustling about their rooms.

Mamacona Yulli took me into her workstation, a place I'd seldom been. I regained my composure soon enough and knelt in front of her table, awaiting her instructions.

She sat on a bench behind the table and clasped her hands together. Finally she spoke.

"You've been selected by the Sapa Inca to submit in marriage to his nephew. After you're wed, you'll be taken into the *panaca* of Huáscar, to which Sapa Inca Manco's nephew belongs. It is my *panaca* as well."

Married to my young prince! My heart seemed to stop, then leap almost from my chest. Yet tears salted my eyes, for at that moment, more than before, I understood what Mamacona Yulli meant about death. I looked into the face of the woman who had been like a mother to me and didn't know if I could ever stop my tears.

"The High Priest will conduct your marriage rites. Unfortunately, joyous celebrations that usually accompany such a marriage will not happen for you. We regret that. And there's something else." She studied me closely. "The mamaconas have decided that you will be the one to carry our story to the Spaniards, who will record it for future generations.

This I had not expected. "What must I do?"

"The story on the quipu in your pouch will have to be

translated for the person to whom you entrust it. Who that person is, we leave to your good judgment."

"I'm honored by the mita you've given me," I said. "But I'm frightened by it. What if I should fail?"

"Your strength of character, which we have nurtured, assures that you'll succeed." Mamacona Yulli moved to stand in front of the table and placed her hands on my head. "We love you and will miss you, but we're happy for your marriage."

I kissed Mamacona Yulli's hand, as I had been taught to do, and bowed my head.

"I will obey," I said.

We, in Santa Maria Monastery, learned that the aclla's husband, a member of the Inca nobility, had fought in the jungles with the rebellion until the capture and execution of the Sapa Inca Manco Inca Yupanqui. Her husband had been in hiding when the aclla was brought to this monastery. Much later, she left our community to re-join him in the remote high jungles, where relatives had sheltered their two sons.

She gave into our keeping the story that was on the quipu in her pouch. After consultation with my council, for we were concerned that our act might be heretical, we have agreed to preserve this legacy.

† Ángela Marie Ortiz de la Navidad, Abbas, Santa María Monasterio

Anno Domini, 4 Agosto 1551, Feast of Santo Domingo, Cuzco, Peru

---

Joanna gently placed the document on the pew beside her. What an incredible story! How did one come to grips with all of its implications?

The central preoccupation of the acllas, and obviously the Incas, seemed to have been with the periodic cycles Earth went through, what they viewed as a birth, death, and rebirth.

Was this the deeper meaning of the elaborate symbolic geo-glyphs carved into the landscape of Peru—that civilizations evolved not in a linear, but in a cyclical fashion?

When she'd studied philosophy in college, she'd memorized a passage from Plato's *Critias*:

> ...with you and other peoples, again and again, life has only now been enriched with letters and all the other necessaries of civilization - when once more, after the usual period of years, the torrents of heaven sweep down like a pestilence leaving only the rude and unlettered among you. Then you start again like children, knowing nothing of what existed in ancient times, either here, or in your own country.

Some people thought that passage could refer to Atlantis, but what if Atlantis was simply a metaphor for all ancient civilizations—those which predated even the earliest cultures of India, Sumer, Turkey, Greece, Egypt, and China.

What if all the coincidences and commonalities of ancient architecture, sacred writings, and early myths were a desperate attempt by our ancestors to communicate something profoundly important?

Joanna slipped the fragile pages back into the linen cover and took off the white gloves. She carefully placed everything into the envelope, went back to the locutorio door, and set it into the turnstile opening. She rang the bell for the extern nun to retrieve the envelope and lingered nearby, reluctant to abandon such a precious document.

Mamacona Yulli mentioned a myth.

That has to be the same myth Sister Elena gave me to decode!

The frequencies of matter looked at cycles. If the cycles of all matter and energy were comparable on macro and micro scales, then humankind might be able to predict the movements of the universe and thus, be prepared for natural cycles that always involved some catastrophe.

She thought back to Mamacona Yulli's words about the death of Pacha Mama. If her theory was right—if this myth and others like it had actually been passed down from a civilization so remote that only the barest traces of it survived, what did that mean for her time, for the *Present Time*?

She heard the turnstile clink.

Whatever it meant, she was determined to find out. After all—what were the odds that she, an astronomer studying the frequencies of matter, should be handed a myth that seemed to relate to the cyclical nature of those same frequencies?

She shook her head and giggled softly. *Rosa would call it destiny.*

Chapter 26

Joanna directed the attention of her graduate assistants to the area near Earth's magnetic North Pole, where a Fermi bubble had been detected. Piggybacking off her frequencies research, there was a chance spectroscopy might reveal previously undetected spheres analogous to such bubbles in the far reaches of the universe.

"Let's review what we know about Fermi bubbles," she said, manipulating, the image currently displayed on the large plasma screen on the wall. "Here's the bubble in the Milky Way Galaxy, discovered in 2010 using NASA's Fermi Gamma-Ray Telescope that gave the name to gases like this figure-8 bubble emanating from above and below the black hole in the center of our galaxy."

"They're emitting high energy gamma-rays from the fission caused by the destruction of matter in black holes," Karina, the youngest assistant said.

"Hasn't a team of SETI scientists started looking at bubbles like those as possible signatures of extraterrestrial archaeology?" Francisco stood and moved to the screen, a huge grin betraying his excitement.

"Dyson spheres and stellar migration by advanced civilizations bent on harnessing the energy of the universe—but that's extremely hard to believe—I thought all that stuff was from a 1945 science fiction novel by Olaf Stapledon," Camilo said.

"Imagine for a moment," Joanna said, "that there might be artifacts out there somewhere that resemble—"

"—resemble molecules of artificial man-made, or we should say 'intelligent-made,' objects not occurring naturally in the universe, but that give off identifiable frequency signals like the ones you've detected, Dr. Nickels-Stewart," Pedro said.

"So, you're saying we might be able to detect those frequencies of "intelligently" made objects in the vast reaches of the universe and find—," Karina said, eyes wide in awe.

"Intelligent life!" Camilo yelled, and looked down, blushing.

"—signs of galactic engineering!" Karina finished.

Joanna laughed, excited at how the students were surfing off each other's ideas in a wonderful game that bore no resemblance to work. She touched the screen of her tablet and shifted the planets in the solar system model on the screen.

"A number of times during the last hundred years, scientists have observed disturbances in radio transmissions when planets such as Jupiter, Mars, and Venus are in a direct line with the Earth and the Sun," she said. "We know high sun spot activity is correlated with electrical disturbances. Is it possible Fermi bubbles increase or decrease those effects?"

"Take a look at this." Francisco touched the central console to change the image again. "These are trace images of charged particles from black holes that NASA scientists believe are disbursed by Fermi bubbles throughout the universe in sort of a chain reaction effect. Could Fermi bubbles be similar to worm holes?"

"Gamma-rays are hazardous to biological material, but because of their short waves, they can become less so and their penetration could be contained with the right material... but what else could the bubbles carry—besides charged particles, I mean?" Camilo looked perplexed.

"Fermi bubbles like worm holes—hey, could they be superhighways through the stars?" Pedro asked, with a pensive look toward Joanna.

"Excellent notions!" Joanna beamed at the assistants. "Now think about this, we know matter exists as a standing wave, vibrating at an 'x' frequency... could *matter* be disassembled and actually *carried* by the Fermi—"

"Dr. Nickels-Stewart?" Ms. Sanchez said over the intercom. "Sorry to interrupt, but there's an important call for you on the office line."

Joanna excused herself and hurried to her office. She pressed the speaker button and sat at the desk.

"This is Dr. Nickels-Stewart."

"How're you doing, sweetheart?"

"Michael!"

"Listen, I've only got a minute—when's your flight to Ulaanbaatar? We've got a belated birthday to celebrate."

"Michael, I tried to call you earlier—I've got to stay at least two more weeks. Rosa's broken up with J.D., and I'm working on something for a friend of Aunt Jane's—"

"You've already stayed longer than you planned." She heard a short, sharp exhale. "Forget it! I'm coming to Peru."

"Michael, please—." The phone went dead.

Michael's flight was due at 11:30 a.m., and Bartles had offered to meet him at Alejandro Velasco Astete International Airport—Joanna was tied up at the observatory.

"Please bring him to the lab if you don't mind," Joanna said. "I'll take him to lunch and see that he's settled into the hotel—"

"No, no!" Bartles said. "Have your secretary cancel that reservation—the family will insist he stay with us. I'll give him lunch and drop him off at the observatory after he's rested—that's a very long flight after all."

Joanna picked up her cell phone. Bartles' number was flashing on the screen—she'd ask him to alert her when he was dropping Michael at the observatory.

She hurried down the stairs and waited by the front door. After Michael's call, she'd swung between anger and delight. Michael loved her—he couldn't possibly have known about the senator sending Granville to spy on her. Still, he *was* a lot like his father. Whose side would he take?

If I don't know the answer, then we have a much bigger problem than I thought.

The car pulled up to the curb. Bartles hurried around to open the back passenger door and Michael emerged in a smooth liquid motion, unfolding his lanky frame and planting his feet on the sidewalk.

Joanna saw him pull a handkerchief from his suit pocket and wipe his hands. He always did that when forced to use some public conveyance—a subconscious prejudice.

She found herself wanting to draw attention to it, scream it aloud for what it was, but Michael would've been baffled.

She went through the door to embrace him. He picked her up, swung her around, and kissed her so hard she almost lost breath.

"Michael, it's so good to see you—sorry I couldn't meet you at the airport... ."

She waved to Bartles and ushered Michael through the entrance. On the way upstairs, she pointed out the views of Cuzco through the high lobby windows, then showed him to the lab where she introduced him to her colleagues.

Dr. Alderez entered the lab, smiling broadly.

"Welcome Mr. Vander Hurst! Joanna told us about the great work you're doing in Mongolia!"

Michael described a half-arc with his hand, indicating the lab. "I'm impressed by *this*."

"We're fortunate to have a well-equipped lab and a brilliant scientist to direct it, even if she's here for only a brief time," Dr. Alderez said, looking fondly at Joanna. "I hope you'll let her give you a tour of the entire facility while you're here."

"I saw a very complimentary article in the international papers on your work," Michael said.

"It's reassuring to have others appreciate what we do," Dr. Alderez said. "But truly, Dr. Nickels-Stewart's contributions are largely responsible for our growing presence in the press. Your own work sounds intriguing, though. Joanna tells us you've been working in the Gobi Desert?"

Joanna saw a distant look come into Michael's eyes and knew he'd lost interest in the conversation.

"He may be in the desert," she said. "But his mind's never far from

D.C."

The smile disappeared from Michael's face. Dr. Alderez hurried to fill the awkward moment.

"Well, do let me welcome you to Cuzco! We hope you'll have an opportunity to visit us again before you leave. Joanna, please feel free to show Mr. Vander Hurst around the lab."

Joanna gave a quick tour and then led Michael to her office. As soon as the door was closed, he enfolded her in his arms, kissing her long and hard.

"I'm afraid you'll disappear if I let you go," he said, still holding her close. "It's been the worst time I can remember. I feel like I'm missing a part of myself."

"I've missed you, too. Do you mind if we have an early dinner at the observatory restaurant? It's really nice and there are excellent views of Cuzco."

He grabbed her wrist and pulled her through the door into the small bathroom connected to her office. He lifted her onto the sink and kicked the door behind him. She felt a rush of emotion.

"Michael ..."

He hiked her skirt and pulled her close. She pushed him away.

"Michael, please, not here."

He backed away, frowning. "What's wrong?"

"It's just... it's not the right place."

"Joanna—how can you ...?" His eyes narrowed. "Do let me guess. Old Carlos has been making up for my lost time, am I right?"

"That's unforgivable." She slid off the sink, jerked the door open, and stumbled back toward her desk. She took a few deep breaths, collected her purse, flipped off the light switch, and went into the hall.

The toilet flushed. A moment later, Michael stepped into the hall. She locked her office, and they walked in silence down to the quadrangle.

"Look, Joanna, I'm sorry—"

"Forget it. Let's go to the restaurant."

Chapter 27

The maître d' showed them to a table with a view of the city. Joanna ordered two bottles of Cusqueña® beer.

"It's the national drink," she said. "You really ought to try it."

"God, you look sensational. Let's leave for Mongolia tomorrow."

"Michael, we need to talk."

"What's keeping you here? Your mother's dead, and if you haven't found your father by now you're not likely to. Hell, he probably doesn't want to be found. Face it—what more can you do here?"

"Rosa needs me, and I have to do something related to astronomy for a friend of Aunt Jane's. Plus, I promised to finish some research for Dr. Alderez."

"Seems to me Rosa has plenty of support, and surely that observatory can manage without you."

"We're on the verge of proving the Incas were highly-skilled astronomers. This could be the beginning of something huge—a complete re-evaluation not only of the Incas, but of other so-called primitive cultures."

He leaned back and folded his arms. "And they can't do that without you?"

She was at a loss. He didn't have a clue!

"Who am I, Michael? Do you even know?"

"I know I'm not waiting around while you act the part of the celebrated scientist in some backwater observatory!"

"*Acting*—I can't believe you—."

"Bottom line, Joanna, I love you and need you with me." He pushed back from the table. "If you really want to marry me, you'll come with me tomorrow."

The Cusqueña® beer bottle hit the wooden table with a thud. The other patrons turned toward Joanna. She steadied the bottle, pushed the bread plate aside, and leaned forward.

"I wanted to marry you all right—that's the whole damn reason I came to Peru."

"What *are* you saying?"

"Your father." She lowered her voice. "He told me I had to 'clear the air,' surrounding this adoption business." She leaned back, picked up her bottle again, and glared. "His exact words: 'It's imperative my wife and I know the ancestry of our future grandchildren.' "

His tanned face went chalk white and gradually shaded to deep rose.

"God-damned-son-of-a-bitch, you never told me—"

"I'm not finished," she said. "He sent his lackey Granville to dog my every step? No doubt, because he thought I couldn't be trusted to tell the truth."

"Why didn't you phone me immediately to let me—?"

"There's one more thing you *really* ought to know. Your father had a meeting with General Moore shortly before your promotion was announced."

Michael pulled his arms close to his body, folding in on himself, shrinking back into his chair.

"How do you know that?"

She took several swigs from the beer bottle. *Why did I do that?* She'd always despised people who deliberately hurt others.

Setting the bottle back on the table, she took a deep breath. "When I met with him—the day he gave me that anonymous letter—he ordered one of his bodyguards to cancel a meeting with General Moore, because he hadn't heard from the officials in Ulaanbaatar yet."

Michael gripped the edge of the table. "Why didn't you tell me that in April?"

"You were so happy about doing something on your own... I'm sorry, I know it was wrong, but—."

"What else haven't you told me?"

"Granville stalked me, intercepted mine and the de la Reyna family's mail, and hired thugs to kidnap me."

"Did what!" A few heads turned in their direction.

"He told the police the kidnapping would hit the international news media," she said, attempting to keep her voice even. "He wanted everyone to know about my family, how my father was a terrorist. That way Senator Vander Hurst could convince you not to marry me. By the way, your father had the U.S. Embassy negotiate his release."

"You can't possibly believe I knew about any of this!"

Just as she feared, there it was—his usual quick rush to self-defense.

Joanna drained the bottle of Cusqueña® beer. "Please inform Senator Vander Hurst that I definitely agree with him—I don't have the kind of ancestral genes he wants for his grandchildren."

"Let's take this down a notch," Michael said. "You know I don't agree with Father's views—all that bullshit about heritage and bloodlines."

He reached across the table for her hand. She pulled back, staring at him.

"Let's cancel the wedding in Charleston. We can get married in Mongolia. Besides, the media doesn't have a clue about your adoption. We need to give my father time, Joanna. He'll come around. I hate what he's done, but I know it's done in our best interest."

"Wow, how absolutely obtuse of me!" She slapped her forehead. "It's *clearly* in our best interest to cover up my heritage so the Senator doesn't ruffle any political feathers, or god forbid, potential voters—."

"Just stop it." He held up a hand. "We'll have a better perspective on this in the morning."

"Tell me, Michael...if Granville *had* managed to get my family history into the headlines, what would you have done?"

She looked out the window at the churning skies above Cuzco. "Don't bother to answer that. You know what... I don't intend to ignore my identity any longer. I'll be lost forever if I do, and we'll both regret it."

"Your identity! What are you talking about? Never mind..." He tossed the napkin down, pushed his chair back, and stood.

"I've booked reservations for both of us on a flight to Lima at 11:00

a.m. tomorrow. No, don't bother to get up. Finish your dinner. I'll get a cab back to the de la Reyna estate. Oh—and Doña Isabella said to tell you she expects us for breakfast at eight."

Joanna phoned Bartles and asked him to convey her regrets to Doña Isabella. Breakfast was more than she could handle—yes, as a matter of fact she *was* feeling poorly—no, probably just a stomach virus—and would he please tell Michael she'd be at the estate at 9:00 a.m., to drive him to the airport?

She nixed the thought of going back to her apartment—sleep would be impossible. She returned to her office, sat on the small sofa, and gazed unseeing out the window.

If there were any rules for breaking up, she wasn't aware of them. The only thing she knew for sure was that she'd staked a position and had to stand her ground.

The night was endless. She paced up and down, berating herself and Michael, his family and hers. Finally, at 4:00 a.m., hoping for a modicum of peace, she sat at the computer to record her thoughts on further study of the Fermi Bubbles. Eventually, she nodded off over the keyboard.

The cell phone sounded 8:00 a.m. She didn't feel tired. Unlocking the bottom desk drawer where she kept a clean sweater and underwear, she grabbed what she needed and slipped into the bathroom to freshen up.

Cuzco's cold morning air slapped her in the face as she emerged from the observatory. The car she'd rented for Michael's stay in Peru was parked where she'd left it yesterday morning. She got in and headed toward Casa de la Reyna.

Michael was waiting, suit bag and carry-on case in hand. She drove under the porte cochère, feeling a surge of relief. She wasn't ready to face Doña Isabella, or anyone else for that matter.

He shoved his things in the back seat and got in beside her. She drove quickly away. On the way to the airport, he said little, feigning interest in Cuzco's passing scenes.

Joanna dropped him off at the terminal entrance, parked the car in a long-term space, and joined him at the security checkpoint. They were passed through, and she walked with him toward the departure gate that led out to the tarmac.

"I hope you're coming with me," he said. "Just get on the plane and go—Rosa can pack your things and send them on to Mongolia."

"I have to stay here."

"I just don't understand." He paused and turned toward her. "I love you. Isn't that all that matters?"

"I love you, too, but it's never going to work."

"Joanna, please—"

She touched his arm. "Promise me you'll find someone who'll make you happy and have a wonderful bunch of kids. They'll be special—just like you. Please, just be happy."

The last boarding call sounded over the loud speakers.

He wrapped his arms around her. "I can't believe this is happening," he said, holding on tightly.

She broke the embrace. He caressed her face briefly and turned away. Grabbing his suit bag, he ran through the gate and over the tarmac, not looking back.

Nauseous, Joanna pressed her hand against her abdomen. It felt like a black hole had just opened inside her. She watched the plane taxi down the runway, lift off, and disappear into the clouds.

Back at the lab, the hours ticked by. Joanna looked up to see the skylight filled with brilliant stars. Where had the time gone?

Probably it was best to go to the office and write a few notes on the day's work before heading home. At least she wouldn't have to worry about sleep—sheer exhaustion would take care of that.

So what am I going to do with the rest of my life?

She thought of Maria Reiche, the German mathematician who'd visited Peru for a brief expedition and spent the rest of her life combing the geoglyphs in the Nazca Desert. The 'old maid of Nazca,' they'd called her.

Maybe I could be the 'Old Maid of Cuzco.'

The night guard buzzed her desk. "Doctor Nickels-Stewart, buenas noches! Doña Rosa de la Reyna requests to see you."

Damn it! She'd wanted to avoid all the de la Reynas, needed to be more in control of her emotions.

"Gracias, please send her up."

Bracing herself for the onslaught, she opened the door. Rosa darted through and pulled up a chair.

"Okay, so tell me."

"Tell you what?" Joanna sat in the chair behind her desk.

"Don't give me that! Mother knew the minute you didn't come to breakfast. She called me in Lima to come home immediately—she's very concerned."

Joanna leaned forward, propped her chin on her hands. "Simple truth?"

"Simple truth. Okay, but you know I need more embellishment."

"You can toss that 'maid-of-honor' dress. You never liked it anyway."

Rosa's face darkened. "Which straw broke the camel's back?"

"He didn't even know me, Rosa. I should have seen it, but how could I—*I* didn't *know me*. I was too caught up in some stupid fantasy about being Mrs. Michael Vander Hurst, the fifth." She dropped her head into her hands. "God, I'm so blind."

"It isn't easy to see what we don't want to see." Rosa looked down at the floor, appearing lost in her own thoughts. After a while, she looked up. "So—what's next?"

"I guess I'll go home to Virginia and start looking for a good position with one of the universities that tried to recruit me."

"Why not take the job Dr. Alderez offered?"

The intercom buzzed. The night guard announced another visitor. The door burst open.

"Joanna, I've been looking all over town for you—I'm firing that damned bodyguard. Where's Michael?... Rosa! When did you get back from Lima?"

"Michael's gone," Rosa said.

Joanna felt the tears well up and threaten to choke. She pushed them back and forced herself to focus on the simple miracle of two friends regarding her with loving kindness.

Carlos glanced about the room, took two strides, grabbed Joanna's jacket from the coat tree, draped it around her shoulders, and assisted her to stand.

"Let's go," he said.

"Where're we going?" Rosa demanded.

"To the Via Làctea for that chocolate cake you two are always talking about."

Chapter 28

The scattered pieces of her life needed to be gathered up. She knew very well what to do. A plan had to be made and she needed to stick to it. That'd always been the solution in the past.

But she'd never been at a crossroads like this before. Marriage plans deep-sixed, no permanent job, failure to find her Peruvian family—well, that wasn't exactly true—there could be relatives Sister Elena knew about.

Furthermore, she'd stumbled onto some interesting ancestors and maybe the frequencies research might be tied to the meaning of the myth. There was so much more she needed to research and analyze about that.

She knew the cycles the myth referenced were linked to the geoglyphs on the landscape of the Sacred Valley, and those had to be tied to astronomy, since the landscape replicated the Milky Way, but she couldn't put together the underlying message the myth seemed to be transmitting. How *did* one get into the minds of ancient people and tease out their meaning?

The locutorio buzzer sounded loudly, and the door opened with ponderous slowness. Joanna's red swollen eye's struggled to adjust to the dark interior.

"Joanna, please bring your chair closer to the grille."

"You called Rosa's mother this morning—she said you wanted to see me." Joanna scooted the chair a foot closer.

"My dear, please tell me why you came to Peru?"

Was the old nun's memory failing?

"I wanted to find my birth family."

"Why?"

This was getting annoying. What was she asking?

"I needed to find my identity—to find me, but that's on a more precarious footing than ever. Not only have I *not* found members of my birth family, but my hopes of having a family of my own have slipped away."

Waves of sadness washed over her, she struggled to keep her voice clear.

"My career's going nowhere—which I'm sure, is a huge disappointment to my father, to James Nickels-Stewart—and my mother's completely devastated over my break-up with my fiancé. She'd hoped I'd soon be happily settled into the lifestyle for which she's groomed me my whole life."

"And your identity's tied to all that?"

Tears flowed freely. She clinched her hands and pounded her lap—how stupid—not being in control of her emotions, not being in control of her life.

"Yes! Those roles would have helped to define me. I'm trying to sort it all out, and I'm not making very much progress."

"Joanna, it may seem like an imposition, when you've already expended great effort working on this myth, but I need you to do one more thing. It's something I can't do myself, and I believe it's vital to understanding the myth. If you decline, it may never be done."

What is she asking? Doesn't she know I'm at my wits end, that I barely have the stamina to get my things together and leave for the states.

"I need you to walk the Inca Trail."

"That's not possible. I'm sorry to disappoint you, Sister, but I don't have the time. May I be frank? What I really want to do—have to do, right now—is hide away some place and lick my wounds for just a little while."

"That's not like you, Joanna. Besides, I was under the impression physical exercise stimulates the production of serotonin, a natural antidepressant. I can't think of a better place to lick wounds and heal than on that trail."

"Touché…," Joanna said.

Sister Elena laughed, and the room sent back echoes like tinkling bells. A rustling sound came from behind the grille, and the gnarled hand reached a small rectangular piece of paper through the bars.

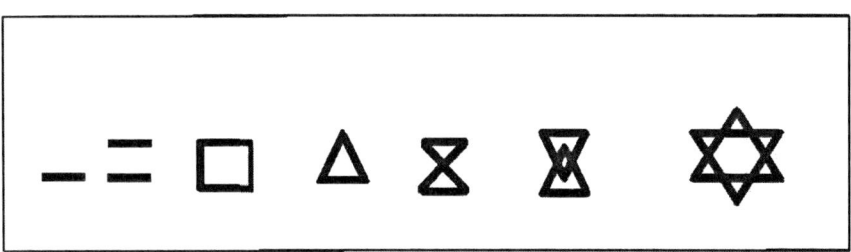

"Joanna, I believe the shapes on this paper, which are an ancient depiction, provide a way to understand the meaning of the life of the acllas. Books could be written about the resonances they generate in the mind of the beholder. In this form, they're a kind of shorthand, a guide for the soul to follow in searching for the divine, a graphic of what happens when the soul recognizes a greater dimension for its development."

"They're geometric shapes—like Egyptian hieroglyphics," Joanna said.

"The Pythagoreans were among the earliest groups to have written about those shapes, Sister Elena said. "Inca acllas and their counterparts throughout history, like the Egyptian priestesses, the Vestal Virgins, etc., were the 'wisdom' keepers, and also knew about them."

"Do the shapes tell a story, then?" Joanna asked.

"The array, I believe, shows the insight into the meaning of man's great journey through this world that was developed by the 'wisdom keepers.' That piece of paper represents that knowledge reduced to its essence."

"You said 'journey through life'—does that single line represent a person alone with self—much as I'm feeling right now?"

"And *so are we all alone*, until we realize there are no barriers and find the way to break through to clear consciousness. It's only when we see persons and things as they really are that we can meet them in pure communication," Sister Elena said.

"I remember discussing Jewish mysticism with a friend in college," Joanna said. "She told me Solomon's *Song of Songs* in the Bible is not, as I thought, an erotic love poem, but rather describes the union of the soul with God. She said there's a breathing exercise—breathing in and out in a rhythmic pattern, while focusing on the breathing—that's supposed to produce an ecstatic state, and it seems Rabbi Simeon Bar Yohai, who lived around 2 B.C.E., attributed that activity, *called the divine breath*, to King Solomon.

"She said Hebrew tradition claims that Solomon wrote his love poem in that ecstatic state. She says the *Star of David* is supposed to symbolize such a union. Are the psalms also 'love poems' to God?"

"The *Star of David,* as you see, is there at the end of the array, and it does depict the 'spiritual marriage,' the union of the soul with God," Sister Elena said, "but the symbol goes far back beyond the Hebrews, and some believe, has an even greater esoteric meaning. I'll leave that for you to discern as you contemplate it on the trail. By the way, Teresa of Avila's book *Interior Mansions* is a superbly practical source for understanding the ecstatic union, called *the spiritual marriage*."

She couldn't believe, of all people, *she* was having this discussion with Sister Elena. She did recall that Mamacona Yulli had hinted at such things in her instructions to the newly initiated acllas. *Was Sister speaking again? Pay attention, Joanna.*

"We cloistered nuns have the privilege of reciting King David's psalms daily. Our *Divine Office* is comprised of them. They're chanted in the beautiful Gregorian chant that expresses so well the soul's longing for union with God. That's the main work of our cloistered lives: to praise God, ceaselessly, by chanting the *Divine Office*, in which we constantly thank Him for the greatest of all gifts, the soul's ability to join in loving union with Him."

"I must say I didn't understand your way of life—actually thought it was such a waste," Joanna said.

"Oh, my dear, it's the ultimate adventure!"

"A special union with God like that must be impossible for the average person. I mean, I can't see myself having time to develop such a focus."

"Union with God may be a little more difficult minus some of the handy 'aids' that our cloistered convent life provides—for instance, the gift of time, without distractions—but it's not impossible. We nuns, like you, and everyone else, must seek God in the humble activity of our daily lives—no matter what the work may be—sweeping a floor or discovering a galaxy. We must seek Him in the moment and consecrate it to Him."

"So, you're saying a person has to be constantly aware of God and invite Him to be present in all they're doing? Frankly, Sister, that sounds impossible to me!"

"But you're constantly aware of yourself, is that not so? God's already there in the soul He created. He just needs to be remembered, now and then! I think He wants us to recognize Him as a *person*."

"Dodi," Joanna said. "The Hebrew mystics called God *Dodi*—"

"Friend…it's a thrilling thought, isn't it?" Sister said. "Extra dimensions of knowledge and understanding become available as we work to know God more and more. I'm sure you've discovered the same in your scholarly work. I believe that's what the acllas did, Joanna. In fact, I'm convinced walking that trail, as they did, will give you more insight into the meaning of their myth."

"Toward the end of writing my dissertation, late one night, I was attempting to analyze the implications of my research, and I came to some point where some new dimension opened up for me. I thought I saw the *unity* of all knowledge. I wondered, '*Is this what it means to attain to the level of doctor of philosophy—have I tapped into some strange repository of universal knowledge? Am I meant to contribute in some tiny way to it?*'"

That sounded pompous, but it had been a strange experience, and she'd gained new insights.

"I think it's true that the more we study and contemplate, the clearer the underlying connections become," Sister said.

"It was weird. Is it possible that that's what the philosophers, priests, and priestesses of ancient civilizations were able to do?"

Joanna was lost in thought, glad the nun hadn't said anything more. There'd been times she felt a strange presence in an eminent way—like two months ago when she and Rosa had gone to mass in Santa Maria Church. The beauty of the chant and the words of the Mass easily transported her, and she'd longed for a lengthier period of communication with—with what?

Perhaps she'd find out, somewhere along that trail. Would she find the meaning of the myth? Grief at not finding her birth parents still gripped her, but maybe by decoding the myth, she'd at least get to know her great to the Nth degree grandmother, Huarana, a little better.

"So... Sister, you're saying this trek could help me solve the riddle of the myth? What would I have to do?"

"There are some difficult physical requirements—practices utilized by serious 'searchers' that are designed to get the job done!" Sister Elena sighed. "I know they'll seem bizarre, but here goes! First, you must fast. That's most important, and please do not take creature comforts along, even your cell phone!"

Joanna was glad the nun couldn't see her face.

You must train your body to be impervious to the weather, especially to temperatures—go unshod frequently—you'll be surprised at the disciplining of self that engenders. All of this forces you to focus away from preoccupations with the *desiring self*, and the last requirement is even more difficult, I fear. You must practice silence, at least during the day."

"Let me make sure I'm understanding you correctly," Joanna said. "I'm supposed to starve, freeze, go barefoot, and remain incommunicado, is that all?"

Laughter rang out from behind the grille. "Touché!"

"I don't mean to be flippant, Sister, but austerity like that would certainly force a person to focus on God, begging for deliverance, if nothing else."

"Your trek won't be for viewing pretty scenery. Do you understand the concept of surrender? You must let go, really let go of will, desires, pain. Think of this as a kind of hero's journey, and, in keeping with the start of that journey, there's something I want to give you."

Joanna watched with growing curiosity as a small white linen-wrapped packet tied with a thin length of purple satin ribbon was handed through the bars.

"It's a talisman for your journey, my dear. Please don't open it until your moment of *greatest need*. Vaya con Dios."

Chapter 29

"You're doing *what*! Wait—stay right there—I'm coming over. Madre de Dios, Carlos—she's having a nervous breakdown!"

There was a thump and the phone went dead. No use ringing back. Rosa wouldn't answer anyway—had probably bolted out the door without the cell phone.

It was no use—no one was going to talk her out of doing the trek—she owed it to herself. It would be interesting to test whether the experience would bring greater insight into the myth, which should certainly help her discover more about her ancestors, and there might be the added bonus of having a personal interaction with a supernatural being. *Hey, it was possible. Game on!*

The click of Rosa's stiletto heels echoed in the open stairwell. Joining them was the sound of heavier footsteps, moving around the balcony, nearing the apartment. Joanna jumped up, took three quick steps, opened the door and found her friend in full fight mode, accompanied by Carlos.

Rosa grabbed her by the arm, propelled to the bedside chair, and perched on a chest opposite. Carlos remained near the doorway, eyes downcast, looking as though he'd be happy if the floor opened and gave him a convenient escape route.

"Good Lord, don't just stand there, we need a stiff drink." Rosa glared at him.

Carlos placed his black leather portable bar on the small dresser and pulled out three silver tumblers, poured scotch and a splash of seltzer in each. He handed a tumbler to Joanna and one to Rosa, picked up his own drink, selected the most distant corner, and sat on the carpet to observe the proceedings from afar.

Rosa took a sip and set the tumbler down. "Okay, Joanna, slowly now—just tell me, what's going on?"

"It's nothing, really. I'm afraid you've gotten all worked up needlessly."

"Please tell us, you know we're here for you. Wait! Don't say a word, tell you what, why don't you come back with us to Casa de la Reyna. We can talk the whole night through, okay?"

"I'm fine—I'm just going hiking, that's all."

"You said spiritual quest…"

"Well, that, too—I need to sort some things out, and the rigors of the Inca Trail will help me to do that."

"Joanna, as I recall, you're somewhat frightened of heights," Carlos said. "I must tell you one of the passes on that trail rises to a little less than three miles high, with steep narrow ledges to navigate, and there's no other way around them."

"I've read about the trail, did a virtual walk on the Internet, and I've talked to some people who've walked it, and yes, I've heard the horror stories, but now is the best time to go, before the high tourist season. Besides, I understand the trail's better maintained since the government has been regulating it."

"Still…it's a dangerous venture," he said.

"Joanna, it sounds awfully much like you're having doubts," Rosa said. "I vote you shouldn't go."

"I don't want to start at Marker 88, the usual trek. I'd like to walk the ancient Milky Way path, the one the priests and acllas walked in their spiritual initiation rites."

Rosa groaned and got up to refresh her drink.

"I knew it!" she said. "Joanna, we can get you help—there's a good therapist in Lima— that god-damned Michael Vander Hurst!"

"This isn't about him!" Joanna crashed her hand down on the bedside table.

Rosa dodged as though she'd been hit, and Carlos stared wide-eyed.

"Who're you trying to convince?" Rosa said.

"Please, understand, this isn't about him—it's about me. For the first time in a long time, I'm doing something for myself." She swallowed hard and lowered her voice. "Besides, Dr. Alderez asked me to do some work related to the trail."

"You can't walk that trail alone. Come back to Peru next year and we'll walk it together."

"Rosa…it's got to be now—"

"Well, if you insist on going now," Carlos said, "Rosa and I'll come with you. It'll be good for all of us."

"Hey buddy! Didn't you hear me? The hell you'll volunteer me, I'll be damned if I'll trek that Inca Trail anytime in the near future—not for Joanna's or anybody's sake!"

"I don't want to impose my whims on you all—absolutely not!" Joanna said. "Carlos, you're much too generous."

Carlos got up and stretched his legs. "It's settled. I'm coming along, never did it before, and can't think of a better time to do it!"

"It'd be great to have you along… I didn't exactly know how I was going to manage everything—guides and porters and such—could you really take a month off?"

"No problema, Señorita!" He raised his glass in salute.

"You're both crazy as loons," Rosa said. "Go ahead, trek all you want, but count me out."

Exactly three days later, Carlos and Jamie stopped at Hotel San Pablo where Joanna, backpack slung over her shoulder, stood shivering at 4:00 a.m. in the cold morning mist. The traffic in Cuzco was sparse, and they were soon driving on the roughly paved road down to the Urubamba Valley, following the river eastward toward Pisac.

The little market town plaza where vendors were setting up stalls filled with vegetables and crafts was already teeming with eager bargain hunters. Some people sat on the ground on blankets with their wares spread around them. They were laughing and chatting with neighbors. The mood was festive.

Jamie unloaded the backpacks from the trunk and waited by the curb as Carlos searched the crowd for the porters who were scheduled to meet them. Joanna spotted four Quechua men in distinctive Ollantaytambo ponchos and colorful highland hats who were hurrying toward them.

"Joanna, wait here, I want to check that they've got all the supplies we need," Carlos called, slinging his backpack over his shoulder.

Jamie returned to the car and drove away. Joanna waved to him and watched as Carlos followed the trail guide and three porters to a mound of camping gear. He'd hired them, he said, not only for transport, but because their numbers afforded protection in case that was needed.

The vendors were haggling over prices. It was a time-honored practice. Bargaining was expected and admiration was reserved for those who were good at it. Joanna was enjoying the repartee between a Quechua woman and her customer, when she realized someone was hovering near her elbow.

She picked up her backpack and moved to the adjoining stall, thinking she might be in the way. The woman followed close behind. There was something familiar about her, but it was hard to tell. She was bundled in a ski suit, all body parts covered except for the triangle of her face, and that was obscured by expensive wrap-a-round sunglasses.

Joanna swerved back to the first stall. The person moved with her, and a strong odor of flowers and patchouli filled the air. That perfume was unmistakable.

"Rosa, what're you doing here?"

"I couldn't very well let the two of you have all the fun, now could I?" Rosa stood back and assumed a pose, with her hands on her hips. "Look at me folks, I'm friggin' trekking." She paused. "Tell me something, why does this show have to start at 5:00 a.m.? Talk about ungodly."

Joanna grinned in delight. Rosa removed the sunglasses and shook her long dark hair out of the skin-tight cap that hugged her head like a nun's coif.

"Does Carlos know you're here?"

"Nope!"

"We need to tell him—quickly. We may need more supplies."

Joanna looked around for Carlos and the porters and saw them staring in her direction. Carlos had obviously seen Rosa. He waved and sent one of the porters away.

"When did you get here?" Joanna asked.

"Came over yesterday evening and stayed with Tina—she's letting me park my car at her place until we get back. She's mother's old nanny and lives here in Pisac."

Carlos arrived and greeted Rosa. "Glad you're here, sis. I've sent the porters to get more supplies and they'll go on to Calca. They'll travel much faster than we do and will have camp set up when we make our first stop for the night. The guide will stay with us—although he'll keep slightly ahead. Of course, when we reach the more remote areas, all the men will stay closer."

"One of the vendors told me there's a path at the back of the plaza, said it winds up through Inca terraces to Pisac ruins," Joanna said.

"I'm thinking we'll want to follow the longer dirt road that curves around the mountain," Carlos said. "We need to become gradually acclimated to the more strenuous climbs."

About two miles along the road leading to the ruins, they took their first break. Rosa climbed on a boulder at roadside and discarded her hiking boots. Carlos sipped water from a canteen. Joanna watched two young boys struggling to corral a small herd of alpaca.

"How different they are from the kids I know," she said. "In America we'd never believe our kindergartners were capable of such responsibility."

"So, intrepid leader, what's our itinerary for this trip?" Rosa asked.

Joanna pulled a rudely constructed map from her pocket and handed it to Rosa.

"This map shows the route. We'll start here at Pisac on the north side of the Urubamba and head northwest toward Ollantaytambo. From there we'll cross the river and trek straight up the mountain to the trail that goes on toward Machu Picchu."

"So, the Land of the Dead is supposed to be here at Pisac?" Carlos leaned forward, peering over Rosa's shoulder. "Does this map have anything to do with Sister Elena's myth?"

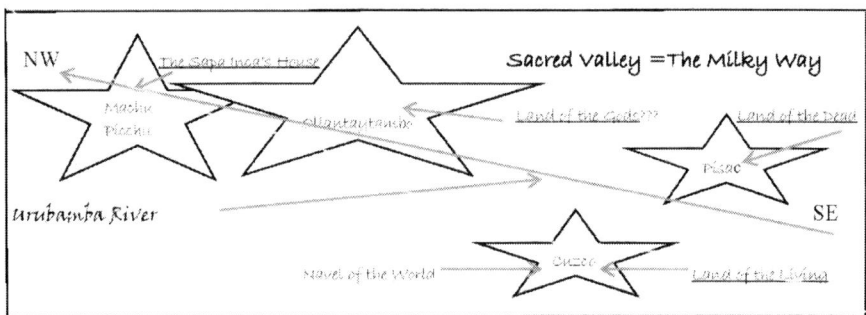

"Essentially I'm trying to find the places *on the ground* that the myth seems to indicate are here in the Sacred Valley. I'm sure the locations are real and not just part of a story—a 'myth'—as we usually understand it."

"What do you know so far?" Rosa asked.

"As you've noticed, the map represents what I've concluded about some of the sites indicated in Sister Elena's myth. We're here at Pisac, of course," Joanna said, pointing to the spot on the map.

"Since the Sacred Valley is supposed to replicate the Milky Way, if we were looking at a star map, Pisac would be the black cloud constellation and, therefore, the place on the ground referred to as the *Partridge*. That bird is a symbol for the Land of the Dead in Incan mythology, as it is in world mythology, and, also, that's the exact spot where the gateway or bridge to the Land of the Dead is located in the Milky Way."

"Cuzco appears to be near the middle of the Milky Way." Carlos said. "Is that why it's called the *navel*?"

"That particular location, in myth, is always near the central axis of the Milky Way. As you can see, Ollantaytambo is probably the fabled 'birth place' of the Incas. That area in the Milky Way is always at its northwest terminus, just as Ollantaytambo is at the northwest end of this valley."

"Why have you got all those question marks by that label for the 'Land of the Gods?" Rosa asked, rubbing each foot and pouring water onto them from her canteen. "It's at the end of the Sacred Valley, isn't it? Shouldn't it be logical that it has to be the Land of the Gods?"

"It just isn't that clear. Ollantaytambo is technically at the end of the valley and, if this valley replicates the Milky Way, that's where the Land of the Gods is supposed to be, of course."

"Well, then, what have you concluded about Machu Picchu?" Carlos said as he inserted his right foot into his hiking boot.

"All the books say it was a royal resort for the Sapa Inca and his entourage. Of course, it has the usual religious shrines within its confines, but, so do all the Incan cities."

"Weren't the Incas supposed to be ignorant of older civilizations in pre-Columbian times?" Rosa asked, turning her pocket inside out where she located a protein bar. "How come so many of their symbols and ideas about astronomy are the same?"

"That's a question everybody should be asking," Joanna said.

"What did Sister Elena say you had to do on this—what was her term? *Pilgrimage*, wasn't it?" Rosa said, munching contentedly.

Joanna took a deep sip of water. "I'll tell you what I have to do, but you certainly don't have to join me. There's fasting, of course, and the goal of the first stage is to let go of negative thoughts about the past. When faced by fears and obstacles, I have to say 'I surrender.' I guess that means surrender to God's will. I have to mean it, though—have to stop struggling to figure out why things have happened, and stop struggling to control everything."

"That's not an easy agenda," Carlos said.

"And then there's the injunction to maintain silence for the whole day with conversations only in the evening. You're right, Carlos. None of this is going to be easy for me, and I guess the fasting and silence are designed to force a turning toward the interior. It's meant to be a spiritual pilgrimage, after all. In addition, of course, I'm 'walking' the Milky Way, just as Sister Elena believes the acllas did. As I pointed out, that's why we're starting here at Pisac Ruins."

"I think I'll join you in the fasting and silence," Carlos said. "It should be an interesting experiment."

"Hey! Don't look at me! I'm just along for the ride—the walk—I'll support you two in whatever you want to do," Rosa said. "How's that? Is everybody okay with that?"

"Rosa, your delightful company means more than your participation," Joanna said. "I'm thrilled you decided to come along."

"Well, I'm no mystic, but I can certainly see how those actions could cause change in a person," Rosa said, licking her thumb and index finger after placing the remainder of the protein bar in her pocket. "Know what? I think I'll join you two in the fast—maybe lose some weight—that'd be great!"

They resumed the trek and soon rounded the highest point of the switchback. The ruins of a vast necropolis opened before them like a colorful Chinese fan spread across the high mountain.

The valley floor was three thousand feet below and exerted a strange pull on Joanna. She turned and hastened away from the outer rim of the road.

Across a wide divide, where the road circled around, the buildings in the temple area could be seen. They were constructed of immense carved stonework that took on shades of faded rose in the sun's slanting rays.

Higher up, tombs were plastered to the sheer cliff walls, looking like adobe swallows' nests. The wonder was how humans could have constructed them in such improbable places, and they were so numerous it was impossible to count them.

The guide stopped a short distance away. Joanna sat on a rock outcropping and was joined by Rosa and Carlos. The site demanded silent contemplation.

"Grandfather de le Reyna brought Rosa and me here just before she started boarding school," Carlos said. "I'm sorry to say I don't remember anything he tried to tell us about the place."

"I feel like I'm seeing it for the first time," Rosa said. "I'm experiencing it the way I imagine you're seeing it, Joanna."

"Dr. Alderez said this site, like Machu Picchu, was probably an astronomical observatory," Joanna said. "Science and religion were inseparable for the Incas. This site may have also been a training center for the priests and acllas."

She believed it was, and she was stunned by how perfectly the place fit the description in the myth. She was definitely on the "trail" of the myth's secrets.

Chapter 30

Joanna found her journal in the backpack and sat down to scribble the first notes of the journey. "Pisac Ruins" she titled it.

Pisac lay at the southeastern end of the Sacred Valley, on the northern side of the Urubamba River. If the Sacred Valley was the Milky Way on the ground then the Urubamba was like the "River Styx" for the Greeks or the River Jordan for Jews and Christians—rivers conceived as celestial rivers, located near the gateway to the Land of the Dead, representing symbolic boundaries on the distant edge of the Land of the Living.

The heroes, real or mythic, who attempted crossing those rivers—Gilgamesh, Noe, Prometheus, Jason and the Argonauts, Ulysses, the mythic Alexander, Quetzalcouatl, Viracocha, Buddha, or Christ—all made that journey, more or less successfully, and all pointed to a *Way*.

Sister Elena had said when you want to make room for the "new self" you have to let go of the "old"—so death to the "old self" had to take place. *How appropriate to contemplate that at Pisac!*

How did one let the "old self" die? Just what did that mean?

Did it mean shedding all non-essential things? Well, that wasn't a difficulty. Lately, she had very little that constituted material things: no home, no furniture, not even a car. Auntie Jane had given up everything on entering the convent.

Did "letting go of the old self" mean letting go of her depression over breaking up with Michael? She'd tried to mask any emotion related to that, but it lurked at midnight, rendering her sleepless, and ambushing her in unexpected ways, like when she tasted a special food they'd shared, or heard some favorite dance tune.

Did it mean replacing residual images of herself as Michael's wife with some new notion about self? That was still a blank.

Maybe it meant letting go of the sense she'd failed her best friend in some way. Rosa hadn't mentioned Juan Diego's name since the incident at his apartment, and there didn't seem to be a ripple on the pond of her happy-go-lucky self—which only made Joanna worry more about what was lurking beneath the surface.

Sister Elena had said this journey might bring greater understanding of the myth. Would that be able to be surrendered, too, if there was no new insight?

One thing she knew for sure, it would be a huge relief to hand all of this stuff off to some Supreme Being and say, "I surrender"—and actually mean it!

I've got to really do this, and, like the needle of a compass pointing north toward God, must say "I surrender" every time a thought pops into my mind to worry me or to draw my attention away from the goal of this journey.

Carlos called to her. "Joanna, do you want to take that short cut down through the terraces to the village?"

She nodded at him and stowed her journal.

Following along behind Rosa, she kept her eyes riveted on the path. She feared freezing on the spot if she saw just how far down it was to the valley floor.

They had no need to stop in the village for lunch. Rosa and Carlos had decided to join her in the fast. The plaza was a blur of color and sound as they hurried past food stalls with tantalizing smells. The water they sipped as they continued walking toward Calca assuaged some of the hunger pains.

When they'd gone a little beyond Pisac, Joanna stopped and looked back at the mountainside. She could see a giant condor geoglyph spread out on the mountainside, just as Fernando Elorrieta Salazar and his brother Edgar Elorrieta Salazar had described in their book. The ruins, the terraces, the natural rock outcroppings—all had been utilized in some way to form part of the bird's shape. Its wings were outspread, in a protective gesture.

She frowned. *Why depict a condor in a place named for a partridge?*

The road to Calca was not a challenge to the three friends who were reasonably physically fit. Since the highway through the Urubamba Valley was well traveled, several trucks stopped, and offered a lift, but Carlos waved them on with a cheery "Gracias."

The valley followed the riverbed. Lush farmland lay in swaths along the road and stair-stepped up the mountainside in wide terraces. On the south side of the river, the mountains were brown, dry, and dusty—when rain fell, massive landslides occurred. On the north side, where rain fell more abundantly, the mountains were fuzzy with "Day-Glo" green mosses, vines, and shrubs that resembled mountains in Hawaii.

Rosa limped along, Carlos plodded a slight distance ahead, and Joanna, who had adjusted fairly well to walking barefoot in the grass alongside the pavement, paced steadily forward.

Her stomach growled and images of food flitted in and out of her thoughts. They were nearing Calca, and Carlos had dropped back to walk beside her.

"I had the porters set the tents up just beyond town in a secluded field off the main highway," he said. "They tipped the farmer for its use. We'll build a fire and rest for a while before turning in for the night. First light will come awfully early."

The warmth of the fire was welcome. Joanna felt lightheaded from the fasting, yet she'd been strangely energetic on the final push toward Calca. It was probably a good thing they were still on level ground.

Carlos tugged his socks away and massaged his feet. Rosa was stretched out full length near the fire, and Joanna sat staring into the flames.

"I've never fasted this long before," Carlos said after a while. "Am I supposed to have a headache and dizziness?"

"I think those are the universal symptoms, but, if we can hang in for a while, both effects will go away."

Rosa groaned.

The guide and porters sat further away playing the ancient game of Pichqa, with pyramidal-shaped dice. They laughed and placed bets as they cast the die on the ground.

The porters were content. They'd eaten their evening meal from take-out boxes ordered in Calca.

Although it was just twilight, Joanna, Rosa, and Carlos agreed that sleep was in order. Tents were zipped shut, and "day one" was logged as accomplished.

Joanna's wristwatch chimed the alarm at 1:00 a.m. She'd set it so she could see the Milky Way in full splendor. She pulled on her parka, unzipped the tent flap, and stood outside, shivering in the cold, looking up into a sky blazing with stars. The hunger pangs were intense.

She took a deep breath. "I surrender," she whispered.

Reaching just inside her tent, she dragged out her backpack, and extracted a water bottle. The water coated her parched tongue and slid smoothly down her throat—cold, refreshing, filling her empty stomach. She drained the bottle and sat down on a thermal gel pad that Carlos had provided for each of them. It felt heavenly. Was this one of the comforts she was supposed to give up? She hoped not!

The tent proved a decent backrest. She leaned against it, staring up at the sky. The southern hemisphere stars were clearly delineated. She could identify the dark cloud constellations that were so prominent in Andean myths. The llama with her baby marched toward the northwest, down the middle of the Milky Way, just as she, Rosa, and Carlos were doing on this trek.

A slight rustling sound caused her to direct her attention back to earth. Rosa came out of her tent and crossed the field to enter the extra tent that had been set up with chamber pots as a makeshift latrine.

Joanna waved to her when she exited. Rosa hurried over and started to speak, seemed to decide against it, sat down instead, leaning affectionately against Joanna's shoulder, tucking her hand into the crook of her friends arm and gazing up at the sky.

"I want you to know I wouldn't have missed this trip for the world—even with this diarrhea I've got," she whispered. "Damn lucky you researched the symptoms people get when they fast! I would *never* have thought to bring *Depends®*!"

"It won't last long. The body has to adjust, and it's going to rebel in several ways." Joanna grinned. "You mustn't be scared when the hallucinations start—like seeing hulking rats."

"Good God! Thanks a lot—some things are better left unsaid until morning light," Rosa said, stretching and yawning. "I'm going to freeze to death if I don't get back to my tent."

She paused and faced Joanna squarely. "Which is better do you think, starving to death, freezing to death, or dying of fright? Step right up, folks, take your pick, either one is guaranteed to get you dead!"

Carlos, awakened by the laughter, stuck his head out of his tent and strode over to join them.

"Are we stargazing?"

"I'm just leaving, please join Joanna. She's still star struck."

Carlos brought his blanket, draped it around both their shoulders, and leaned back against the tent alongside Joanna. "Who knew the sky was this wonderful out here," he said. "So, my Exalted Professor of Astronomy, please tell me about the Milky Way."

"You're sure I won't bore you?"

"You actually think I wouldn't take advantage of a free lecture on the stars?"

She smiled and pointed. "Remember when we were at Pisac I told you and Rosa that that location, lying to the southeast end of the Sacred Valley must be the replica on the ground of the partridge constellation, which marks the *Gateway to the Underworld*, where dead souls go? Do you see the constellation, over there?"

"Duh! So that's why there's a huge cemetery there ..."

"You've got it! Now look to the northwest at the other end of the light band, toward Ollantaytambo. That bright star there is Vega and it's supposed to point to the *Land of the Gods*."

"So Ollantaytambo really is the *Land of the Gods*?"

"Well, I don't think so, but it may be. According to a scholarly work by William Sullivan, the Incas named that star *Paco*, 'father of the llamas.' Paco was a male llama that stood guard over the flocks and sounded a warning when danger was near." She felt a tingle of joy at Carlos' absorbed interest. "Strangely enough, Babylonian astrologers referred to Vega as a priest who guards the 'bridge' to the *Land of the Gods*, and the Inca/Amara word for priest is also *paco*."

"Did other ancient peoples have locations on the ground that they also associated with those important locations along the Milky Way, just as the Incas have here in this Sacred Valley?" Carlos asked, a look of wonder on his face.

"That obsession to mark those locations along a sacred river seems to be ubiquitous around the world. It seems to be part of a common heritage of humanity from some very ancient time, when we were all one community, whatever that may mean."

"So the *Land of the Gods* has to be somewhere over there to the northwest, opposite Pisac in the southeast, right?" Carlos asked.

"Yes, if the Sacred Valley is really engineered to be the Milky Way."

Chapter 31

The journey wound through Ucay, Urubamba, and onward to Ollantaytambo. Although flat land, it was a grueling exercise in endurance and seemed interminable. The only distraction was the awe-inspiring scenery. Snow-covered peaks of distant mountains appeared to play "catch-me-if-you-can," hiding in sudden mists, reappearing in dazzling sunlight.

It was August, the season of early springtime in the Andes. Irrigation ditches were being cleaned, the terraces shored up, and the fields plowed in preparation for planting.

Joanna was listless, lightheaded as she plodded along. The walking sticks the porters had provided proved to be very handy. Rosa and Carlos were slightly ahead of her, moving with studied determination.

Sister Elena had told her to practice silence. That was becoming increasingly easy—no one even had the energy to talk. She'd made some futile attempts to assure her companions that they were experiencing the worst part of the hunger pangs. It was true, their stomachs would shrink, and, after a while, preoccupation with food should subside.

"Good thing we have no other challenges," Rosa said. "I don't know if I can—"

"Wait a minute—I didn't say *no* other challenges."

"How encouraging…" Carlos said and kept trudging.

Near Ollantaytambo, Joanna spotted a wide curve in the river overhung with bushes. It was well hidden and she suggested they stop for a while. Carlos said he would occupy the attention of the porters so she and Rosa could bathe.

The two splashed and dived like playful dolphins. "I've never enjoyed a bath so much," Rosa said, squealing with delight.

"Don't expect another for quite a few days." Joanna climbed out of the water and grabbed a cotton towel.

"I would've never left Cuzco if I'd known we couldn't bathe," Rosa said.

"When did you say your last camping trip was?" Joanna asked, beginning to entertain serious doubts about Rosa's wilding skills.

"I don't do camping," Rosa said, tying on a warm robe and running to her tent.

Carlos took his turn at bathing and then joined Joanna and the porters around the campfire. It was mid-day, but the consensus was that a siesta was necessary—it had taken three days to walk from Pisac to Ollantaytambo. A rest was well deserved. The ruins could be explored later in the afternoon.

The historic town was the traditional starting point of that part of the Inca Trail that tourists usually walked. Joanna calculated that it would take four more days of reasonable trekking to reach Machu Picchu. The plan had been to take a full eight days, spending two days at each major site where there were ruins.

The most rigorous part of the trek lay just ahead on steep mountain paths. She was glad they'd started at Pisac and walked to this point because they were able to adjust to the deprivation of hunger while the physical demands of altitude weren't present.

It was difficult to sleep in the middle of the day and it was stifling in the tent—may as well make use of the time. Only, how was she to go about the business of mapping the constellations depicted by the geoglyphs when she was in the midst of a personal crisis?

Many hours of the last two days had been spent coming to terms with thoughts of Michael. The hunger had forced her even deeper into some region of regret. She hadn't stopped loving him—a silly notion. How did you stop loving someone?

What had the last year and a half been about? Why hadn't she seen Michael's deep resentment of his father's control tactics? How had she missed that he idolized his father despite that control? She'd been around the family long enough, should have perceived the dynamics, but would the result have been any different if she'd let herself be aware? Doubtful that!

Talk about being aware! Why hadn't she noticed how Rosa had put up an impenetrable façade to hide her depression over J.D.? Here she was, supposed to be Rosa's best friend and yet she'd been too busy to see what was happening.

Good thing she didn't have to worry about Carlos. He seemed to accept the rigors of their journey with cheerful bravado. Were there issues he was confronting? She knew he worried about Rosa—he'd said so—but there had to be other things that haunted him. What about Camille Pizarro? Rosa once told her there'd been an understanding from the time those two were children that Carlos would marry her someday. Lately, neither Rosa nor Carlos mentioned her.

Sister Elena had admonished Joanna about tying herself in knots analyzing everything. She'd said what was needed, at such a time, was to make a conscious effort to invite God to be with one in the moment and to surrender. What was the term in the Jewish Kabbalah? *Devekuth,* cleaving to God—she certainly needed a lot of devekuthing.

Rummaging in her backpack for a bottle of water, she saw Sister Elena's gift. Was this the time she needed it the most? She picked it up, turned it over, and examined it closely. The contours were obscured by the sturdy linen wrapping.

"Not now," she said aloud, and put the little packet away. She returned to her cot and commenced a deep breathing exercise to reduce stress.

Blood-curdling screams reverberated through the calm afternoon. Joanna leapt from the cot, scrambling to find her shoes. *Who was screaming?*

She tore out of her tent and ran headlong into Carlos, who was charging from his tent at the same instant. They collided in a front-on tackle, as the screaming became a howling screech.

"Rosa!" Carlos yelled, trying to disentangle himself.

Joanna righted herself and dodged past him, running toward Rosa's tent.

Carlos caught up with her and unzipped the tent flap. Rosa was sitting upright in her sleeping bag, rocking from side-to-side, in a stupor, staring into the distance.

"Rosa, what's wrong?" Carlos bent toward her, gently touching her arm. She gazed at him blankly.

"Was it a bad dream, Rosa?" Joanna sat beside her and pulled her into her arms. Carlos moved to the other side and helped cradle her like a baby. They joined her in the hypnotic rocking and spoke directly into her ears, alternately whispering endearments.

She seemed to relax, closed her eyes, and dozed fitfully. They continued rocking and soothing her. "We love you, Rosa. You're okay, Rosa. It's okay, sweetheart."

Gradually her agitation stopped and she opened her eyes again. "I can't do this—I can't go on," she said. "There's nothing left inside me, nothing."

They held her more tightly, swaying with her. Joanna smoothed hair away from her face, and Carlos kissed her forehead. Finally, she sat up and pushed them away, asking for water. Joanna reached for the water bottle and opened it for her.

"Just now," Rosa said, "I heard someone say, *'Let go, Rosa—just let go,'* but I don't know who that was." She shivered and pulled her sheet over her lap.

"I'm getting you some hot soup from the porters," Carlos said, "I'll be right back."

Joanna found a light blanket, placed it over Rosa, and sat back down with her arm around her.

"I'm empty inside," Rosa said, "like there's no 'me' left *in here.*" She pounded her heart. "I don't know what to do—is it the fasting?"

"Fasting often does force us to face things we usually keep from our consciousness. I've been crying uncontrollably as we walked along—mourning what I considered my losses." Joanna paused, choosing her words carefully. "Rosa, I've worried that you and I haven't really shared our thoughts since you ended your relationship with J.D."

"I couldn't, don't you understand? It's like I would've exploded into a billion pieces if I admitted how much I was hurting." She took a sip of the water. "If I didn't say it aloud, it wasn't real. I've known J.D. since I was a child... what's *wrong* with me that he can't love me?"

"Oh, Rosa!" Joanna stood in front of her. "That's the stupidest thing I've ever heard."

"Well, what about, what the fuck's wrong with him? Is that good enough for you?" Rosa angled her tear-stained face up at Joanna.

Carlos returned at that moment, soup in hand, and opened the tent flap. Joanna and Rosa were bent double, howling with laughter. He halted in astonishment and looked down at himself, as though checking to see if he'd zipped his pants. His reaction produced even greater mirth.

In the early evening, they explored the ruins of Ollantaytambo fortress and temple complex. Rosa seemed subdued but eager to climb to the top of the fortress. Joanna ran from one vantage point to another exclaiming how the whole valley, where the Patacancha River met the Urubamba, could be seen.

"I've read that these ruins probably date from a very early period," Carlos said. "The edges of those huge monoliths are precision cut, and archeologists say the stones aren't from this area. It must have been difficult to transport them up to these heights over those steep cliffs."

"Dr. Alderez told me that Ollantaytambo is where the two branches of the Milky Way were believed to converge and might be the area the Incas called their 'place of origin.' This is where the bridge to the *Land of the Gods* was believed to be located," Joanna said.

"In grammar school we learned that the Incas placed all the ashes from the previous year's llama sacrifices and all sorts of other offerings, even gold and silver objects, in the streets of Cuzco," Rosa said. "Then they flooded the whole city so the offerings would be carried via the Urubamba River to the bridge here in Ollantaytambo, where they were sent on as gifts to Con Ticci Viracocha."

"I remember that, too. People were stationed all along the river with torches to light the way," Carlos said. "The offerings were pushed along the river thirty miles to the bridge here. The newly initiated Inca warriors raced along the Urubamba and tossed their own symbolic offerings into the river here. Joanna, isn't that what your ancestor Joré did? That's one cool story."

"Joré said he wanted to win first prize in the race. Wasn't that the carved salt figure of a war lance?" Rosa said. "It must have some significance. Do you know anything about it, Joanna?"

"Vega is a first magnitude star that rose heliacally—just before the sun at the summer solstice. For the Incas the star was both the male llama and the priest/shaman who carried the war lance, the illaca. That's probably the symbolism behind the war lance salt figure, but Ollantay was their greatest warrior, for whom this place is named, so who knows, it may stand for him."

"Vega represented the ram. A llama would have a close resemblance. You said it stood for the priest/shaman. Wait a minute! In Old Testament stories mother read to Rosa and me, Moses and Aaron were pictured wearing headdresses with *ram's horns*! Those two were also high priests, right! Joanna, just what are we dealing with here?" Carlos asked.

"As I said before, it's a long story, but suffice it to say that the same underlying images and concepts reverberate throughout the whole long history of world mythology. There's a book *Hamlet's Mill* by Georgio de Santillana and Hertha von Dechend, which does a great job of compiling all that information."

"Do you know what the second and third prizes were?" Rosa asked.

"A bird is the second, possibly a condor—birds were the messengers to the gods. The Swan constellation is near the middle of the Milky Way, where it appears, from our vantage point on Earth, to separate into two branches. A cluster of stars that represented birds for the Incan astronomers is also located there. The third prize, the toad, is a constellation beyond the southern tropic, near the abyss—where the Earth's southern celestial axis of rotation is located. So those three prizes were symbolic of some very important locations along the Milky Way."

Carlos and Rosa's interest was invigorating. Having to answer their questions helped her form clearer ideas about Incan mythology.

"The guidebook says those are supposed to be granary silos on the mountain opposite us," Rosa said. "Why would anybody want to place them so high up on the mountain? And there's something else I remember, when I visited here as a child, I was told the cliff beneath them is supposed to look like a man's head."

"Fernando and Edgar Elorrieta Salazar in their book, *The Sacred Valley of the Incas:Myth and Symbols*, say the carved head represents Viracocha as he appeared when he came to teach the Andean peoples about the calendar and agriculture," Joanna said. "The four granary silos depict the four-cornered headdress he wore, possibly representing the four cardinal directions."

"That makes sense then," Rosa said.

"In addition, the silos may represent the four solstice and equinoctial points of celestial earth. The cliff at Viracocha's back is in the shape of the 'burden' he carried, and the crags, to left and right, are shaped to be his hands supporting that burden. The Salazars say the temples situated to either side, as though they're extensions of his hands, seem to mark the positions of the sun at June Solstice."

"I'd like to climb up there someday," Carlos said.

"Dr. Alderez told me there's a heated debate among archaeologists about where Pacaritanpu, the *place of origin* for the Incas, was supposed to be located," Joanna said.

"I've read that many historians tried to make a case for Machu Picchu," Carlos said.

"The *place of origin* is always located at the convergence of the Twin Rivers of the Milky Way," Joanna said. "The convergence here of the Urubamba and the Patacancha River forms an alluvial fan. Within that area, the Elorrieta Salazar brothers believe the Incan irrigation canals seem to outline a tree and that most likely is meant to depict the 'world tree,' which is always at the *place of origin*. There's a newly discovered terraced pyramid, off there to the right of us. It apparently has two doorway indentations that are lit by the sun at winter solstice. I'd place my money on Ollantaytambo as the *place of origin*."

"Then that means the *Land of the Gods* has to be here in Ollantaytambo," Rosa said.

"In Egyptian mythology the constellation of Orion lies at the entrance, or gateway, to the *Land of the Gods* and that spot is always the *place of origin*. If Ollantaytambo is the Incan counterpart of Orion, as I suspect, then this is the gateway."

"So then, you're thinking Machu Picchu is the *Land of the Gods*?" Rosa asked.

"That's the crux of the problem. Machu Picchu, as I said before, isn't technically in the Sacred Valley. The experts can't agree as to its age, whether the Incas built it, or what its purpose was. Some say it was meant to be a lookout post and first defense against hostile jungle tribes. Others contend it was built by Pachacuti Inca as a pleasure palace. Excavations proved it was never a fortress, nor was it self-sustaining as an agricultural site. Scholars have finally concluded it had to be a resort for the Sapa Inca and nobility, and, in addition, that it was probably used as an astronomical observatory."

"Bummer! It just seemed to make good sense that that spectacular site had to be the *Land of the Gods*," Rosa said.

"If Machu Picchu isn't a candidate for the dwelling place of the gods, then it has to be Ollantaytambo, right? Wait a minute! You said *Ollantay* could be the constellation Orion ..." Carlos dropped his hands to his sides and stood very still, a dumbfounded look on his face.

"Go figure!" Joanna said. "Ollantay is the great warrior in the famous Incan drama who has woman troubles with Chasca Coyllur, which is Quechua means *bright morning star*, the one with the long hair—that means streaming rays—which happens to be a description of Venus in all world mythologies. And wouldn't you know it—in all the myths Orion also had the same kind of problems with Venus!" Joanna said.

"Hey! I just thought of something! Our trek is a vision quest, like Joré and the young Inca warriors had to make!" Rosa said. "It's our very own race along the Milky Way."

"Highly unlikely!" Carlos said. "The term *race* can hardly be applied to our pace."

Their ascent rose steadily upward, and everyone appeared exhausted, especially Rosa. All agreed they'd had a good night's rest, tired as they were after having climbed all over Ollantaytambo ruins the evening before. No matter, no one had been elated about rising at daybreak to start the up-hill climb.

They'd reached the next stopping place and the porters were pitching the tents when it was discovered that part of the camping gear had been left on the banks of the river at Ollantaytambo. It was decided that two porters would retrace their steps down the steep mountainside while the guide and remaining porter would cook the noon meal.

José, the leader of the guides, prepared the food at a distance so it wouldn't taunt the fasting trekkers. Carlos busied himself laying charcoal and large kindling pieces inside a stone circle to build a campfire. Joanna searched in the gear for the box of matches and struck a long match to ignite the wood. Rosa stretched her toes toward the fire.

"I can't believe those porters have already returned with the gear," Carlos said. "I'm nearly prostrate from the climb up here, and they're still running at a trot. It exhausts me just thinking about it!"

The campfire sizzled, ejecting volcanic chunks of glowing embers around the stone circle. Joanna had taken a seat on the ground next to

Rosa, and leaned forward on her knees nursing a water bottle.

"This water is really exceptional," she said. "But it has to be savored to get the 'full' effect—and do permit me to emphasize that 'full' is the effect I'm hoping for."

"At what point will my innards start dissolving?" Rosa asked.

"I'd like to see those ruins down there," Carlos said, pointing toward Llactapata, the city above the terraces. "Anyone want to come along?"

"I'm going to take a short nap now that the porters are back with the sleeping bags," Rosa said.

Joanna and Carlos descended to the ruins. The vista was different from the high terrains Joanna had been on in the past. This mountain rose almost perpendicularly from the valley floor and gave the impression that, if one fell and started rolling downward there'd be nothing to break the fall—it was straight down. She shuddered, lowering her eyes to pay attention to her immediate surroundings.

"Quechua are genetically adapted to these heights," Carlos said. "Of course, chewing the coca leaf with lime certainly helps."

"I'd begun to think I was addicted to maté de coca tea. From the moment I arrived in Peru, everyone served it to me. And it worked its magic, because I adjusted to Cuzco's high altitude fairly quickly."

The remains of the terraced village had a Sun Temple in which two trapezoidal windows faced east. Joanna entered the temple and peered through the windows. She'd read that the constellation Corona Borealis, viewed through those windows, appeared to rotate over time, from one window to the other, showing first the summer and then the winter solstice.

She peered through the openings and saw Carlos examining the precision of the carved stones in the semicircular wall of the Sun

Temple. She searched the horizon, imagining the priest/astronomers observing the winter skies of the June solstice.

"Every single one of these ruins has astronomical significance," she remarked as Carlos entered the building. "For instance, these windows indicate the solstices."

Carlos laughed, giving her an admiring glance. "I'm sure glad I waited to walk this Inca Trail with you as my guide. Where else could I have found someone with such a storehouse of pertinent information?"

They left the ruins and returned to the campsite in companionable silence. It was time to consume their last bottles of water for the day. Joanna went to awaken Rosa.

"Rosa, we're back," she called, "come out and have some delicious water. Just think—it's aged since we filled our canteens at Ollantaytambo!"

There was no answer.

"She was really tired," Carlos said. "Maybe we should let her sleep."

They sat by the campfire and took off their hiking boots. With less exuberance, each sipped on their umpteenth bottle of water. Joanna felt chilled and got up to get an extra sweater. As she passed near Rosa's tent, she heard low moans.

"Carlos, get over here, quick!"

Carlos threw down the water bottle, leapt to his feet, and was immediately by her side. He heard the moans and unzipped the tent flap. Rosa lay on her back with her right leg bent at the knee. Her foot was visibly swollen.

"José," Carlos yelled.

Joanna darted passed him to tell José Ramos to bring the emergency kit, but Carlos' voice had signaled the danger. The guide ran toward them, kit in hand, with the three porters trotting behind in close succession.

He entered the tent and fell to his knees, examining Rosa's foot. "Snake bite! Put this constriction band on her ankle, Carlos—not too tight—be sure you can insert your forefinger between the band and the skin."

He laid the sterilized scalpel out on a rubber sheet and spread a non-alcoholic antiseptic gel on the area he intended to lance. He handed one of the porters the intravenous bag he'd hooked to Rosa's arm and filled a syringe with antivenin.

Carlos applied the constriction band while Joanna cradled Rosa's head, keeping her heart above the level of the wound. She noticed Rosa was burning with fever and asked for a wet towel to wipe her forehead.

"Who are you? ... I didn't know. ...I didn't know," Rosa mumbled.

José, balancing on his knees, lancet in hand, cut the foot in two places to access the bite area. He applied a suction pump to each bite mark—repeating the routine several times. Dusting baking soda over the foot, he wet it to form a paste and piled it on the wound.

Next, he ordered the porters to get all the battery powered thermal pads from the other tents. When they returned, he covered Rosa with the pads and placed her in the sleeping bag.

Joanna stood nearby wiping Rosa's brow with the wet cloth that one of the porters had provided. It was probable some of the poison had traveled throughout her system, but the medications administered by José would eventually cleanse her and counter the poison. Still she was in for a rough time. It was a good thing she'd chosen to fast—any other toxins in her system would have long since precipitated out.

"Joanna, come with me," Carlos said, indicating she should let one of the porters apply the cold cloth to Rosa's brow.

"How on earth did she get a snake bite?" Joanna asked. "I thought there were no snakes at these heights."

"It probably got into the bedding we left behind on the river bank and there *are* poisonous snakes near that river. We have to try to find it. The porters have already searched Rosa's tent. We need to check the other tents and equipment."

From behind Rosa's tent, one of the porters yelled. They could hear him hitting the ground with his walking stick, flailing something. Carlos and Joanna rounded the tent. The porter picked up the snake on the end of the stick and brought it to Carlos.

"A coral snake! Joanna, if you hadn't checked on Rosa when you did, she'd be dead."

"How did José know which antivenin to use?"

"The only poisonous snake around this area is the coral snake," Carlos said. "Our guide is a full time paramedic. I hired him because I didn't want to risk something terrible happening to you or Rosa on this trip."

"I thought using suction for a snake bite was usually a bad idea," Joanna said.

"He used sterile instruments, of course, and, since the wound was on the foot, he knew the venom could be extracted more easily than if it had been in a large muscle area, higher up on her body. He did everything an emergency room doctor would have done. Unfortunately, in these remote areas, we have to be our own 911 service."

Joanna was thankful the paramedic knew what to do. Still, she worried about Rosa reaching a hospital quickly. "Carlos, we need to return to Cuzco with her."

"José has handled many snake bite cases. The truth is we'll be a hindrance to the porters. We simply can't travel as fast as they can. You saw how quickly they descended the mountain to get the camping gear. Rosa has the portable oxygen mask with the tank, and they'll carry her in an almost upright position. When they're down to the five thousand foot level, José will call in the med-vac helicopter from Cuzco to lift her out. He'll phone my parents to meet them. In less than an hour she'll be in Clinica Pardo, and José and the porters will return to assist us."

"I'm so frightened for her," Joanna said.

"Trust me, she'd be furious if you ended your trek. My parents will make sure she has excellent medical care. They'd want you to continue on here, and, while Rosa recuperates, she'll be happy to know you've finished your goal."

Chapter 32

They had climbed to Dead Woman's Pass, 13,776 feet above sea level. The terrain was barren with scarce patches of ichu grass, a favorite food of llamas.

It was like being on top of the world—bitterly cold as night came on, and the stars seemed to drop down and surround them. Joanna was helping Carlos prepare the campfire when a storm struck with raging displays of sleet, hail, thunder, and lightning. They grabbed their backpacks and scrambled into Joanna's tent.

Carlos sat near the tent's front flap and opened his backpack. Joanna darted toward the rear and stripped off her wet clothing. She was struggling into thermal underwear when she saw Carlos look away, apparently concealing a deep blush. She dissolved into laughter.

"I'm not sure I haven't put the top on my bottom—it's like trying to fit into a hospital gown—"

The storm drowned her words. It was like a band of furies, wind hands whiplashing through camp, dagger sharp fingernails ripping at the tent. Hailstones pelted the rubberized canvas, sounding like the tympani section of an orchestra. It was an operatic performance of epic proportions, *The Ride of the Valkyries* in full Technicolor with lightning strikes for added effect.

"I've finished my wardrobe wretchies," she called to Carlos, and laughed, remembering it was one of Rosa's favorite expressions.

He stood with an apologetic look. "I'll make a dash for my tent when it lets up."

She patted the floor, indicating he should take a seat near her at the back of the tent, and produced her canteen, offering to share its contents. The campfire had long since gone out, and it was beginning to get very cold— it was clear this was to be their "dining hall" for the evening.

"I'm thinking we're in for a stormy night," she said.

"You're sure you don't mind sharing your tent—cause if you'll share your blanket, I'll fall asleep right away. This has been the hardest climb I've ever done, and I'm fairly fit."

"The altitude's become a problem for me, too, since I haven't been drinking my quota of maté de coca tea. Do you think Rosa's safely back in Cuzco? I wish we'd gone with her—I'll never forgive myself if she's—"

"José Ramos is a smart, skilled paramedic and the porters are sure-footed as llamas. We would've really slowed them down—I mean it! She'll be okay. She'll have some pain, but the bite will be watched and treated by the hospital staff. I would've insisted on going with her, if I'd believed it was necessary."

"It was lucky you chose such reliable porters."

"They're hard workers and loyal to a fault," he said.

"I've heard that companies building tall skyscrapers in New York City hire workers from Peru to construct the girders because they're not afraid of the heights."

"Our national congress needs to do more to improve their livelihood. Their working conditions have become a little better now that we've passed legislation mandating tour companies pay a fair wage, limit the gear weight, and provide minimum insurance." Carlos sat on the floor of the tent and took the canteen Joanna offered.

"I want to introduce even more measures that will improve conditions in the highland villages. That's what motivates me to continue as an elected official," he said.

"That's very noble," Joanna said.

"May we change the subject? Let's talk about what you've discovered on this trek, okay. I was wondering—has this journey really helped you to decode Sister Elena's myth? What can you tell me about it? By the way, I must confess, this fasting's been a pain for me. I've persisted because I didn't want you to think I was a wimp."

"You and Rosa didn't have to fast. It wouldn't have bothered me a bit to have you all eat whatever you wanted. Well, it would've bothered me! But still—"

"It's been a good discipline. My short stint in the army toughened me up for such deprivation. I even miss the old boot camp days. At least I exercised regularly."

"Tell you what—light that kerosene lamp. I'll be glad to bore you to death with my ruminations on the myth."

"Fire away! I can't think of a better use of my time, in the midst of this stupendous storm, than attending a lecture by the famed Professor Nickels-Stewart."

She handed him a blanket. "Wrap up in this, I'll put the sleeping bag around my shoulders. Good thing you put the back wall of this tent against a huge boulder, let's lean against that—it'll make a great sofa."

There was one thermal gel pad remaining after they'd packed the others in Rosa's sleeping bag. Joanna got the spare, placed it on the floor in front of them, and they huddled together, their stocking feet toasting on the pad.

The seating, in no way, resembled a cushioned sofa, but it was adequate. The only illumination was the small kerosene lamp sitting on the floor near the tent's entrance.

"To answer your question, I believe I *have* made a little progress on the myth. I think it's some kind of guide, sort of like an initiatory path toward higher knowledge." Joanna paused a moment, eyes cast to one side. "The thing is, Rosa may have been right when she guessed our trek was like a *vision quest*. I believe that's why Sister Elena insisted I make this pilgrimage."

"Sister's a wise old bird, isn't she?"

"She's convinced—and I think she's right—that the Inca acllas and priests traversed this trail as a kind of walk along the Milky Way."

"Sounds like you've been serving an apprenticeship with Sister Elena. Hey, I have it! You're the sorceress' apprentice!"

"That's probably a very apt analogy, although I hadn't looked at it that way." She paused, staring at the central pole of the tent, and quoted Don Juan Matus, the "sorcerer" of Carlos Castaneda's writings.

" '...*every warrior on the path of knowledge thinks he's learning sorcery, but all he's doing is allowing himself to be convinced of the power hidden within his own being ...'"*

Carlos leaned forward, taking the canteen from her. "This trek has certainly *jerked me out of my usual context* and shifted my *assemblage point* as Don Juan Matus would say!"

The lightning strikes and the wind had died down. The rain still drummed steadily and the cold was even more penetrating. Joanna reached for her wet jacket and took a penlight and a piece of folded paper from the pocket.

"Take a look at this," she said. "Sister Elena gave me a kind of 'guide' for the interior journey one makes on pilgrimages. I researched it to see if there were other guides in other religions. This is a graphic of a compilation I did of several of the spiritual paths."

"Spiritual paths ...," he said. "Sounds like you're *really* serious about your trek being a vision quest!"

He put the canteen down and took the paper from her, unfolding it, scrutinizing it as he would a legal document, while she held the pen light.

"What are these paths supposed to mean?"

"The top part is the Islamic Sufi Mystical Path—the Whirling Dervish's spiritual quest. The middle is Christian, and the bottom is taken from the Jewish Kabbalah. Sister Elena said she believed the acllas followed a path similar to the Christian path."

"They're all essentially the same," Carlos said.

"That's what I found so astonishing, too."

"So, tell me about them."

"Well, for example, when the Sufi dervish—by the way, 'dervish' means doorway to union with the divine—when the dervish performs his 'whirling' or spinning ritual, he's actually going through all the levels of the spiritual path. I'll demonstrate what I mean." She jumped up and stood in front of Carlos.

A Compilation of Spiritual Paths

Sufi Muslim Path

1	2	3	4	5	6	7	8
I am alone	I am seen by the Beloved	I reach for my Beloved. He reaches for me	I search for my Beloved it is all I do	I am in the arms of my Beloved	I am Pure Love I am Pure Being	There is no I There is no one here	There is THIS and I must return

Christian Path

— = □ △ ⋈ ⋈ ✡ ○

Jewish Path: Madregot (Levels of Mystic Assent)

Devekuth	*Toward God*	Kisupha	Tevunah	*With God*	Dodi	*In God*	Yechidah	*Return*
'Cleaving to God In aloneness'		'Yearning for God' 'Kavanna' (one-pointed concentration)	'Separation of man as subject & God as object disappears'		'Dear friend' -mystic is bound by love		'Union with Absolute' 'Hitpaalut' (rapture following union)	

"The dervish starts by placing his left foot on the floor, grounding himself," she said. "Then he pushes counterclockwise with the other foot, like this." She started a slow twirl.

"His right hand points to the ground, while his left points heavenward, and then he gradually increases speed. I won't demonstrate that because fasting has made me wobbly." She flopped down beside him. "Anyway, with increased speed, the dervish enters a kind of 'flow,' and finally achieves ecstasy—union with the divine. He describes feeling as though he's one with all creation."

"I've felt a kind of *flow* like that when I was jogging," Carlos said. "Even more so, when I'm playing a piece of music with friends and we enter a sort of trance while we're jamming!"

Joanna could see Carlos' face in the dim light. He was fully awake now, and his eyes twinkled with excitement. She kept pushing back thoughts of similar times, when she'd shared exciting ideas with Michael. The difference was Carlos was genuinely interested.

"I've a theory about what may happen in the body that causes those states of ecstasy," she said. "It's a scientific explanation, of course—but, that's what I do! Do you mind listening?"

"I'm your captive audience." Carlos placed his hands on either side of his head, like an elephant flapping its ears. "See, both ears are wide open, although I can't say the same for both eyes."

She laughed. "Here's what I think happens. When the dervish spins counter-clockwise, I suspect the spinning actually creates an electrical current produced by positive and negative charges on ions in the nuclei of the body's cells. The electrical current arcs from one nucleus to the next, and, like a lightning strike shooting through every cell of the body and on into the brain, it induces neuronal firing. Natural chemicals, such as serotonin, pour into the bloodstream, and a *super* 'natural high' occurs as the spinning body's electromagnetic field aligns and connects with Earth's own electrical charges, or even with those in the whole universe! The dervish then experiences a sense of enlightenment and exclaims in an ecstatic 'union' with everything, 'My God, my God!'"

Joanna changed position to face Carlos. "I'm convinced that, not only is Sister Elena's myth referring to astronomical facts that are reflected in the sites along the Sacred Valley, but that it's also referring to this same phenomenon of divine union, of spiritual enlightenment as, say, the Sufi mystic is experiencing."

Joanna moved her feet nearer the gel pad and reached down to massage her toes. "The thing is, ancient people conceived of the union of sky and earth, of the divine and the human soul, in terms of the sexual union between a man and woman when the two had reached the highest level of an orgasm, really an ecstatic union."

"Tell me, Joanna, is that what Solomon's *Song of Songs* in the Bible is really all about?" Carlos took up the pen light and examined the piece of paper more closely. "Remember, I told you about mother reading the Old Testament stories to Rosa and me when we were in grammar school. Well, she skipped Solomon's descriptions of his experiences with the Queen of Sheba! Of course, we looked it up in father's library when she was out visiting."

"Those writings attributed to Solomon did express the sacred union between God and humans in sexual terms," Joanna said. "Strangely enough, Buddhist monks have also described the mystical union with all things in the universe as being like one long unending orgasm!"

"I guess there's no other way to describe such a transcendent effect," Carlos said. "Do you suppose that same effect is sought by Christian 'snake handlers' and Voodoo dancers, who dance until they go into a trance and their bodies ache and their feet bleed?"

"Pain can force the mind inward and ultimately beyond," Joanna said. "It's a gruesome thought, but monks and nuns and other Christian mystics used an instrument of flagellation, called a discipline. It was a sort of whip made of loose leather strips, tipped with sharp metal points that was held in the hand and whipped across the shoulders."

"Are you saying those monks achieved some sort of sexual climax—like the Marquis de Sade?" Carlos' face registered shock.

"They struck their backs in a rhythmic motion, first on one side and then the other, probably attaining a trance state and producing that same kind of 'flow' and climax, and ultimately the feeling that they were transported into union with all things."

Carlos sat very still for a while, minutely examining the floor of the tent.

Joanna stifled a laugh. "In the monks' minds it was a spiritual act, in imitation of the flogging that Jesus received from the Romans, and when they endured that, they believed they were granted the ecstatic union."

The pen light formed a slow arc as Carlos' hand fell to his lap. His blanket slipped to the floor. "The dervish goes into a flow and enters the doorway to divinity…," he recited, eyelids drooping, voice trailing off.

Joanna reached to retrieve the blanket and his eyes popped open.

"Like in great sex…wow…! Like in the Chemical Wedding! Right, Joanna? Hey, I'm betting old Newton knew all about that!"

"The Hieros Gamos, yes—as depicted in 11th century European courtly love poetry and very like the sexual union described in Tantric Buddhist documents, as well as in Muslim practices, and, as you surmised, also by King Solomon."

"That's the Greek word for *sacred marriage*, isn't it?" Carlos sat up with his eyes wide open.

"It's a very ancient rite. All the texts stipulate that the sex act, in the sacred marriage, must be practiced with complete 'unselfish' focus on the partner's pleasure. It's engaged in not just to reach climax, but to transport the participants into union with divinity—at least that's how all the spiritual paths of the ancient religions viewed it."

The storm had returned with increased strength. The wind howled and sleet pounded the tent. They listened a while in silence.

"Joanna, will the fasting we've been doing produce some kind of trance effect like that?"

"Who knows, it may, because it's a repetitive action with focused concentration."

"I know it's a whole other tangent, but do you think prehistoric priest-astronomers could have discovered how to sharpen their perceptions in ways that surpass our abilities?"

"Jesuit paleontologist Teilhard de Chardin, in *The Phenomenon of Man*, wrote that everything in the universe is on a continuum from lesser to greater consciousness. Modern particle physicists know when we even think about doing some action, an experiment for instance, directed at one of those 'conscious' particles, then the other particles seem to respond to our *intended* action, even before we act." She moved her hands in a broad circle. "It's like the web in the Vedic conception of the universe, where all matter is connected, and ditto, all forces."

"So you believe we *can* know things that may not come directly from our own experiences?"

Her attention had been focused on Carlos. She looked away, staring unseeing toward the center tent pole.

"I guess those priest/astronomers were skilled observers and obsessive record keepers and learned from those who came before who had been recording observations from very distant ages," Carlos said. "You said the Incas re-engineered Cuzco and the Sacred Valley to replicate the Milky Way. Did they believe they were attuning themselves to some cosmic order, to Viracocha's plan?"

She heard him, jumped up and grabbed the paper, holding it near the kerosene lamp.

"It astronomy," she bellowed at him and then lowered her voice. "It's Viracocha's Plan, the god Saturn's Plan." She pointed at the geometric shapes. "Those 'spiritual paths' are some kind of symbolic way of representing the ancient knowledge of the precession of the equinoxes! Carlos, I can't believe what I'm seeing."

"Careful, you're hyperventilating—remember you have lowlander lungs, and you're up on a very high mountain!"

"Look at that hexagram in the Christian Spiritual Path— those interlocking triangles that we call the *Star of David*. That symbol looks just like the equilateral triangles Johannes Kepler used to depict the conjunctions of Saturn and Jupiter. Those conjunctions are the keys to understanding the whole system of precession, of understanding about the universe in motion, and that idea didn't originate with Kepler, nor with Plato, nor Aristotle, who both referred to it. It was ancient even in their time."

"By the way, I saw Kepler's manuscript with those drawings in a Paris museum," Carlos said. "So, you're saying those ancient people knew about precession, is that possible?"

"The angles of those triangles in Kepler's drawing move through only 1/3 of the zodiac in forty conjunctions, which takes about 720 years. Imagine the zodiac circle of constellations, which parallels our celestial equator like a clock face. Multiply 720 years by three (the three angles of the triangle) and that equals 2160, which is one double hour on the zodiac clock, and that's called the double hour of the Greatest Day. Those 'hours' of the Greatest Day are terribly important."

"I know where you're going with that," Carlos said. "Every two and half thousand years we have a new zodiac sign, right? Like we're in Pisces now, but next we'll be in Aquarius."

"Our vastly distant ancestors called the passage to a new sign of the zodiac, a new world age. As the angles of Saturn and Jupiter's conjunctions turn through the twelve constellations of the whole zodiac, marking each 2160 years, they finally reach the Greatest Day of 25, 960 years (12 x 2160 = 25,960) rounded to 26,000 years."

"What happens after 26,000 years? I mean, is that number some kind of benchmark that's as significant for us as the 2160 years?"

"Well, there's some proof we may have ice ages associated with that cycle."

"Oops! Sorry I asked."

"Carlos, world mythology seems to be permeated with precessional information related to the conjunctions of Saturn and Jupiter. To show you what I mean about the symbols of the Christian Spiritual Path being astronomy, I need to remind you of a story that repeats in Mesopotamian, Egyptian, and Greek mythology that tells about Saturn, the Titan, separating his world parents Ouranos (sky) and Gaia (earth), who are imagined in sexual union."

Joanna sat back down and placed the paper on the floor in front of her. "Saturn emasculated his father and ever afterwards 'controlled' the movements of the Earth and the cosmos. He and his siblings, the Titans, move at will through the heavens, but he controls the axis around which everything turns."

"So, old Saturn is the Titan who did that! My memories of mythology are a little fuzzy," Carlos said.

"Time is said to have begun with that act of separating the world parents, the earth and sky. How mind shattering that concept must have been to our far distant ancestors. After very long periods of time watching and recording changes in the sky they finally realized that the earth and sky weren't all one thing, they were separate and in motion."

"Why haven't I heard of these things before, they're terribly important, aren't they?" Carlos said.

"Unfortunately, although many archaeologists and historians have heard of precession, they seem to ignore it. Look at those symbols of the Christian Path again—those symbols are ancient, go way back beyond Pythagoras. I'm betting that *single line* symbolizes when the earth and sky were believed to be one, when we were in blissful ignorance, in paradise! Those two *parallel lines* show the concept of the separation of earth and sky; the *square* is celestial earth—not that people believed the planet was flat, but they realized they could locate their position by observing the stars that rose with the sun, heliacally, at the solstices and equinoxes, the 'four corners' of earth. You could say those 'star markers' were their original GPS!"

She could barely contain herself, was embarrassed to find she was almost prancing in her eagerness to convey her ideas.

"So, those ancient people really knew the Earth wasn't flat? Wow!"

"There were many 'indicators' that they observed which proved their Earth 'home' wasn't flat. The star markers, at the four 'corners' of the solstice and equinox 'cross' of the celestial plane, which they observed on the horizon, changed over time," Joanna said. "After a little more than two thousand years—remember that Saturn and Jupiter mark this passage of time on the zodiac—the sun rests in another constellation, rises within a new zodiac sign, and, therefore, has a new set of star markers rising before it at the solstices and equinoxes. When the new age begins, new star markers have to be re-established."

"So, what does the *triangle represent*?" Carlos stood and opened the tent flap a few inches. Rain pelted his face. He sat back down and pulled the blanket around him.

"Early man knew the heavens turned around a 'pole star' that remained unchanged for vast periods of time. He imagined that pole running through the Earth and believed it was controlled by Saturn. That axis was the *world tree*."

"Then, do the *two triangles, point-to-point* represent the north polar area and the south polar area with the *world tree* running through the center?" Carlos asked.

"The earth's tilted axis projected into space forms a circle like the top of a cone as it rotates about the celestial equator projected into space. The bottom cone represents the same thing at the southern end of the axis.

"The 'X' shape that the triangles make may symbolize the obliquity of the ecliptic, the intersection of earth's projected celestial equator and the sun's apparent path, the ecliptic plane, as the view from earth makes the sun appear to intersect earth's celestial equator at the solstices and equinoxes. The most important intersection is when the sun is 'resting' in a particular constellation at spring, vernal equinox, as I mentioned above. The sun, for two thousand one hundred and sixty-six years, *a world age*, will rise at spring equinox in that same constellation.

"There's a medieval symbol called the Chi Rho, an X with a flagpole and lamb superimposed, which symbolizes Christ, who has entered the world of man. That flagpole symbol, with flying banners, superimposed on the X, is an ancient symbol for Saturn, who controls the Earth's axis. The Chi Rho would have resonated with people who were aware of the older symbolic representation of how the Sun's path intersected Earth's celestial equator."

"I read about the Dogon tribe in West Africa having cave drawings showing a point-to-point cone shaped figure like that. It was called the *world egg*. A spiral inside each cone was meant to show the motion of the *world tree*," Carlos said. "That's like the *world tree* we saw at Ollantaytambo, isn't it, and so that's the axis of the world? Fantastic!"

"That sixth figure, of two triangles with points intertwined, may represent the Earth's celestial plane—the *navel of the world and the Land of the Living*— with the *Land of the Gods* above, and the *Land of the Dead* below, *all on a vertical axis*."

"Are all ancient symbols crammed with such vast storehouses of information, like these?" Carlos took the paper from Joanna.

"Our distant ancestors seem to have devised many such symbols, like those interlocking triangles that we refer to as the Star of David, to pass on to future generations their knowledge of celestial mechanics. Of course, the *circle* at the end of that array means the cycles are eternal, that they repeat! That astounding knowledge, represented by Saturn and Jupiter's movement 'around' the zodiac constellations—that knowledge of precession, led directly to the arts of civilization, like the calendars, agriculture, religion, even how kings rule!"

"You're saying the forty conjunctions of Saturn and Jupiter are signifi—" Carlos nap-jerked, fell sides ways and caught himself mid-fall, grabbed the pen light that had fallen onto his lap, shook his head, and once again began a slow list sideways.

Joanna pushed him gently, and he settled prone onto the tent floor. She covered him with the blanket and sleeping bag, and lay down near him.

Chapter 33

Sleep wasn't going to happen for her. She was too excited. Sitting up, she reached for her backpack and pulled out the map of the Sacred Valley on which she'd 'highlighted" Pisac, Cuzco, and Ollantaytambo.

Searching in the backpack again, she found the transparency printed from the astronomy computer program she'd used to find the Milky Way constellations as they might have appeared above the Sacred Valley in 650 A.D. She placed the transparency over the map and watched the sites line up perfectly.

There was Pisac, the partridge, lying near the southeast. One of the sequential lines running from Coricancha in Cuzco pointed toward the southern celestial polar-region. Several of the Incan dark cloud constellations lay at the southern end of the Milky Way, near the area marking the Land of the Dead.

Joanna let her hand trace the Inca Trail on the transparency from southeast to northwest along the Urubamba/Vilcanota River, from Pisac toward Ollantaytambo. She remembered looking back at Pisac and seeing the huge condor geoglyph on the mountainside.

The little country church in southwestern Virginia where James Nickels-Stewart's mother had taken her on a Sunday morning when she was six-years-old inserted itself into her thoughts. She heard the congregation singing "…on the wings of the snow white dove, He sends his pure sweet love..." Birds were the messengers to and from the gods.

The Swan constellation, the Northern Cross, the cosmic bird, was a ubiquitous image in mythology and religion. It was symbolic of the spirit in humans, the spirit of the gods, and the energy of life. That constellation lay across the center of the Milky Way, where astronomers had detected a huge black hole, in which they believed life might have originated. The exoplanet Kepler 22B that may closely resemble Earth had recently been discovered in that constellation.

The "cosmic bird," in Incan lore was the condor, and it flew from Pisac—Land of the Dead, the underworld, *ukhu pacha*—toward

Ollantaytambo, bearing souls to their re-birthing place near the highest heaven, where they perched on the *World Tree* until they were born again.

After a short while, those souls were believed by the Incas to be reborn at the headwaters of the River in the Sky from where they would return, via the river, back to the Land of the Living, *kay pacha*, back to Cuzco, the center, the navel above the abyss.

Nothing ever lost—neither matter nor energy—a basic tenet of science. The whole Inca story, their vision of the cosmos, as well as the visions of other ancient civilizations, Joanna realized, could easily be written in scientific terms without losing anything. One just needed to understand what myth was. Aristotle said Plato was the last person to understand what myth really was.

Joanna looked at the map again. There was Vega, right where it should be at the other end of the Urubamba/Milky Way, supposedly pointing toward the *Land of the Gods.*

Ollantaytambo, the hunter, the great warrior hero of the Incas, located near that juncture, could be the constellation Orion.

Astronomers had observed the birth of stars in the Orion Nebulae, which was near the upper "arm" of the Milky Way. Vega, near the Swan/Lyra constellation, was in that vicinity and was the constellation that had always marked a celestial "sacred" spot for ancient people—it was their "place of origin." Ollantaytambo was the site of Inca geoglyphs representing the Tree of Life,' so it really had to be the Inca's ancestral birthing place.

Since Orion was thought to lie near the bridge to the Land of the Gods, did the Incas also consider Ollantaytambo to be at the entrance to Machu Picchu?

It was obvious that Machu Picchu was special, because it marked the terminus of the Inca Trail along the Urubamba, but archaeologists agreed on only one thing about the site. The buildings were of the best design and construction of any in the Inca Empire, an empire whose capital city, Cuzco, had impressed the Spanish Chroniclers enough that they wrote home about its magnificence.

The Incas had chosen Machu Picchu, a spectacularly beautiful, nearly inaccessible site, and lavished all their efforts on making it more beautiful than any other place in all of Tahuantinsuyu. Recent discoveries had dated earlier occupations of the site to nearly two thousand years before the Incas. Yet the site had been of no interest to the Conquistadors. Contrary to their usual practices, they'd left it alone.

It was said that Machu Picchu was well preserved when Hiram Bingham stumbled on it in 1911. Why would the Incas and later the Quechuas have abandoned the place and been so secretive about it that the Spanish never knew about its grandeur? What were they hiding?

Joanna let herself relax a little, pretending she was swinging in a hammock, letting her mind sift slowly through the facts. The Spaniards had systematically destroyed every other sacred site. She'd read that somebody among the Inca nobility had finally gotten a Spanish land title for Machu Picchu in the late 1500's, saying it was just undeveloped land that had belonged to Sapa Inca Pachakuti, and besides, it was on an incredibly high, remote ridge, really it was useless land, they'd said.

In 1613, eighty-one years after the Spanish Conquistadors had landed on the coast of Peru, Juan de Santa Cruz Pachakuti Yamqui Salcamaygua, an Inca/Quechua nobleman, told the chroniclers about a fabulous "house" built on a hill, next to a river. He'd said, "... they say that a house was built for Tunupa Viracocha to dwell…and the Sapa Inca commanded that it be serviced and maintained for Viracocha…and the house was on a hill, next to a river… ." Where had she read that line before? She'd seen it somewhere before ...

It was in Sister Elena's myth! She pulled a copy from her backpack. The passage was highlighted in yellow. "Pachakuti Inca made beautiful above all others the home of Viracocha and all things are revealed there. In his abode, Viracocha bids the condor to bear the souls of men to the Life Tree, near the entrance to his home in the sky …"

"... *the house was on a hill, next to a river* ..."

Her heart thumped wildly, she jumped up, yelling, "That has to be it!"

"What! What is it?" Carlos sprang to his feet prepared to fight the intruding army.

"Sorry! Go back to sleep, I'll tell you tomorrow."

He lay back down, pulled the blanket over his head and was soon snoring.

They were protecting it! Everybody in the empire was concealing it! They'd deliberately let it be forgotten!

When the bridge to the Land of the Gods went below the horizon, due to precession, Viracocha was said to "leave" the Earth going into the celestial sea. He was no longer in residence on Machu Picchu.

The Incas weren't about to let their sacred huaca be desecrated. *Fantastic!* They were hiding their most valued treasure right in plain sight. *Why didn't anybody notice it before, why hadn't she?*

Well, she knew the answer that accounted for her own ineptitude—and it was shocking, totally contrary to her usual trait of questioning the experts. She'd taken for granted that scholarly opinion was correct. She'd believed their conclusions—that Machu Picchu was simply a site built by the Sapa Inca as a resort, and that it just happened to be used for observing the heavens—were unassailable.

The site that Sapa Inca Pachakuti commanded to be built and, every succeeding Sapa Inca had scrupulously maintained, was Machu Picchu, the "house" of Con Ticci Viracocha!

Machu Picchu, the Land of the Gods!

She wanted to dance around and scream it to the high heavens. *Not a good idea!* She'd let her heart do the dancing, instead.

Bravo, Quechua peoples! You hold the absolute record for one of the longest kept secrets—kept long enough for future generations to have enough sense to preserve the great treasure as a United Nations World Heritage Site.

Excitement gripped her, like when she'd gone to *Walt Disney World* as a child.

She sat up and pulled her backpack near, opening the outside pocket. She'd put two things in that pocket for safekeeping. One was a contour map of Machu Picchu and the other was the linen-wrapped small package Sister Elena had given her.

Placing the gift on her lap, she used the pen light to study the map. The Urubamba continued a good distance beyond Ollantaytambo and flowed through a gorge that surrounded Machu Picchu like a horseshoe, like a snake, an OUROBOROS, the snake swallowing its tail, the ultimate ancient symbol for eternity and for the vision quest, the journey of self-discovery, of realization of the divine.

The Llama Road clearly ends at Ollantaytambo, because the Land of the Gods, eternity, is beyond the Sacred Valley, beyond the Milky Way. This is truly thrilling.

She leaned against the back of the tent and closed her eyes, imagining the terrain around Machu Picchu. Sister Elena's gift fell to the floor. She reached to pick it up. Sister had said to open it when it was needed the most. The trek would be over tomorrow. Maybe now was a good time to open it... to celebrate her discoveries.

The ribbon came off easily, along with several layers of the linen cloth wrapping. Inside was a small pouch with woven straps that could be tied around the waist or around the neck. The handiwork was exquisite. Embroidered on the front in colorful threads were a caiman and a large rat-like creature. Each was outlined with gold threads.

Joanna examined the pouch more closely, turned it over, and opened the tiny flap. A folded piece of paper was pushed down inside. She pulled it out. It was a song, copied in Sister Elena's distinctive handwriting.

The Caiman and the Capybara, it was Huarana and Coco's song.

Chills assaulted her already cold body. Was this really Huarana's pouch, the "good luck talisman" delivered to Joré by his sister?

It seemed impossible that such a fragile object could have lasted for all those centuries, but Joanna had seen textiles woven by the acllas in museums in Lima and they were still well preserved. She gently inserted the song back inside the pouch and held it cupped in both hands, thinking about Huarana and Joré.

Was Huarana the aclla who brought the myth, the aclla's legacy, to Santa Maria Monastery? That aclla had been chosen by the Sapa Inca to be the wife of one of his nephews. Was Joré that nephew? He was certainly a great-grandson of Huana Capàc.

If the pouch had been made by Huarana and belonged to Joré, why hadn't Sister Elena told her?

Her feet were numb, had gone to sleep, her fingers were nearly immobilized from the cold. *What a predicament!* Here she was, in the middle of the night, on a very high mountain in a violent storm, smack dab in the middle of executing Sister Elena's fantasy trek, with no way to get to the nun to demand answers. *Something else she had to "surrender"...*

Good thing the trip would be over tomorrow. She'd confront Sister Elena as soon as she was back in Cuzco, because the nun definitely owed her answers.

It was midnight, she had to get some rest so they could finish walking the most difficult part of the trail, but she could barely contain her excitement about Machu Picchu and her ancestors. She wished she could wake Carlos to tell him.

The gold threads on the pouch gleamed in the lamp light, like a vibrant chain linking her to Huarana, her N^{th} degree grandmother. She smiled, thinking about Carlos' term for distant ancestors. Tying the talisman around her neck, she pressed it to her heart, lay down next to him, and curled into his back for warmth.

Chapter 34

It was densely dark. Someone was bending over her. She groaned to think it was morning already.

"Carlos, please let me sleep—just one more hour—"

She was jerked to a sitting position. Rough rope pinned her arms to her sides. She heard grunts, someone struggling and a dull thud. Something had landed on the floor next to her. A strong gust of wind blew through the tent. A voice shouted. She could translate only bits and pieces.

"... on their feet ...on that back trail."

"Go faster... you're not... ."

Joanna counted two voices, one sounded familiar. Where had she heard it?

"Hurry, get um up... we got to go... got to get out of here."

"Wait a minute... dark as the Potosi Mines... trail's closed... stay here and leave at daybreak."

They'd been sleeping for some time. Joanna listened intently. The only sound was an occasional snore. She wriggled to loosen the rope around her upper torso and felt it give slightly.

Maneuvering fingers under the rope, she pushed outward and felt it tighten, forcing air out of her lungs, causing her to gag at the smell of perspiration and beer.

She couldn't just sit idly and not attempt to escape. It sounded like Carlos had been knocked unconscious. The men were armed, she'd felt the cold steel of a gun while the rope was being tied around her.

Wind thumped against the tent, mimicking her heartbeat. She touched her wrist, counting pulse beats, keeping track of time. She struggled against the rope again and caused the backpack at her feet to shift across the floor.

She froze. The snoring continued. Time passed, and the heated air from extra bodies became stifling, adding to her tiredness, causing her to doze.

Heavy footsteps sounded outside the tent, startling her awake. Light appeared as the tent flap was unzipped. She prayed the medic and porters had returned.

One of the men awakened, rolled forward, and stood with his gun drawn. He kicked his companion who jumped and drew a gun from his jacket pocket. Both adjusted their ski masks and waited on either side of the tent flap. A tall man bent to enter.

"Manuel! You said meet you in Maldonado."

"How long does it take to carry out simple orders?" the man asked.

"Hold on, now—"

"Outside. ¡Tengo prisa!"

Carlos stirred, rolled over, and sat up. Like her, a rope secured his arms to his sides. He wiggled across the space between them and sat next to her. Leaning into her side, he punched her arm with his shoulder.

"Good morning, old sport! Say, I sure do hope we had a rousingly romantic night."

She tried to contain herself. It was impossible. The stressful situation, added to the lack of sleep, caused her to emit sounds like Joré and Huarana had made when they listened to Coco singing and chortling.

Her laughter rang out above the loud argument the men had been having outside the tent. There was a period of silence, and all at once shouting and scrambling could be heard.

"What the hell? Is he dead? ¡Escucha me!"

"There's a flask in his pocket. Get that, ¡vámonos! Check his pulse, maybe he fainted."

"¡Vámonos! ¿Listo? Put him in the tent—on the cot."

They carried Manuel inside. One man went back out, and the other remained, looking down at Manuel lying inert.

The second man returned with a flask. "Manuel! Manuel!" The man slapped his face and forced his mouth open, making him drink some liquid. Manuel coughed and sat up. Leaning forward, he held his face in his hands.

"Boss, you all right?"

Joanna eyed the man sitting on the cot and searched her memory. He looked familiar. She glanced at Carlos. He showed no signs of recognition.

The man straightened and stared at Joanna with a stunned look on his face. He had a distinctive, angular, craggy face. Above hazel eyes, his brow rose high to thick shiny black hair that formed a widow's peak.

She watched as he struggled up from the cot and made a motion to leave the tent. One of the men offered to help, but he signaled them to go out ahead of him. He followed, halted mid-stride, turned around, and came back to stand in front of her. She looked up and met his gaze, wondering what he intended to do.

Reaching down, he lifted the pouch that she'd tied around her neck, and examined it for a long moment, then gently placed it back against her heart. He looked deeply into her eyes and smiled, communicating a strange mix of bewilderment and respect. She smiled in response. He stepped back, bowed low, and left the tent.

She checked Carlos' reaction. He seemed to be as astonished as she was. Just outside the tent door the man could be heard issuing orders. "You lead, Rico. Tie a rope between the man and girl and tie another rope from the girl to yourself. Tomàs, you walk immediately behind the man. That trail is treacherous."

"I'm not taking orders from you, old man. I'm bringing up the rear," Tomàs said. "We're going to take Summit Trail over the top of Old Mountain and down the far side."

"That ledge is barely two feet wide in places," Manuel said. "They could stumble and all would be lost."

Rico came into the tent, assisted Joanna to stand, and pushed her ahead of him as he dragged Carlos along behind. Billowing curtains of fog surrounded them as they emerged from the tent.

Tomàs waved a gun at Manuel. "We're not going to release that girl. Are you loco? I'm giving orders now, old man. The pair of them will ensure my retirement."

Rico knotted the rope around Carlos, tied it to Joanna, and secured the other end of the rope around his own waist. He set a fast pace as they jogged out in single file, over the pass, and onward toward Runkuray.

The men were fighting among themselves. Was Tomàs implying that Manuel had intended to release her? Then, why had they bothered to take her and Carlos hostage? What did they hope to gain? Would they be held for ransom? Most likely, but Manuel seemed sympathetic.

Joanna could barely see the ruins at Sayajmarka as Rico rushed them along, skirting the cliffs. They passed Puyapatamarka where she'd hoped to investigate the stone baths and the aqueduct system, which the guidebook said still functioned. There was a magnificent view, through the thin sunlight, of the 20,000-foot holy mountain, called Salcantay. To the left was a relatively smaller green mountain that Joanna had seen on the virtual tour and beyond that was Machu Picchu.

Rico pulled them forward as they stumbled down steep steps and continued through a copse of jungle vegetation. They climbed again, descended, and climbed again, going through a length of tunnel before finally reaching Huinay Huawna. At the pace Rico had set, they'd covered territory usually requiring a full day.

The canyons were obscured by fog. Joanna was glad she couldn't see how far down it was to the valley floor. They were passing through incredible ruins.

She hoped she could come back someday to explore Huinay Huawna. The site was reputed to have some of the best stonework on the Trail.

If she and Carlos had been completing the trek alone, they would've gone from here to Intipunku, the Sun Gate, where the trail descended into Machu Picchu. Instead, Rico headed for Summit Trail.

It had been a relentless forced march, and now they were ushered onto the most dangerous part of the path. Summit Trail was a granite scar cut into the mountainside. Only a few saplings clung to fissures in rocks.

It was like walking the ledge of a very tall skyscraper, one foot placed gingerly forward and the other drawn cautiously up behind. A false step and a person would become airborne in a swan dive, with no parachute and no safety net. Death was the only possible outcome. It was terrifying.

Mist swirled up from below, obscuring the abyss that loomed only inches away. Rico, just a few steps ahead, could barely be seen. Joanna shivered. She was glad to be roped to Carlos.

Somewhere along the trail, she'd remembered why Tomàs' voice had sounded familiar. He was one of the pair who'd tried to kidnap her when she'd visited Machu Picchu that first time. She was snapping mad to know he'd finally succeeded.

He and Manuel were at odds. Was there a chance the older man would assist her and Carlos once they were safely off the trail? Manuel didn't seem like the others, so he might help. Why was he interested in Huarana's pouch? He looked to be Quechua. Had he recognized those symbols?

Carlos leaned forward and whispered. "I thought there was only one path from the Inca Trail to the Sun Gate."

Joanna turned her head slightly to hear better and saw, where the clouds had parted, a sharp drop-off. She trembled. It looked to be nearly a mile straight down to the river.

"Joanna, are you okay?"

"My whole life I've had a recurring nightmare. I'm on a high cliff, on a narrow ledge. I glance sideways, and it's miles down to the valley floor. I feel pulled toward the edge and I freeze, trying to hug the rock face. I lie down near where the ledge cuts into the mountain and crawl along, clinging to the rock as best I can. I'm too close to the precipice, about to fall, and I wake up screaming."

"¡Callete, ¡Calete!" Tomàs shouted.

"Listen, Joanna, just look in toward the cliff," Carlos whispered. "Don't look at the edge. We'll make it. They're not going to let us fall—they need us for ransom—just take a step at a time. That's my girl."

Joanna shook with terror, lifted one foot, and leaned into the mountainside. Her heart did a flip-flop as she forced her gaze inward and maneuvered her shoulder to contact the cold granite. Focusing her eyes away from the sheer drop-off and onto the black and gray light-reflecting granules of the rock face, she willed herself forward.

The path was obscured by fog. Even Rico was inching his way along the rough rock surface. Joanna had to slow her pace to keep from stumbling into his back.

"God almighty!" Carlos shrieked.

A pterodactyl, wings stretched outward at least seven feet, sharp beak locked into position, swooped toward her like a deadly missile. She froze.

In her peripheral vision, she saw the monstrous black shadow wheel away and fly out over the gorge. Moments ticked by. The condor dipped it wings and circled back.

It hovered above her, talons extended, and plunged toward her face. She dodged left, dragging Carlos and Rico with her. Horror-stricken screams split the thin mountain air.

Glancing up, as she fell into the abyss, Joanna saw Carlos spinning round and round, grasping at a lone tree below the cliff's edge.

Suddenly the rope around her waist jerked upward. Carlos was still clinging to the tree, kicking at the rock face, trying to get a toehold. Stones pelted down on her head.

Loud cursing and sounds of desperate fighting came from Manuel and Tomàs, who were still on the ledge above. Off to her right, Rico had grabbed onto an outcropping and was fumbling at his waist, attempting to untie the rope that bound him to her.

She felt the rope slacken. Rico had freed himself. A thundering roar shook the mountainside and the rock ledge to which he'd been clinging crumbled into the gorge. Chilling cries echoed upward as he disappeared into the fog-enshrouded canyon.

The rope that secured her to Carlos jerked upward again, nearly squeezing her breathless. The other end of the rope that had been tied to Rico was looped in a noose and dangled freely below her.

The mist cleared, and she glanced upward again. Carlos was swinging slowly, side to side, gripping the tree, trying to support both their weights.

Tears stung her eyes. She loved him, always had—weird time to acknowledge it—and he loved her... that was clear... only a fool could've missed it.

That tree's not going to hold.

She tried lifting her hands, but her arms were still fastened at her sides. Back in the tent, she'd managed to slip the rope slightly, but Rico had tightened it again when he'd secured the other rope to her waist.

Sucking in her breath, she angled her elbows out, maneuvered one hand between the coils and pulled down. The rope loosened almost imperceptibly and she resumed pulling on the coils until she'd lifted out each arm. She rested a moment and then, climbing hand over hand, hoisted her body upward.

If she could just get enough slack on the portion of rope around her waist, she could remove it, but it was tied in a slipknot. She needed to decrease her weight, and then she'd be able to tug at the other end and wriggle out.

She hitched her body higher and pulled harder. The rope gave, allowing just enough space so she could lift it up, first over one arm, and then the other.

It was impossible to hear what Carlos was yelling. She concentrated on the rope. Her fingers gripped it tightly. It seemed glued to her hands. He yelled again and his words drifted away on the wind.

She pried her fingers loose, one-by-one, smiled up at him and let go.

Chapter 35

Her body contorted, folding in on itself. She fought gravity, knowing it was futile. Involuntary screams shook her. The abyss, monster of her childhood dreams, drew her inexorably downward. There was nothing to do—nothing...

At the moment of greatest fear, fall into the loving arms of God and say, "I surrender."

"I surrender," she screamed, trying to concentrate on the "loving arms of God" and not the awful pull of inevitability.

She drifted, spun around, and the spinning stretched on, defying the physics of the fall. Everything slowed.

Fear ebbed away, even thoughts of bones breaking on sharp boulders below. Huarana's pouch slapped at her neck. She clutched it and closed her eyes, writhing in a macabre slow dance, spinning and spinning, on-and-on.

The cells of her body came to a sudden halt, rearranged themselves, and slid into perfect harmony with everything in the universe. No words, no images flitted by, just sensations of completeness, like pieces of puzzles falling into place, melding into a transcendent flow.

Ribbons of rainbows enveloped her, appearing, disappearing, striking melodic chords with each dissolving and re-forming.

"I surrender," she whispered, sinking deeper into the flow. Undulating waves swept through her and she floated on a sea of unending pleasure.

A vise gripped her chest, shoving air from her lungs. Jagged wood ripped her thigh. Blood spurted, drenching her leg. Pain seared through her body. She screamed. A dark curtain descended, enshrouding her.

Time passed and she forced her eyes open, shook her head, and glanced around. She was moving, swinging, slowly rocking.

The rope that had tied her to Rico still encircled her waist and upper torso, forming a halter under her arms. She glanced up, trying to see what held her.

The noose on the end of the rope was looped around a rotten log. The log jutted out from a stone platform about five feet above her head.

I'm suspended in mid-air.

She angled her head down, dreading to know the remaining distance between her and the river. Clouds floated below.

Okay, I know this rotten log's going to break any minute... but I can deal with it... I have to breathe, breathe rhythmically... can't panic.

She snuffled breaths in and out, feeling the calming endorphins start. A disembodied voice sounded in her ear, "Surrender, Joanna, surrender."

Was she hallucinating? That sort of thing typically happened after a long period of fasting. Why hadn't it started before?

The voice came once more.

Sister Elena?

She laughed hysterically and remembered she needed to hold her body still. The log could break any minute.

Am I meshuge! Disembodied is the only way I've ever heard that nun's voice!

"Surrender is the only possibility," the emphatic voice announced again. "When the initiate meets with imminent death, she must surrender, that way she becomes fearless. What is there left to fear?"

Joanna ignored the voice and looked upward, assessing her situation. Maybe she could climb the rope, heave herself onto the log, crawl along it, and reach the stone platform. She studied the sliver of wood. *Definitely meshuge!*

Even the slightest jerk would splinter that rotten wood and she'd plummet into the boulder-studded Urubamba.

Surrender really is the only choice.

She closed her eyes and felt the searing pain. Breathing in deeply, she held the air, let it expand her lungs, breathed it out, held the expulsion, in and out, held the air, forced it out, in and out, in and out, letting go, breathing deeply, holding the breath, forcing it out, breathing slowly in and out, in and out... dozing. She'd been tired forever. *So tired... so sleepy.*

Back and forth, she rocked in the cradle, back and forth, back... and... forth... her mother's voice crooning a lullaby. "Rock-a-bye, baby in the treetop, when the wind blows, the cradle will rock ..." There were more words... she knew them... it was okay... she'd remember... back and forth, back and forth....

> Rock-a-bye, baby, in the treetop,
> When the wind blows, the cradle will rock.
> When the bough breaks, the cradle will fall,
> Down will come baby, cradle and all**.**

Great God! Her eyes flew open. *When the bough breaks, the cradle will fall.... That's awful! Why would anybody want to sing that to an infant?*

She felt her body tense, uncurled her legs, stretched them straight down, instantly drew them up. Emptiness loomed below.

Why was that cradle hanging in a tree anyway?

Her body ached. She was beyond tired. Her mind fought drowsiness.

The World Tree—it's in all the myths. The World Tree—Earth's axis! Of course, that's it.

Her father's explanation came to her about the "breaking tree." It broke because the axial orientation and movement of Earth changed over time. First, she was to consider that it takes 26,000 years for the axis to describe a small circle in the heavens, counterclockwise to its rotation, pointing at different constellations—*precessing.*

Second, he said she needed to remember that the axis tilted ever so slightly over 41,000 years from an angle of 22.1 degrees from the vertical to 24.5 degrees—that change in the axis' tilt was called its *obliquity*.

Third, the path of Earth's revolution around the sun was not a perfect circle. That circle could change to an ellipse over 100,000 years. That was called its *eccentricity*.

Eccentricity was mainly due to an interaction with the gravitational fields of Saturn and Jupiter, as well as, with those of the sun and moon.

The interaction of those three things, he'd emphasized, could cause erratic changes in the seasons and in the amounts of the insolation—radiant energy from the sun. For example, when the tilt angle *increased* its obliquity—the degrees of its tilt—summer, in both hemispheres, was warmer, winters were colder; when the tilt *decreased*, then summers were colder, winters warmer.

But, all that could be greatly exaggerated by the change in Earth's path around the sun, as it moved in an "ellipsis" which would bring the planet sometimes even closer and then sometimes further away from the sun. The result was probably long-term shifts in climate, alternating between interglacial and glacial periods—*Ice Ages*!

During times like that, humanity could really be said to "fall from cradle Earth," as the axis, the *World Tree*, would feel like it was shaking and causing terrible upheavals.

Could ancient memories of such catastrophes really produce a nursery song about a breaking world axis that brought on events like Ice Ages?

Did other nursery rhymes have mythological/astronomical resonances, too? She needed to take a closer look at *Jack and the Beanstalk*. That could certainly be a reference to the World Tree, and what about *Old King Cole*—the name meant "cold"—could that actually be Saturn, the "Old" King, and *cold* because the planet was the most distant from the sun that the ancients knew about?

Was that particular nursery rhyme supposed to remind future generations of the conjunctions of Saturn and Jupiter, which marked the world ages and signaled changes in the Earth's axial orientation, which could also be heavily influenced by Earth's nearest neighbors: Mars, Venus, and Mercury?

Were those planets the "fiddlers three" of Old King Cole, with their differing gravitational pulls causing Earth to "dance" to their *fiddling* as the axis became oriented differently? Did Old King Cole's "pipe" represent Earth's axis, and did the "bowl" represent the "half" celestial dome—that part of the sky that was visible "above" Earth?

What bizarre thoughts, maybe I've been too long without water ...

However, Saturn and Jupiter's long-term patterns of conjunctions did seem to coincide with Earth's axis cycling through its period of 26,000 years. Were those conjunctions, tracked over time, meant to be "predictors" of cataclysms? Many recent archaeological digs had unearthed civilizations dating back to half that cycle, which corresponded with the end of the last Ice Age.

How touching to think our earliest ancestors might have composed a lullaby like *Cradle Song*, to remind us, warn us, that the cycles do occur and can be very painful. At least, it sounded like a reasonable explanation for why our first parents might have composed such a gruesome ditty to sing to infants.

Their desperate attempts to send an important message to future generations through a cradlesong had certainly succeeded. Here we were—eons later—mindlessly singing to our children about a breaking bough and a falling cradle.

Mindless, until you ferreted out the whole story!

Shifting positions, now and then, was important. She flexed her fingers and gingerly moved each leg around. She had to keep circulation going, but, also, she needed to balance the gravitational pull on her own rotten log "world tree."

She was growing dizzy again—couldn't think anymore. The air was getting warmer. Mists were rising from the river, and the fog was clearing.

It had to be late in the afternoon. She licked parched lips, sighed, and settled once again into a deep sleep.

The gentle touch of sunlight on eyelids awakened her to a room of intense blue sky with thin cirrus clouds. Her bed was swinging. *Why was her bed swinging?*

She looked above her head and gasped, remembering where she was. It was a rude awakening. Her body ached. Thirst was a worm boring into her mind. She flexed her fingers, moved her toes, the circulation improved only slightly.

Venturing a glance into the gorge, she gagged, realizing it was still a great distance straight down to the riverbed. She scanned the horizon, turning her head slowly, worried even a slight movement might send her crashing down.

She could see snow covered Mt. Salcantay off in the distance, and directly ahead, 500 feet below her, Machu Picchu's ruins glowed emerald in the sunlight. What an amazing view from the condor's perspective.

Her gaze lingered as she scanned the ruins. She could actually do a virtual tour from up here. *My eyes can do the walking, instead of my fingers, a la the old phone book commercial. Gallows humor, that... but...*

At least a virtual tour would be a distraction from her present situation. She focused on the Gateway of the Sun that led into Machu Picchu and pretended to walk the outline of the ruins that was supposed to be built in the shape of a condor.

Slowly, she trained her sight on Huayna Picchu, the most distant feature opposite her position. The Quechuas, after the conquest, had referred to Machu Picchu as "Old Mountain" and Huayna Picchu as "Young Mountain."

The shape of Huayna Picchu, *Young Mountain*, was like a crouching puma, according to Fernando Elorrieta Salazar and his brother Edgar. They believed Huayna Picchu and the whole landscape had been deliberately sculpted to depict the life cycle of the Puma, thus representing Viracocha from youth to old age.

To the right of Huayna Picchu were three smaller hills, which, taken together, actually did look like a fledgling bird. Viracocha, at times, had been called "young bird" and "old bird." Could that mean he was associated with the "cosmic bird?" It certainly made sense if Machu Picchu was indeed the Land of the Gods.

Glancing toward the ruins again, Joanna slowly traced the other shapes incorporated within the condor outline of Machu Picchu. All totems in Incan cosmology—constellations in the celestial sphere associated with Con Ticci Viracocha— were etched into the patterns of buildings and on the landscape of this *city above the clouds*, as many people called it.

According to the Elorrieta Salazar brothers, a puma appeared to be stretched out on the north side, on one of the raised wings of the condor. On the opposite raised wing, on the south side, they believed a winged lizard was depicted. She'd read that the Incas always divided sacred spaces into two lines of descent, even Cuzco and Ollantaytambo, with its "tree of life," were divided that way.

The north side always represented *hanan pacha*, the line of descent that included the Sapa Inca and nobility, whose lineage *huaca* was the puma. The south side, *urin pacha*, was the oldest line of descent, which included the priests, the acllas, the Coya who was the Sapa Inca's sister-wife, as well as, all the other common people, whose lineage huacas were the "fixed" stars. The Incas claimed that no one knew how old that line of descent was.

How appropriate to represent the oldest lineage system as the "flying lizard." Could that really be an association with Draco the Dragon? Five thousand years ago, Earth's axis, in precession, pointed toward that constellation, when Thuben was the polestar. A curious anomaly was that ancient people in the Southern Hemisphere, who never actually saw the northern polestar overhead, still thought of north as up.

The sun's rays beating down on Joanna's head felt good. The cold temperature, at nearly a mile above sea level—even though equatorial—

was almost unbearable.

How long could she hang here? Best not to think about that—she'd think about Cuzco.

The Incas referred to Cuzco, just like other ancient worldwide sites of religious import, such as Jerusalem, Babylon, and Gobekli Tepe in Turkey, as the "navel of the world." Like those sites, the Inca's Sacred City was believed to be the axis that connected the three worlds.

Cuzco was situated high above the Urubamba Valley, on the southern side of the vast canyon where the river flowed from southeast to northwest. It was sacred to Viracocha, who seemed to match all the worldwide mythological characteristics attributed to the god and planet Saturn, who was "in control" of the heavens. Viracocha was also associated with the puma in all of Andean mythology. Cuzco was shaped like a puma with its head located at Sacsayhuaman, with its body running southeast to northwest, and positioned to look northeastward.

A puma's head, the mountain lion…the Sphinx…it couldn't be, could it?

The fabled monument loomed above her. She was twelve-years-old and stood with her father watching the sun rising over the Nile. The river flowed from south to north, replicating the Milky Way he'd told her. Did she know when the zodiac constellation Leo, the Lion, had risen with the sun at vernal equinox?

She must count back by periods of 2160 years from the present sign, Pisces, in which the sun 'rests' at spring equinox to the time when Leo was the constellation in the zodiac in which the sun rested.

Math was her favorite subject in school, so she'd announced her answer proudly. He'd told her that Graham Hancock in his book *Fingerprints of the Gods* (New York: Three Rivers Press, 1995) believed the Sphinx might have been built during that very ancient time to commemorate its own reflection in the sky at the vernal equinox.

"But couldn't the Sphinx be commemorating an even earlier time when Leo rose with the sun?" she'd asked. "How do we know if the Sphinx is commemorating Leo in 11,000 B.C.?"

Her father had said many geologists believed the erosion on the surrounding walls of the Sphinx was caused by water erosion, not wind abrasion. He said the last time the Giza Plateau had enough rain to erode those walls was around 11,000 B.C.

Then he'd asked her if she knew of any important events that might have occurred nearly 13,000 years ago. She said she'd recently read in her Geography textbook about the melting of the glaciers at the end of the last ice age, which nearly matched that date.

That was when he'd given her that lesson on celestial mechanics about the changes in Earth's axial tilt, its orientation, and movements around the sun.

He'd said, "The earth is affected by the gravitational pull of the sun and nearby planets so that it tilts through a 41,000 year period from 22.1 to 24.5 degrees from the vertical. We are presently at 23.5° in our tilt, so where are we in the range of Earth's declination?"

"Nearly in the middle," she'd answered.

"When we've gone only 1° more and reached the 24.5°, the tilt starts back in the other direction. It never goes beyond that. That slight change causes Earth to point at different sections of the sky over time, which causes our pole star marker to be different. Where is it pointing now?"

"Polaris, the North Star, in the Little Dipper," she'd exclaimed and added, "And I know where it was pointing 5000 years ago—Draco the Dragon. Our science teacher said so."

He'd pointed out one other very important fact. "Over the 41,000 years it takes for Earth's axis to change its degree of tilt, it gradually becomes positioned differently in relation to the sun, and that can cause cataclysmic changes."

"Like ice ages," she'd guessed. "Are we going to have an Ice Age soon?" she'd asked, fearing the worst.

"Milutin Milankovich, back in the 1930s, proposed the theory of ice ages advancing and receding within a 26,000 year period because of the effect of Earth's pole changing its degree of tilt."

"That's a little more than half of the 41,000 years," she'd observed.

"Scientists disagree about the causes, of course. They believe ice ages don't necessarily correlate with the approximate 25,776-year-cycle. They cite all the other conditions related to Earth's other physical properties, such as the torque in its rotation and revolution due to gravity exerted by the sun, moon and planets, that have to be in play for an ice age to begin. Still, ice core samples and seabed samples collected by scientists at Ohio State do seem to indicate a cycle like the one Milankovich suggested. So, Joanna, when do you think the last great Ice Age ended?" he'd asked, watching her closely.

"Around 13,000 years ago?"

Delighted, he'd picked her up in his arms and danced around. That kind of celebration of her ability had made her strive to please him. She'd always suspected she was an over-achiever for just that reason.

She'd confided again that she was worried about an Ice Age coming soon. He'd reassured her it wouldn't happen in her lifetime, but it would surely happen again, because that was *Earth's natural cycle.*

In light of the ancient focus on that 26,000-year period, did her pet theory of the rise and fall of civilizations really have some merit? Well, it certainly did if you considered the upheavals that occurred at the end of the last Ice Age.

Could it be that it took approximately 13,000 years—half the cycle of the 26,000-year period—for humans to reach a high level of civilization after wipeouts? What other ruins did she know about that showed devastation 13,000 years ago?

Bolivian archaeologist Oswaldo Rivera determined a date of around 12,000 B.C. for Tiahuanaco, and those incredibly sophisticated buildings showed signs of being destroyed by a wrenching cataclysm. The tumbled ruins of Pikimachay, near Ayacucho, were believed to be at least 14,000 years old.

Belgian engineers Robert Bauval and Adrian Gilbert in their book, *The Orion Mystery* (London: Wm. Heinemann, 1994), demonstrated that the placement of the Giza pyramids aligned with the three stars in Orion's belt, as they would have appeared at least 13,000 years ago—the pyramids were probably built later to commemorate that earlier time.

The Egyptians recorded their observations of the rise of the constellation Orion from a point on the horizon to a point directly overhead, which, on the equator, would be above the three pyramids. It took 13,000 years for Orion to rise to that point.

Then it took 13,000 years more for Orion to descend to the horizon again, thus completing the 26,000-year cycle. *Neat to think the Egyptians had been trying to communicate information like that.*

Earth's natural cycles seemed to be the preoccupation of all ancient people as they watched recurring events in their surroundings. Was it possible that all those cultures were trying to "remember" a very important, vastly distant time-period?

The First Time, the Golden Age—a special time held as a *common* memory by humankind, say, a time before the last Ice Age. Did the aclla's myth record that common human memory, that First Time, that first cycle?

Mankind first noticing the cycle of the apparent conjunctions of Saturn and Jupiter—which taken together would have been the brightest light in the night sky—would have told stories about it around their camp fires, stories handed down through the generations, and someone eventually drew the conclusion that the cosmos was in motion. Then they came to the realization that vast amounts of time could be measured by the motions of the planets.

They'd realized they could mark the passage of time over aeons and those cycles repeated, which made them predictable. Sister Elena's myth seemed to reference that phenomenon of the two giant planets conjuncting:

I am Con Ticci Viracocha. I weave the pattern endlessly. I am born, I live, I grow old, I die, and I am reborn again. I look on the place of dawning, at the confluence of the Twin Rivers, where I give to Pirua the means to measure all things. I give to the people the cluster of seeds that is their treasure, the seeds that grow near the place of the First Time.

Machu Picchu, the Land of the Gods, had within its confines all the "instruments" for understanding celestial mechanics. It recapitulated all the geoglyphs. They could be lost to the ravages of time or destroyed by human will, but every thought form related to Inca science and religion was enshrined in this one spot.

The pattern the planets made had actually given ancient man the concept of time. Forever afterwards, they had something by which to mark their seasons, their lifetimes, and their aeons. Best of all, they were aware that the cycles repeated, just as the aclla's story and myth described.

Machu Picchu—Land of the Gods—the eternal place…

Was that it—was that what the myth was trying to communicate?

That there was never going to be an end—fear of eternal destruction could be let go—of an eternal death—because there would always be a *First Time*! It isn't personal life, but LIFE that is eternal.

That's the message of Sister Elena's myth—Life is eternal. That's the aclla's legacy.

She wanted to jump up and down in exuberance, but remembered her predicament and glanced up at the jagged log that had broken her fall. How ironic that a condor had caused her fall, and the geoglyph condor on Machu Picchu had triggered her insights into Sister Elena's myth.

Now, if only a condor would fly by and rescue her! She lowered her eyelids slowly, fearing the slightest move.

Chapter 36

The sun dipped low in the west, and shadows crept down the mountainside. Joanna tried to close her mouth but her tongue was swollen, making swallowing near impossible. She'd had no food for almost seven days, but that was bearable compared to the thirst. She'd hoped death might come quickly. That would have been merciful compared to this creeping, excruciating inch-by-inch death.

"Dear God, I thought I'd lost everything already. I didn't find my birth parents, I've broken up with Michael, and my career's pretty much down the drain. Carlos is probably dead. I've tried to surrender everything on this trek. I'd actually begun to visualize an incredible journey that might lie ahead for me, and now, I guess I'm required to give up even that. Well, I surrender. I mean it. Anyway, here I am, God, my life's all that's left. You can have it. Amen."

One more thing to think about, that "amen"—she repeated it mindlessly, like everyone else—but what it meant was "Amon, make it so." It was the Old Testament writers hedging their bets by calling on the Egyptians' *one-true-god, Amon* to answer their prayers—they definitely weren't taking any chances.

Evening mists were rising, signaling night would soon envelop the cloud forest. Animals prowled, jungle cries sounded far off. Fear crept back. Would the hallucinations start again? How much longer did she have? *God, please help me surrender, amen.*

She startled awake, heard branches breaking, something falling, sliding, tumbling down the mountainside, scattering scree. A full moon had risen while she slept... *Mama Quilla.*

She strained to see where the noise was coming from, slowly moving her head towards the sound. It was coming from the right. Had a wild animal picked up the scent of her blood?

In the shadows, she saw a man making his way towards her. It had to be one of the kidnappers. It didn't matter. She'd die soon enough anyway.

The man sat down, still a good distance away, and looked for a long time in her direction, apparently calculating whether the structure holding her would support his weight. Finally he stood and worked his way closer

Struggling through more underbrush, he approached the stone platform and, lying down, began to crawl toward the fragile wooden frame.

"Hola, Carlos, what took you so long?"

He halted, gripping the sides of the log, and sat upright, laughing and swiping tears.

"I guess I've gone hysterical on you," he said. "I was afraid you were dead."

"If I breathe, I'll be swimming in the Urubamba River," she said. "But that's not necessarily a bad thing, because I've peed all over myself."

"Know what?" he said. "So have I."

She glanced down at the abyss. "Well, all I can say is, this sure does provide a whole new venue for a pissing contest."

Laughter released tension. Carlos wrapped his legs firmly around the edge of the splintered log. He inserted his hand inside the tangled looped rope from which she dangled and lifted it briefly above the log, wresting it clear of the sharp tip.

He edged backwards, repositioning the rope as he jostled his way toward the stone platform. Joanna swung in a circle each time the rope was lifted.

When he'd gained sturdy footing, he reeled the rope up, hand-over-hand, until he could grab her arms and hoist her onto the stone platform. Her world swirled, making it difficult to stand.

Carlos gently lowered her to the surface of the platform. He sat down beside her, reached for her hand and helped her crawl away to solid ground. Clear of the platform, he stood and lifted her in his arms, hugging her tightly to him.

He found a level area and lowering her to the ground, unclipped the flask of water from his belt and made her drink slowly. The water trickled down her throat. It was the most precious liquid she'd ever tasted. She'd never take it for granted again.

Carlos gathered a pile of dry leaves, removed two flints from his pocket, struck a flame and burned the leaves. He mixed the ashes with sap from a nearby tree and made a poultice.

Stripping away her shredded ski pants, he touched the places where the splintered log had torn her flesh. She winced as he rubbed the poultice into the wound. He unzipped her torn parka and applied the homemade salve to her other wounds. When he'd finished, he lifted her in his arms once more. She relaxed against him as he held her.

"You took my breath away when you let go of that rope," he said. "I thought I'd lost you forever."

There was a cave not far from the stone platform, an Inca tambo. Carlos carried her into it and placed her torn clothes on the ground to form a pallet. He slipped out of his jacket, wrapping it around her shoulders, and took off his pants to cover her legs.

"You look like a mummy bundle!" he said. She smiled and lifted her right hand to touch Huarana's pouch still nestled between her breasts.

He lay down beside her and pulled her close to warm her. She thanked him with her eyes. They lay for what seemed a very long time, clinging to one another, no words spoken, lost in a world apart, enfolded by the cave's darkness and the glory of being alive.

Carlos was sleeping. Joanna arranged the parka to cover them both and fitted herself more closely to him in her need for warmth. His eyes fluttered open and he turned toward her.

With grace and focus, she wrapped her legs tightly around him and began to stroke his face, moving her hands slowly down his body. She kissed his eyelids and brushed his lips with a whisper of a kiss. Like a doe licking a fawn, her hands rhythmically stroked Carlos, and he followed her lead.

He kissed her lips gently—no hurry—everything with perfect attention to her pleasure. The pulsations she sensed in him made her want to take him inside her, but she knew they had to postpone the final union until both were in the flow.

The electrical charges quickened, she felt Carlos respond, felt the charges align from the tips of her toes to the crown of her head, kindling a dance of union choreographed by life from time immemorial between two loving spirits.

I am in the Beloved. The Beloved is in me.

Positive and negative charges joined, erupting in an aurora borealis, coursing through neuronal pathways, playing in sync, like perfectly matched harmonic chords. Joanna, jolted by a fusion of particles and energy, felt herself no longer existing as a separate being.

I am pure love. I am pure being.

Lightning flashed around them, permeating cells, igniting golden sparks, radiating waves that merged and came together in a single pulse, a standing wave, a unity of being, the alchemist's dream. Like the Sufi dervish, in union with the Beloved, they cried out.

My God, my God.

Chapter 37

Joanna and Carlos stumbled through Intipunku, the Sun Gate, into the ruins of Machu Picchu, clothes in tatters, skin gashed and bruised, hair matted, feet blistered and caked in mud. They were greeted by José and the porters who shouted with joy and rushed to bring blankets and thermos bottles of water.

José told them that he and the porters had returned late yesterday and found their camp abandoned. They were very worried and hurried forward onto the trail leading to Machu Picchu. It had never occurred to them to look on Summit Trail.

They'd scoured the ruins, hoping to find the pair resting somewhere, and then they'd decided to backtrack in case Joanna and Carlos had gotten lost in the fog. On the narrow ledge, along Summit Trail, they'd found one man dead and a badly wounded fellow who said his name was Manuel.

Josć had patched him up as best he could. Manuel had been agitated about what had happened to Joanna and Carlos. He said Joanna stumbled off the ledge, and that Carlos and Rico, tied to her by ropes, was pulled after her.

He and Tomàs had fought, he said, and he'd killed Tomàs to save himself. Afterwards, he'd searched but there was no sign of Joanna or Carlos. He believed they must have died in the fall from the ledge.

The porters had conducted a futile search below the trail and then proceeded to transport Manuel down the mountain. He'd died as they descended. They took his body to the morgue and reported the missing hikers to the local police. They'd described the fight between Manuel and Tomàs and told the police Tomàs' body was still up on Summit Trail.

The police said they'd pulled another body from the Urubamba the day before. The porters described Carlos to them, but they'd insisted the man did not fit that description.

José hadn't tried to reach the de la Reyna family because he'd hoped it was still possible to find Carlos and Joanna before alarming them. The police had returned with the porters to Machu Picchu to begin a renewed search. Hours later, having admitted defeat, they were all overjoyed to see Joanna and Carlos hobbling through the Sun Gate.

José and the porters escorted Joanna and Carlos to Machu Picchu Pueblo Hotel, secured a comfortable room, and told them they could register later. Carlos used the hotel landline to call home and report that they were safe. They would stay the remainder of the day and night at the hotel. Don Remondo insisted he'd send a helicopter to fly them back to Cuzco the next day.

From the hotel gift shop, Joanna, who still had her passport and credit card in a pouch pinned inside her bra, ordered, via room service, white cotton t-shirts embroidered with colorful birds and the hotel logo and jeans for her and Carlos.

They consumed their first meal after the long fast. By necessity, it was beef consommé and dry toast points.

The ambiance of the rustic dining room, overlooking the Urubamba, with the plaintive Inca tunes played by a small band on panpipes and a half-moon harp, made the occasion a festive celebration. Joanna set her mug of consommé on the table and picked up a toast point.

"Carlos, I'm so excited. I think I've decoded Sister Elena's myth. It's difficult to condense it into just a few words, but the gist is that our remote ancestors conveyed messages through stories, with very accurate science concealed in metaphors—and that message is the same the world over."

"What's the message?" Carlos' eyes held and reflected her image in the candlelight.

"That the Earth goes through cataclysms in a natural cycle—it always has, always will."

"Cataclysms—you mean…?"

"Like ice ages building up and melting down based on changes in the Earth's polar tilt over time." She took another sip of beef consommé. "And, those ancestors made sure to convey loving assurances that mankind is eternal. Bottom line, as Rosa says—we do go on forever."

"But what do the geoglyphs in the Sacred Valley have to do with the 'messages' from our distant ancestors?"

"It's a pattern…like a concept map written on the landscape. The Great Pyramid, the Mayan Temples, the Temple at Angkor Wat, all contain patterns that are really very accurate astronomical correlations related to a 26,000 year period."

"So the Sacred Valley really has been modified to resemble the Milky Way ... "

She nodded. "And they all deliver the same message. How cool is that!"

Carlos paused, deep in thought. "How many of these cycles do you think mankind has lived through?"

"Who knows? Archaeologists keep finding ruins of civilizations even more remote than the Egyptian or Mesopotamian—like Gobekli Tepe in Turkey. All show signs of some catastrophic destruction, like Puma Punku near Lake Titicaca, which can be dated to 13,000 years ago. It seems our ancestors became obsessed with getting the cycles into their records, to warn their descendants—but also to pass on hope of an eternal resurrection from the chaos."

"Please take it easy, Joanna. I fear all this excitement is going to wear you out more than the ordeal of hanging above the Urubamba on a rotten log!"

"Remember when I told El Presidente that civilizations may rise and fall in a pattern related to celestial mechanics?"

"What I remember most is the look of absolute incredulity on his face!"

Joanna chewed on another toast point and watched Carlos as he hungrily drank his second cup of beef consommé.

"Mythology and astronomy have been a huge interest of mine since childhood," she said. "But it's only *now* that my accumulation of knowledge has yielded a sort of unified picture. I suspect from the first day I met her, Sister Elena has been guiding me to a point where I could integrate all this knowledge. She gave me the myth to decode, introduced me to the aclla who brought the myth to the monastery, and then insisted I walk the Inca Trail."

He smiled. "... and now you know the secrets of the universe."

"Don't tease me! What I do know is that our far distant ancestors, who first evolved into fully conscious humans, and subsequently, experienced a full cycle that Earth goes through in the 26,000 years, believed their real purpose in life was to get down the particulars of that experience and transmit it to us."

"I think you're certainly on to something, Joanna. I'm really in awe of your conclusions!"

"Each time those worldwide climatic changes, like Ice Ages, occurred, people very quickly reverted to savagery as they eventually lost all knowledge. If the ice ages persisted for generations, perhaps prolonged by reduced sunlight from massive volcanic eruptions, then all the advances in knowledge, in technology, in culture, would simply be forgotten."

She grabbed two more toast points and sipped her beef consommé. Looking up, she saw Carlos regarding her intently. He was such a dear to listen to all this.

"After each rise and fall of those civilizations, there would always be remnants of 'Knowers,' those people who had the wisdom that was needed to restart civilization. Just think about it! If that happened today, our people in the international space station would be the survivors, provided they had a way to get back to Earth. Anyway, the 'Knowers' would be the Viracochas who traveled about, teaching the arts and technology of the lost civilization. They would have seemed like gods to those poor people who survived the calamities. Those ancient 'Viracochas' would have made provisions before devastations occurred to preserve their knowledge, just as worldwide governments have done in so many ways today."

Carlos dipped a toast point in his consommé. "You quoted a passage from Plato once that I found interesting. I believe it had something to do with what you've just described."

"Plato said Solon's ancestor visited Egypt and was told by priests at Heliopolis that the Greeks and other people believed their lives had only recently been 'enriched' by the the things they considered necessary for civilization. The priests said that the cycles of destruction had come repeatedly and, I quote, '... after the usual period of years ...' people had to start again, 'like children, not knowing what existed before.' I think that phrase '... after the usual period of years ...,' is very significant and probably refers to the 26,000 year cycle that I've described to you."

"Joanna, I'm totally eager to hear about more of your discoveries, but don't you think we should get some rest?" He held up his right hand, "I solemnly promise from this moment forward, always and forever, to be your devoted listener, but, please, may my promise start tomorrow?"

Chapter 38

Bartles was at the airport with the estate limousine to meet Joanna and Carlos and drive them to Casa de la Reyna where Rosa, Don Remondo, and Doña Isabella eagerly awaited their arrival. Joanna called Santa Maria Monastery en route to the estate and asked for an appointment with Sister Elena. The extern nun said Sister Elena would see her immediately.

Joanna asked Carlos to convey her apologies to his parents, and requested that Bartles drop her at the monastery locutorio. She pressed the buzzer and entered to find Sister Elena already behind the grille. The two antique chairs were pushed far back against the wall. She selected one and moved it near the grille.

"Benedicite! Joanna, I'm delighted you asked to see me. I'm eager to hear all about your adventures."

"How did you know walking that trail would change my life?"

"I think every person who commits to such a pilgrimage finds it life-changing."

"The acllas knew that, didn't they, Sister?"

"I'm convinced they did. I'm convinced every human soul has the capacity to know it. I'm guessing you worked out that the spiritual paths of all religions are essentially the same."

"How did you know I did that?"

"Because it's what I did, many years ago. I made a pilgrimage across Europe following the *la voje làdee*, another very ancient trail recapitulating the Milky Way Path."

"I can't believe you made that journey!"

"I'd just graduated from the Sorbonne and needed 'time out' to consider what I would do with my life. Back in those days, it was easier to travel that path, it wasn't as heavily populated and traffic was at a minimum.

"It actually took six months. It was believed to have been a path of pilgrimage for the Druids, and, before them, many other peoples held it sacred. The *Camiño de la'Estrellas*, the Road of the Stars, is the part in northern Spain. The ultimate destination was Rosslyn Chapel—Rosslyn means 'ancient knowledge,' you know.

"You might even say that Rosslyn Chapel is the Machu Picchu of the *la voje làdee*, because it's also the northwest destination point of the European path."

"You didn't need me to decipher that myth, did you, Sister?"

"I needed you to validate my findings—isn't that what a good scientist does?"

"Bien entendu," Joanna said, barely above a whisper.

Has this nun orchestrated all my actions? To what end?

Admittedly, it was exhilarating to have gained insights into the myth, which, obviously, could only have been done by walking the trail... but...

The electric torch hummed an annoying counterpoint to the silence in the locutorio, becoming almost unbearable. Joanna continued to puzzle over how readily she'd complied with Sister Elena's plans for her.

"Joanna, if you could reduce your experiences on the trek to one simple phrase, just what might that be?"

One simple phrase... impossible! So many things had happened, but there was one moment that loomed above the others—the ecstatic union.

"God is frequency ..."

"*Il est extraordinaire*! So... He chooses to reveal Himself to each of us through our own frames of reference," Sister Elena said, her voice tapering off into thought.

"He's like a pulse, beating at the heart of all creation. He's the essence of all things, distributed throughout the universe. He's light frequency—color frequency—music frequency—matter as frequency—humans as frequency." Joanna paused, amazed at what she'd said. "God is vibrating at the core of everything, and because of His vibration, all things spring into being, and are sustained in being. He's the proton, electron and neutron in the nucleus of every atom. He's the subatomic particle, and, as we probe deeper into energy and matter, He's in all the minute divisions we make in our attempt to find ultimate matter and energy. I'll never look at the universe in the same way again because I see Him pulsating in everything—everything glowing with His essence!"

"My goodness, you sound like Teilhard de Chardin!" Sister Elena's laughter ascended the musical scale. "Now tell me about your insights."

"The acllas wanted us to know that Earth inexorably passes through periods of destruction but that it rises from the ashes and we, as humankind, will flourish again. We each have our own minor cataclysms, our own death, which is also inexorable, but we have the eternal promise that life will renew itself and humankind will go on. That's what the myth is all about—what the acllas knew! It's their legacy!"

"Joanna, why did the acllas call their legacy *The Llama Road*, do you think?"

"My ancestor Joré referred to his ordeal race along the Urubamba as 'racing along the *Llama Road*' and, at that time, I assumed it was just another name for the Inca Trail. The more I've thought about it, the more convinced I've become that he and the acllas were referring to the literal Milky Way. When they walked or ran along the Urubamba from Pisac to Ollantaytambo, in their minds, they were moving along the Milky Way with the mother llama and her suckling—the Peruvian dark cloud constellations that move down the center of the Milky Way, the Incan tribal huacas. For Joré and the acllas, that journey represented the ultimate act of their lives. When they did that, they believed they were 'in touch' with divinity, moving along that road toward the Home of the Gods, which was just beyond the Milky Way—'as above, so below.' "

"The Llama Road ..." The room grew silent. Joanna's mind raced through the many resonances the words raised

"So, what has this journey meant for you *personally*?" Sister Elena broke the silence.

Joanna had thought about that during the long hours she'd hung above the Urubamba. Now she knew.

"I hadn't realized how much I'd lived in the past or in anticipation of the future—never really in the present moment. Mamacona Yulli told the acllas, 'The Land of the Gods can always be present to us, here and now... .' Sister, I believe that's a metaphor for eternity. What she meant is that when we always live as though we're in eternity, we're always living in the present moment, not anticipating the future and not regretting the past, just **living** in the 'now.' I've never felt so happy and at peace."

"So, like the *Hero's Journey*, along the Milky Way, you've endured the *great sacrifice*, survived the *gruesome death*, and *divine revelation has been vouchsafed* to you. Now you have *the obligation, the mita,* to share the knowledge in some way."

"How did you know about my fall off the mountain?"

"My dear, we cloistered nuns have our ways, but really there's a simple explanation. Doña Isabella and Rosa came to see me while you and Carlos were recuperating at the hotel in Machu Picchu Pueblo. They made an offering to the monastery for a special Mass of Thanksgiving to be celebrated for you both."

"That fall stopped my fear of death. I think I understand why Mamacona Yulli said the acllas didn't need to fear a cataclysmic destruction of the world. We're made of God's essence—we are eternal, and like energy and matter, we're indestructible."

"I'm thrilled you experienced the ecstasy of the Hieros Gamos," Sister said.

The silence between them lengthened. Joanna breathed a sigh of contentment and thought how their friendship seemed like one of long duration, with no words necessary.

"Joanna, will you accept the guardianship of the legacy?"

Was that it? The task, *the mita,* that was required at the end of the Hero's Journey because the "hero" was not allowed to remain in *Paradise*, but had to "return to mankind" to share the revelation, to share the new knowledge. It was strange where this search for her birth family had taken her.

Family suddenly meant not only her immediate personal set of relatives, but a city, a country, and a world, with a past, present, and future, and a *mita* she had to fulfill in their name.

"I don't know what to say, but it seems I have no choice. So, is the Aclla's Legacy, which has been your legacy, supposed to become my legacy? I must say, as the aclla did, 'I'm frightened by this mita. What if I should fail?' "

Sister Elena laughed. "And I'll quote Mamacona Yulli's reply, 'Strength of character assures that you'll succeed.' There's not one bit of doubt in my mind about that, Joanna."

"It's true that the meaning of the myth *has* become clearer to me, but I don't know what to do with it, I can hardly go preaching in the streets!"

"God forbid! Please listen. You can't—even, in your wildest imagination—conceive of the wondrous things that are about to happen in your life. You must be patient, let them come to you, let the future happen, and someday the appropriate candidate will come to carry the myth forward, just as I have found—"

The monastery bells asserted their authority, clanging the hour. Sister Elena halted mid-sentence and rose to leave.

How horrible to have bells control one's life like that.

The bells continued sounding the hour and the noon Angelus. Joanna automatically whispered the words she'd been taught in boarding school. *"The Angel of the Lord said unto Mary, 'Hail Mary, full of grace, the Lord is with you, blessed are you among women, and blessed is the fruit of your womb ...' "*

There was a slight noise behind the curtain. Footsteps approached the grille. The heavy curtain parted. A tall thin woman, enshrouded in black, stood behind the bars. She lifted the veil covering her face and placed it over the back of her head.

Joanna has a visual of herself at the observatory in Virginia, discovering eruptions on Rhea, awe-stricken at what she had seen, at what she saw now. The countenance was ageless—like the Pieta—with an unfathomable sadness, yet a luminescence that radiated peace and contentment. The eyes regarded her with pure unconditional love, the kind she believed only divinity could express.

"Huarana, how wonderful! You're just as I always imagined you would be."

The voice was the same, but how different to see words shaped by the mouth and expressed on the face. There were so many things to ask her, to tell her.

"Mother Abbess gave me permission to see you for only a moment, my dear. We'll visit again soon. God bless you."

The curtains closed, muffling the voice, creating a vacuum where the nun had stood. On the other side of the curtain, the door settled softly into its frame.

She called me Huarana.

Chapter 39

The click of the Italian made stiletto heels announced Rosa's arrival. Joanna opened the office door and embraced her.

"How's the foot?"

"Fine, really fine, José and the hospital staff are brilliant medicos!"

"Thanks for dropping by today. I really needed your advice on this décor thing," Joanna said.

"I don't get it. Why would you fix up this office when you're leaving for the states?"

Joanna turned toward the window. "So, what do you think for curtains, I mean, should I have curtains? I know the mini-blinds ensure uniformity on the building's exterior, but I hate the look—couldn't we disguise the blinds by putting up…"

"Joanna, look at me! What *are* you saying?"

"Dr. Alderez made good on his original offer. He's given me a paying job!"

Rosa grabbed her arms and twirled her about the room. Extracting herself, Joanna got two Inka Kolas® from the small icebox and placed them on the table.

"We need to talk." Rosa plopped on the sofa and pulled the coffee table near.

"Talk away, I'm listening." Joanna said, sitting on the sofa beside her.

"Did Sister Elena tell you I came to see her? No? Well, I did—I needed to talk to a—well, to someone about what happened to me on that Inca Trail."

"Why didn't you come to me?"

"I was too embarrassed—thought I needed to go to confession, and then I remembered Sister Elena, and how sophisticated she was, besides, that locutorio is really like a confessional, right?"

"Are you kidding? You embarrassed, that can't be—my hearing's gone bad."

"I'm serious, Joanna. That snakebite was excruciating. I felt the poison shoot through my veins like an electrical current and... and then, well, I saw something, actually heard something."

"Hallucinations happen when you've been fasting—"

"It wasn't that. There was a voice, very clear. It said, 'Don't be afraid. I'm the one who loves you. Don't turn back.' I said something stupid. I said I didn't know, but, Joanna, I do. I do know."

"Carlos and I hoped you'd tell us about your experience."

"I can't stop thinking about it... and there's another thing. I'm almost ashamed to say it—that's what I really wanted to talk to Sister Elena about, but I was sure glad she was behind that curtain."

"What happened, Rosa?"

"Well, according to Sister Elena, my body reacted in a normal way to an encounter with a supreme love. That's what she called it."

"Wait a minute, are you saying—you're not saying you actually had an—"

"Yes," Rosa whispered, "and you're not going to believe what Sister Elena said next!"

"I can't wait!" Joanna turned her back briefly, feigning interest in the computer screen to hide her amusement. Rosa's face was burning brightly enough to light up Lima.

"You're not going to believe it. That old nun said, 'Dear child, do you think an orgasm is sinful? Do you believe any natural reaction your body has is unholy?' and, Joanna, swear to God, I almost fainted."

"That I can believe," Joanna said.

"Then Sister said, 'You aren't the first to experience such a thing. Julian of Norwich gives an excellent account of a woman's orgasm. Presumably, she'd never experienced sexual stimulation from neither a man, nor a woman, nor was she autoerotic... .' Joanna, so help me to God, I was absolutely speechless." Rosa reached for her Inka Kola® and took two long swigs.

"She actually said that ..."

"Can you imagine the commotion she'd have caused making those remarks in front of the nuns at our boarding school? She told me to check my father's library at Casa de la Reyna, because I'd find a long list of authors, like Teresa of Avila, who described incidents just like mine."

"Did she say what you're supposed to do when something like that occurs?" Joanna asked, in awe that Rosa may have had some kind of mystical experience.

"The truth is—I've actually become obsessed with pursuing whoever this *being* is, even if it takes the rest of my life. I was totally fulfilled, like nothing I'd ever experienced. I seemed to understand that this fulfillment resonated throughout the universe, making even *it* more complete. Something is expected of me, but I still can't figure out what that means."

"Maybe, I understand just a little bit, because something happened to me, too, that made me feel like I 'owe' something. Rosa, we need to talk a lot more about this, but I promised to meet Carlos for lunch. Will you come with us?"

"Can't—Mama's expecting me to go to the nursing home to visit Grandmother de la Reyna. Have fun! I'll see you tomorrow at dinner." She enclosed Joanna in a hug. "I'm so glad you're my friend. Thank you, Joanna ..."

Rosa was out the door, but a moment later stuck her head back inside. "Don't worry we'll design this office brilliantly, make it a magnet for all those home decor magazines. Bye!"

Joanna entered Carlos' office and found him at his desk, going through stacks of papers. He looked up, smiled a welcome, then came from behind the desk and held his arms wide for a hug. "I need to finish signing these papers and then we'll go. Do you mind?"

She shook her head and patted her purse. "Got reading material, I'll just perch at your conference table."

The intercom buzzed. Carlos pressed the lever and said, "Yes?"

"Don Mario Garcia to see you, Sir, shall I show him in?"

Carlos glanced over at Joanna with a stunned look on his face.

"Thanks, Teresa."

Joanna started toward the door, prepared to wait in the reception area.

"Don't go—it's Juan Diego's father. I've no idea what he wants, but I'm worried I'll lose my temper. I haven't seen him since Rosa broke the engagement."

Don Garcia came in, hand outstretched to Carlos, and stopped, staring at Joanna.

Carlos moved to his side and shook his hand. "May I introduce you to Dr. Joanna Nickels-Stewart?"

"It is a pleasure, Dr. Nickels-Stewart. I've heard wonderful reports of your work at the observatory."

"Thank you," she said, and returned to her seat at the end of the conference table.

"Don Mario, please sit down," Carlos indicated the chair in front of his desk. "What may I do for you?"

"Forgive me for interrupting your day like this." The older man's demeanor changed, his shoulders slumped. "May I have a word with you privately?"

"Dr. Nickels-Stewart can be trusted to keep our confidences, I prefer she stays. May I get you a drink?"

Carlos poured two tumblers of whiskey, neat, and returned to give Don Mario the glass.

"Sir, this visit's a surprise."

Joanna resumed her reading. Don Mario appeared to forget her presence.

"Carlos, you and Juan Diego have known one another since grammar school—no one could know him better. I—we—that is, you...." Don Mario was visibly shaken. He sipped his whiskey and squared his shoulders. "Carlos, under no circumstances must my son be allowed to become *president* of this country."

Carlos didn't respond. The moment lengthened, became awkward. Joanna looked up from her reading.

"Make no mistake about it, I do love him." Don Mario took another drink and continued. "But I love my country more. It has become clear to me that J.D. is a profligate woman-chaser and, I must admit, his costly education hasn't done a thing for him. He's about to bankrupt me, and he'll do the same for this country. I've come to ask you to put your name up for this election, and I want to throw my support behind you."

"I don't think that's a good idea—"

"I'm so sorry about Rosa." Don Mario' pulled a large white handkerchief from his pocket. "You know that, and I ..."

"Sir, I'd rather we didn't discuss Rosa, but I will say this: J.D. did her the greatest favor ever by showing his hand *before* marriage."

"I haven't been much of a godfather to you, have I?" The Don paused to take another sip. "But, my boy, I beg you—for the sake of this country—make a bid for the presidency. If you'll run, I'll make sure you're successful."

"I won't be in debt to you, nor to anyone else, for that matter. I can't say that I *will* run—I need to discuss it with my family—but, if I do, you may be sure it will be on my own, and it'll be a clean campaign."

"I never doubted that," Don Mario said.

Joanna had stopped reading. She hadn't considered that Carlos might be interested in running for the presidency, although he'd talked about needing a higher position of authority, if he was to make any real contribution to the welfare of the Quechua people.

"Sir, I suspect circumstances have caused you to become somewhat over-wrought." Carlos indicated the Don's drink, "May I give you the other half?"

Don Mario nodded. Joanna saw him watching Carlos pour the drink at the breakfront. He swiped his handkerchief across his eyes again.

"When you've thought this through," Carlos said, "I'm sure you'll feel better about whatever it is J.D. has done. Just give it time."

"I may be many dastardly things, Carlos, but I'm no fool. That boy is not presidential material, and I'm too old to be his puppet-master. If he wins, some of his very rich and powerful friends, who have their own ideas about being his puppet-masters, will run this country and, all I can say is, God, help us."

Don Mario belted down the last of his drink and stood to go. "Please think seriously about it. Adios!"

Carlos came to the conference table, sat in a chair near Joanna, put his elbows on the table, lowered his face into his hands, and stayed that way for a while. Finally, he sat up.

"I must admit I've been rehearsing possible scenarios that include running in this election. Since our experiences on that trek, I've had a notion I need to give something back for all I've been given. Only thing is, if I did run, and Don Garcia's backing meant the difference between winning or losing, I'd rather lose than have the Garcia name associated with my campaign."

"I imagine his influence could tip the scales, essentially eliminate the strongest of the twenty candidates the newspapers say are running against J.D. Oops! Sorry, I've no right to get involved in this—"

"What do you mean? You've every right!" Carlos stood, took her hands, and went down on one knee.

"Joanna Nickels-Stewart Huarana Ayaviri γ Almagro, please do me the greatest of honors. Say you'll become my wife, the Doña Joanna de la Reyna, and who knows— maybe even the esteemed First Lady of Peru!"

Chapter 40

The Nickels-Stewarts were on their way to Peru with Vivian and Sister Mary Jane Howell in tow, as well as, a complement of eight of Joanna's and Rosa's BFFs, who were finally about to star in a wedding—with a new set of fashionable bridesmaid dresses, minus giant dahlia bows. Doña Isabella insisted everybody should stay at Casa de la Reyna.

Earlier, Carlos and Joanna had called her parents to tell them about the engagement. Mary Ellen and James expressed sheer delight, as did Sister Mary Jane, who was visiting the farm, and shared in the phone call. She confessed she'd always prayed for such an event, and had been very disappointed when Joanna became engaged to Michael.

"God certainly works in mysterious ways," she remarked. "I can't wait to hear all about your Inca Trail pilgrimage."

"I'm not sure I'd credit God with *all* those mysterious ways! I've been wondering lately if He hasn't had more help than He actually needs or wants from you and Sister Elena," Joanna said. There'd been a quick intake of breath and a hurried 'Good-bye!' from Sister Jane.

The plane had no sooner touched down than everyone wanted to hear, in minute detail, all the recent happenings in Joanna's life, especially about her engagement. The bridesmaids said they'd been stunned by the news.

"What kind of soap opera are we in here?" Marva demanded. "I declare, I can't keep up with you, Joanna. I think I've missed several episodes."

"I must admit I haven't grieved too much over exchanging Citadel Cadets for Carlos' devastatingly handsome hidalgo groomsmen," Wilma said.

"I like dancing the *Shag*," Sandra said, "but, I'm dying to try the *Marinera* with these Peruvian macho males!"

"How *did* you get cloistered nuns to do your music and flowers?"

Mary demanded.

"Do we have to address you as Doña de la Reyna, after the wedding?" Dollie asked.

Many special events were on the schedule. Dr. Alderez had been exuberant about Joanna's news and insisted on personally conducting a tour of the Cuzco Observatory for her family and friends.

Tonight there was a dinner at the Posada del Inti restaurant. Joanna looked around at the dearly loved faces and thought how lucky she was. It was ultimate happiness having them with her in Peru.

"This is one of the best places for authentic local food in Cuzco," she said. "Many other restaurants serve typical tourist fare. Mama, you and daddy promised you'd try the cui—it's really very good—something like chicken."

"Go ahead, James, you order some and I'll taste a little bit," Mary Ellen said.

Joanna laughed. It was so like her mother to dip just the tip of her toe into strange waters.

"When Barbara, Linda, and Gail and I toured the Cathedral today, we saw a circa 1753 painting of the Last Supper by Marcos Zapata Inca," Marsha said. "Can you believe it, Jesus and the apostles were dining on roast guinea pig, chili peppers, potatoes, and corn-on-the-cob!"

"I've got to tell you all about something that happened recently at my apartment," Joanna said. "As you saw, my room has windows with screens, but no glass. Only shutters separate it from the interior courtyard—I can hear everything.

"One morning, about 4:30 a.m., I was awakened by shrill-pitched whistles and squeaks. I looked out between the shutters and saw a little ole plump black and white guinea pig running for its life. It was oinking bloody murder, circling the balcony like on an exercise wheel, short legs moving so fast they were just a blur.

"A man, holding a tall chef's hat on his head with one hand, was wielding a huge meat clever with the other, and chasing madly after that poor little guinea pig. Round and round they went down the circular stairs and into the courtyard. All I could think was, '*Good God, there goes breakfast*!' "

"Joanna, *pa-lease*, I really don't need that image ambushin' my thoughts whilst I'm trying to consume my meal," Mary Ellen Nickels-Stewart said, waving away her husband's offer of a bite of the delicacy on his plate. "No thanks, James, you go right ahead and eat all that li'l ole cui all by yourself."

Jamie, who was providing transportation, collected Joanna's party in the stretch-limousine after dinner and delivered them to Casa de la Reyna. Carlos greeted them at the door.

He ushered everyone into the library where Don Remondo was serving drinks in front of the carved marble fireplace. The library was cozy and approximated a 'family room,' as nearly as the palatial de la Reyna home permitted.

It was an instant celebration, and everyone was enjoying the occasion. Rosa, however, seemed subdued. Joanna wanted to get her alone later and find out what was going on. Rosa could light up the room when she was happy. It was disappointing when she was so serious.

Don Remondo was in the midst of recounting a story about touring the American South with Rosa and meeting an elderly farmer in a small town who asked where they were from.

"When we told him we were from Peru, the old farmer seemed taken aback. 'Well now, that's alright for you folks,' he said, 'but I do declare I ain't never been to Indiana, and I ain't got no reason to go to that Yankee state, any old how.'" The Don smiled broadly, delighted at the laughter from his audience.

Rosa left her seat on the sofa and went to stand beside her father. She appeared to be waiting for an opportunity to speak. The Don paused, raising his eyebrows at her, apparently resenting the imagined interruption. He motioned for Bartles to refill his champagne glass.

"There's something I want to tell you all," Rosa said, looking around the room, glancing at each person in turn. "I've been waiting for the right moment. We're about to become very busy with all the wonderful celebrations for the wedding, and I suspect I won't find another time when just my close friends and family are together like this."

Her serious mien cut the joyous atmosphere like snuffing out a lone candle in a room.

Joanna turned toward Carlos, forming a silent "What's going on?" He shook his head, mouthing back, "I don't know... ."

"I've made a momentous decision," Rosa said. "It hasn't been easy, but I'm certain it's the right thing, it's what I *must* do. I'm entering Santa Maria Monastery to become a cloistered nun." Rosa plowed ahead despite the gasps from her audience. "My entrance date is set for December 17th, just before Christmas. Mother Abbess says I have to enter then to prove my commitment to my vocation."

"Rosa, oh please, please God, not that." Doña Isabella hid her face in her hands. Mary Ellen patted her shoulder. Sister Jane moved quickly to her side.

Don Remondo, who'd just raised his glass to his lips, spilled champagne on his waistcoat. "By God, young woman, you'll do no such thing," He mopped at his stomach with a napkin. "I'll disinherit you—do you hear me?—cut you off—totally!"

"Do you think I care about your money?" Rosa said.

"You'll care well enough when Abbess Antonia demands an exorbitant dowry," he shouted. "How else do you think those nuns will support you?"

He advanced toward Rosa as if to grab her by the shoulders. Carlos jumped between them, putting his arms around both.

"Father, please listen to me! Rosa's decision needs to be respected. She's a mature woman... it's her life."

Don Remondo jerked away, went to his wife's side, pulled his handkerchief from his suit pocket and handed it to her. "There, there, my dear," he said, glaring at Rosa and wiping his brow with the back of his hand.

"I'm sorry my announcement has caused such a disturbance," Rosa said. "Everyone, please forgive me." She took her champagne glass and moved away from the fireplace.

Bartles bustled about the room, refreshing drinks and laying logs on the fire. He directed attention to hors d'oeuvres he'd placed on the library table.

Joanna, trying to reach Rosa, was ambushed by Vivian, who wanted to speak with her about the shocking news. It was nearly impossible to focus on what the housekeeper was saying.

The bridesmaids had been drifting by to speak with their old friend from boarding school, who was now nursing her fourth glass of Dom Pérignon. Joanna knew it didn't take much alcohol for Rosa to execute a howling dance on the tables. For that very reason, Rosa had always been assiduously circumspect about public consumption of spirits.

Extracting herself from Vivian, she dodged a brace of bridesmaids heading her way. She hurried to claim a window seat near where Rosa had sunk into an armchair in a distant nook.

"Rosa, you know I support anything you choose to do. I won't say I'm happy about it, but it's not about me. I love you, no matter what." Rosa got up, gave her a half hug, and made her way across the room to the drinks cart that Bartles had just reloaded.

Joanna scanned the room to find Carlos. He was with her father, sampling hors d'oeuvres. She turned to permit Bartles to refill her champagne glass and saw the bridesmaids swooping toward her. They clustered around, talking all at once.

Don Remondo and Doña Isabella were on the far side of the room, backs turned away. They were engaged in conversation with Sister Jane. Now and then, Joanna saw Don Remondo look over his shoulder, casting an aversive look at Rosa. *Please God don't let her see that.*

Moments passed and everyone returned to seats around the fireplace and the lively conversation progressed to the wedding and Carlos' campaign for the presidency. Joanna saw Don Remondo rise and hold his champagne glass high. He'd been snagging every possible occasion to toast Carlos' choice of a marriage partner, and his potential success in the up-coming election for the presidency of Peru.

He proposed a toast to Carlos and everyone responded, clinking glasses and shouting, "Salud!"

"Carlos, I've noticed you're ahead in the polls," James Nickels-Stewart said, coming to sit beside him. "From what I've read in the *Washington Post*, you're the most 'celebrated,' I think the next word was 'beloved' candidate to run for election in Peru in the last fifty years."

"I hope that's a good omen, sir. Unfortunately, many Peruvian voters, like some in your own country, have unsophisticated reasons for choosing a candidate. Campaigns can quickly become personality contests here."

Doña Isabella came to stand behind the sofa where Carlos sat. "Everyone in Peru knows and loves our son," she said, smiling down at him with adoration. "Ours is an old and illustrious family, descended from both the Spanish and the Incas. That's why Carlos is so—"

"—inbred, see, we all are—just look!" Rosa jumped up, put down her wine glass, and held up her hands, palms outward, giggling and wiggling her pinky fingers, exhibiting the rare misshapen curvature of each inwardly tilted top joint.

"Hey, everybody, see, observe centuries of inbreeding," she shouted.

Joanna held her breath. At boarding school, in sophomore World History class, during a lesson on the Incas, Rosa had declaimed her theory about the de la Reyna family's inbreeding, maintaining that she was the product of incest, because her mother was descended from Inca kings, who, like Egyptian Pharaohs, had married their sisters. The headmistress of the school, Sister Angela Marie, had clutched at her heart and hurriedly called on another student, but Rosa had prevailed, managing to get her point across.

"Silencio, Rosa, don't be ridiculous!" Doña Isabella scolded. "As I was saying, we can trace our roots to the Conquistadors and Inca royalty on both sides—"

Rosa waved her wine glass around. "Friends, Peruvians, Countrymen, rend me your peers—lears! I ask you, whose sin... age—lineage—can compare? There's none greater, I tell you... . Hear! Hear! All boast—toast—the Contiskador and Hinca Club." She held the wine glass higher, brandishing it wildly toward everyone. "Les cheer that old scrusive 'C & I' Club—all hail, the heathens—chievtains!"

Don de la Reyna coughed, his face succumbing to *purple-rising-apoplexy*, a condition Joanna had heard Rosa coin while observing the Don's angry frustration as he described people he dealt with daily, whom he considered jerks. She sent a pleading look toward Carlos.

"Father, why don't you tell everyone about your newest venture to promote modern agricultural methods among the highland Quechuas?" Carlos said.

Rosa stood, weaving her way toward Carlos. "Hey, Carlos, lemme tell 'um." She swept her wine glass around to include the whole room.

"Loosen up—lissern up, everybody. Dear old pater's gonna stand ass stride that old cordillera and pee *real hard*. Les all boast hinnovative messdids!"

Joanna looked askance at Sister Jane who had just lowered her head and pulled a handkerchief from the wide sleeve of her religious habit. She was obviously letting her black veil conceal what would've been termed *unseemly mirth* in her convent's weekly chapter of the confession of faults against the rule.

Doña Isabella glanced mournfully at Rosa, glided to the door, and pulled the bell cord. Bartles appeared. There was a whispered conversation and then Doña Isabella spoke loudly, so the others could hear. "Bartles, please bring coffee. Thank you."

The door closed. Almost instantly, there was a knock. A maid entered.

"Perdón," she said. "Doñita Rosa, someone in the parlor wishes to see you."

Rosa smiled broadly, waved to everyone, and staggered toward the door. Doña Isabella hurried to grasp her arm and, amid loud protests, executed a strained navigational dance as they exited the room.

Mrs. Nickels-Stewart stared at Joanna in stunned silence. Mr. Nickels-Stewart fiddled with his coat buttons, alternately buttoning and unbuttoning them. Sister Jane, laugh lines clearly visible, coughed, covering her mouth with one end of her handkerchief while attempting to wipe tears with the other. An increasingly rosy hue appeared on Carlos's face. The eight bridesmaids gazed searchingly about the room, pretending great interest in high bookshelves and the coffered ceiling, deliberately avoiding eye contact.

"Don Remondo, I'm really interested in your methods," Joanna said, hoping to diffuse the situation. "I would imagine major population shifts occur when—"

Sister Jane gave a convulsive hiccup and headed for the door, shoulders shaking. En masse, eight bridesmaids arose to follow, dropping excuses about assisting Auntie Jane.

The door slammed and sounds of muffled guffaws issued from the hall. Carlos, who had just taken a sip of brandy, sputtered and dabbed at his mouth. He stood, beginning to inch his way toward the door. Joanna glared at him, daring him to leave.

Doña Isabella returned. "Rosa sends her regrets. There's some sort of business requiring her attention in the parlor. She wishes you a peaceful goodnight. Do you mind if we skip coffee?"

Everyone accepted that the party had ended and thanked Doña Isabella. On the way out of the room, Joanna stepped up beside Carlos. He winked at her and slapped her on the derrière. She reached out to pinch him, but he jumped away and hurried forward to escort the Nickels-Stewarts to their rooms.

Chapter 41

El Presidente Emilio Duarte had insisted on hosting a party for the happy couple. All Cuzco was abuzz, eager for an invitation. Significant money had even exchanged hands, proffered under the table to officials in order to secure an invitation to the most coveted social event of the season. The party would be at the palatial colonial hacienda on the Almagro Estate in the Urubamba Valley.

The estate had become a museum depicting life on a sixteenth-century encomienda. It had been given to the government of Peru for official functions when Don Almagro died, leaving no direct heirs to inherit the estate. His only relative was in a monastery.

However, the deceased don's daughter did benefit indirectly as a cloistered nun from the interest on revenue producing ventures associated with the farm. The proceeds were entailed, in perpetuity, to Santa Maria Monastery.

Joanna emerged from the limousine as Jamie opened the door and Carlos took her hand. Arc lights played all around. It was a huge media event.

All cameras were trained on Carlos' fiancée. She had chosen to wear a pearl gray strapless dress that dipped low in back. An iridescent filmy cape, with a hood, stiffened by thin pliant silver wire around the edges, enveloped her head and shoulders and formed the scantest suggestion of a mantilla that was fastened at the crown by silver, emerald encrusted combs.

"I'm damn proud to be escorting Dr. Joanna Nickels-Stewart to this party," Carlos said.

"No prouder than I, to accompany Peru's next president."

The paparazzi maintained a respectful distance. Carlos and Joanna had agreed to grant a brief interview with pictures. In appreciation, the press promised to vacate the premises as soon as the interview was over.

El Presidente greeted the couple effusively at the door and told them to have a drink in the library while the other guests assembled in the main salon.

Joanna's hand remained tucked into Carlos' arm as he led her into the library and made her sit on a carved Tuscan chair just inside the door, where it faced a long row of tall windows overlooking the gardens. When she was seated, he pulled something from his pocket.

"You didn't ask about an engagement ring when I proposed to you," he said. "I had to request Grandfather de la Reyna's permission to get it from the vault. It was one of the items from his second cousin's estate. The fellow died without an heir and my family inherited all his possessions. I used to go with Grandfather to the bank when I was a child, and, on one trip, he showed me the ring. He said I should give it to my bride someday."

Joanna opened the mother-of-pearl box. "Carlos, it's stunning, emeralds are my favorite."

"You think I hadn't noticed!"

The ring had been correctly sized so it slipped easily on her right ring finger, per the European custom prevalent in Peru. The large green center stone was set in an old-fashioned pierced setting, exquisitely designed in platinum.

"Who was it originally made for, do you know?"

"Someone very special to Grandfather de la Reyna's second cousin, I think it was his fiancée, but something tragic happened."

"It's a treasure, Carlos! I'm so thrilled to have it."

Carlos pulled her up from the chair and embraced her tenderly, kissing her. When they stood apart, Joanna was facing the massive carved marble fireplace.

Her heart did a quick staccato beat. She was looking at a life-sized portrait hanging above the mantel.

The woman in the portrait had delicate features with dark curly hair forming a widow's peak on her high forehead. She was wearing a pearl gray formal dress, with a mantilla of some soft transparent pearlescent material that enveloped her completely and fell over the chair where she sat. Her hands were crossed on her lap with the right hand resting on top of the left. The ring on the woman's right hand was an exact replica of the one Carlos had just placed on Joanna's hand.

She swayed toward Carlos and braced herself on the chair arm

"What is it, Joanna? What's wrong?" He caught her, lifted her to a nearby sofa, and reached to pull the bell cord by the door.

A steward appeared immediately. "Please bring a glass of port," Carlos said.

"That painting over the fireplace," Joanna said, "who is she?"

Carlos gave a cursory glance toward the fireplace. "I've been here a million times since I was a small child, but I don't recall seeing a painting there." He continued watching Joanna.

The steward entered and placed the port on the table with a glass poured for Joanna.

"Thank you," Carlos said. "Wait a moment. Do you know who that is in the portrait?"

"Sir, I don't know. It was in storage, as were the other contents of this room. The manager of the estate asked that we put the things out for this occasion." He bowed, left the room, and closed the door.

"Joanna, I can't imagine who it must be, except that I do recall that Don Hernando de Almagro had a daughter." Carlos ignored the painting and lifted the glass of port to Joanna's lips again. "Maybe that's who it is."

Joanna heard his words and lost consciousness. Seconds later, she awakened to Carlos patting her face and hands.

The door opened. El Presidente Emilio Duarte entered the room. He rushed to Joanna.

"My dear, what's wrong? What's happened? We must send the guests away—you cannot possibly greet them now, you are pale as a ghost!"

"Emilio, that portrait seems to have disturbed her," Carlos said, turning toward the fireplace to inspect the portrait for the first time, now that Joanna was sitting up, fully recovered.

El Presidente glanced at the portrait and stared back at Joanna.

"¡Madre de Dios! *It is you, Joanna*! But it can't be."

Chapter 42

In the locutorio at Santa Maria Monastery, Joanna sat shivering, awaiting Sister Elena's arrival. Her parents and Sister Jane were with her. She'd managed to get the appointment for late afternoon and had spent many anxious hours waiting for the time to arrive. She'd hoped to introduce her parents to Sister Elena at an opportue time while they were in Cuzco, but today she'd demanded they and Sister Jane accompany her to the monastery.

James Nickels-Stewart commented excessively on the architecture of the locutorio, while Mary Ellen occasionally wiped at the corners of her eyes and emitted a tittering little giggle at her husband's remarks. Auntie Jane was quiet, and that was the most disturbing thing of all.

Someone entered the room on the other side of the iron bars. The black curtain was swiftly drawn aside, and Sister Elena stood there lifting her face veil, draping it back over the veil that covered her head.

"James and Mary Ellen, I'm happy to finally meet you," she said. "Sister Mary Jane has told me many wonderful things about you both."

Mary Ellen smiled, and James stood and reached his hand through the bars to shake her hand. Sister Elena responded with a warm handshake.

She sat down and turned to Joanna. "Doña Isabella called to say you saw the portrait at Almagro Estancia. Sister Mary Jane, your parents, and I owe you an explanation. I was waiting for the most appropriate time to reveal this to you, Joanna."

"Seems to me the *appropriate time* was several weeks ago when I begged you to tell me what you knew about my birth parents."

"It saddens me to think this has upset you so terribly. First, I want you to know I love you very much—dear God, where shall I begin?"

Joanna sat motionless, looking at the faces surrounding her. They obviously knew one another very well. Mrs. Nickels-Stewart was rummaging in her purse. Sister Mary Jane reached over to put an arm around Joanna. Mr. Nickels-Stewart came to stand behind her chair. The elderly nun left her chair and stood close to the grille, looking down at Joanna.

"My darling girl, you are my granddaughter."

Joanna's hand flew up, warding off the unexpected blow. She was on the ledge, above the abyss, careening toward the edge. Minutes ticked by, and she became a heated glass rod, pulled past the point of cooling, shattering into a million pieces. A high thin keening wail split the air.

"Joanna—" Sister Mary Jane started.

Her body shook of its own accord. Aunt Jane embraced her. Her mother and father hugged them both, supporting Joanna who was now folded in on herself like a small child.

Sister Elena sat behind the bars, helpless, wracked by sobs.

Grief consumed Joanna in waves. Sister Elena sent for a glass of water and handed it through the bars to James who helped Joanna sit up and drink from the cup.

Pushing the glass away, she looked at each of them in turn. She'd searched so hard, worried through long nights, felt such despair. Still, they'd kept this secret and let her suffer.

"I'm angry—angry with *all* of you! You especially, Sister Elena! You let me run up and down exhausting every avenue to find my family, and all the time you knew and never said a word. How could you be so cruel?"

"I've much to answer for," Sister Elena said. "I wanted to tell you before now. I'm so sorry it's happened this way. Please let me try to explain, to tell you how it all came about."

The old nun reached back, pulled her chair alongside the grille, and sat down near Joanna.

"Your birth mother, Sarafina, was my daughter by Don Rodolfo de la Reyna, a second cousin to Carlos and Rosa's grandfather, Don Augustin. I was affianced to Don Rodolfo when he died in a horrible accident. We had been intimate once, I was secreted away to give birth and then my family sent me to Europe. Don Augustin and his family adopted Sarafina and reared her.

"She attended college in Ayacucho where she met your father, Alejandro Huaman Ayaviri. They were married despite Don Augustan's objections, and you were born shortly before your father was imprisoned."

"In those days, it would have been a great disgrace for Clara de Almagro's family if she'd given birth to a child out of wedlock," Sister Jane said. "She really had no choice but to let them arrange the adoption of her daughter, who was destined to be your birth mother."

"I loved my child very much and wished I could rear her myself, but one didn't cross one's family back then, Joanna. My fiancé, your grandfather, was dead, and I didn't want to marry anyone else. I believed it was best to take the veil in this monastery.

"As time went on, my grief became less, and I grew to appreciate my vocation here. I don't regret that part of the tragedy. But I do regret the negative repercussions for you, my dear child."

"Sister, I admire the courage you've shown in revealing this to Joanna," James Nickels-Stewart said, as he reached through the grille and patted Sister Elena's arm.

Sister Elena turned once again to Joanna. "Mary Ellen and James have been the best parents a child could possibly have—please don't mourn that they didn't tell you about your adoption. We all believed it was best to protect you, while you were growing up, from anyone here in Peru who was either intent upon an Inca restoration, or intent upon preventing one. Through Ayaviri, as you've already discovered, you're a descendent of Huarana and Joré and, therefore, you're directly descended from Sapa Inca Huayna Capàc, down through Huáscar. You are most certainly Incan royalty.

"People say your father, Ayaviri, became a revolutionary during his college years in Ayacucho, out of compassion for the poor beleaguered Quechua people. Huarana's legacy belongs to you by blood, Joanna, but also, by the fact that you've earned the right to guard it now, and to use that knowledge for some good purpose in the future.

"Your initiation into that heritage from the moment you came to Peru is why we've not revealed your identity before now. It was necessary that you learn as much as you could for yourself. You could say your initiation has been like the vision quest tradition that your ancestors practiced."

Joanna used the backs of her hands to wipe her eyes, like removing an obstruction. She was fascinated by Sister Elena's words.

"I think I met Ayaviri," she said, clearing the tremor from her voice. "When Carlos and I were kidnapped on the trail, a third kidnapper arrived in camp after the two others had tied us up. I was terrified, but his eyes seemed so full of compassion and love. It's strange, but I felt that I knew him. He came over to me and picked up Huarana's pouch that I was wearing around my neck and looked at it for the longest time. Then he smiled, bowed to me, and left the tent.

"The police told us he'd killed that kidnapper in a terrible fight after I fell off the mountain and pulled Carlos over with me. They said Ayaviri was badly wounded in that fight and died before they could get him to a hospital."

"He must have discovered you looked exactly like his wife," Sister Elena said. "I'm sure he guessed you were his daughter. Dr. Alderez called me and said the body was identified as Ayaviri's, but the warden in Lima asked that it be kept quiet. After all, they'd already given out that he'd died in prison, and the last thing they wanted was a massive public demonstration of grief on the part of the Quechua people.

"Joanna, I know that you'll grieve that you had no opportunity to get to know him, but his was a difficult life, hiding always from one faction or another. You may pay your respects to him when you wish. Dr. Alderez claimed the body and had him entombed in our burial vault beneath this monastery church. We intended to tell you about it after your wedding."

How could she ever wrap her mind around the twists and turns her life had taken since the letter with the birth certificate had arrived in D.C.?

"Sister, I need to ask you something. Did you send that anonymous letter to Senator Vander Hurst?"

"I'm so sorry for the pain that caused you. I was so fearful that, if you married in the states, you would never come to Peru to claim your heritage."

"So, you plotted all this…"

"I know we can't control the consequences of our actions. I know it so well, and I'm haunted by it. Please forgive me, Joanna."

If she chose to let it, the resentment and anger she felt would consume her. It couldn't be denied, it *was* a despicable thing they'd all done. There was really no difference between Sister Elena and Senator Vander Hurst.

They'd both tried to play God and shape another's destiny, and that was unforgiveable. Yet Joanna had to concede that the scientist in her also recognized that both the senator and the nun had goaded her into finding a new existence with broader horizons than she'd ever imagined, and, for that, she owed them immensely.

She left her chair and pulled both Mary Ellen and James to her. "You're my parents, the greatest set anybody could ever want, and I'm not about to think of you in any other way. Mama, I need to say that your dear sister Mary Jane is also fantastic, except for her damned interfering ways! But I do love her despite that."

Sister Mary Jane reached for her hand. Joanna pulled her into the circle. When she'd extracted herself from their hugs, she went to the grille, put both hands through the bars, and pulled Sister Elena to her, embracing her as best she could. She felt the nun's frail body touch hers and cried silently for the beauty and gift of having a grandmother, but also for the time that was lost to both of them.

She felt Sister Elena trembling from the emotion and caressed her cheek, wiping tears from the porcelain skin. Gradually, she lowered her arms, but continued to hold her grandmother's hands. It was still jarring to think of the nun in that way.

Sister Elena glanced down at the engagement ring. "It's your emerald," Joanna said. Carlos' grandfather gave it to him. You were wearing it in that portrait."

"Joanna, darling, you're so very precious to me."

"I can't deny that I'm torn between being angry with you and being way beyond excited that you're my grandmother—it's such a wondrous thing."

The convent bells chimed and Sister Elena reluctantly rose to go. Joanna thought about the many infractions the nun had accrued against the Holy Rule in the time she'd spent with them. Rosa had told her those infractions included touching and being touched, missing the bells to chant the Divine Office, and revealing strictly personal information. She regretted that her grandmother would have to bear the humiliation of confessing all of those.

Sister wiped tears from her eyes and expressed regret that she had to leave. She begged everyone to visit again soon and closed the curtain. The extern nun appeared immediately and pressed the buzzer to open the massive door to the street. Joanna, her parents, and Sister Mary Jane exited into a mild star-filled evening on Calle Santa Maria.

"Okay, you all, I know just the place to warm the cockles of the heart and to celebrate our newly extended family," Joanna said. "We need to go to Via Làctea for chocolate cake and some good rounds of drinks for you, Daddy. And, if you all don't mind, I'm calling Rosa to ask her to bring the whole de la Reyna clan to join us."

They arrived at the pub to find Rosa already there with two large tables pulled together on the balcony. The wide doors leading to the balcony had been thrown open and the view was of a fabulous movable feast with Cuzco as a backdrop. The whole family was gathered there, even great Aunt Catarina Diego γ Garcia.

"You said *celebration*, so I collected everybody, including the bridesmaids, and asked Jamie to chauffeur us all to Via Làctea ," Rosa said.

"I've got the champagne bottles in ice buckets and Rosa has commandeered the staff to bring several chocolate cakes with plates and forks. We are ready," Don Remondo de la Reyna said, smiling at Joanna.

She returned his smile, pulled Rosa aside, hugged her, and whispered, "You're not going to believe the latest news!"

Everyone settled into chairs around the table. Carlos found a place next to Joanna. Don Remondo, assisted by James Nickels-Stewart, served the champagne.

The waiters served cake while Don Remondo held up his glass, moving it in a gesture to include the whole table. "Joanna, please tell us your news so we can get this party started. Salud, let's celebrate, everybody!"

Joanna stood up. "I want you all to know I've found my family—one close member in particular, and numerous other relatives. My grandmother is alive and well and, this you're not going to believe, I'm a distant cousin of all the de la Reynas!"

There was silence all around—in fact, the other patrons in the pub ceased talking and every head turned toward Joanna.

"Carlos and Rosa, I'm your cousin—I haven't counted what 'n^{th}' degree—but we're cousins somewhere down the line! And, most astonishing of all, my grandmother is Clar—"

Don Remondo grabbed Joanna and hugged her, cutting off her words. "Don't announce her name here," he whispered.

Rosa reached Joanna just ahead of Carlos. Both enclosed her in a hug. The bridesmaids jumped up, joining in, and everyone pranced around, embracing.

"Just so everybody's clear about this," Carlos called loudly, "you may be sure Joanna and I are far enough apart in kinship that it won't interfere with our marriage—just so everybody knows!"

There was a roar of laughter from all the pub patrons.

"You're serious, Joanna, we're really cousins," Rosa said, looking like a five-year-old with a new puppy. "Who would've believed it? Only, that's not the most important thing, because we're about to be sisters! Bona fide sisters-in-law! Wait a minute, who is your grandmother?"

Joanna leaned in close, signing the name to Rosa.

"¡Madre de Dios!" Rosa screamed. Carlos put his arms around both of them. Everyone else continued exclaiming over the news. In fact, the pub had exploded into shouts and warm congratulations. Rosa recovered and hugged Joanna again, crying and laughing at the same time.

Don Remondo ordered another round of champagne for everybody in the pub. Perfect strangers came to the table to congratulate Joanna. Someone texted a photojournalist, who arrived at the pub, hurriedly snapped photos, and headed out to post the story.

Carlos intercepted him, made him erase the digital photos, and paid him handsomely to squash the story.

Everybody talked long into the evening. The pub served dinner *on the house* and when it was time to leave, the de la Reynas ditched the young people and had Jamie chauffeur them, along with Joanna's family to a night on the town.

Carlos drove Joanna's rental van, which she'd decided to lease while her family and friends were visiting. The decision was made to go to the Observatory Tower, since Joanna had a key. They all wanted to see sunrise over Cuzco.

Inti rose, enveloping Coricancha in bright light, while the group of friends sat watching.

"Rosa, I wish you wouldn't enter that convent," Gail said.

"Please everybody, I need so much for all of you to support me. You saw mother and father's reaction the other night. They've been awful to me, treating me like a child."

"But, Rosa, why enter a cloister, why not enter an order like Sister

Jane's? Those nuns don't shut themselves behind bars," Barbara said.

"I've thought about that—believe me—and it's tempting. I could probably teach college classes, but I feel this call to the cloister so strongly. I believe I've been asked—called—to give back in some way. I've come to believe, absolutely, that our prayers can influence, through our own life choices and intentions, everything in this universe. And the most direct, efficient way to do that is to live a lifestyle that has been practiced for millennia by experts in the spiritual life."

"But you've such a wonderful future ahead," Wilma said. "What about the modeling job with that top agency, *People* magazine said you were offered?"

"I've been wondering how you intended to use that degree from M.I.T.," Marva said.

"From what Joanna tells us, Sister Elena seems to utilize her many degrees quite effectively," Dollie said.

 "I can't imagine you locking yourself away when Joanna's about to be your sister-in-law and live here in Peru," Mary said.

"I know it may seem a waste and doesn't make sense, but then it's not supposed to. I just know I have to do this. I'm as sure as anyone could ever be that it's what I must do. It makes me peaceful and joyful. Please be happy for me."

Joanna saw Rosa look toward her, directing the last statement at her. She smiled her approval and felt Carlos grip her hand. His gentle, empathic capacity to be aware of another person's angst was one of the many things she loved about him.

Chapter 43

Joanna, teary-eyed, face red and swollen, waited for Rosa outside the wrought iron gates of Santa Maria Monastery. It was hard to believe only a month had passed since her wedding had taken place in this very same church.

All her childhood dreams of such an event were realized. Doña Isabella had insisted on taking her and Mary Ellen to the Almagro Estate to locate her mother's wedding dress. Sarafina Almagro Ayaviri's exquisite gown had to be slightly altered to fit Joanna's tall thin frame, but she'd been proclaimed the most beautiful bride anyone could remember. Afterwards, she and Carlos had adjusted seamlessly to living together and had been ecstatically happy as they campaigned for the election.

Now she was desolate waiting for Rosa, recalling how they'd stood here less than a year ago at 4:40 in the morning, trying to attend Mass and seek permission to visit Sister Elena for the first time.

The de la Reyna limousine drew near the curb. Jamie jumped out and hurried around to open the rear door for Rosa, who alighted and ran over to embrace Joanna.

"I can't believe you're doing this to me. I'd hoped, somehow, you'd change your mind."

"Please don't make it any harder for me," Rosa said, reaching up to adjust her white fur 'Jackie Kennedy style' pillbox hat. Jamie retrieved the matching fur muff from the back seat of the car, and handed it to her. He bent to kiss her cheek.

Joanna waved to him, noticing his eyes were misting over, as he jumped into the car, started the engine, and pulled away from the curb. He honked the horn, scattering several paparazzi who had gathered to snap photos of Rosa.

Cuzco at 12,000 feet above sea level had turned colder than usual in the middle of an already cool December summer morning. Joanna still had difficulty remembering the switched seasons. She smiled at the irony of the outer clothing Rosa had chosen for this occasion.

Her best friend wore a cinnamon-colored full-length fitted cashmere coat with a shawl collar. Well concealed, beneath, was a drab black serge dress with a cape that came to the waist. The regulation outfit included a black leather belt and heavily starched white linen cuffs and collar. The stiletto heeled Pradas® and silk stockings would be exchanged inside for black cotton stockings and the rope sandals worn by the nuns. Rosa had said that Abbess Antonia, in a private ceremony, would place a black net postulant veil on her head.

"You're probably the most fashionably dressed postulant who ever entered a monastery," Joanna said, laughing through tears.

"Hey! I'm betting that honor goes to Sister Elena, Clara de Almagro, your grandmother!"

Joanna wondered why the bishop had granted permission for a truncated six-month Postulancy—probationary period —for Rosa. The trial period usually extended from one to two years, but he'd made an exception for Rosa. Was it because he was aware of the "vision" she'd had on the trail?

Rosa hadn't mentioned that experience in the last few months. Joanna assumed she had gotten spiritual direction, which was what Sister Elena had recommended.

Earlier, she'd confided to Joanna that if she successfully completed the rigorous requirements of the probationary period, then at the end of the six months, she'd be inducted into the monastery as a novice, in an elaborate reception ceremony, staged like a wedding.

"I'll miss you so much," Joanna said. "I can't bear it!"

"I love you more than life, Joanna—both as my good friend and now as my real sister, well, sister-in-law—but I can't turn away from what I know. Whatever it was that happened to me has altered my life. Like Francis Thompson in his poem, *Hound of Heaven*—that our beloved Sister Angela Marie loved to quote back in boarding school—I must '...*seek Him down the labyrinths of my mind...*' because He's pursuing me like the Hound in that poem. The vision I had is etched in my memory and permeates every fiber of my being. Please try to understand."

It was 17th of December—Rosa's entrance date into the monastery. The Incas had given sacrificial gifts to Viracocha, during the Summer Solstice around that time.

Sister Elena told Joanna that Abbess Antonia had declared that if Rosa wanted to show she was serious about her vocation she had to enter now, despite the fact that it was near Christmas time and her unwrapped presents lay under the beautifully decorated Christmas tree in the drawing room of Casa de la Reyna.

Rosa's resolve to be a nun was being tested by the abbess, Sister Elena had explained. In fact, Rosa would be tested during the entire time she was a postulant. The nuns would observe her reactions and attempt to determine if this was truly the will of God for her.

The hardest part Joanna could imagine was that "The Rule" required that Rosa remain totally separated from her old life during this time. Sister said Rosa would have to submit to tests of humiliation designed to break her self-will, would have to do all sorts of menial tasks, would even have to repeat the same task over and over, with hands raw, knees aching, until the postulant mistress judged that the "task" had been done perfectly.

Worst of all was that Rosa would have to force herself to consume unpalatable foods in order to curb her natural responses. It was all part of the training in discipline, a trait essential for a nun, Sister Elena said.

At the end of the probationary period, if Rosa remained steadfast in the pursuit of her vocation and the choir nuns had not 'black-beaned' her, a concept that actually had its origin in monasteries—that is, voted her out as unsuitable for the life—then she'd be admitted to the novitiate.

The six months of Rosa's probationary period at the monastery passed more quickly than Joanna could believe. She and Carlos had campaigned vigorously and the election for the presidency would be held soon. Don de la Reyna noted that the publicity surrounding Rosa's reception into the historic monastery most certainly wouldn't hurt Carlos' popularity; rather, it was sure to secure even more votes.

Don Remondo and Doña Isabella de la Reyna had sent out engraved invitations asking everyone to their daughter's clothing as a nun. A formal reception would be held afterwards at Casa de la Reyna, but Rosa wouldn't be permitted to attend. Instead, Don Remondo would formally unveil a portrait of his only daughter that he'd commissioned earlier.

Thousands of candles illuminated the inside of Santa Maria Church and the mosaic mirrors scattered their images like shooting stars. Flowers blanketed every altar and the pews, pulpit, choir grille, as well as the bishop's throne chair, had been polished to a high sheen. It was the most solemn event to grace Santa Maria Monastery in many years. There hadn't been a clothing of a novice for forty years.

Silver trumpets sounded and The Bishop of Cuzco, with his entourage of priests and acolytes, enacting colorful medieval pageantry, processed to a triumphal march from Verdi, down the center aisle of the church and took up places on the highest step of the main altar.

El Presidente Emilio Duarte, wearing full governmental regalia with the presidential sash, accompanied by his coterie of national police agents, followed the procession down the aisle. He was seated in an honored place in the front row pews with Rosa's family and friends, where his wife had already taken her place. Occasionally, he sniffled and wiped his eyes with a large white handkerchief.

The monastery bells pealed joyously and then there was a hushed moment as the congregation stood and turned en masse, staring expectantly toward the back of the church. Joanna imagined she could hear an ant scurrying along the stone floor.

Abbess Antonia jingled the skeleton keys, a harsh counterpoint to the silence, as she unlocked the door to the grille at the back of the church. Moments later, she and Sister Elena, totally concealed in their black habits with white mantles sweeping the floor, face veils in place, led Rosa from behind the bars of the cloister and left her standing alone in the middle of the aisle.

Unseen behind the grille at the back, the choir nun's *á cappella* voices intoned the age-old antiphon, *Veni, Sponsa Christi,* "Come spouse of Christ," calling the young bride to the nuptials with her Heavenly Groom. Joanna felt a ripple of awe sweep through the church.

Rosa wore Doña Isabella's antique champagne-colored wedding gown, fashioned in princess style. It was of handmade Alençon lace with a portrait neckline and long lace sleeves ending in a pointed-"v," extending just to the middle finger of each hand. She carried a bouquet of white lilies. Her black hair was drawn severely back and braided into a band secured at the base of her skull. A fitted-lace cap covered her head but left the braid exposed. The cap ended in a sharp v-point on Rosa's forehead with v-points on either side of her face, covering her ears about half way down. Grace Kelly had worn a similar lace cap on her wedding day.

The filmy veil, trimmed in transparent lace appliqué roses, was placed as one piece over Rosa's head so that it fell to the hem of the dress in front, and ended in a small train at the back. She looked altogether otherworldly. Her only jewelry, gifted by Joanna, was a necklace of antique ivory pearls with teardrop pearl earrings that glistened in the candlelight.

Every pew in Santa Maria Church was occupied. People even stood in the ambulatories along each side, under the windows. They held their collective breath, fearing even to sigh, lest the vision in front of them would vanish.

"Come, Spouse of Christ, receive the crown, which the Lord has prepared for you from all eternity ..." the choir nuns exquisite voices rang out, and Rosa, eyes cast down, glided gracefully down the aisle.

She knelt on the first step of the altar, and, above her, the Bishop intoned the ritual words, "What do you ask, my daughter?"

"God's mercy and yours, your grace," Rosa replied in a high, clear, confident voice.

"Do you wish to receive the holy habit of religion and to observe the Rule of Santa Maria Monastery?"

"Yes, Bishop Eduardo, this I wish, and desire, by the grace of God."

"May the Lord, who has begun this in you, bring it to fulfillment."

Joanna, kneeling in the front pew, wondered if the bishop recalled Rosa taunting him about the cloistered nuns sleeping late on Saturdays. Knowing he understood English, she'd translated his Spanish words for Joanna, altering them, so that the bishop said the nuns were slothful for not rising at 4:00 a.m. on a Saturday. Thinking about Rosa's humor made tears start again.

The choir nuns summoned the Holy Spirit to bless Rosa, singing, *Veni Creator Spiritus*—"Come, O Creator, Spirit Blest, and in our souls take up Thy rest, come with Thy grace and heavenly aid to fill the hearts, which Thou hast made."

The Bishop descended the steps of the altar and stood quietly praying. After a moment, he raised his arm and, with a grand flourish, lifted the veil away from Rosa's head.

An acolyte took the veil and laid it aside. An extern nun stepped forward and extracted the hairpins that held Rosa's braid in place. The braid fell in a long dark, glistening coil down her back.

Another acolyte handed a pair of large decorative silver shears to Bishop Eduardo, who positioned himself behind Rosa. The acolyte grasped Rosa's braid and held it out horizontally for the bishop.

The congregation's collective eyes were riveted on Rosa as Bishop Eduardo snipped the braid off at the base of her neck. He and the acolyte returned to the high altar where he took a seat in the throne chair off to one side.

Rosa knelt motionless, the beautiful lace cap mercifully concealing her mangled hair. The church was deathly silent. After a long moment, she stood, moved inside the communion rail and went to the side altar where she laid her bouquet of lilies on the altar in front of the sculpted marble statue of Mary, the Mother of Jesus.

Joanna knew what was coming next. Sister Elena had warned her earlier. She watched Rosa return to the steps leading up to the main altar where she ascended them and knelt once again.

Lifting her head, Rosa gazed briefly at the cross above the altar then extended her body to a full prostration before the tabernacle. Two extern nuns came from the sacristy, carrying a black rectangular shroud. They placed the pall over Rosa's prone body, signifying her aloneness in her sacrifice of self to God.

Joanna had been with Rosa in all the major events of her life. It broke her heart to think she couldn't follow her into this one, but her sacrifice was at least on the same par, for she was losing her best friend. They'd played a game of concentrating on one another when they were far away, so one or the other would call to see what was up. It usually worked.

Rosa, please hear me, now. Don't you dare think you've left me behind, I'll always be by your side, do you hear me…

Muffled sobs sounded throughout the church. Doña Isabella cried quietly, her head turned in toward Don Remondo's shoulder. Joanna cried openly. Carlos put his arm around her.

The choir nuns sang with full hearts, *Posuit Signum*. "He has placed a seal upon my countenance that I may admit no lover but Him."

The extern nuns came forward, removed the pall, and exited to the sacristy. Rosa arose and returned to kneel on the top step of the altar.

An acolyte stood to one side, holding the folded black habit of the Santa Maria nuns. The bishop intoned a prayer over the habit and blessed it with holy water. He lifted the habit and placed it on Rosa's outstretched hands.

Joanna thought how the "fashion plate of Peru"—as the news

magazines referred to Rosa—would no longer be preoccupied with such things. A black shift with a floor length white woolen mantle would be Rosa's new "haute couture" for the rest of her life.

The bishop blessed the scapular, which represented the yoke of Christ, and placed it on top of the habit. Next, he laid the white veil of a novice on top of the scapular and sprinkled it with Holy Water. Finally, he blessed the triple string of large black Rosary beads and gave them to Rosa. She would wear the prayer beads on the black leather belt at her waist.

After the blessing and prayers, the extern nuns took all the items from Rosa and waited to escort her to the enclosure where she would be clothed in the habit.

An acolyte placed a tall white candle in Rosa's right hand. The light from the candle flickered across her face as she stood and turned toward the congregation with eyes cast down.

She walked ahead of the extern nuns, down the aisle to the enclosure. The choir nuns sang of the "wise virgins," in the Gospel of Matthew, whose lamps were trimmed, whose candles burned brightly, whose lives were in order, and who were prepared to meet Christ, the bridegroom.

Rosa had told Joanna that Abbess Antonia and Sister Elena would assist her in putting on the habit. Novices were considered incapable of dressing properly their first time. Joanna imagined getting into that garb did require a bit of practice.

The bishop addressed the congregation in a short homily while Rosa was being clothed. He mentioned the vibrant young woman who was giving her life to God and lifted his hand to brush away a tear. He finished with an exhortation to all present to think about the great sacrifice they were witnessing and to examine their lives to see what they might offer to the Creator. He turned from the pulpit and took his place again at the center of the altar on the highest step.

The congregation watched the new novice emerge from the enclosure, and the choir nuns intoned *Exuat*, "May the Lord strip you of the old person and clothe you as a new person, who, by the grace of God, is re-created in justice and holiness of truth."

Rosa floated down the aisle. She was transformed. Only the small triangle of her face could be seen. She wore the black habit and the white veil of a novice. Around her shoulders was a white choir mantle that fell in graceful folds, touching the floor as she walked. She seemed to glow like a crystal from some inner source, making it nearly impossible to keep one's eyes on her for long.

Joanna remembered only once before, at a rock concert, when she'd seen an audience so melded together by an experience. They'd seemed like a massive organic amoeba, responding as a single unit. This congregation was similarly united in their adoration of the vision that was passing by them.

Carlos appeared awe-stricken at the sight of his little sister. The Don and Doña de la Reyna looked saddened, but proud. The congregation, turning as Rosa passed, genuflected and crossed themselves.

At the back of the church, Joanna glimpsed Juan Diego Garcia sitting by the wall near the rear door, lurking like some insect. Was Rosa aware of his presence? She laughed silently. *There wasn't the slightest possibility!*

She found it difficult to attribute altruistic sentiments to Juan Diego. He was probably using this as a press-op, had, no doubt, alerted the media so they could photograph him attending church on a weekday, being terribly religious.

Rosa is way beyond that bastard now. Let him look on her and grieve his loss! Joanna mopped her eyes with a tissue. She wanted to run out of the pew, grab Rosa by the arm, drag her out of the church, and take her home so they could go shopping and eat chocolate cake at the Via Làctea and laugh together.

Rosa knelt at the foot of the altar and Bishop Eduardo held two crowns above her head, one of roses and one of thorns. He intoned the ritual words once again.

"Behold, dearest daughter, two crowns. Choose the one with which you wish to be crowned."

There was a dramatic cessation of sound as the congregation awaited Rosa's response.

"I choose the crown of thorns," she said, in a voice resolute and melodic as the monastery bells.

Bishop Eduardo handed the crown of roses to the acolyte and came to stand directly in front of Rosa.

He lifted the crown of thorns high and forced it down around Rosa's head.

"Receive, dearest daughter, this crown, in memory of the Lord's own crown of thorns."

Joanna saw the piercing sharp thorns cutting into Rosa's white veiled head as they encircled it. She cringed in sympathetic pain.

Head bowed, Rosa calmly endured the pain. The bishop looked up and addressed the congregation in a booming voice.

"Henceforth, Doña Rosa de la Reyna will be known in religion as Sister Mary Clara of the Incarnation." He dipped an evergreen branch in the silver aspersorium of holy water, held by the acolyte at his side, and sprinkled it over Rosa's head. Then he cast it in all directions toward the congregation, who made the sign of the cross.

The choir nuns sounded a jubilant *Te Deum*. "We praise Thee, O God. We acknowledge Thee to be Lord of all creation. All the earth doth worship Thee, the Father Everlasting. To Thee all angels cry aloud, Holy, Holy, Holy, Lord God of Sabaoth, heaven and earth are full of your glory."

Rosa, Sister Mary Clara, stood and turned toward the congregation. Her eyes were cast downward and inward. For a brief moment, she glanced toward Joanna and her family with a smile full of light and love, like a blessing.

The Bishop took her right hand, led her down the steps of the altar, down the central aisle in measured steps, toward the enclosure. Once again, the congregation genuflected and made the sign of the cross as

Rosa passed.

The Abbess Antonia opened the wrought iron gates to admit the young novice into Santa Maria Monastery.

In glorious celebration, the choir nuns' *Te Deum* resounded, once again, throughout the church, and all the bells in all the church towers of Cuzco rang their sonorous peals of joy.

That was the last view the family had of Rosa. From this day forth, they would contact her through the locutorio. She was "dead to the world and all it represented"—a coded phrase, often quoted from the Bible, meaning, as Rosa had told Joanna, that one could transcend the veils of reality and awaken to eternity.

Chapter 44

Joanna watched as Carlos left the private quarters and walked briskly down the hall toward the tall Palladian windows overlooking the parade grounds of the Gubernatorial Palace in Lima. He was dressed in a dark suit, conservative tie, hair well groomed. There wasn't a single point for criticism in his appearance.

She'd seen to that, inspecting every detail. Following him down the length of the room, she reviewed the events leading up to this day. She recalled the sightseeing tour when Rosa had sprung the CEDAR Surprise of a luncheon with El Presidente Duarte, the futile search for her birth parents, but the glorious discovery of her ancestors, and the decoding of Sister Elena's myth—Sister Elena, her dear grandmother, and, of course, the incredible insights into mythology and astronomy.

Then there was the wedding—was she really using that phrase? The wedding had been the talk of Peru, and the timing was just right, everyone had said. Don de la Reyna said it brought serendipitous publicity, adding many votes to Carlos' bid for the election.

Carlos had said Peru should be thrilled to vote for such a beautiful and brilliant First Lady. Added to that, he'd said, the Quechua people believed it was a restoration to power of their beloved nŭsta, their very own Inca princess.

The newspapers had been reporting for days that Joanna was descended from Joré Inca, a great-grandson of Sapa Inca Huayna Capàc, the last great emperor of all of Peru before the Spanish conquest. Her maternal side was equally illustrious, the papers said. Two Conquistadors were counted in that line of descent.

The streets teemed with people. Not only was it Inauguration Day but it was July 28, Independence Day. Excitement was running high.

People clung to the wrought iron fence surrounding the palace grounds. The guards were colorful, grand in their uniforms. The historical regiments with their famous military bands stood ready to parade. Security forces were everywhere. The Peru National Police Service shadowed Carlos' every move.

There'd already been threats on his life. The country's history of doomed presidencies would be almost comedic, if it weren't so tragic. There'd been presidential terms of office that lasted for a few hours, a day, a month, six months, and the causes of interrupted terms were listed as civil wars, coups, terrorist violence.

Joanna watched Carlos nervously scanning his inaugural speech. He'd memorized it days ago, practicing incessantly. Because he was so passionate about the reforms and programs he hoped to sponsor, he said he had to deliver the address perfectly. It was clear he could have delivered it extemporaneously.

Reforms were needed. He'd even appointed Joanna to serve in the Ministry of Science and Education. Her job would be to arrange the training of scientists for the newest space program that was being required of every member nation of the U.N. He'd said she was the perfect person to accomplish that work. With her at his side, he could rejuvenate this great nation and set its course for the future.

"Joanna, this is our *mita*, our personal mission," he'd whispered to her when the election results came in, and he'd known he was the winner.

She'd thought that, too. Perhaps, Ayaviri's passion for reforms that would help the Quechua people would finally be realized during Carlos' term. Maybe she, Joanna—Huarana—could prove to the Peruvian people how important the acllas' legacy of the myth was to their understanding of the great place Peru occupied in the progression of world history. Their civilization had been as great as that of Sumer or Egypt and they had shared in the same "world-wide-data-base" of ancient astronomy that had been so important to hand on to future generations.

Joanna hurried to stand near Carlos in front of the window that opened onto the balcony. She put her arms around him and leaned her head against his heart.

"I'm so damned proud of you. Did you sleep well? Are you ready?" she asked.

"Believe me, I've never been more ready—I'm standing at the gates like a race horse, pawing and chomping at my bit. I can't wait till that bugle sounds."

"Carlos, am I dreaming this? How *did* we get here?"

"Are you kidding? You worked your little butt off! Actually, the reality is, we might not be here if J.D. hadn't been exposed as the principle investor in that copper-mining company. That made the whole Quechua population turn out in droves to vote for us."

"I'm worried about you. I don't think you slept more than four hours a night after you filed those campaign papers."

"My vitality's at its peak—I feel so blessed, doing exactly what I believe I was meant to do, but how about you, my love?" He stroked her chin lightly as he looked lovingly at her.

"Well, after you left the banquet hall last night—to get your beauty rest—I partied 'til dawn with our family and friends and then slept just a little while." She frowned, worry lines appearing where bright laughter had been. "I had a horrible nightmare, Carlos, but I'll never, ever, be able to tell you about it. However, there's another dream I do want to share with you, but I can't tell it before breakfast!"

"That's a strange notion! Why ever wouldn't one want to tell a dream before breakfast?

"Long story—suffice it to say, it's a Southern thing, bad luck, etc…but maybe I will tell, I guess it'll be okay, because you said the Inauguration Breakfast will be a brunch. That means there'll be no breakfast for the dream to be told *before*."

Carlos lifted her chin, kissing her tenderly. "You're an amalgam of the most interesting contradictions of logic and superstition I've ever seen. Do I need to tell you how much you fascinate me?"

"I think the dream was about you."

"What do you mean *think*? Is there someone else, so soon?"

"Silly thing—Carlos, I dreamed we were on Machu Picchu. It was in Incan times. You were the high priest and I was an aclla. A pestilence had decimated the population, and we were the only people left alive. We were making a last offering to the sun at the Intihuatana because we didn't have long to live."

"That *is* a disturbing dream!"

"Yes, and there's more. I actually had that same dream when I went to Machu Picchu that first time, shortly after I'd arrived in Peru." She stopped, looking at him intently, reassuring herself that he was listening.

"I'm convinced now that the first dream was about Huarana and Joré, because the last time I visited Rosa—Sister Clara—at the locutorio, she was telling me that Mother Antonia had assigned her to digitize all the sixteenth-century records. Rosa said she'd found a record that told how Huarana had returned to her childhood home where her husband had been living after the rebellion. Carlos, that means that they were both at Machu Picchu after Huarana left Santa Maria Monastery!"

Those stories about your ancestors are priceless. I'm so glad Ayaviri preserved the records, and apparently so did Santa Maria Monastery," Carlos said.

"Yes, but the dream I had last night was the same dream, except it was about you and me. I dreamt I recited a poem for you. I remember the first line, but can't recall the rest. It's driving me crazy. I was aware that it was important to us. Do you think the dream is some sort of portent for our future?"

"How much champagne did you say you drank?"

Slapping his arm, she laughed and put her hand to her forehead, pushing the hair back from her face. She glanced up and saw the look of adoration in his eyes.

"You said we were on Machu Picchu?"

"I remember a little more of the poem now. Want to hear it?"

"Of course, I'm your worshipful audience."

"Once, on a moon-bridge, we glanced into waters that smiled back lilies of every hue. Hand-loved canoes, sky lanterns, spunned-glass fish starred our world ..."

Carlos took her hands. "... while you recounted strange tales I heard only in your eyes." He continued, "For we knew we would taste the frozen ice, not the substance of dreams. In celebration, we drank the only toast we could, I with fruit chilled by early rending, and you with that warmed in distillation. You would have carried away ticcis too big for us, only people might have laughed or cried. Ticcis weren't for sale anyway, who could have bought them with multi-hued lilies, on a moon bridge?"

She joined him on the last stanza. "But... they *were* ours—we'd paid the price, long ago, in temple chimes and memories, and with an infinite love, needing neither hands nor eyes."

"Don't you realize what that is?" he asked. "Here, let me show you." He took his wallet from an inside pocket of his suit coat and opened a small compartment. Taking out a folded, dog-eared, yellowed slip of paper, he displayed it on his hand for her to see.

"Good grief, Carlos, that's the silly poem I wrote in high school—"

"*Con Ticci*—you wrote it for me after I escorted you and Rosa to that Polynesian restaurant in D.C., just before you two graduated," he said.

"I can't believe you kept that!"

"Dear, dear girl—you should have guessed long ago. When I first met you, you were only fifteen, and I was twenty—but I knew, no matter how long I lived you'd always be in my heart."

"I had a crush on you all during high school," she said. "When you took Rosa and me to our first grown-up restaurant, I knew I'd fallen badly for you, but I thought you regarded me as a nuisance of a little sister, because you were so much older."

"Hey—not that much older! I've treasured that poem. You actually sent it to me after I returned to Cuzco. Whenever I came to visit Rosa, you always introduced me as your honorary older brother, remember?

Then we lost touch because I went to school in England, and you went on to the University of Pennsylvania. So, I thought there wasn't a chance for me ..."

"Carlos that dream *isn't* a portent for our future. We have eternities to live and love."

Carlos reached for her hand, raised it to his lips, and kissed the palm. Stepping through the tall window, he went to the front of the balcony, near the podium where he would take the oath of office and deliver his inaugural address. The applause and cheers were deafening.

Waving to the crowd with one hand, he motioned with the other for Joanna and their family members to come up and join him. "Thank you for always being by my side," he whispered to Joanna, pulling her close. The crowds cheered louder. He released Joanna, waved harder, turning in an arc to include everyone and then spoke just before moving to the podium.

"A high priest, you said? Was I good-looking in that loincloth? You really *must* tell me all about the other roles I've played in our eternal drama."

"Well, you were a little over the top as Moses."

Chapter 45

EL PRESIDENTE CARLOS DE LA REYNA ASSASSINATED

Enormous crowds, gathered in the plaza to celebrate the success of this popular couple, witnessed the massacre. Peru continues in deep mourning as the military seized power to stabilize the central government. Air Force General, Manuel Bustamoro, declared a week of mourning and vowed vengeance on the assassins who opened fire shortly after the swearing-in ceremony for El Presidente Carlos de la Reyna.

First Lady, Doña Joanna de la Reyna, was caught in the spray of bullets. Other guests on the inauguration platform sustained wounds of varying degrees.

The President will lie in state at the Palacio de Gobierno. The closed casket will be guarded by the Order of Santiago. Burial will be in Cuzco, in the vaults under Santa Maria Monastery Church that have been maintained since the 16th Century by the de la Reyna family, who are patrons of the monastery.

The interim government will…

The emergency vehicle turned onto Calle Maria and approached the side gate leading into Santa Maria Monastery. No sirens blared, but the huge wooden gates swung open immediately.

Through the window, she glimpsed a nun and a tall man in a white coat waiting by the curb as the vehicle drew to the service entrance inside the walled courtyard. The three EMTs jumped from the back of the truck and pulled out the gurney containing her sheet-draped figure. She was being administered an intravenous drip bag.

Another person emerged from the vehicle dressed in a black veil and a white religious habit with an International Red Cross band around her sleeve. Behind the gurney, the physician fell into step with the nun who had accompanied the emergency vehicle.

"Please follow me," Mother Abbess said, hurrying ahead to show them the way into the infirmary.

"How bad is it?" The physician opened the glass door to the infirmary.

"She's alive. It is still 'touch and go.' It's a miracle anybody survived," the Red Cross nun said.

"Have they any idea who the assassins are?" He indicated that the nun should go ahead of him.

"Many are blaming elements who held resentment toward an Inca descendant who happened to be the wife of El Presidente. Some are even blaming Garcia Family supporters who may have fanned the flames of the leftist factions who campaigned against Carlos."

"It has devastated this country—I've never seen such a beloved couple elected to that office. I shudder to think where we'll go from here," the physician said.

Who are these people? She struggled to understand what they were saying and felt herself pulled swiftly down a long dark tunnel.

The room glistened like the inside of a seashell. The sun intensified the creamy luster and gently nudged her to wakefulness. Wide windows opened on flower-filled gardens, and a breeze lifted the mosquito netting above the bed.

An elderly nun sat by the window nodding over a book. She looked familiar, but the room seemed strange, and why was a nun in her bedroom?

"Sister, please help me. Where am I?"

The nun dropped the book and jumped to her feet. She was at the bedside in an instant, crying and laughing at the same time. "You're in Santa Maria Monastery, my dear."

"Why?"

There was a commotion at the door. The nun turned and knelt as another nun entered the room and came forward with her right hand extended. The first nun kissed the ring of authority on the extended hand and rose to her feet in a swift motion.

"Mother Abbess, shall I summon—?"

"Please go quickly. I'll stay with her."

The nun called "mother" seemed familiar. She was sure she knew the other one, too. Why were they being so mysterious? Surely, they could tell her why she was here.

"Would you like something to drink?" The abbess inquired, fluffing the pillows.

"Thank you," she said, taking the glass and sipping at the straw. The liquid was warm—citrus— lemon. It tickled her throat. "Please tell me why I'm here."

The door opened again and a younger nun came hurrying into the room.

"Rosa, why are you wearing that costume?" she asked. "You look ridiculous. It's really bizarre, what're we doing here?"

Tears streaming down her face, Rosa rushed over to hug her. It felt good to have arms around her. She clung to Rosa, basking in life and warmth.

"We were so worried," Rosa said. "We thought we'd lost you, too."

"Lost ..."

The Abbess turned to the other nun, "I'm calling Dr. Val-Ponte."

The Abbess left the room and the other nun, who was old, hurried over to Joanna, taking her hand. Rosa's arms tightened around her.

"Joanna, I can't bear to tell you, but I must. It's so awful. You've been in an induced coma for two months." Rosa paused, gripping her tighter. "There was an assassination on Inaugural Day."

She heard the words, saw Rosa brush tears from her eyes. *What did that have to do with her? What was Rosa saying?*

She looked closely at Rosa again and then at the old nun who was crying now.

"We had to hide you here," Rosa said. "The police are worried the assassins will return to finish the job, if they know you're still alive."

"... if I'm alive?"

"Joanna, darling, Carlos is dead."

The seashell room was a comfort and the warm sunshine streaming through the windows, affirmed she was alive. It was good that she didn't have to think or leave the bed. It was hard enough just to open her eyes. *Why didn't I die? I should've died.*

Rosa sat with her each day, coaxing her to take food, convincing her to be pushed about in a wheelchair, round and round the paths in the orchard. Each afternoon she was wheeled to the far side of the monastery where there was a tiny wayside chapel.

In the chapel, she fixed her gaze on the cross. Maybe God would see her staring. She couldn't manage much more.

She tried to read the books Rosa—Sister Clara—brought, but the words made no sense and she grew weary with the effort.

Sister Elena was her grandmother they'd told her, and she accepted that. The elderly nun was teaching her to knit baby clothes for the homeless shelters in Cuzco. At least that gave some purpose to her days, and she had soon grown to welcome Sister Elena's loving approval of everything she did.

"Joanna, explain to me once again how the message of the myth may fit in with your research into frequencies of matter?" Sister Elena asked.

"That's all so long ago. I don't remember."

"Wasn't it about standing waves and cycles?"

"Don't you see I can't deal with all that? Why're you bothering me?"

"My dear, you must deal with it. It's time—time to pick up the pieces and start—"

"Don't you lecture me, you can't possibly understand. I don't care about picking up pieces. He's in my dreams—that's the only place I want to live. Leave me alone." She threw down the tiny cap she'd been knitting and pushed the button on the arm of the wheel chair, propelling it toward the door.

"But I do know, Joanna. I know the sheer pain of being awake ..."

The wheel chair halted, turned. "Please forgive me ..."

Sister Elena was at her side, embracing her. "There's nothing to forgive, my darling."

The doctor insisted she exercise every day. She trundled through the halls, concentrating on every muscle, steering the walker ahead of her. No chance to re-live dreams in the midst of that.

When she could stand without assistance, Sister Clara forced her to traverse the paths in the apple orchard twice daily. The sunshine and exercise made her stronger, but it was difficult being with Sister Clara—Rosa—who reminded her so much of Carlos. She'd made up excuses in the beginning for remaining in the solarium, but gradually looked forward to the visits, to Rosa's laughter and stories of humorous incidents in the cloister.

She'd started to wonder how long Mother Antonia and her Council would let her stay in the monastery. Maybe, she'd petition them to permit her to enter the order, become a nun, like Rosa. The order had a long-standing tradition of accepting widows. It certainly offered one way to "end" her life without doing violence.

Rosa said it had been three months since the assassination. She'd been brought to Santa Maria immediately afterwards, so two of the months were spent in a medically induced coma and then another week in semi-delirium. She was finally taking on weight, which pleased the doctor, because she'd been pencil thin.

Now that she was no longer in the coma, she'd had to contend with nausea, which was definitely a new condition for her. She'd been one of those individuals who'd never experienced illness, just the usual childhood maladies.

Abbess Antonia and Rosa entered the infirmary with Dr. Val-Ponte. Rosa came to her bedside and kissed her on the forehead. "How're you feeling?" she asked. "Sister Trina told us you were vomiting earlier this morning."

"Remember how we felt when we ate those three day old hamburgers we'd stashed in our lockers at boarding school when we were twelve? Well, that's pretty much how I'm feeling now."

"Joanna, I've done some tests. I repeated them—I needed to be sure," Dr. Val-Ponte said. "I was surprised at the results, but I'd started to suspect something earlier. I've asked your grandmother and sister-in-law, as well as Abbess Antonia, to be present this morning."

Sister Elena hurried into the room, stood on the other side of her bed, and smiled down at her. *Why did the doctor want all these people in her room at a time like this?*

Another wave of nausea assaulted her. She wished they wouldn't smile and be cheerful.

Didn't they know Dr. Val-Ponte was probably about to reveal that she had some terrible life-threatening disease? She caught her breath as he gazed at the chart once again and then looked directly at her.

"Joanna, you're approximately three months pregnant."

She stared at him, unbelieving. Tears flooded her cheeks. Sister Elena, Sister Clara, and Abbess Antonia stood like automatons, gawking at her in silent shock. Suddenly each one became animated, emoting in sequence, laughing, crying, embracing, congratulating her—

proclaiming their happiness.

"You're absolutely wonderful, Joanna. I can't believe I'm going to have a niece—maybe a nephew—it doesn't matter! I'll take either one, or both!" Rosa grasped her hands, dancing a little jig beside the bed. Suddenly she looked down at her habit, dropped Joanna's hands, and glanced shyly toward the Abbess who was smiling broadly, appearing as though she wanted to join Sister Clara in the jig.

Joanna reached for Rosa's hand again, held it to her heart, turned her head to the side, and looked far beyond the monastery windows, out past the Cordillera, out where Machu Picchu glowed emerald in all its glory.

Carlos' baby... *Carlos' baby*!

He'd insisted on going back to Machu Picchu Pueblo a few days before the inauguration ceremonies. They'd walked over the ruins, tracing places that marked the equinoxes and solstices.

When the tourists left and the ruins closed for the day, he'd requested special permission for an evening hike with overnight camping at the cave where they'd sheltered after he'd rescued her when she'd fallen from the ledge. Exquisite memories came rushing back of their first time there and the glorious recent time.

Still holding Rosa's hand, she let her gaze return to the room. Sister Elena stood nearby, beaming---her precious grandmother, who'd forced her to return from that grief-filled parallel universe and made her remember the insights.

Pachamama's cycles—the cycles of the whole universe, constantly moving into and out of existence, standing waves pulsing with conscious matter and energy, pulsing with Infinite Being. The same matter and energy that was Carlos, whose love would live again, even as it lived now in her womb...

Sister Elena, eyes bright and deep as the evening skies above The Sacred Valley, leaned over her, and placed both hands on her abdomen.

"Sicitur ad astra, Huarana. The legacy continues . . ."

AUTHOR'S NOTE

The Incan myth in this novel is fictitious. The authentic myths were dictated to the Spanish Chroniclers by Inca Quipucamayocs, the record keepers and translators of the quipus—the unique color-coded vertical knotted cords of various lengths tied to a horizontal cord—used in the Incan Empire to communicate about and remember important events, names and numbers of persons, places, and things.

Early on, had the Incas and their predecessors received the scholarly attention long focused on "old world" classical empires, they would have ranked among the greatest of those past civilizations. Indeed, they would have taken their proper place as a rival to the grandeur of Rome.

Had that been the case, the reader of this novel would have known who the *acllas* were. There would have been clear explanations, rather than a paucity of information, or even omission of the word in reference works.

Put simply, the *Acllas* were the Incan cultural ambassadors to the conquered tribes of an empire that spanned the length of Andean and coastal South America from Ecuador in the north to Chile in the south. In the top echelons of their hieratic, initiatory institution, the Mamaconas were celibate priestesses who were dedicated for life to the moon goddess Mama Quilla. They were the highly educated teachers of the newly chosen eight-year-olds who were destined to join their ranks or, who, at the appropriate age, would be given in marriage—a marital contract brokered by the Sapa Inca himself—as prized brides to the kings or chieftains of conquered tribes.

Soon after the conquest of Peru, the Spanish Conquistadors saw the efficacy of such a system and its reflection in Spain's cloistered monasteries of Catholic nuns. They petitioned Church authorities to found "new-world" monasteries of nuns in Cuzco to educate their mestiza children, whom they'd sired with the royal women of the Sapa Inca's household—thus copying the Incan system of "benevolent control" to assure the future of their newly formed empire.

ACKNOWLEDGMENTS

Gratitude is owed to the following people: Father Lawrence J. Bayer, the person who was always there and who baptized me to spiritual gifts that have brought lasting happiness; to Sister Angela Marie, CDP, headmistress of my boarding school, the greatest teacher and role model for my professional career, a wonderful surrogate mother to the children in her care; to Dr. Marva J. Larrabee, inspired professor, skilled chair of my doctoral dissertation committee, friend, 'sounding board' and cheerleader for this manuscript in late night phone calls and extensive marathon reading sessions, and for the precious friendship of her foster son Frank Torres Arciniega; to Jane Marshall Howatt, fellow writer, dear friend, former student, who first heard of *Huarana* on my return trip from Peru, many years ago in the Barnes & Noble café in Augusta, GA, and without whose constant encouragement the novel would never have been written, who, with her husband, Jim Howatt, M.D., hosted the Oak View, CA Writer's Group, that brought together creative writers, skilled editors, & terrific friends whose editing and suggestions for this manuscript were right on target; to Marsha Maulhardt, Sean Maulhardt, Terry Maulhardt, Robin Winter and Cheryl Price, talented writers, editors, friends and fans of the novel; to the 4 friends: Linda McGarity Franks, Dan Franks (and Bean), Kristy Lynn Gossett & Jack Hugill, all who stood by me during the years of caring for my mother; many thanks to Kristy and Linda for reading the manuscript and for good advice; for help and wonderful baked goods to Joyce & Doug Wright; to former students and dearest friends: Greg & Nicola Davis, Debbie Johnson & Lee Bultman, Dr.Victoria Nufal Sanders, and Kathy Iwashima (who insisted they enjoyed hearing innumerable chapters read aloud and offered constant encouragement); to dear cousins and friends of my heart & youth: Fred & Bobby Fuller Adams, Sandra Adams Caraviello, Joe Caraviello, Robin Caraviello Hartline, & Joe (Joey) Caraviello, Jr., Freddie Adams Wallen, Richard Adams, Mike Adams, Gary Adams, Mary Adams Jacobs, Perry Jacobs, Anthony Adams and Zack Jacobs, Randy Adams, Jeffery Adams, and Jack Adams, Jr., Myrtle, Richard, Harrietta, Darnell, & Rita Bowens; and dear cherished friends Wilma Cantey Deddish, the inspiration for Rosa & organizer of my first 'fan' club, & her husband, Michael Deddish, a most gracious host; to dear friends: Gail Stafford, Ruby Martin, Jan, Jim, Laura, Brian, & Cari Messick, Joan Johnson, Sylvia Jordan, Peggy Schalmo Meeker & Chester Meeker; Terry Blanton Rexroad, Dustin Rexroad, and Greg Rexroad, who gave the manuscript glowing reviews with astute suggestions in the 2nd revision, to Colonel Alan F. Blanton, excellent writer, whose generous supplying of 'White Shoulders' perfume is always appreciated; many thanks to Toni Lapopolo (Abbess Antonia), literary agent, along with Shelly Lowencoff, both renowned writers, editors, teachers, and presenters at *Oak View Writers' Boot Camp Workshop*, for their sound advice; great gratitude also goes to beloved pets: Misty, Lab-Mix Pup, Vida, Hahn's Macaw, & LaGris, gray kitten (companions of all night writing vigils); to dear cherished Charleston friends : Mary, Ron, Laura, & Wesley Thrift, Dollie, David, Davy, & Denecia Brown , who shared the happy 'teaching' years, and to dear friend Barbara Ferer (Benedícite!—you alone share the Dominican 'war' stories) & her brilliant husband, Dr. Del Woods (who slogged bravely through the manuscript after its first revision and whose critique & praise meant the most); to dear friends Renate Sorensen & Delmarie Rose for loving encouragement always; to dear friend Gail Dickinson Dennis for nutritious meals & unending encouragement, and to her sisters Janie & Cheryl, brother John & his wife Joan, & little Lucky Pup, Much gratitude to Dr. Jana Sandarg for leading us to Peru & especially to Mary Louise Icenhour (You stormed the monastery gates with me!); thanks to Sara Griswold for her insights into her homeland. Thanks to the librarians at Royston Public Library, especially Ms. Rose Chitwood, who patiently hunted down every book of my whims; to Dr. William Mareska, Cindy Hooker, Debbie Glass, & Gina Marsh, whose cheerful optimism and encouragement are appreciated. My gratitude to Shari Spokes, author of children's books the <u>Stepping Stone Stories</u>—*Sara's Flower Garden*, & Sandy Lagno, the "Animal Whisperer." Gratitude to all my very dear students, always my inspiration.

GREATEST GRATITUDE GOES TO RENOWNED, LONG-SUFFERING, SUPERB EDITOR-MIDWIFE TO THIS MANUSCRIPT: SHANNON ROBERTS of *The Editorial Department*. Thanks to Renni Browne, *The Editorial Department*, for much appreciated initial editing and encouragement. Her comments still bring laughter. Her editorial balloon screamed, "Shut up! Shut up!" in response to the paragraph where I felt impelled to editorialize on the action after having depicted, apparently very well, the Hieros Gamos: i.e., <u>*showed*</u>*!!!, didn't tell.*

Many thanks to you, my future readers!

Heartfelt thanks to Farris Yawn and Nadine Yawn, of Yawn's Publishing, Inc. and Farris Books, who along with their line and copyeditors, labored diligently by my side to "birth" this novel.

CPSIA information can be obtained at www.ICGtesting.com
Printed in the USA
LVOW11s0239170816

500723LV00001B/62/P